monsoonbooks

ISLAND OF DEMONS

Nigel Barley was born south of London in 1947. After taking a degree in modern languages at Cambridge, he gained a doctorate in anthropology at Oxford. Barley originally trained as an anthropologist and worked in West Africa, spending time with the Dowayo people of North Cameroon. He survived to move to the Ethnography Department of the British Musem and it was in this connection that he first travelled to Southeast Asia. After forrays into Thailand, Malaysia, Singapore, Japan and Burma, Barley settled on Indonesia as his principal research interest and has worked on both the history and contemporary culture of that area.

After escaping from the museum, he is now a writer and broadcaster and divides his time between London and Indonesia.

T0150023

ALSO BY NIGEL BARLEY

The Innocent Anthropologist
A Plague of Caterpillars
Foreheads of the Dead
The Coast
Smashing Pots
Dancing on the Grave
The Golden Sword
White Rajah
In the Footsteps of Stamford Raffles *
Rogue Raider *
Toraja *

(* published by Monsoon Books)

Island of Demons

NIGEL BARLEY

monsoon

monsoonbooks

First published in 2009
by Monsoon Books Pte Ltd
52 Telok Blangah Road, #03-05 Telok Blangah House
Singapore 098829
www.monsoonbooks.com.sg

This second edition published in 2010.

ISBN: 978-981-08-2381-8

Cover painting: "Rehjagd" by Walter Spies. Courtesy of Walter Spies
Foundation.

National Library Board Singapore Cataloguing in Publication Data
Barley, Nigel.
Island of demons / Nigel Barley. – Singapore : Monsoon Books, 2009.
p. cm.
ISBN-13 : 978-981-08-2381-8 (pbk.)

1. Spies, Walter – Fiction. 2. Bali Island (Indonesia) – History – 20th
century – Fiction. I. Title.

PR6102
823.92 -- dc22   OCN313646912

Printed in America
13 12 11 10   2 3 4 5 6 7 8 9

Introduction

Between the two world wars, the island of Bali in the Dutch East Indies was a unique place of special power in the Western imagination. Only recently colonised, in a great effusion of blood that shocked even the Western democracies, it had become the jewel in the colonial crown of Southeast Asia. The Dutch had appointed themselves guardians of a rich and ancient culture distinguished by lavish ceremonial and spectacle, where beautiful women went bare breasted and handsome men were allegedly available for those of more unconventional tastes. Bali was an obvious site for Western fantasies about Paradise and underwent an influx of foreign visitors. Some were artists, musicians, dancers and writers, attracted by the staggering aesthetic experience that was centred on complex and exotic Hindu rites. Others were scientists, keen to capture the secret of this tantalising and enigmatic culture so that Margaret Mead and Gregory Bateson, the foremost anthropologists of their time, came here and sought to record and interpret what they saw, as they forged the tools of the burgeoning new discipline they served.

Foremost amongst all these expatriates was a charismatic German, Walter Spies, who chose to live in the upland town of Ubud and formed such close links with the Balinese that all subsequent foreigners depended on him as a means of gaining access to the islanders and their world. He was all things: a painter, a musician, an ethnographer, a linguist and a dancer. To his house, flocked the rich and famous of the age: Charlie Chaplin, Miguel and Rosa Covarrubias, Noel Coward, Vicki Baum, Leopold Stokowski, Barbara Hutton and many others whose names, prominent at the time, have now been forgotten. His house by the river at Campuhan, shone like a beacon of enlightenment, scholarship and intercultural understanding for some twenty years.

But such an oasis belongs only in the imagination and cannot endure in the real world, for the foreigners not only brought the idea of

Paradise but also their demons with them. Small-minded Dutch colonial administration, personal tragedy, the darker drives of the human soul and the deepening shadow cast by the outside world in a planet headed for another world war – all conspired to bring him down and lay waste Walter Spies's project, so that he too is now largely forgotten outside Indonesia. Changing ideas have naturally also led to a re-evaluation of his life but – oddly perhaps – least on Bali. There, the school of painting that he founded still flourishes, the musical arts that he supported have continued to transform and grow and he is remembered with genuine affection by both the new Balinese intelligentsia and the children of the ordinary peasants who were his friends.

This is a work of fiction not of history. I have not hesitated to tamper with chronology where the narrative demands it. Thus, the reader should not be shocked to hear that I am fully aware that Rudolf Bonnet could not have encountered Ni Polok on the beach in Sanur as the wife of Le Mayeur in 1929–30, though I have described that meeting. The Japanese occupation of Manchuria happened *after* the Paris Exposition of 1931 not *before* as I depict it. The records of the trial of Spies remain inaccessible so the version presented here is invented. Also, it took place in Surabaya, not Denpasar, and Margaret Mead was not actually present but authorial economy dictates the change of venue and personnel. The names of many Balinese associated with Spies have been deliberately changed (though the most prominent have not) so that the decision to invoke that association remains with them.

It is also not a work of autobiography. I am not Rudolf Bonnet or Walter Spies – least of all am I Margaret Mead. Although I have done some small ethnographic fieldwork on Bali, I am not a Balinese expert and do not speak Balinese – as Spies was and did – and I have had to depend on the generosity of knowing others, Western and Balinese, who have been as liberal with their knowledge and friendship as Spies himself was with visiting researchers. Deformations are not necessarily mistakes but mistakes remain, as always, my own.

Canggu, Bali

I

"There are no ghosts in Bali," I said and did my grand-old-man-of-the-arts face, ravaged by its burden of knowledge. In my later years it has served me well and stares out at the world imperiously from a dozen book covers bearing my name and cataloguing my works. I took off my glasses to show my profile. "A famous anthropologist told me that, so it must be true. On cremation, classically, the souls of the dead soar away as doves released at the high point of the ceremony and come back to this earth as the morning dew. Nowadays, for reasons of economy, they may substitute chickens which, I know, debases the image. The Balinese imagination animates trees and rocks and so forth, and creates witches, naturally, *leyak-leyak*, that often appear as blue flames dancing across the fields in the dark. When I first came here, the bicycle was a novelty that had somehow got into the Balinese brain and so witches assumed the shape of riderless bicycles pedaling themselves furiously through the streets at night, tinkling their bells. The other odd thing about these infernal machines was that their tyres inflated and deflated themselves rhythmically like panting dogs ..."

"Yeah. Like, I've already read Covarrubias, Powell and those other old guys, Mr Bonnet. That wasn't the sort of ghost I meant."

My interviewer pronounced it "bonn-ay" to rhyme with "Chardonnay".

"It is properly pronounced 'bonette' almost like the American term for a lady's hat but with an equal stress on the second syllable. Quite simple. People tend to get it wrong. Doubtless, they are associating me with Mon-ay or Man-ay. A sort of compliment then."

I smiled with old, yellow teeth to show that I modestly accepted that compliment. My interviewer yawned and pandiculated, luxuriantly, displaying blinding American dentition but pencilled no notes, instead stretched long, golden – surely Californian – legs, flecked with hairs of still-lighter hue, and smoothed back thick, honey-blond curls. A memory, as of a forgotten language, tickled at my brain. For most of my life, I had been tuned to a different idiom – dark Asian hair, dusky brown skin, almond eyes. These eyes were blue and very bored.

"Miguel," I pronounced irritably, "was not always reliable. He wrote the first, definitive work on Balinese culture but he lumped together too much. The Balinese only have culture so that they can argue about what exactly it is. What they do and say in one village is quite unlike what they do and say in the next. Of course, in those days we were pioneers. Knowledge has progressed since then."

He smirked condescendingly. "The Western myth of progress? Yeah, right. Covarrubias. I said that I had *read* him, not *accepted* him."

"Margaret Mead," I said, "sat in that very chair and expressed her admiration of his work."

Unwillingly, he was awed and looked down at the chair where he … where she … It was almost true, too. She *had* said that but, of course, the chairs had been bought long after. An artist never loses his touch for the significant object that brings a whole tableau to life.

I had agreed to this interview only out of a misplaced sense of duty to scholarship, an American student come thousands of miles to crouch at my feet, a thesis, one of the swarm of "researchers" descending like flies on the corpse of still-twitching Bali. God knows I had done little enough in my life for art and learning. It was clear that I was proving a disappointment. Irritation prickled at the back of my neck.

"What exactly was the title of your thesis?"

He yawned and stretched again. I had forgotten his name and glanced down at the card on the low table by my elbow. It told me – reminded me – that he was James Grits, a graduate student from an East Coast college I had never heard of. He was still stretching. He was a well-built boy. Under the shirt was definite rippling. His large, betrainered feet executed a sort of rapid, rhythmic tattoo to stamp out the final muscle contraction as the soft cotton of his shorts rode up the tanned skin of firm thighs to create a zone of transition fascinating to a painter's eye. Even at my age, having long laid down my brush once and for all, the artist's instinct dies hard. I inclined my head to imagine how I would grasp form and shadow of that dusky triangle in my habitual pale pastels, aware that my hands executed involuntary sketching motions. I almost missed the answer when it came.

"Colonial discourses of the exotic Other and the paratextual constitution of the aesthetic fallacy."

"I see." I did not, of course, see. This was yet another strange language. In my life I had had to wrestle with so many and now the world was playing me the extreme disservice of changing those that I thought to have mastered. I took a draught of iced hibiscus tea. My companion had ordered Coca-Cola brought by pattering Nyoman and left it untouched and warming in the sun. I remembered the days when Americans wept at the sight of Coca-Cola as a witness of a separate and distant world from which they were exiled and clutched at ice cubes like diamonds. Had he been Indonesian, I should have had to coax him into sipping before I could decently taste my own drink. Now, I swigged. There are some compensations for being a mannerless Westerner amongst other mannerless Westerners. I tweaked the folds of my *sarong*, a tasteful handpainted *batik*, tied in the Javanese not Balinese fashion and given to me by President Soekarno, that explored the muted shades of an old sepia photograph. There was a time when we – they, the Dutch – punished Westerners for wearing local dress.

"And how exactly may I help in this endeavour?"

"You know your English is kinda weird – like you swallowed a dictionary."

"Perhaps the people I learned my English from were kinda weird. As to the dictionary, I once started compiling a Balinese–English dictionary. A lot of people did. Perhaps I learned more English than Balinese."

"Right. Like I'm saying. It seems to me Bali is still full of ghosts, the ghosts of that clique of privileged Westerners who invented Bali as a site for Western fantasies of paradise, back in the Twenties and articulated the sexual metaphors of domination that underpin it. You're ... like ... the only one left."

"Ah. You mean like the last of the dinosaurs."

He giggled boyishly in a manner I found charming and then spoilt it by headshakingly returning to the shibboleths of his faith.

"There's that old misplaced evolutionism again."

The communists had talked like that, back in the heady days of the Revolution; nothing but endless chains of judgemental notions and "isms". The writers of the period – Idris, Toer and the others – were now unreadable because of their stilted dialogue. But people had really talked like that. I thought of Sobrat, McPhee's little friend, shot in the head during some ideological tiff in Indonesian abstract nouns. All those years of refining and schooling his body as a perfect instrument of classical dance to have it thrown contemptuously in a ditch just down the road from here. I gripped my glass of tea in a liver-spotted reptilian claw and tried hard not to slop it on the *batik*. To retain the beauty of its organic dyes, it had to be washed in a special herbal extract brought from Java. Nyoman had warned me the jar under the sink was running low.

"Some metaphors, Mr ... er ... become realer every day." I swallowed hard, enjoying the iron chill on my throat.

"Exactly. That is why they have to be brought out into the light and subjected to critical review and DE-CON-struction." He had an irritatingly etymologising stress pattern.

I looked round at the light as it fell on my garden. Like all painters – like Mon-ay – I had once been obsessed with light. In old age, I fled it. We were seated, as Margaret Mead had not been, on the elegant Balinese copies of eighteenth-century Dutch furniture that they handcarve a few miles away, as they sit, themselves more comfily, on the cool floor. Above us a shading canopy of purely Balinese CON-struction, serried ranks of razor grass thatch resting on polished coconut trunks and beams that met in a central boss of a raging Garuda bird, rich in fang and claw. My neighbour had done that, the peaceful little old farmer I talked to most evenings as he pottered around and watered his orchid pots and complained of his ungrateful family. Underfoot, we trod simple red Balinese tiles of baked earth. That one there was loose and tripped the unwary. Over the years, I had learned to step round it. With age, one learns to adapt oneself rather than try to change the world. During the construction, I had joked saucily with the women who baked the tiles, made them laugh, even drawn one of the younger ones, her youth already sunk and shrunken by hard labour but the red dust caricaturing rude good health in her cheeks. It had been exhibited recently at,

I think, Surabaya.

The whole building was cool and practical – and very cheap. I had not made much money but had learned to value physical comfort, judiciously purchased. Any fool can be uncomfortable, as my friend Walter used to say to excuse some new extravagance. Around us, tinkled water and ponds, the remains of the ancient water palace, rehabilitated, planted with reeds and blue lotus. I had seen them on my first visit to the sacred springs at Tampaksiring and asked a delightful, bathing farmer their name. I knew them, of course, as the ancient Buddhist symbol of the human striving for Enlightenment, the soul struggling up from the mud, through the murky water to the light it somehow knew, even from the seed, was there. As a fugitive from another, colder Enlightenment, I treasured them too. He had shrugged and grinned. "Don't know their proper name," and towelled off unselfconsciously a barbarous magnificence of genitals, "but I grow them for the pigs. They love 'em. Just gobble 'em right down."

"… the centre of it all was Walter Spies," he was saying.

"Mmm?"

He finally took a swig of the Coca-Cola and grimaced – made what Walter called a *schiefes Gesicht*, a "crooked face".

"Warm." Then said again the name. "Spies." He spoke louder, obviously assuming I was deaf, as if the distraction of boredom were the exclusive privilege of youth. "It's time to lay the ghost of Walter Spies."

Yes. I had thought it would end up there. One way or another, it always came down to dear Walter. And being laid, as a ghost, now *that* would have amused him greatly. Walter had never outgrown the very worst schoolboy humour.

***

I too was young at the time. I know that is no excuse and these days, in my dotage, youth itself seems to demand its own extenuating circumstances. Nevertheless, there it is. I was young and Walter was simply the most magical person I had ever met. There was a golden glow about him. It was always as if the sun were somehow behind him and his features were blurred by its radiance and there was a force of enthusiasm in him that knocked you down – like one of those big-pawed puppies that rushes at you, expecting your love, overwhelming you with its lapping tongue until all you can do is laugh and submit.

You must understand that I had been raised in grey, wool-stockinged Amsterdam, in a home of solid bourgeois comfort where God and his disapproval daily cast a long shadow. Only the presence of six brothers and sisters created a sufficient pool of anarchy to dent the obsessively regular existence of my parents. My father was a schoolteacher who had worked himself up to be a successful businessman so there were no foolish notions about the value of education for its own sake to be found lurking in that house. Mathematics was studied so you could keep accounts, literature so you could write a sound business letter. It was my misfortune to be attracted to art. To my father that signified poverty, vice – worse – impractical improvidence. My mother, learning of the reason that her son – one of her several sons – was crying himself to sleep at night, avoided confrontation but undermined him slowly with nocturnal whispers. She saw herself as artistic and had executed several fine works of embroidery in the English style. A compromise made my vocation acceptable. It was decided that I was to become a commercial artist. To my father this meant the acquisition of a sensible, useful skill where visual seduction would not exceed that of the corpulent ladies of a certain age to be sketched for the whaleboned corsetry advertisements. (In fact, the few of these ladies that I ever met were both immodest and rapacious women.) As I completed the course and filled my folder with loving depictions of shoes and hats, my mother began to whisper again and I found myself the assistant of an art dealer, Jacob Vorderman, a surprisingly coarse and unaesthetic man who constantly puffed cheroots. The shop was full of perfectly presentable Dutch paintings of cows and windmills and bowls of fruit but, in the back, he pursued a guilty passion for the crazier contemporaries – people like wobbly Kokotschka and poor mad Kandinsky. The walls of his upstairs apartments blazed with their deluded colours.

"What do you think of that?" he would ask, shoving a mass of Kandinsky polychrome spaghetti under my nose. He always wore patent leather evening shoes that crackled as he walked, like a man treading on hot coals.

"It shows a rudimentary sense of form and arrangement," I opined in my self-righteous schoolboy voice, turning it this way and that. "But what is it? Art cannot be self-referential. It needs a subject. What *is* it?"

He laughed and snorted, coughed on his cheroot and firewalked away. "The future, lad."

By now, a further string had been added to my bow. I had started to be offered scholarships and nothing was more tragic to my father than to refuse a proffered cheque. True, they were not large cheques but it was to him an overwhelming idea that I might be paid for doing – as my father saw it – absolutely nothing. All I needed now was to unworthily encourage his suspicions that the art dealer – a man whose thoughts were very far from God – was seeking to convert me to Judaism and I was finally released into the arms of the Muses.

Their embrace, alas, was less warm and more marmorial than I had expected. At the Keyserschool, over the next few years, the ensoured staff taught me to translate a work of art into the rules and techniques that underlay it, into a series of obstacles to be serially overcome. I imposed grids, balanced compositions, calculated perspective. I framed and counterposed. On free days, I crept through the galleries, hitherto closed to my eyes by parental disapproval, to coldly probe, according to instruction, the bosomy flesh of Rubens, the withered skin of Rembrandt, the feral teint of Breughel and reduce them to well-documented visual devices. Caravaggio, alone, moved me strangely. Who knows how long this would have continued but I was saved by – of all things – a resented family holiday.

My father had sold a ramshackle property on the Jodenbreetstraat for an unexpectedly high price and, in an equally unexpected response, resolved to carry off the whole family to Italy. A rambling villa, the country property of a line of dilapidated noble pretension, complete with well, chestnut trees and squabbling retainers, was hired in the mountain village of Lansoprazole and we all set off – children, grandchildren, sons- and daughters-in-law – like a caricature of an Italian extended family, for six weeks of *dolce far niente*. I hated the idea. I had work to do. But my mother shouted and then whispered. I gave way.

Predictably, as we travelled, first by train and then by cart into sunshine and – yes – light, it was as if sudden electricity began to course through me, as if eyes and ears and nose, sealed for so many years, abruptly unthawed and popped. I discovered a world of softened forms, bevelled by time, grown organically and not in accordance with civic ordinances. Everywhere the picturesque lay in ambush, ready to be made back into pictures. Every wall and path exuded a symbolism of passing time, the cycle of the seasons, the mutability of human endeavour. Even my father felt it and slipped off his jacket to parade around in shirtsleeves and braces. As I looked from my window into the trees that tumbled down the broken slopes into purple heat haze, I was not the first northerner to be seduced by a fiery southern orange, each one a miniature sun nestling in deepest green. Nor, come to think of it, by Luigi, the stableboy.

I am shy of the depiction of the sexual act in my work. Its shadow is to be found there, by the observant, in the cast of a glance or the tilt of a shoulder. But with black, flying locks, olive skin and muscled thighs, it seemed to me that Luigi was the perfect model to pose for me in emulation of David and – it was revealed – had been more blessed by God in one aspect than David by niggardly Michelangelo. Moreover, it became apparent that his duty or privilege had always included the matter-of-fact servicing of tenants who might require it. He immediately understood my unarticulated needs better than myself and I was astonished to be swiftly mounted with the smiling uncomplicated complaisance with which he would have greeted a similar desire in my sister or – I was almost sure – the donkeys that he cared for out of season. I shall draw a veil of discretion over the long, sultry afternoons spent amidst the smell of horses and tumbled straw as I explored his endlessly affable body with my sketching charcoal and trembling fingers. Language played little part in our relationship as we worked our way through the poses of the entire classical canon and the worship of his flesh flowed into the worship of my art as I hotly deployed all the devices I had so coldly mastered in the north. Luigi presented and preened and laughed and disdainfully kicked my own body into poses for his own pleasure as he saw fit. At the end of an afternoon, he would yawn and pout and – in an eloquent gesture – swipe his palm across his chest to flick the sweat and such other of our fluids as had accumulated there to the ground, before silently holding it out, still damp, for his fee. Then he would stalk away with a not-unfriendly tweak to my nose as I gaped at the departing

– almost Florentine – buttocks. So, little by little, my unknown senses were coaxed into life and stretched their stiff muscles as my scrawny, white body hardened and blossomed in the reflected sunlight. I grew a moustache.

"When you all return home," I informed my mother with careful casualness at breakfast one morning, "I think I shall stay on for a bit. I'm getting a lot out of Italy. " Several teaspoons clattered simultaneously onto the tabletop. My father paused in the slicing of ham.

"Impossible!" She breathed sceptical cologne into the coffee smell. "How could you possibly keep on a house like this on your own?"

My brothers and sisters, sensing an approaching storm, seized bread, fruit, slices of ham and sidled away from the table to the bright sunlight of the garden.

I smiled reasonably. "I didn't mean to stay on here, mother. There is a boarding house for hikers just up the hill where I can get a room very cheaply out of season – the place where Luigi takes care of the donkeys." I blushed. "It is my chance to build up a portfolio of my own work. I can travel around the hills, the villages, record the daily life." I addressed my father. "That is the business capital of an artist," I hazarded. "The development of an artist's career must follow a certain logical progression."

He pursed his lips and pared cheese with the folding knife he carried always in his pocket.

I took a deep breath and drew a piece of paper from my own. "It will save money. It is so much cheaper for me to live here than Amsterdam. I have all the figures." I passed them across and my father dug out pince-nez and ran a doubting finger down the columns. I had naturally omitted certain items, such as Luigi's ... fees.

My mother returned to the chase. "But what of your commitments at the school? Your professors? You have not yet received your diploma."

"There is nothing here for laundry," observed my father, papertapping.

"I have submitted all the necessary course work, mother. My diploma can be mailed to me. I am completely free." As I said it, I knew it was true and felt a sudden fear grip my heart. There is nothing more terrifying than absolute freedom. I have hidden from it all my life.

"Surely this figure is inadequate for painting materials. Are they cheaper or more expensive here, so far from the city? Have you even checked?"

"You are too young to live alone, my son."

"I am twenty-three, mother. Most of my contemporaries already have their own place."

"What about footwear? If you are trekking through the hills you will need a lot of boots."

"So that is it. You want to be alone to do as you wish, to live the wild life of an artist. It is not, I think, drink. You have only taken the wine here in moderation. Do you have some model?" She looked at me coldly and her mouth shaped with distaste. "Some woman?" Only another woman could put so much contempt into the word.

"No woman," I said carefully but the words caught in my throat. I coughed and tried again. "I can assure you there is no woman, mother." How little we really deceive our mothers. "I wish only to work undisturbed."

"That I do not believe. It is something else," she said, fumbling at her bosom for a handkerchief. Her voice dropped to a hiss. She was whispering again, this time not for my father's ears. "Something much worse. Something I don't want to even think about. I have read about such things with artists. The other day, I happened to look in your portfolio and did not greatly like what I saw. Too many naked bodies, men's bodies."

I was stung. "Mother, you had no right ... That is to say ..." I smirked condescendingly. "Those are not naked bodies. They are nudes, part of the tradition of Western art. Where bodies are concerned, the artist is like a doctor. He is above the excitement of ... of ..."

"Socks!" shouted my father, waving the page at us like holy writ. We both turned open-mouthed, having heard something much worse that we did not want to think about. He took off his glasses and stared into our astonishment. "Socks," he urged. "You will get through six pairs or more a month. You know what Italian men's socks are like. Cheap, yes, but wear them for three days on the trot and they go all in holes. And, say what you like, you can't go without socks for long. No man can. Not even an artist."

And so I won the argument, by default, by putting in my mother's hands a weapon so devastating she dare not pick it up.

I settled in comfortably with the Widow Traverso and her hollow-eyed daughter, Gabriella. There was a vast and cosy kitchen, with bubbling stockpots, strung-up hams and sausages and a great fireplace haunted by cats. Its flanks were lined with pots of dried herbs and fruits and from it emerged big, heavy dishes involving dumplings, beef bones, offal in a hundred forms. She and Gabriella were the local wise women, midwives, herbalists, bone-setters and, like all people credited with special powers, they were at the margins of the social and had a whiff of witchcraft about them. Local boys walked past with their hands thrust deep in their trouser pockets to protect the glory of their manhood with propitiatory gestures of clenched fists and horns made with fingers. But Western medicine had yet to reach this remote valley and was anyway too costly for the local farmers, so they were tolerated and the fact of their not going to church was never mentioned in Lansoprazole.

We were to spend long open-windowed evenings here, struggling through an ancient, dog-eared almanac whose runic dictates ordered the affairs of the house, the women knitting, or me deciphering an occasional newspaper with a dictionary or talking to one of the rare hikers who stayed overnight, till last thing, usually before nine, the Widow would brew us all a cup of citronella as a nightcap.

Upstairs were three plain bedrooms, one shared by the ladies and two for guests. At the back lay the stables where Luigi plied his trade. The Widow was more than glad to have me, a rare permanent guest, unfussy, grateful and out most of the time, ranging the hills and valleys with my friend Luigi and his other mounts. One evening I drew her and her daughter in a hasty, slipshod charcoal that she received with cries of ecstasy and set up over the mantlepiece, behind the holy almanac, with much joyful handclasping. If only all audiences were so easy to please.

And so that hot summer passed in slow content. On my daily excursions, I sketched and looted the area for the picturesque, to be worked up later in oils. Even the women were pretty and I captured their bursting bosoms with bold manly strokes of pencil and charcoal, just as readily as the sculpted torsos and pert buttocks of the local men. I made my first attempts at the local tongue, words, simple sentences.

Luigi sometimes schooled me but was incapable of sustained effort and his attention flickered. Mostly I simply talked at him in Dutch, as I did the kitchen cats, with exaggerated assumptions of his comprehension. For his part, he occasionally sang in a lusty, inaccurate tenor – local songs that may have had some religious burthen but, judging from the thrusting gestures of his fists and leering grin, were probably all happily about wine and women. I tried to probe him on the family history of the Traversi. He informed me by rotating his finger rapidly at the temple and whistling, that the Widow was a little crazy, by pinching his fingers together against his chest that Gabriella's tits were too small and by triggering his thumb against his head and letting it loll, that Signor Traverso had been shot – or perhaps shot himself at least an extended hand ago. Then he gestured down to his balls, clenched a fist and laughed. That, I took to mean that, as a great stallion, he had nothing to fear from their female powers.

Our journeys were punctuated with "interludes". Luigi and I rutted like Arcadian woodnymphs on rocks and in sylvan glades fragrant with rosemary, thyme and the cliches of Poussin as we tore ravenously at the ham, cheese and bread provided by the Widow, washed down with pitiless black wine. A sort of tradition of the afternoon siesta imposed itself, where, fuddled by drink, we bathed or sunned ourselves or slept muskily intertwined in the undergrowth. The world buzzed happily like crickets in my ears. I had never done such good work.

And then the season began to change in Lansoprazole as summer gave way to autumn, the leaves of the few deciduous trees turned to gold and my portfolio bulged with harvest scenes, the benison of nature's foison, in heaped up grapes, olives and sheaves of wheat. A cold wind howled from the north, blowing up the dust. It was now too cold to swim and, when it came to the much anticipated "interludes", Luigi was suddenly all pouting reluctance. It was too windy, people might see, he was tired. I sighed and accepted that a point had been passed in our relationship – saddened it is true – but impressed by my own emotional sophistication. I sought refuge in the imagery of nature. The grape had given its first juice but there were still second pressings and these were often the sweetest. I took to working in the empty guest room, painting, pasting, shaping what I had gleaned, getting it all down on canvas as my breath steamed in the icy air – with occasional, and increasingly rare, furtive assignations in the stable to still my appetite and fire my inspiration. The room was so cold, the paint would not dry so I paved the boards with canvases, like so many paving slabs and then worried about the padding cats.

Then, as I lay sleeping one night, he was suddenly there, hard and urgent, garlicky breath in my ear, hands strong round my waist, panting in anticipation. I was glad that I had taken the end room. Emptiness lay between us and the women. We filled it with groans and gasps.

The next morning, I was as one beguiled. Had it really happened? The happy soreness of my body confirmed that it had. After that, he came a couple of nights a week, unannounced, like some hot, desirable succubus, threading in and out of my fantasies. And on those nights when he did not come, my sleep was of a dreamless depth I had never known before. I was ... fulfilled.

It ended, one mid-morning, as I was waiting for Luigi to arrive for one of our promenades. He had been three days without coming. There was blown snow outside, the gleam of icicles to be captured, the chilled huddling of peasant and livestock. In a dream, I had seen him enter my room silently in the night and leave with just a chaste kiss and a grinned "Ciao". A ghost. I was worried. The superstition of the house was infectious. He had never disappeared like this before. The Widow shrugged. He was a man. Regularity was not to be expected of men. I was different, perhaps, being an artist, but possibly not. Maybe he had gone to the city to look for work. He would return when he was ready. In the meantime, Gabriella would look after the donkeys.

First came the scream that sounded like the heart being torn from the chest of a living person. Then a low, agonised moan: "*Il tessore. Il tessore.*"

I was in the kitchen, cold, trying to stroke a little heat from one of the resentful cats, coaxed aboard my boney knees. The scream came from above. Then feet pounding up the stairs. Mine, I realised. The door of the Widow's room stood wide open. I had never been inside this female space before. It was much as I had imagined – bare floor, hard, wooden furniture and, in the middle, the great, wallowing bed that was the centre of the house. Here had been enacted her marriage, the conception and birth of Gabriella, perhaps the death of her husband killed by his own thumb – hand. Beneath the bed was stowed every valuable thing of the household, now strewn in all directions – an ancient shotgun, a motheaten fur coat, deeds to the land, a clutch of sepia wedding pictures, powerful herbal specifics, a vast Bible fit to beat demons to death and – clearly – the economies of the household.

"*Per la nozze di Gabriella*," sobbed, red-eyed Widow Traverso. Her wedding costs or – more likely – her dowry, then. She crouched there, wailing, skirts immodestly pulled up to display despair in woolly knickers. Between her legs lay the biscuit tin that had held the "treasure" whose disappearance she was currently grieving, clutching her hands to her twisted mouth. Was I suspected? I could not tell. And then she lifted her eyes and looked at me with a terrible hatred and pain that seemed to distill the suffering of all betrayed mothers. As I began to stammer denials and protest my innocence she extended a grim hand and I saw that all this was not for me but for Gabriella, standing terrified behind me and a fearful truth dawned on all three of us.

"Luigi!" I still don't know which of us spoke the name. It evoked a further eruption of female wailing and shouting from which I hastily withdrew to my room, not venturing out until driven by evening hunger into a silent, brooding house.

The next few days were intensely difficult. Only slowly did I piece the whole the truth together from the Widow's cursing into her cooking pots, or shouting after Gabriella words to be found in no dictionary. It seemed that, on the evenings when he did not come to me, Luigi had visited Gabriella. And the sleeping Widow danced sympathetically as he enjoyed her daughter's too-small charms there in the great bed. The lacing of our citronella with verbena or some other somniferant explained our depth of sleep. I was agog at the idea of Luigi plunging into Gabriella as the slumbering basilisk lay inches away snoring through her moustache and then extracting the dowry, as the daughter – mission accomplished – lay, in turn, smiling in sated sleep. Yet, in a way, I understood. For Luigi, after his own fashion, was an artist too. He had done this, I knew, not just for the money but to take his art to a higher plane. Wherever he was, he would not starve – at least not until pasta and grappa had done their work to sap and sag that splendid facade. And, if my dream was to be believed, he had at least said goodbye.

But it was time for me, too, to say goodbye. Blame could not be laid at my door. I had not, after all, introduced Luigi into the household. But our friendship associated me in his guilt. Not only was the house poisoned by slow-burning rage, even to my innocent eye, Gabriella was beginning to swell and bloat. Luigi would naturally be bursting with a quite unnecessary fecundity and it was only a matter of time before the shotgun and the wedding pictures under the bed coalesced into a single idea, bringing the Widow's eye to rest on me as the one way to save both the honour and fortune of the Traversi by a swift marriage. I hastily packed my traps, quick with a more artistic fertility and returned to grey, rain-sodden Amsterdam.

Mynheer Vorderman had laid out the canvases all round the living room as in the spare room in Lansoprazole. My father appraised him pince-nezed as he, in turn, appraised my work. Women had been banished since this was considered a matter for men. He held up a delicate study of a mother and daughter, based on the charcoal of the Traversi, crackled his feet and nodded.

"Breasts," he puffed happily. I had somewhat idealised Gabriella, lending her the bosom of Luigi's dreams. It positively exploded. "The lad does good breasts and in Amsterdam people like a nice solid pair of breasts from elsewhere over the sideboard. Not Dutch breasts mind. That's another thing entirely. Get you in a lot of trouble Dutch breasts." He cast his gaze over the other paintings in nodding content. "Peasants, ruins ..." he looked down again "... breasts. Not my taste of course. Scarcely *avant garde* as you'd be the first to admit but there's a market for these. The art of small houses and tidy minds. We'll do an exhibition – one of those little places down by the canal – a few bottles of wine, some Italian cheese, the stuff with the grape pips on the rind. I'll cover costs and framing. We split the take 50–50. You get rid of that moustache." He meant mine not the Widow Traverso's. "What do you say?"

"He's delighted," said my father, stepping forward to shake his hand and accept one of the poisonous cheroots. And so I became a professional artist, standing on my own feet, making my own decisions.

* * *

My Italian pictures, it was quite generally agreed, were a commercial triumph. At first I thought I was unlucky with the weather, one of those misty evenings lit only by the gleam of rain-slicked cobblestones, whose chill discourages nocturnal outings. But that made the glow of the warm south, in which my pictures were steeped, irresistible to these pale northerners. The air was heavy with mothballs and compensating cologne, the smell of a middle-class crowd. Jacob Vorderman had combed his little black book to entice them out and here they were, good solid people with money in their pockets, the dentured classes, who might be interested in a picture of something they could recognise by an artist on the way up. There were a few expensive and elaborate oils to tempt the extravagant but these were heavily padded out with bargain-price pastels and gouaches that held out the hope of turning into a good investment.

In one corner was the mayor, his eyes dancing round the crowd, identifying, annotating; in another, the doyenne of female society, Mrs van Damm – each surrounded by their court with Jacob firedancing back and forth. And already more than half the pictures were decorated with the red dot of success, signifying that they had been sold. It is always a shock for a painter to see his pictures, for the first time, mounted and framed, closed and complete. Hung on a wall, they now have to hold their own against all the other works in the world that could stand in their place. They are no longer a work in progress. They define you.

My parents were there, glowing. The exhibition had somehow defined them too. Father was finally a successful businessman among his peers, talking money, banks and investments to those not too proud to listen. Mother was in something towering and black that set off her eyes, with matching gloves buttoned to the armpits. She was, above all, relieved by the bosoms – on the walls not in the room. Blatantly heterosexual, they swelled and throbbed from every corner, but always constrained and tightly bodiced, the obvious face of thwarted schoolboy lust. This was not, she was thinking quite rightly, the archive of a sated satyr. This was what Dr Freud was teaching us to call "repression". Lust, yes, but still safely unslaked. I was glad to duck behind them like a rampart.

Jacob led me over to be presented to Mrs van Damm. We still kissed hands in those days after the First World War. It took a second war to stop the handkissing. This one, presented with coyly bent wrist, was sallow, blue-veined and liver-spotted, the skin almost transparent beneath the rings.

"So young!" She cooed cupping my newly unmoustached face. "I want you to know I have bought one of your pictures – that adorable little one in pastiche over there." She pointed.

I frowned in incomprehension. Then the penny dropped. "Oh, I see. Not 'pastiche'. You mean in pastel." Her mouth set hard. Clearly, she was unused to contradiction.

Jacob intervened. "I think you misunderstand," he hissed, footcrackling. "Not the other one. Mrs Vorderman means that one *in pastiche*."

"Oh right."

She resumed. "What I loved about it was that sweet little doggie in the shadows."

"Oh that's not a dog. That's … oh I see. The dog … right. How clever of you to spot it."

"But it has no title." She looked piqued. "Every painting has to have a title."

"It's not strictly a painting. Oh, right. Well … it's 'Doggie in Pastiche'." I glared at Vorderman who oleaginated back.

"Would you like Mr Bonnet to write it on the reverse for you?"

"Lovely," she cooed. Jacob relaxed and smirked. I went and took down the painting, pulled a pencil from my inside pocket. I hesitated at what I knew was another defining moment. I could jot down something obscene and insulting, draw a vicious caricature of Mrs van Damm, sketch my own face with extended tongue. Instead, I looked at my happy parents, Vorderman chestswelling and relaxed, sighed and wrote "Doggie in Pastiche". Yet in some strange way, I was enjoying this, biting down on my own pain and humiliation in a toothache-sucking fashion. Dr Freud was teaching us to call that "masochism".

Over by the drinks table, knocking it back without dissimulation, was a bunch of my contemporaries at the art school. As I approached, they turned to face me and greeted me with undisguised sniggers.

"At least the food and wine is the real stuff," smirked Bakker, a skinny, stooped figure in a threadbare jacket, who passed for something of a radical in student circles.

"Meaning the art isn't?"

He fluttered fingers of protesting innocence. "Did I say that? People come for different things." He poured another glass to show what he had come for. At least they were using glasses, not swigging directly from the bottle. "The last public event that was sure enough of an audience to go uncatered was probably the crucifixion. But what happened to constructivism, expressionism, surrealism ... even impressionism, for God's sake?

"This stuff ..." he swung the glass unsteadily round the room "... isn't what you'd call directly destructive of late capitalism is it, old man?" He smiled with false sweetness and slipped a condescending arm around my shoulder. I shook myself free.

"Is that what art is to be measured by, its power of destruction? What about the giving of innocent pleasure, the struggle for form and mastery of technique – the purely aesthetic?"

They fell about in simulated humorous collapse, slapped each other on the back, gasped for air, clutched at the table. The silent films, with their exaggerated gestures, were upon us.

"True art," he smirked as one imparting a sad lesson to a slow child, "is the expression of the will of the proletariat."

"But, but ..." I thought of my firm-chested peasants, my noble horny-handed sons of toil "... does not every line here speak of the dignity of labour, the integrity of the peasant?"

His eyes blazed with anger. "Bourgeois false consciousness," he snarled. Red spots of sale appeared in his cheeks. "The rural masses collaborating in their own exploitation?"

I pointed to my own red spots. "Does it count for nothing that so many have been sold? You lot would give your right arm – arms – to sell like that."

Bakker, suddenly calm, regarded me with genuine pity. "Dear boy. The fact that so many people buy you is the clearest proof of all that, either you are no good, or you are being tragically misunderstood." He pursed his lips to deliver oracular judgement. "My own view is that they understand you only too well." He sneered. "Go on. Go back to your ..." he campily lisped the word and did something showgirly with his legs "public", making it obscene.

I turned abruptly, eyes full of tears, only to cannon into something small and hard – a diminutive person, all in black with prominent teeth and hand outstretched, a sort of bucktoothed Toulouse Lautrec.

"Tidmans," he sucked inspiration from the teeth, "*Telegraf.*"

Tidmans, the famous art-critic whose articles were like little polished jewels, collected to be published every year in book form. He was justly famous for his insight, his uncanny ability to go beyond the particular in an artist's work to seize some point of more general validity. He sandwiched my single hand warmly in both of his and nodded at the students.

"The adulation of one's coevals," he ducked his head modestly to show he had had his share of it. "This must be a wonderful moment for you," he chuckled. "A young artist's first exhibition! But it won't be all like this, you know." He twinkled avuncular wisdom. "There will be bad times too, when it seems you are not getting the recognition you deserve and it is as if the whole world is conspiring to bring you down. That's when you must think back to the rare moments of unalloyed triumph like this!"

After that, there were other trips to Italy, other exhibitions, in the course of which I established a small but faithful clientèle or, to use Bakker's word, public, still interested in the classic depiction of the human form. But these suffered from a law of diminishing returns and, little by little, I felt my art drying out and withering beneath my fingers. I knew I was treading out a final pressing. I sought other Italian valleys and mountains, served my artistic apprenticeship in Florence at the feet of Michelangelo's Luigi – I mean David. I hunted out new suns. By a drunkard's logic, if heat-soaked Italy had been good for me, perhaps blazing North Africa would be even better. All I found was unromantic dust, tedium, pilfering and unwashed, disobliging youths. I toured the cathedral cities of Italy, lit candles in a dozen basilicas, bathed my blank Protestant soul in the light of stained glass, prayed for a new path, a sign. Then, on a journey to Rome, in my twenty-eighth year, inspiration abruptly came to me, not as an angel, a visually transformed altarpiece or a message from God but in the form of a small, podgy Dutchman in shorts and high, laced-up boots.

"Nieuwenkamp." He had the limp, boneless grip of all Dutchmen who have worked in the Indies where the natives touch, but do not squeeze, white hands. "Wijnand Nieuwenkamp."

I was – we were – staying in a small *pensione* near the Spanish steps run by another widow – this time Dutch – who kept canaries dotted about the terrace in small cages. It was the year of 1923 and there were three of us at the table, the last being MC Escher, an artist with a huge though diseased graphic talent, that condemned him to an obsession with the transformation of geometric forms. As we spoke, he was bent over the tabletop of pierced metal, his dark hat held underneath, his head cocked sideways in an attempt to transform the floral swirls that made up its solid surface into the empty ground of the dark shapes thus created with the hat. As I say, he was obsessed. His gift was mathematical rather than purely artistic and mathematicians are often more than a little strange. Escher looked at the whole world through a mop of dark hair with the innocent gaze of a child staring at a turning tin angel above its cot and Nieuwenkamp talked about him as though he weren't there. He poured red wine into our glasses from the carafe and I could see Escher juggling his eyeballs, mentally converting half-empty into half-full and back again.

"Come up to my room," said Nieuwenkamp, "and see my etchings, as the actress said to the bishop." Then he saw Escher's swimming eyes. "Wait, no. Better you stay here and I'll bring them down. It's the hall, the stairs you see – they're all covered in square, black and white tiles and up on the first floor, someone has set two mirrors on the walls at forty-five degrees to each other. Once he sees them, he gets frozen in the perspective, can't move, the sorry bugger. Are they going up, are they coming down, approaching us, receding? He's there for hours every day staring at those bloody tiles. The second floor's worse. There they've got a convex mirror."

Escher had started sketching, dribbling, turning pages, unaware that we were even there, threading his pencil in and out of his beard. It was the window now that had him. The ratio of height to breadth of the individual panes of glass, it seemed, was the same as that of the whole casement to the frame. The sun, shifting round the patio, hit the canaries and they burst into sudden song.

"Nested structures," sighed Nieuwenkamp ambiguously. "Recursive something-or-others. He's always on about it." He shrugged and clattered off upstairs in the boots, reappearing, several minutes later, with a large, elegant book. "My Balinese pictures!" He glowed with authorial pride, lay the book down with a comforting thump, pushed it across at me. "You say you've sucked Italy dry. Bali, latest jewel of our eastern empire, a whole new world just waiting to be captured! Privately published of course."

As usual I noticed the style before the form, rather crude drawings, weak use of shadow and colour, clumsy figures – the work of a book illustrator, not an artist. Escher was now on his knees under the table looking up at the cover with wonder through the pierced tabletop. It occurred to me that both had lived lives softened by family money, no need to compromise, to earn a living. Neither would have cut his teeth on the ladies of the corsetry trade. I turned the pages, scarcely able to breathe. It was all there – ancient temples and palaces, dances, markets, towering volcanoes, trees so old and twisted they were rooted in time itself. Money for old rope. One picture showed rice terraces cascading down a hill, each sinuous mudbank in counterpoint to the next. Escher, now peering at it through his fingers, danced on the spot and whimpered, like a dog watching a squirrel up a tree. If you imagined the image in two dimensions, it was as if a giant had flung a rock into a lake and sent out rippling reverberations from a hidden centre.

"I was there when the troops went in in 1906," said Nieuwenkamp. "Cycled all over the island, drawing. Been back since, of course. Oh, yes, it's changed. We have brought them the blessings of corrugated iron and syphilis but it's still special. Friendliest people on earth. Best of all ..." he turned another page and pointed, "... tits! Lots of 'em. Only the harlots and Dutch women wear blouses. No point in giving away what you can sell, eh?" He had painted a chubby woman doing her hair, with elbows up, in an awkward pose better calculated to exhibit her breasts. "Brazen!" His epiglottis was working away. "Blazing!" With an effort he calmed himself. "Actually, of course, it's a form of innocence. Eve not knowing she's naked and all that. I seem to remember from your last show you're a tits man, Bonnet? Thought so."

All that came to mind was corsets. But I could see myself reworking that picture, making it better, shifting the torso more to one side, cocking the sinews of the thighs, catching the tone of the muscles moving under the skin, the play of shadow, the delicate planes and contours of the face that Nieuwenkamp had turned into a featureless blob. From somewhere came a whiff of coconut oil and patchouli, the authentic smell of the East. It was Escher's hairoil, he standing close behind me, working away at a sketch. He held it out to us smiling, a savant child wanting his parents' praise. By a series of slow transformations across the page, a volcano – belching flame and smoke – had become a bare-breasted maid with elaborate plumed headdress had become a smiling, muscular youth with a suitcase marked "Bonnet" on his head, the whole quite beautifully drawn.

"Well would you look at that," said Nieuwenkamp, wonderingly. "Not so daft, then."

2

You might reasonably expect, at this point, that I would return to the subject of Walter, allowed to drop in the previous digression, but the moment is not yet right. You left me in Rome. I have to get to Java and that getting was no small matter.

My mother, her mind haunted by images of colonial heat, insects – possibly even Komodo dragons – was convinced that I would die.

"Why is it we worry more about you than all our six other children put together?" she sobbed.

"The Indies is not Africa, mother. Our people live long, healthy lives there, given the proper precautions. Anyway," I added with the heartlessness of youth, "everyone has to die somewhere."

Proper precautions were much on the mind of my father, certain that I would fall foul of the exotic women he knew to roam abroad not just singly, as in Amsterdam, but in great wild herds. His parting gift to me, slipped into my pocket on the harbour jetty, was a large, flat tin embossed with the names of Goodyear and Hancock. In my innocence, I had assumed it was a puncture repair kit for the bicycle I had declared I would buy in emulation of Nieuwenkamp. Only later, when stowing my gear in the tiny cabin, did I open it to find a confusing sausage of sturdy rubber with instructions for scrubbing in hot water after use and regular airing to prevent the growth of mould.

The little boat, *Bintoehan*, of the KPM line was a smart tin toy. Nearly new and brightly painted she was somewhat too frisky for many of the passengers in the slow swell that set in immediately we left Rotterdam. Deft Javanese stewards roamed the corridors with tinkling dinner gongs and hips that swayed to the memory of other gongs in childhood *gamelan* orchestras, trying in vain to tempt the passengers off their sickbeds. My own stomach withstood the pounding, indeed the sea air had lent me fierce appetite. I dined virtually alone in the dining room, sumptuously over-served, under a poster that sang the charms of Bali. At that time it seemed to me wonderfully evocative. It showed a beautiful slant-eyed maid sitting erect and cross-legged and holding a lotus flower as a Madonna her child. The older eyes of memory reveal it as nothing but – to use Mrs van Damm's word – a hopeless and embarrassing pastiche – an obviously Javanese girl with Javanese covered breasts, sitting awkwardly in a male pose, Balinese headdress slapped on her head and holding a Buddhist icon. It was the sort of thing that nowadays Professor Grits would write humourlessly about in grim erudition – "Colonial Photography – no Photgraphies – and the Framing of the Cultural Negative", or some such nonsense. Never mind. It fired my imagination as I chewed my way through endless dishes spiced with chilli and turmeric – the Dutch *rijstafel* – a meal for the indecisive that allows you to taste everything without finishing anything, served on a bed of steaming rice. It was still the jazz age, a fact confirmed by a list of cocktails illustrated by a sophisticated sketch of a dancing glass. Embarking cautiously on the path of adventure, I worked down daily one spot from the Americano to the Zanzibar, judging that I would reach the Singapore Sling at the same time as the eponymous port. Few other concessions to modernity had been made. Syncopated rhythms had not seduced the ship's band, a bunch of gnarled old tooters and scrapers with shiny jacket collars, dusted with dandruff, who ground out endless arthritic foxtrots under the ticking ceiling fans.

Other figures began to appear, inevitable Dutch planters in crumpled alpaca suits, faded wives, plump and pushy administrators, a young pig-faced Lieutenant van Gennep of the sappers. All were swiftly and jealously appraised for a touch of the tarbrush and spontaneously sifted themselves into a rigid colonial hierarchy of race. The ship itself was a model of empire in miniature: stern-faced white officers; unseen helots, Chinese and Indian, toiling below; and trim, cool Javanese as the acceptable face of the East. The problem of a large but wealthy Eurasian family, the Niemeyers, always in white and displaying a beautiful chromatic range squeezed from the burnt sienna tube, was tactfully defused by allotting them their own dining table "to keep the family together". As whiter than Cremnitz white and direct from the homeland, I was able to delude myself that I had opted out of any such classification – a citizen of the world. As a bachelor, I fell as prize to the shipboard spinsters, the Van Tonk sisters of Haarlem or tortoise-necked Miss Timms, on her way to rejoin her brother's clerical vocation in Singapore following a little home leave in a missionary house in Stoke Newington. Endless games of deck quoits, bridge and sticky foxtrots were my penance, interspersed with coy jokes of romance: "I'm setting my cap at you Mr Bonnet", "The ladies trump you again with their fluttering hearts, young man", "A game of table tennis, Mr Bonnet, unless you are afraid of losing to love?" and so on. It was the most sustainedly athletic period of my life and I was glad to be accepted as part of this brave little community, to be assumed to be just another element of the normal world. Meanwhile, the real face of normality, Lieutenant van Gennep, sat at a corner table and sipped endless gins, crotch visibly bulging, as he appraised the Eurasian girls with hot, frustrated eyes and eased his tight colonial collar.

We were to take the Cape route via South Africa and steamed slowly down the west coast, calling briefly at some of the minor ports – Dakar, Takouradi, Lagos, Fernando Poo – to embark deck cargo and a mass of seething steerage passengers. At the time, it was considered more healthy than the route via Suez, allowing a more gentle acclimatisation, as the thermostat was slowly turned up by divine hand and a plague of flies buzzed in from the armpit of Africa to crouch thickly on every surface. Having tired of jokes about Biblical plagues with Miss Timms, I sat in my cabin, or on the foredeck, batting the flies away and practising my Malay vocabulary with the stewards.

"*Lalat*, 'fly'?" I pointed questioning at a huge bluebottle.

"*Lalat!*" confirmed dark-eyed, smiling Hamid with a flick of a flyswat, plucked from his waistband, that sent it tumbling to the deck.

As we eased towards Cape Town a sudden cold mist descended and as the sun burned it off the flies evaporated with it, revealing a deep and peaceful harbour and a town of neat Dutch buildings and tree-lined streets strung out along the foot of Table Mountain laid with its cloth of white cloud. Miss Timms and the Van Tonks embarked in an open horsedrawn cab on a tour of the cathedral and lesser places of worship, climaxing in tea at the Mount Nelson Hotel. I had intended to escort them but was surprised, at the last minute, to be waylaid by Lieutenant van Gennep who was waiting at the bottom of the gangway at the wheel of a large and disreputable Buick convertible, its engine already throbbing.

"Quick Bonnet!" he hissed. "Before the old girls see you." The door was thrown invitingly open and, without thinking, I got in. It was one of the more unusual days of my life.

I had expected to be driven round the town centre, the little squares, the grandiloquent buildings of national identity, the odd monument to some person of inflated local importance before going somewhere dark and cool to taste the local wine. It was not to be.

Van Gennep skirted all such temptations and headed inland with a purposeful look, crunching gears in the overworked gearbox. Over the roar of the engine, communication was difficult but there could be no doubt where we were heading – Table Mountain. He drew up and applied the handbrake with relish, as a man might apply sauce to a sausage and nodded at a sign indicating a hiking trail.

"We've been sitting around too damned much, Bonnet. Now we can get the stiffness out of our legs." He set off at a cracking pace, leaving me no alternative but to follow, panting after him. Dressed as I was for visiting cathedrals, it was not an enjoyable experience. My thin-soled shoes slipped and skidded in the dust, I had no hat, my tie blew in the chill wind coming off the sea. At one moment my legs went from under me entirely and it was only by seizing a prickly plant with my bare hands that I avoided a nasty, possibly fatal, fall. My cries and protests went unheard or at least unheeded. Everywhere, nameless things slithered and scuttled and stones from Van Gennep's feet showered my head and face. After some two and a half hours, I emerged, sweaty, cold, thirsty, filthy and whimpering, at the peak or rather the plateau. Van Gennep was standing one foot comfortably raised on a rock, as on a barrail, hands thrust in pockets, puffing a cheroot and savouring the salt-spiced view, a vast vista of land and glittering sea.

"Damn and blast you, Van Gennep!" I cursed. "You could have got me killed."

He turned in astonishment. "Now what way is that for an artist to talk? Just look at the panorama, old man. I should have thought you'd show more interest. Still," he shrugged as one greatly miffed, "if that's how you feel perhaps we'd better just go back down."

He turned and retraced our steps at least twice as fast as before, crying out with joy at each headlong skid towards the edge. I abandoned all pretence of dignity and performed most of the descent on my backside. When I arrived at the bottom, dithering with rage and fear, he was dozing comfortably at the wheel. He tipped back his hat and looked me over.

"Righty-ho. I see things of the spirit are not your thing, Bonnet. Time for the flesh."

We drove in broody silence due south, or at least as much silence as could make itself heard over the roar of the engine, but the landscape thawed our mood. On our right lay the ocean, curling surf on sand and rock, on our left a softly, undulating valley, neatly combed into vineyards. Smiling black faces peered out at us. The air was scrubbed clean and cool by fresh rain. I began to turn it into tableaux in my mind, curling vine tendrils, capturing the spray off the surf, worrying over the shine on nose and cheekbones of black faces, easy enough to render in oils but what would be the best technique in charcoal or pastels? Mile after mile lay behind us. A sign urged us on to Constantia. We passed small *dorps* with bales of wire and barrels outside wooden stores and glimpsed white, step-gabled Dutch houses in the distance. Finally, we turned through wrought-iron gates and crunched up gravel to an imposing building set back from the road and shaded by old trees.

A smiling coffee-coloured face appeared and a delightful young man bowed us in and waved us to a table set in an arbour. Van Gennep ordered a bottle of the local white and it was brought, proffered for inspection and delicately poured. The cool taste of gooseberry and cinnamon, overtones of lime. It seemed to me that the waiter smiled over his shoulder as he walked away.

"You have been here before?" I offered appreciatively.

"Not at all." He sipped and leant back with a sigh. "The recommendation of Van Hunks, a fellow officer, a Cape Boer. *This*," he leant forward again for emphasis, "is the best house in the whole province."

I looked around. It was a nice house, old, solid, certainly comforting, but was it the *best* house? I decided to keep my reservations to myself.

After a while the waiter appeared again, still smiling. He really was a very handsome young man. Perhaps, he invited, the gentlemen would care to the see the stock of the house. I was quickly on my feet. As I say, I have always delighted in wine-cellars, the long ranges of barrels stretching away in the gloom, the peace, the still time. He led us across the garden and through a French door. I froze, my jaw dropped.

Arranged around the walls of an elegant room, on a variety of chaises and sofas were sprawled young men of colour, all in very white underdrawers. The air was a musky, velvety exhalation. They smiled and stretched, demonstrating the muscular perfection of their limbs. One leant forward and gently stroked the back of my hand. He looked up, huge brown eyes, from under long lashes and asked, in a husky voice, "So ... you want to taste the African banana?"

Blood thundered in my ears, sweat gushed over my whole body, a huge erection drained the blood from my brain so that world turned and swivelled in greyness. "I ... I ..." Dimly, I perceived, a "house" was a house of ill repute – though this was a house of ill repute of high repute. "I ... I ..." Then Van Gennep was there behind me.

"What the fuck? Out, Bonnet! Out!" I felt strong hands grab me and was dragged, in zombie trance, legs left-and-righting like a mechanical toy and thrown into the car.

"I ... I ..." I dimly heard the engine revving, shouts, giggles and suddenly I came to to the sound of Van Gennep's own hysterical laughter as we hit the road and fish-tailed back towards the city, plumes of dust twisting behind us.

"I'll get the bastard," he chortled, slapping his thigh. "Good one though. Fancy Van Hunks sending us to a *male* whorehouse! He must have laughed himself silly. Wait till I get back to the mess. Thank God we got away before they got stuck into their pitch. Could have turned nasty. The evil bastard. If we were happy to settle for that, after all, we could have just given the steward a poke."

I shook my head. "What? How?"

"Oh come on Bonnet, for Christ's sake." He accelerated viciously. "When were you born? Everyone knows that any KPM steward is happy to oblige a passenger for a couple of florins. It should be on the ticket – a sort of right of passage."

I gaped, then ... "But shouldn't we perhaps go back and ... er ...

perhaps we should at least offer to pay for the wine?"

Van Gennep snorted. "This is no time to play the gentleman, Bonnet. Filthy buggers. Serves them right. Lucky I didn't give them a good thrashing." Blood suffused his piggy face. His hands tightened on the wheel as if strangling it.

"What he said ... about the African banana ..."

Van Gennep laughed again. "Yes. Now, that was good. Never heard that line before. Tasting the African banana! There are two ways you can take that!"

"Actually," I said dreamily, "I can think of at least three."

* * *

My parents back in Holland, to whom I wrote gushing postcards of the natural beauties of South Africa and my pencil itching to do its work, did not know. Miss Timms clearly did not know and had not the mental categories to make knowing possible. The Eurasian paterfamilias, Niemeyer, did know and curled his lip whenever he saw me, taking pains to gather his brood more closely about him as though against a pollution. The ordinary stewards all knew and no longer bantered with me in Malay. The head steward, chubby, smirking and deeply unattractive, most particularly knew and came to my cabin at all hours of the day and night with fresh towels and offers to pose for me. Van Gennep knew, of course, but to him it was nothing, simply part of a soldier making the best of a bad billet and living off the land.

But then it was all his fault. Those lightly spoken words of the accommodating nature of stewards had led me, heart pounding, to pluck up my courage and place my hand quite firmly on handsome Hamid's equally firm buttocks one morning as he bent across my bed with the breakfast tray. It had been an act of genuine attraction, liking, even respect. The result had been spilled coffee, shock, horror, manly tears and the display of photographs of his wife and children as proof that he did not, could not, and the takeover of his post by the chief steward with the cynical eyes and the breast-pocket always gaping for a tip. I had felt shame, guilt, self-disgust and anger in equal measure, the responses I had been conditioned since my childhood to feel towards my own tenderest emotions. I was well in advance of the age in learning to dismiss attraction and desire as mere allotropes of cultural oppression. My crime somehow communicated itself galvanically through the very metal of the hull, reaching all parts of the ship, including – I was sure – the engine room that I had never visited. The vibrations in the air were subtle. No one was openly rude or offensive. The captain did not cut me dead. But suddenly I was no longer part of the group. The Miss van Tonkses of Haarlem ceased to tease me, now a walking dirty joke, with offers of romance. I was no longer sought out for bridge and table tennis. Van Gennep, I saw, had quietly sidled into my place and seized the opportunity to move in on the Niemeyers, swapping bluff jokes with the father, telling stories of military life as he let his eyes rest on the vanilla-scented eldest daughter.

I took pains to be absent from the cabin when the chief steward made the bed. He responded by twisting and folding the towels into swans, roses, and then more directly anatomical expressions of thwarted interest that were left propped on my pillows as a dog might have cocked its leg. And so, most mornings, I sat alone on the foredeck, practising my Malay now without the help of the stewards, as the little ship ploughed across the ocean towards Colombo. Hamid, occasionally on duty there, would serve me coffee with the averted eyes of cold professionalism and I would tip him too lavishly. I had devalued the currency of our friendly relations, converted the gold of simple humanity to the dross of rutting bodies. Sometimes, I would draw the hands of fellow-passengers at the dinner table, or their feet on the dancefloor. Whole people seemed, for the moment, beyond me.

One morning, after the visit of the chief steward, I drew my own face in the looking glass. I still have it. A self-portrait is always a taking of stock. Remember those appallingly dispassionate self-portraits by Rembrandt – born incidentally just across the road from me though some time before, as I tell the young – executed at various stages of his life and charting his descent from youthful enthusiasm to senile dismay. In the mirror, I saw before me a man of some thirty-three years, tall, blondish hair still thick and cut short. The individual features were well enough though each flawed – the nose a little long, the cheeks a trifle too shallow, the neck somewhat scrawny, the weak blue eyes honest but small, imprisoned behind wire-rimmed spectacles – yet somehow they did not go together to make a satisfactory face. The fault lay, perhaps, principally in the mouth – small, thin-lipped, inescapably prissy and ungiven to the expression of joy. It is a cold, blank face, not radiant with innocence and yet lacking in self-confidence – worse – lacking in self-liking and spontaneity. There is something in it of a disillusioned undertaker.

* * *

The coast of Ceylon appeared in the early morning light as a thin moustache on the lip of the ocean. Little boats swept across our prow like swifts, manned by joyful people. Tones of magenta, cinnamon, Aztec gold and – appropriately enough – Indian yellow. Already I was translating it into the painting I would have made of it and sadly aware that the achieved painting would bring me more pleasure than the actual experience. Innocence was fled.

On cue, Van Gennep appeared and leant on the rail, chewing a cheroot.

"I wondered, old man, if you were up for a bit of how's-your-father like in South Africa?" he whispered. Why did he whisper? No one was there but us. "Van Hunks gave me another address."

I gave what I hoped was a withering glare. "No thank you."

"No need to be prissy about it, old man. It wasn't my fault it turned out the way it did. Anyway, from what I hear, you've made the adjustment. But maybe you're right. I wouldn't put it past Van Hunks to pull the same trick again. A sort of double bluff. One hell of a card-player Van Hunks." He shook his head, savouring it.

"Er ... where exactly did he suggest one went."

Van Gennep tapped his nose – a gesture that recalled Luigi. "Ah! A bit complicated. Got it all written down but I'd never forgive myself if you went on your own and got into trouble because I wasn't there to watch your back, as it were. Perhaps you should stay on board and draw the seagulls. I think I'll try for a bit of time alone with the number one Niemeyer girl. I think I'm well in there." He puffed up like pastry in the oven.

"Is that possible? Doesn't her father keep her under lock and key?" His confidence was irritating. His motives disgusted me.

He grinned. "Normally yes. I grant you. But Miss Timms is taking her on the cathedral and tea tour and I'm going to attach myself as escort to beat off the lustful natives. Strictly between you and me, I have high hopes." I pictured him fumbling, hot-crotched, under the tea table while smirking over the fine china. None of my business.

I did not, of course, stay on the boat. Instead, I was an ideal tourist. I admired the stripy extravagance of the Jami Ul Alfar mosque with its red and white brickwork; I ruminated poignantly, in ancient buildings, on the arms of the Portuguese, overlaid by those of the Dutch, overlaid by those of the British. I watched the little boys running on the beach screaming with joy as their kites battled the wind to get airborne. I soaked in the sounds of normal life as in a warm bath. Then, as I was passing the verandah of a large hotel, I heard my name being called.

"Mr Bonnet! Mr Bonnet!"

It was Miss Timms, dressed all in white, like one of the Niemeyers. She waved me over.

"Oh, do join me Mr Bonnet. Have some tea. Fresh Ceylon tea. Quite delicious." I looked down. Three dirty cups. She fussed at a boy – dressed like an extra from a Gilbert and Sullivan operetta – called over for fresh china and hot water. The furniture was all bamboo and rattan, warped and wobbly from the sea air with minimal privacy achieved by the insertion of potted palms. "A slice of walnut cake, Mr Bonnet? I am afraid you have to order a whole one and it is such a waste!" She sliced like a carpenter sawing a plank.

"You are alone, Miss Timms?"

"Oh yes." She looked coy. "The young people have gone off to have their fortunes read in the bazaar and left me to recover. There is so much to see here. It is all too much excitement. Normally, I do not approve of superstition, you understand, but it is only a little harmless fun for the young people. At the house in Stoke Newington the missionaries ran a summer fair with a fortune teller: Mrs Gibbs, normally a quite serious lady, dressed as The Amazing Madame Zodiac. It was such fun. She told me I would go on a long journey and meet a dark stranger. Well, that at least was true!" The house? Not, I presumed, a Van Gennep house. "I must say, they have been gone quite a while. I was beginning to worry a little, Mr Bonnet."

"Where exactly did they go?"

She looked confused, and reacted to the confusion by pouring more tea into the already abandoned cups. "Well ... I am not entirely sure. Lieutenant van Gennep had an address from a fellow officer."

"I see."

She looked around at all the English tea-takers and dropped her voice. "I know it is a lot to ask, Mr Bonnet, but I wonder if you might see if you can find them. Quite frankly, I hesitate to confront Mr Niemeyer without his daughter."

So there I was, in a strange city, charged with the protection of a young girl's honour and a missionary's shame, coerced by a morality that sneered at my own feelings, indeed, regarded my tenderest emotions as criminal. Why should I collaborate in such hypocrisy? Why did I not declare proudly who and what I was? I decided it could do no harm to take a walk in the immediate environs of the hotel. It would set Miss Timms' mind at rest and would otherwise achieve precisely nothing. I turned down a side road, then another, then another and found myself swiftly lost in a seething warren, some sort of market, echoing with sound and smells of sea and land. The stalls were so close together that I had to push between them, heaps of nameless vegetables, piles of cheap mattresses and oil lamps, a woman was gutting a fish. Suddenly, my passage was barred by a big man, a big man with a evil-looking monkey on his shoulder.

"Yes, sahib, yes." He showed big crunching teeth. "Portrait. I do portrait for loved ones back in Blighty."

"No thank you." I was coolly firm. Then, I added foolishly, "I am not British." He seized on it as the start of a negotiation.

"Where you from? From French? Spanish? Maybe you American? It not matter. My portraits work in all languages. Ha, ha! You make picture with monkey. Back home, they like."

I tried to work my way past him but he locked in place and began to howl.

"No, please don't push me. You hurt me! Show me some respect. I old man!" He must have given some order to the monkey for, without warning, it suddenly jumped from his shoulder to mine. Unbalanced, I twirled round, trying to dislodge the beast which responded by leaping on top of my head and ripping at my hair.

"Ow! Ow!" I spun like a Dervish, cannoned into a cheap liquor store, sloshing neat alcohol down my shirt, ricocheted and sat down into a pile of curry paste. I desperately tried to loosen the creature's scrabbling paws and it responded with nasty screaming bites to my own fingers and face. Now the stall owners launched their own complaint, shouting and waving fingers in my face while an old woman began to belabour me with an enormous fat-soaked spoon and I sprawled back into other forms of curry as the monkey, no observer of Queensbury rules, continued to bite and scratch. A man who had no part in it came up, raised my glasses gently and poked me very deliberately and factually in the eye before going away and I howled louder and fell back again as glass crashed and warm oils seeped and oozed and then, thank God, there came police whistles, thudding boots, comforting khaki uniforms. I was seized by two skinny constables, lifted to my feet and presented to a dumpy sergeant, with a swagger-stick, who might have been the head-waggling brother of the chief steward.

"What is all this mess and noise?" he waggled. "Why are you disturbing these good people?" He sniffed alcohol fumes. "Are you drunk?"

"The monkey," I slurred through puffy lips. "I was the one attacked." We looked. There was, of course, no monkey, its owner having wisely decamped at the onset of the forces of law and order. The stall owners shrugged. "Monkey? What monkey?" They rolled their eyes and shook their heads. "He is crazy," they seemed to say, "crazy as the Widow Traverso."

"Look," I said. "I am from a ship, the *Bethoen*, down in the harbour. I was assaulted." I slithered in spilt curry paste and nearly fell, clutching a policeman for support.

"Drunk!" shouted a small man at the back, a barrack-room lawyer. "He is drunk! He is not even English whose right it is to enter the market drunk and break things and insult people."

"I think, sahib, you must pay these good people for the damage you have done and then my men will escort you back to your ship. It is not good to come here and do bad things. You, who are a man of learning from his wearing of glasses, should know better." He waved his cane.

"We have these sticks for whacking wicked fellows." He whacked a stall top in demonstration. "It is either paying or whacking." It was paying.

I arrived back at the ship in time to see Miss Timms serenely climbing the gangplank with her two lost sheep – now found – in tow, all three aglow with feigned innocence and spotless white linen. At the top, I was greeted by a grinning chief steward, who looked me up and down and winked. Black eye, bites all over my face and neck, stinking of alcohol, trousers torn and besmirched fore and aft, escorted by two huge, panting, dark policeman. Now that was his idea of a satisfactory day ashore.

* * *

It finally occurred to me that, in shunning the chief steward, I was denying a part of myself that I would do better to embrace, at least metaphorically. So I confronted him, staying boldly in my cabin in face of his towelling perversities. He spoke excellent Dutch. His name was Anto and he was from Central Java, Solo – more properly Surakarta – proud cradle of Javanese high culture. He was actually a very nice man. He was married with three beautiful children – "But of course Tuan, all men must marry" – but since he was much away from home he had needs, needs that he preferred to satisfy with his own sex. This enabled him to stay faithful to his wife since only relations with women counted. Did she know this, Anto? Perhaps, but, in a marriage, Tuan, some things are best left unsaid. And while he was away, was she free to … ? Absolutely not. If he even suspected anything of that sort, he would beat her within an inch of her life, so great was his love for this woman. And now, Tuan, this business of you and me. Ah no. I shook my head. It had been a moment of madness from my too great affection for Hamid. Tuan really liked Hamid then? Then things could perhaps be arranged so that he should become, again, my friend. I had been too crude. He had been startled and ashamed. He was very young. The pocket gaped in expectation and was fulfilled.

The next day Hamid served me coffee and was all smiles. He put his hand chastely on my shoulder as he poured. Matters had been explained to him by Anto. Of course, he was my friend just as before. Being my friend seemed to mean that he was prepared to flirt with me and roll his eyes at any suggestive remark, to look over his shoulder smiling to see whether I watched him as he walked away. He would hold my hand, interlacing his little finger with mine, as he did with his friends in the village, when we walked together. He chatted happily to me – told me of his life in Java, his hopes and dreams for his children, his excitement at the approaching end of this his first voyage. I loved his beauty and his innocence and he accepted my admiration without offence and, alas, without consequence. I realised that I was trapped, not at all unhappily, in a medieval romance of courtly love. This must stop. And yet ... it enabled me to savour and express my own most delicate feeling, notably a delicious pain and required me to do absolutely nothing. I was a part of the human race again, more, almost family, for he called me *kakak*, "big brother" and as a sign of his affection came to rub sea slugs in my face.

"It is *minyak gamat*," he explained, "from an island to the north. It cures everything, all wounds, all skin diseases. There is a story." All good medicines, in Java, come with a story. "Once there was a fisherman who trod on a sea slug and it oozed all over his leg and set so hard he could not get it off. So, in his anger, he took a machete and chopped up all the sea slugs he could find around his boat. When he came back the next day, the pieces had all joined up again, healed and bore no scars. So, people realised the oil from the slug made the body heal itself." He daily rubbed generous amounts into my wounds in a curiously maternal way. It stank like rotten fish. "What a monkey hurts, a sea slug heals." For him, it was all part of the neatness and balance of life, a divine design that worked. For me, it was his gentle fingers that healed.

For the rest of the ship I had ceased to exist, bearing my albatross of shame around my neck. Van Gennep evaded me, seemingly always at the elbow of paterfamilias Niemeyer and complicit in his looks of contempt. From the troubled and guilty eyes of the eldest daughter, I suspected his pursuit might be progressing nicely.

At Singapore, Miss Timms left us with a clutter of old bags and umbrellas, being met by a choir of Chinese children on the quayside who sang Christmas carols in the hot sun in incomprehensible English. "Ha car hear all anger sing, Gory toad a nude porking."

She expressed her thanks by throwing down handfuls of boiled sweets rather as Cleopatra must have cast down rubies from her scented barge. "I have not quite forgiven you for your conduct in Colombo, Mr Bonnet. At a time when I was in need of your help as a good Samaritan you chose, instead, to go off and become drunk as the Prodigal Son."

I thought of the many complexities of the story of the monkey and decided that the strength of her compassion greatly exceeded that of her comprehension.

"I sincerely apologise Miss Timms."

She softened at once. "Well, that being the case, no great harm was done." She looked down and clasped her handkerchief to her nose. "Do you know, Mr Bonnet, I am suddenly aware of the most appalling smell. I do believe they have stored my luggage next to some fish that was not at all fresh and it has become permanently tainted."

I had arranged to meet Hamid just beyond the dock gates of the new terminal building and far from the prying eyes of Van Gennep and other Pharisees. It was my first time in a large Southeast Asian city and I was alive to sights, sounds and sensations crowding in on me, the sheer number of people, the density of the throng, the mix of Chinese, Indian and Malay under a European flag. Only later would I learn that what I saw as Malays shivered into a dozen other identities: Buginese, Boyar, Madurese, Dayak and so on.

We spent a happy day visiting the landmarks of the city, crushed side by side in a rickshaw, myself only too aware of the sweat where his thigh pressed against mine. I knew better than to take him to the Raffles Hotel or some other Western haunt where he would feel uncomfortable and eyebrows would be raised against us. The Islamic restaurant in Arab Street met our needs, my first and best mutton biryani, with Hamid soothed by the big *halal* signs in green tiles and being able to eat with his hands, not inconvenient forks and spoons. Then, back to the rickshaw, Hamid with shining eyes and shaking drips of water from his fingers ...

"We cannot go to the animal garden, *kakak*, to find monkeys for you to fight with. They do not have one here. Instead we must look for cocks. A friend on the ship gave me an address."

Ah no. I know what you are thinking but you must remember that I was taking my first halting steps in Malay, a sensible tongue, where Hamid's term, *ayam*, has no hidden undertones or sordid *double entendres*, being merely an innocent thing of beak and feathers. I can be quite sure of that since I had not mastered the word and Hamid had to mime it with elaborate beating of elbows and cock-a-doodle-doing so that the rickshaw-puller, pounding between the shafts, stared round in wonder, stumbled and nearly needed the application of sea slugs.

That afternoon was my introduction to the Malay world. It was not what we did or what befell us for we did virtually nothing and suffered no real events but it was the easy manner of our doing and experiencing nothing that struck me at the time, the absence of any sense that we had wickedly wasted time. We left the main road down by the shore, whirred down a smooth dirt track that ran out in sand and stopped at a simple wooden house on stilts, graced by a little carved tracery over the eaves and windows. Walter would no doubt have been able to tell you exactly the ethnicity of the style. Underneath the house was a mess of wood and bicycles, displaced doors and buckets amongst which children swarmed, a sort of attic in reverse. To one side, a man in a sarong was pouring buckets of water over his own head and slapping his chest as though in self-congratulation. Hamid climbed down and called up at the first floor, like Romeo to Juliet, where a fat woman appeared, knotting her sarong and smoothing her hair. She shouted something back and giggled.

"Javanese," smirked Hamid, with relief. It appeared that we were in a Javanese *kampung*, a sort of home from home, then. We were welcome and the men were round the back. The Chinese rickshawman sat down on the house ladder and refused all attempts to be paid. We now owed him money and he would not allow this relationship to be so brutally cut. He would sit here until Tuan wanted to go back to the city and then both fares could be paid together. He was, it seemed, now *our* dedicated and loyal rickshawman, nobly refusing all other offers. The woman brought him cold water to drink from a can that made him gush with sweat and waved us again round the side of the house.

About a dozen men were squatting there under a tree, most old, some young, surrounded by cockerels under airy baskets like cloche hats. Their poses struck me at once. There is a posture you find all over the islands, a hunkering down, legs together, the elbows resting on the knees and flapping as from a loose hinge. It is a pose of relaxation but provokes a tension in the thighs, lumbar region and across the shoulders that I immediately yearned to capture with my charcoal. Hamid indicated the tree, lush and big leafed.

"Wherever you see this tree, there are sailors," he explained. "It has big seeds that float so they use them to stuff the jackets to keep sailors afloat when they fall in the sea. The jackets get broken. The seeds get out. It is a tree we respect, a holy tree, for it saves the lives of sailors."

There followed a long conversation in Javanese. The woman, embarrassingly, reappeared to bring a single chair and insisted I sit on it in majestic isolation in the shade while I was ignored by the men who seemed locked in some headshaking disagreement with Hamid.

He turned and spoke in Dutch. "There can be no cockfight today, *kakak*." He smiled regret. "It is an unlucky day for fighting." He gently pressed the hands of the old men. "*Tidak apa apa*." No what what. Never mind, it does not matter.

But if there could be no fighting, there was no reason not to examine the birds and they compared them and showed them off with a passion no less intense than that of Vorderman with his Kandinsky and Prokoschka daubings. First, they passed round a magnificent, haughty bird with black plumage, edged at wings and rump with gold feathers like flames, bounced it on the ground, stroked its throat, felt its treading thighs, nodded and Ooh!ed and Aah!ed – or rather Wah!ed – in admiration. Other birds followed, bigger, smaller, some beautiful high strutters, some tawdry street-fighters, arguments raged, cigarettes were flung on the ground, birds squared up to each other – only to be put back under their baskets. They sat a huge cock on my lap and laughed when it pecked me and knocked me off my chair. I laughed too, stayed on the ground and lit a cigarette. *Tidak apa apa*. No what what. Then, they taunted me with the hundreds of different words for type and size and colour of cocks until my head was spinning, then tested me and stamped and cheered when I got one right by sheer luck. No what what. They soothed me again with cigarettes and coffee. The rickshawman crept round the corner and shyly joined us by slow degrees, an expert, it emerged, on betting on bad cocks. Soon we were all sitting in the kicked-up dust as they explained what to look for in a fighting bird. Checking the tight closure of the anus with poking fingers was, it seemed, a key factor. Hang on, said one, what was that smell of fish? It smelled like dirty women. It must, said one wizened man enthusiastically translated by Hamid, be the white man who spent all his time and money with bad, shameless women and ended up with their smell on him. Best keep him away from the cocks. No what what. I tried to get them back to the birds. They smirked, then sniggered, then fell about. No I could not say that. *Burung* "bird" was at best ambiguous, at worst a dirty word. It meant ... They pointed between their legs. Back to the cocks. What then of breeding? How was that organised? Well, you could not have hens around really strong cocks. If one had been with a hen, it was weakened, lost the will to fight, would be swiftly defeated. If a hen came here, with all these cocks, Oh God, it would be torn to bits. So, how was it managed? Where did they get their eggs from?

They screamed and slapped their thighs. Hamid reached over, smacked my hand lightly and giggled. I could not use that word like that right out loud, "eggs". He blushed. It was a slang word for men's balls. Had I, finally, no sense of shame at all, no modesty of language?

* * *

It was only between Singapore and Batavia that I finally began to sketch Hamid. This did not lead, as I half hoped it might, to some new Luigi-like activity. Across from me in the hot, little cabin, he remained warmly distant and I returned to the familiar sensation of viewing my most selfless emotions as something not to be reciprocated but atoned for. And yet to explore the tilt of his nose, the flare of his nostril, the soft angularity of his neck and the spiky halo of his hair was a protracted act of permitted intimacy. I lay awake at night unsure whether I was being privileged, exploited, treated with sweet compassion or wilfully tormented. I was paralysed by fear of losing his regard and thus my own. As St Paul and Miss Timms would have put it, I *burned*.

The first scattered islands appeared, little clots of sand and palm with a house or two clinging on. I packed my bags, miserable and alone, as we edged through the Buginese sailing fleet of high-nosed vessels with lines of washing where Westerners would have had bunting. I dumped my language notebooks in a grip. *Bunting* was a Malay slang word meaning "pregnant". I tightened the straps on my linen. Why did they have so much washing, I wondered, when no one wore any clothes? On all sides, bare bums, neither derisory nor seductive but simply nautical and indifferent, welcomed me to the archipelago.

Blasts on the ship's siren bullied the smaller ships out of the way as a very dirty tug with Chinese crew took our bowlines aboard and, appropriately, tugged. Anchors thundered down and we entered that long period on ships where nothing happens and no one can get on or off though gangways are locked in place. The other white passengers from Singapore were virtually unknown to me. Van Gennep had simply disappeared. The Niemeyers were there on deck, the younger children squabbling, the father shouting, the eldest girl in tears. I filled gaping pockets, Anton, Hamid, with apology for my love, given with accompanying ritual minuet. Please I wish to thank you. No, no, I cannot, you are my friend. Yes, yes, even friends have to pay for their rice. No, no, I am ashamed. Yes, yes, it is not for you but your children. In that case, I thank you – you are a kind man. Pocket buttoned. All over.

Hamid took my hand-luggage to the top of the gangway and set it down, unallowed to go any further. For the first time he unashamedly hugged me. There were genuine tears in his eyes that I felt damp on my neck as his cheek touched mine. What was he thinking, feeling? I had no idea. I knew nothing about anything any more. But here was a new place, a whole new world. I could be anything I wanted here. If I chose not to, I need not think about how to capture the light on the waves or the billowing smoke hanging over the stern. I was free. Then, I looked over hugging Hamid's shoulder and, as I blinked away my own tears, there on the dock, by some enchantment, stood two familiar figures – my mother and my father, staring up and frowning.

3

They had come by the quicker Suez route and beaten me by three days, driven, it seemed, by a mixture of parental panic on my mother's and commercial adventurism on my father's part. Largely as a result of the contacts made through my social elevation, he had become interested in colonial wares which, that year, set records in the sugar trade for production and price.

"Who is your friend?" My mother's eyes were, as ever, sharp.

"A bright young man who taught me some very useful vocabulary. The Javanese are, as you see, a hot-blooded race whose passions are easily moved."

All about us, Javanese, doubtless hot-blooded, were easily moved, indeed running at the imperial trot, carrying sacks, hauling baggage, coiling ropes, sweat flowing over gloriously muscled limbs yet still smiling when their eyes met mine. White overseers ticked clipboards and shouted orders from the shade.

"We are at the Hotel des Indes," declared father with a certain pride. "Room 374. We'll head off and make arrangements while you check your luggage through the customs shed. They say it will take about an hour. You won't need to hire any of the guides. Just take a car, everyone knows it." This being a moment of great emotion, he touched me lightly on the shoulder.

"You will not," urged mother moving off on his arm, "I am sure, allow yourself to become distracted by the ... picturesque." I did not greatly like her choice of the word or the emphasis she put on it as she waved her arm at the male dockside bustle.

In the great echoing hall with its smell of dust and mildew, officials were ready with their regulations and chalk. A British couple were arguing about their luggage: "No, Kitty. There were *three* brown suitcases and the small black one with the dodgy handle", "Cedric, you know full well that broke in Singers and we got the grey one with the brass fastener", "Yes but then you bought so much in Cold Storage I had to take it *back* out of the rubbish and use it to put the shoes in".

My single bag was hauled up onto a bench like an exhibit and I stepped forward. A man with brilliantined hair and a permanent sniff yawned, asked, "Reason for visit?"

Absurdly, I was nonplussed. "Boredom, a sense of loss, perhaps the search for some meaning and inspiration in a pointless life of artistic failure but popular success, also the extreme beauty of your male subjects whom I hope to thoroughly debauch whilst painting them and so liberate myself from shame and frustration at my own disgusting sexual perversion." I did not, of course, say that, contenting myself with a vacuous "Er … tourism." Come to think of it, they probably mean the same thing. He yawned, sniffed and sketched a cross on the leather as if in apostolic blessing.

The Hotel des Indes was a brilliant white creation in the new art deco style, a thing of exaggerated concrete horizontality, like the towering superstructure of a vast underground ship. It stood on a busy street just down from the prestigious Harmonie Club whose heavily moneyed members ruled this sprawling colonial domain. Trams, more modern than those of Amsterdam, clanged past it and the parking lot was clogged with the latest American cars. To one side, squatted an immemorial banyan or *waringin* tree, a congealed mass of buttresses and trailing aerial roots, its branches hardly able to bear their own weight. The Javanese, recognising it as a creature of power, whisperingly pressed offerings into the fissures of its trunk It was the haunt of tolerated natives – shoe-shine boys, a bicycle repair man, a seller of fried eggs that turned out to be delicious sweet confections of coconut – offering services that did not impinge on the economic activities of the hotel proper. I knew at once that I would sketch it.

As I approached the doors, my suitcase was whisked away with cries of distress in a process that seemed to involve three Javanese. A white man could not possibly carry such a burden, such a thing could bring the empire to its knees. The staff outnumbered the guests by at least five to one. I clip-clopped across the front hall, all coral and gold stucco, fat lamps, fat furniture and engaged the front desk, a rather odd sight with half a dozen Eurasian clerks working under a Dutch supervisor who was seated – the better to supervise – on a sort of high throne. I explained who I was, who my parents were, had a room been booked? The supervisor looked up. Ah no. That had proved, alas, impossible. Did I not know there was an important governmental conference in progress? Hotel rooms could not be found in Batavia at any price. Instead a day-bed, meaning more properly a sofa that became a bed at night only, had been installed in my parents' drawing room. So there it was. My proud independence had been converted back into sleeping with my parents.

My parents raged around the European quarter of the capital for weeks. We went to the Dutch theatre. We ate in Western hotels. We shopped in the European quarter. We made little expeditions to the cool hills of Bogor and the tea plantations beyond. I continued to sleep in my parents' day-bed amongst my old paintings which they had brought with them.

"What am I to do with these? I can't cart them around with me." To look at them depressed me. There was tired old Gabriella with her false bosom. Either they were good and I lamented my present ineptitude, or they were so bad that I despaired of ever achieving anything. It had never occurred to me that European oils would melt in the Indies. They seeped and merged and sagged. I was becoming an involuntary Impressionist.

"You never know," said father. "You might need them for a quick exhibition. I met a bloke the other day that has space." I sneered and pooh-poohed and then he organised an exhibition in a publisher's building in three days flat and, suddenly, I was the talk of Batavia.

"Forget about sugar. Rubber's the coming thing," so bank director Poos a few months before the Crash. The Indies were booming, with collapsing labour costs and rising commodity prices. Even to me the market seemed diseased. Poos was the sort who could only succeed in the Indies. At home he would have been, at most, a chief clerk. He had terrible dandruff in his eyebrows. Here he was on the committee of the artistic circle. There had been some hard drinking at the opening and now we were sweating our way through the inevitable *rijstafel* with copious amounts of beer, the glasses weeping with condensation. Hot, musky air steamed in through open windows as if from a laundry.

"The new Sumatran fields won't come on stream for another three years and production can't meet demand." He sucked prematurely on a fat cigar, a *Sumatra cum laude*, rudely not waiting until everyone had finished eating, and one of the hotel's staff wafted across and lit it before he could reach for his matches. He puffed and an ashtray was extended for his flicking into. "Bloody marvellous, the service. Can't do a thing for yourself. Mind you," he leaned forward and winked extravagantly, "it gets a bit much when you try to go the lavatory." My mother, over the other side of the table, choked on her chocolate dessert. Poos exhaled fragrant smoke, unconcerned whether it spoiled her pudding or not.

"They'd be lost without us, the natives. What would they have to do? I suppose you've been following the news about the calls for independence, the PNI and all that? It'll never happen of course. Once Soekarno's locked snugly away, it'll all be forgotten." It is impossible to convey now the incredible sense of solidity of colonial rule. The Dutch after all had been in Java for three hundred years and everywhere were the signs of their – our – military power and absolute technological stranglehold. Did I really look around, see the countless brown faces of the staff and read them as a statement that one day a great wind would blow and sweep us all away while they would endure like the rooted *waringin* tree I had sketched that afternoon? If not, I do it now.

"Talking of artists ..." Poos must be about to say something embarrassing since he was speaking louder, "... one of my managers had a bit of bother with one on the boat out." My ears pricked, sensing danger. "Niemeyer from Probolingo, nice fella, though not quite white and even the white bit's Jewish so it hardly counts – but we're pretty tolerant and relaxed out here as you've doubtless had occasion to see, Mr Bonnet. Anyway, thanks to that particular artist's activities, he's left with a daughter in the club and ..." He became aware of his own sallow daughter, seated beside me, dripping onto her plate. I thought that would lead him to break off but no ... "so I want to see you, young man, keep your hands firmly on top of the table, if you know what I mean." He guffawed roundly, sucked his teeth and bit on the cigar, flicked more Javanese-assisted ash.

"Is he sure it was the artist, Mr Poos?" My own father, anxious to save the honour of his son's profession. Mother seemed unsure whether to disapprove generally of heterosexual lust or take comfort in the mere possibility of it amongst artists.

"Oh, no doubt about it, Mr Bonnet. A thoroughly bad lot, apparently, a prey to every human vice, whereas everyone else on board was totally respectable."

"Tell me. What was the name of the ship–"

"Mr Poos," I interrupted hastily, "would you advise me to convert my Dutch currency into Indies money immediately or should I wait?" I was aware that a foot was caressing mine under the table.

"Oh no need to be hasty seeing as the two are tied together. The only real problem is the denominations, once you get into the native economy. You'll need smaller notes out there or coins and no one has change. You'll need an account too, what with all the pictures you'll be selling and I'll be glad to set that up."

My father looked pleased that I was finally taking an interest in business. My mother abandoned her pudding and it was whisked away by a delightful gazelle-eyed young man in a very tight, starched uniform. The whole East Indies empire ran on starch as a bulwark against the enervating effects of limpid heat.

Poos launched into, "Of course, even rubber pales when compared to the possibilities of oil ..."

"Are *you*," whispered Miss Poos excitedly through sharp, little teeth, "a thoroughly bad lot?" Inexplicably, she smelled of parsnips.

"Actually, no," I said with sudden clear insight, revealed to myself and tucking my foot under my chair and out of her range. "I don't think I am. You know, I think my problem is that I really rather want to be good."

* * *

The next two months were spent in the company of my parents. We toured the spiny backbone of Java, leaping from vertebra to vertebra – Bogor, Bandung, Yogyakarta. I thrilled to forests, mountains and volcanos, gorges and valleys, to limpid oceans and the huge waves that crashed on the southern coast – all glimpsed briefly from train windows. I saw palaces and princes, emerald rice fields and gushing springs – from passing cars. And I met many Dutchmen. We lived in hunting lodges and slick hotels and, for excitement, visited plantations and factories where the back of nature was bent in toil and hammered into shape with Dutch steel. My haul of sketches was slim. Javanese remained unknown to me except as the hands of brown helpers and the teeth of servile smiles. As was to be expected, I managed a small number of brutish encounters in the margins of my sketches – a palace guard in Yogya, our panting tryst completed in an impossibly hot sort of shed full of ceremonial yellow silk umbrellas and the flutter of moths that ate them – a young Chinese, working in his father's shop, whose deliberate spite appalled me – but they served merely to stoke my lust and self-disgust until finally my father said, "We are headed for Surabaya tomorrow. I must get back to Rotterdam to take care of my sugar shipments. Come with us."

We were in Gresik, a small white-painted town north of the main port, famous chiefly for the landing there of holy Sheikh Maulana Mahil Ibrahim – may God preserve him – who brought the faith from Arabia, and for the manufacture of tinkling gongs. But all that was to change. They were dredging the harbour and tearing up the coconut palms and turning the coastline into brown soup. Factories and chemical plants were going up and there was talk of building the biggest cement plant in the East. The café around us was full of plump, pink young men in clean shorts: engineers, planners, accountants. They were even filming down by the harbour to show the taxpayers back home what great changes the ethical policy was bringing to the grateful masses.

"I can't possibly," I said. "I haven't seen anything yet. You know this was all about Bali, the untouched East, undefiled and unchanging" An old man was arranging buckets, a bamboo ladder, brushes, sloshing a new coat of whitewash over the wall behind us. "I haven't painted anything yet."

Father sipped beer. The engineers laughed as though I had said something witty. Mother took off her tortoiseshell sunglasses, a new American affectation, and shivered slightly in the wind. It was a mark of the speed with which she had acclimatised.

"How long?"

"Oh a month or two, three at the most. You know the way I work. I have to immerse myself completely in the locals, then it all comes quite quickly in a great rush."

She pouted. "I hate to think of you out here alone. If only you were married. Perhaps your father could go back on his own." She turned to him in supplication and he opened his mouth to answer in the affirmative. Oh no.

"Mother!" I seized her hand in a fit of hot filial passion. I had noted and not greatly liked the way she had included that swift barb about marriage and hoped it was not the opening shot of a larger campaign. "Then who would look after poor father? I am not alone. There are fifty million people here! You know I have to be free to move about, follow my nose. Then I can come home and paint it all up, take my time. You have seen how it is here, perfectly safe."

She disengaged herself and held up the local paper, the *Oetoesan Hindia*, pointing grimly to thick, black headlines, like a lawyer in court. "But there is talk of these nationalists, strikes, political chaos."

We always look in the wrong direction for trouble. No wonder so many are killed crossing the road. It was only thanks to my father's sheer pigheadedness that, when The Crash rocked the world's finances in a couple of weeks, he would be safely at sea with his assets tied up in neither worthless paper nor plummeting guilders but a precious food cargo that kept its value on the Dutch market and buttressed the family in the harsh years to follow.

"All that is hot air mother. You heard Mr Poos. Nothing ever really changes out here. Besides, that is Java. Bali is outside all that."

The old man, having painted the wall to his satisfaction, now began to paste a poster to its still-wet surface, fighting the fresh sea-breeze that tried to tear it from his grasp. Job done, he stood back, lit a cigarette and admired. I pointed, in turn.

It was an announcement of the impending Surabaya Regatta, with promised – and eagerly awaited – return visit by the Royal Singapore Yacht Squadron, marchpast of schoolchildren in ancient Batavian costume and special promotion of locally produced cheese.

"You see?" I said triumphantly and with an irrelevance that was thoroughly compelling. "Nationalists don't eat cheese. But it's a pity he put the poster up upside down."

4

Imagine yourself suddenly set down surrounded by all your gear, alone on a tropical beach close to a native village, while the dinghy which has brought you sails away out of sight. I was at Buleleng, in the north of Bali, with the KPM ship fretting and treading water out from the shallow bay. But wait, I was not quite alone. A large cock came and inspected me, decided I was not a worthy adversary and stalked haughtily away.

All travellers' tales are lies. This was not the beach recorded by Cornelis de Houtman who wrote so lavishly of the beauties of Bali in the sixteenth century and whose crew were seduced into desertion by the velvet eyes of the ladies. This was not the paradise of Nieuwenkamp's lush pictures and the posters of the KPM. The sand was volcanic black, coal-dust not gold, an industrial product. A miasmal stench arose from the water and the sea reached out to grasp and suck in, not coral, but a rich deposit of human excrement daily dotted below the high-tide line. Crabs came and waved their claws at me in pathetic bullyboy bluff. I picked up my luggage and tramped wearily towards a straggle of buildings in rough brick where nasty yellow curs opened their throats and howled at me, gathering from the diaphragm, the way opera singers are trained to do, so that their rage lifted their front feet clear off the ground. Of course, the people here were Hindus, not dog-shy Moslems as in Java.

Everywhere people were stirring – coughing, shifting phlegm, sloshing water, groaning against the effort of another wretched day. I wandered pointlessly down a dusty main street where Chinese in dirty white pyjamas were opening shutters and rolling out purely literal barrels and finally found a coffee shop where fires were being stoked and the aroma of coffee to come promised a breakfast of some sort. I collapsed onto a metal stool and a man came and looked, smiled and went back inside, shouting something over one shoulder. Then a stool scraped and a voice came from a dark corner.

"You'll be looking for Walter, then?"

"I'm sorry?" I looked up and tried to focus. A dark form rose up like a wave and extended a pale hand into the light that fell through the open door and then a big man followed it and pulled up a stool. He plonked a bowl on the table, full of fishy rice porridge. It looked and smelled like the product of an elephant's ejaculation.

"Behrens," he nodded. "I'm the government doctor round here." His eyes found the symptom of the collapsible easel strapped to the side of my suitcase and he nodded his chin at it. "An artist," he observed and smiled sadly. "Yet another one."

I was dismayed. "Are there so many?"

The man returned with two mugs of coffee that he set down with surprising grace and began spooning in sugar by the tablespoon.

"Enough," said Behrens with a cup-seizing gesture but whether he meant artists or sugar was not clear. He stirred, tasted and grimaced. "More than enough. We have French and American and Swiss and German and Austrian and even the odd Dutchman. We even have them homemade – born in the Indies. It's all the work of Krause and that book of pornography he published and then Nieuwenkamp and his great big breasts."

"Nieuwenkamp," I said. "I met Nieuwenkamp in Rome. He spoke of Venus or was it Eve?"

Behrens nodded. "Aye, well there you are then. You'll know what I mean. The poor Balinese don't know which way to turn. As soon as they drop their drawers or try to have a bit of a wash there's a *bule* there with a camera or an easel."

"A *bule*?"

"Aye," he gestured vaguely. "A *Belanda*, *orang putih*, *Matt Saleh* – dammit man, us!"

"Oh, I see."

"As a doctor, I can only approve of the Eastern affection for water, regardless of morality, but the tourists are getting out of hand. In Denpasar, the natives are having to hide in their houses at dusk instead of heading for the river. I've talked to the Resident about it but he's only interested in getting the tourist count up to please Batavia. It'll end up leading to disease."

"Is there a lot of disease?" I did not like the sound of that.

He sighed. "Less than you'd expect. More than I can cope with. Down south there's malaria – don't forget your quinine. Then there's smallpox, cholera and diphtheria. Every couple of years we get an outbreak of yellow fever brought in by the illegal Chinese, like as not, or maybe the *haj*. The big scare is leprosy, they think that's tied up with breaking religious taboos and such so they hide it till it's too late, then make a great fuss about it and chase the afflicted out of the village like criminals. Apart from that, it's mostly skin diseases up where it's too cold to wash or too dry to waste the water or where we make them wear clothes. They wash themselves but not the clothes, d'ye see? In the rainy season, rinse your ears out with alcohol every morning, just a drop, to stop the mould." He was giving automatic advice, too many years in the job, answering the same daft questions. I thought of my Hancock and Goodyear, by now probably green with mildew and disuse, and blushed. "Drink tea or coffee, not water, then at least it's been boiled." He lurched to his feet. "And now, if you'll excuse me, I have to get off on my rounds. I'm heading down east today. If you're a friend of Nieuwenkamp, maybe you'll want to take a look at the temple at Kubutambahan." He pointed. "You see that shop? That's where you'll find Fatima. Give my regards to Walter when you see him. Tell him I'll drop by in a month or two."

"Who is Fatima? Walter who?" But he was gone, shuffling down the street, mind already elsewhere. My coffee tasted foul but I drank it anyway. At least it had been boiled.

The shop had an Arabic name over the door and sold tourist stuff, locally woven scarves, filigree silver bowls, rough earthenware, painted carvings to give you bad dreams, all stacked on shelves thick with dust and buckled by heat. There was no counter, just a table littered with paper and dirty cups at which sat my first Balinese Eve. No wait, this was definitely a Venus. Spotting me, she let out a screech, leapt to her feet and almost dived at me. Then she did a strange thing. She turned sideways, dropped her hand to her crotch, smiled coyly and waggled her wrist vigorously up and down, whilst leaning back and thrusting with her pelvis. "Shake the bottle!" she screeched in English.

"What?"

"Shake the bottle! Welcome to bloody Bali. You just come? KMbloody-P?" She continued shaking.

"Er, right. Shake, er ..." Where had she learnt such an extraordinary greeting? The vocabulary argued a more than passing acquaintance with sailors. There was surely something Australian about the routine and the accent and somehow it seemed even more obscene in a man than a woman to perform this little dance so I blushingly curtailed it into a limp handwave. She was a big woman, elaborately robed in a grubby blouse and sarong.

"You want go bloody Denpasar? No worries, I fix, mate." She smiled demurely, finally stopped shaking, sat down again, puffing slightly, and beckoned me over to an empty chair.

"Er, do I?" Did I? She pushed papers off onto the floor and reached for a receipt book.

"Course you fuckin' do. All tourist go bloody Denpasar. Big hotel. Dance. Jiggy jig. Fatimah superbloodybagus car only way."

Bagus meaning "fine", more specifically "beautiful". It was not a moment for long reflection. I had been wondering what on earth to do. I certainly did not want to stay in superbloodynotbagus Buleleng. She came, after a fashion, medically recommended. Soon she was charging me a princely sum to hire her car. The tariff was a complicated affair of miles, petrol, days and wear and tear on the chauffeur, who, it was now revealed, was also called Bagus: a slender, quiet man of my own age with a kindly, homely – not at all *bagus* – face but a sweet moustache and simple, considerate Malay and enough English to tide us over when my own broke down. My luggage was strapped on the back, the car was fed petrol, water and oil and Bagus tucked his sarong chastely between his legs and kicked free his sandals to drive barefoot with splayed feet that did not so much rest on the pedals as grip them. He was all eagerness to be off, like a horse too long shut up. We stoked each other's excitement and soon I too was flaring my nostrils at the upcoming adventure, freedom, the open road in an open car. Shopkeepers appeared at other doors and watched us resentfully, Arabs with their shirts hanging out, Indians with fierce beards like spades, knowing we were escaping from the world of tedium and care.

"Selamat bloody jalan!" meaning have an emphatically safe journey, screamed Fatimah and we jolted off, her profile shaking its bottle again in staccato salutation, chubby hands clutching too many of my banknotes, watched by Bagus in the rear view mirror. We looked at each other afresh, laughed and were immediately friends over the hot leatherette.

"Bagus?" I asked. "Is that your real name?"

He frowned. "It means I am a Brahmana, the highest caste, only Brahmana can be priests – real priests."

"But you are not a priest?"

He had long, thin, artistic hands that stroked the wheel rather than turned it. On the marriage finger he wore a nasty cheap ring set with a chunk of red glass.

"I was not called to become a priest. I was called to become a driver. That is my destiny."

So there it was. Was I called? And was it my destiny to be an artist or merely a vain aspiration?

"Who *is* Fatima?"

He stole a sideways glance. The moustache twitched. "What did she tell you?"

"She told me nothing."

He bent over the wheel as if in respect and lit a cigarette, offered me one – declined – and inhaled, sending glowing clove fragments cascading down the front of his shirt.

"People tell different stories," he spoke softly. "According to some, she is a widow of the King of Bali, the Rajah of Klungkung, who refused to throw herself on his funeral fire when he was killed by the Dutch. But then his body has not yet been burned. Some say she was just a concubine. There were many concubines in the palace. Some say she never had anything to do with Klungkung. Her Balinese is wrong for a person from there but she says it was in the palace she learnt her excellent English. Perhaps she sounds like someone from Lombok. Lombok people are *noisy* and without culture. She is Moslem and I do not know her Balinese name. She converted when she married her husband but he is never there. Some say he is Javanese. I have not seen. I do not know."

We were driving through Singharaja, the biggest town in the north, centre of the administration. This part of Bali had been Dutch for eighty years, unlike the south – conquered by Nieuwenkamp – and the marks of established colonial rule were everywhere, women with covered, not bare, breasts, neat stucco villas, schoolchildren in pressed uniforms, barracks edged with white-painted rocks and dark-faced Ambonese troops with fuzzy-wuzzy hair.

"Beh! Black," commented Bagus dispassionately in passing and pointed with his thumb.

A sign rose up, indicating Kubutambahan off to the left. It lit a flare in my brain.

"There!" I said, stumbling over the name. "Kubutambahan. Is that on our way? Dr Behrens said I should see the temple there. Is that possible?"

He smiled. "You like to see temples? Okay." He executed a smart three-point turn and we bumped up a rising dusty track with overarching trees and suddenly, after a kilometer or two, there it was, the most extraordinary structure I had ever seen in my life.

It stood like sherds of white stone fired into the earth, each one carved with huge figures – gods? demons? heroes of yore? I had no idea. They crouched and reared and leapt, surrounded by flames and flowers and curlicues, forming and framing a gateway. Bagus stopped the car, took my hand gently and led me inside, up a fantastical staircase, through a series of rising courtyards, open to the sky, each more exuberant than the last, where every inch of stonework exhibited a baroque *horror vacui*. He would occasionally drop my hand to make a courtly gesture of respect in the different directions with his own, fingers pressed together and raised to the face, a *sembah*, and then shyly hook up my little finger again. To copy him in his devotions would have been impertinent so I stood embarrassed like a stranger at a funeral who lacks a proper gesture. The place was totally deserted except for cooing doves and zithering lizards. Butterflies flitted in and out of sunlight. I looked around at the statues, the murals – ancient products of an alien civilisation that was surely the equal of Greece or Rome – staring in silence. I caressed a curvaceous stone thigh that was Mycaenean in its purity. This was the Indies as I had wanted it, pristine, unpolluted, unchanged throughout immemorial time, like the *waringin* tree that was the refuge of local culture at the Hotel des Indes. I was transported. My step was lighter, my hips more sinuous. Then the dull schoolboy need to know burst out as if in a definition of the adverb.

"How? Why? When?"

"It is a temple for Ratu Ayu Sari, husband of Dewi Sri, goddess of the rice. It is for the farmers who do not grow wet rice but the other crops." He gestured towards the whole fertile plain spreadeagled before us. "For maize, coffee, fruits, vegetables. The god brings them the harvest."

Everywhere in the temple were carved flowers, vines, a tropical prodigality of vegetation frozen in masonry, the poignant contrast between the transitory and the eternal. I was amazed to see so much creativity, mastery of technique, wealth of skill, so much love, devoted to a small village like this. It was comforting to hear of gods that had familial relations instead of logic-chopping metaphysical status. And then I glimpsed it, the reason Behrens had sent me here, and ran over to make sure I had seen aright. On the inside of the furthest courtyard was a shallow relief that made me gasp, then laugh like a rude misericord in a cathedral choirstall. It was a man on a bicycle, the turning wheels rendered as great bursting blossoms. There was no mistaking it. It was Nieuwenkamp, a frangipani flower gallantly tucked behind his ear in Balinese fashion, pedalling off to sketch a bosom. Moss was growing up his legs.

The gravel-topped road began to climb soon after and the houses thinned and disappeared. Only sporadic hamlets, blowing with woodsmoke, spoke of human habitation. We whined up in low gear, fog and cloud clinging to the windscreen, great stands of bamboo leaning out over the void, the engine coughing in the thinning air. The people looked wilder, long-haired and wrapped in blankets, struggling upwards on foot or riding small, shaggy ponies up towards Kintamani. This was the crest that divided north from south, a place of fantastic vistas and rainbows of light where the still active volcano smoked black against the sky and rode on a sea of meringue. At its foot lay the hot springs feeding into the lake, outlined in black lava like a cheap Japanese print, and alimenting the rivers of the south. In the distance reared the bulk of Gunung Agung, the highest peak, the seat of the gods, the centre of the world by which Balinese constantly orient themselves like homing pigeons. We stopped to drink coffee at a stall piled high with oranges and hugged our cups in the thin, chill wind. Bagus recalibrated the carburettor, pointed and sucked air, shivering, through his teeth.

"There Bali Aga people. Bad people, very dirty. Bali Aga have great magic." He shuddered and his voice dropped. "Bali Aga people do not burn their dead."

"White men do not burn their dead either."

He shrugged. "That is different. They know no better."

A jog-trotting satay seller panted up, his own world slung at either end of a bouncing pole over one shoulder, set up his brazier, fanned it back to life and began roasting little sticks of meat. The delicious smell and spicy peanut sauce conquered my hygienic scruples and I wolfed them down taking care not to use the plate provided for which no proper washing provision could have been made. A man with no teeth and a harelip appeared from nowhere and whipped back his cloak like a stage villain to show a fat, furry puppy. He said something in a language like a prolonged belch and kept poking it out at me and grinning like a lecher.

"You buy," giggled Bagus, cooing and stroking it. It wagged its tail and glopped air. "Dogs from here are famous all over Bali, maybe all over the world. This be a very good dog for you." It looked at me with soft brown Balinese eyes and lunged with its tongue. In vain I told myself this was not love but the smell of satay for I felt love. Yes, I yearned to make it my dog but it would have been a stupid and improvident act, the sort of thing Walter would have done without a second thought, except of course I did not yet know Walter. A dog required a settled existence, commitment, responsibility. I shook my head.

"One day," I said. "Maybe one day when I too have moss growing up my legs."

At that moment the clouds parted on an Old Testament sky and a hazy path appeared, as to Moses crossing the Red Sea, a corridor leading down to the warm south where, in the distance, ricefields of an unbelievable green cascaded down hillsides, like a giant's staircase, and in redemption of Nieuwenkamp's inept picture. We drove on, heat and lushness slowly rising about us like a flood. Ancient temples dotted the roadsides, water gushed and flashed silver like a shattered mirror. Above us, towered coconut palms, their delicate fronds dancing in the breeze with the sound of a rustling silk dress. The world was suddenly gentle and caressing.

Bagus talked steadily into the afternoon, like trickling water bouncing from rock to rock, of ceremonies and gods and women and Fatimah and someone called Walter Piss till my head began to nod. What seemed a few minutes later I awoke with a start and a stiff neck and cursed myself like a fool. We were in Denpasar, back in a world of concrete and corrugated iron and paradise had abruptly vanished. To one side white men in still whiter flannels were chortling and playing tennis on a great field, lavishly attended by ballboys and waiters. There were the usual ugly shops and drains. A sluttish woman was leaning, appropriately, on a large sign advertising the wares of the Goodyear rubber company. We turned into a gravel drive and there was the Bali Hotel. I was slightly relieved not to find my parents waiting on the verandah, peering out from the dusty box trees.

Suddenly Bagus was by the side of the car, hands clasped in respect, head bowed, reaching for the door as my luggage was unstrapped by two strapping, bare-chested lads. It seemed that for Bagus I was now "*Tuan*", "master", and existed only in the third person. If Tuan would like to enter the hotel, his slave would attend to the car. Did *Tuan* wish for the car later? Then his slave would wash it and see *Tuan* again in the morning at ten o' clock if that was acceptable to *Tuan*.

"Bagus, what about you? Where will you eat and sleep?"

He blushed. *Tuan* should not concern himself about that. His slave would sleep in the car, the better to guard it, and they would feed his slave in the hotel kitchen.

The hotel was a thing of potted palms and white tile floors with something of the disapproving air of a sanatorium. At the desk, a neat Eurasian signed me in and noted my easel. Perhaps I was a friend of Mr Piss? No? A pity. A most amusing gentleman, Mr Piss. Would I care to see the menu? The *plat du jour* was boiled gammon and cabbage. No thank you. Just a pink gin in the room that came with a white-painted hospital bed and enough white netting for three brides.

I retired to the bathroom, ladled cool water over my head from the big maternal earthenware pot and felt the suffocation of the still air. It was the dry season and the refreshment of rain lay months off. I stretched out undried on the bed, barely resisting the temptation to throw off the mosquito net that gathered the heat down around me so that I flowed with sweat and groaned against the Dutch wife, a cool bolster that you draped yourself around to allow the flow of air. I finally fell asleep to the whine of the mosquitoes circling the net in frustration, like hungry flies around a meat safe.

Like our Lord, it was only on the third day that I rose again for, the next morning, I awoke with a raging fever, a sharp throbbing in my head and my legs danced of their own volition. I staggered to the bathroom to heave drily for several hours. Shirtsleeved Dr Stove, irritated to be disturbed at breakfast, palpated indifferently as he chewed. A waiter stood beside him with bread and cheese on a plate.

"Stay in bed for two days, drink plenty of water, quinine every four hours, aspirin for the headache and to lower the fever." He reached out blindly, wrapped bread around filling, popped it into his distended mouth and a thermometer into my own.

"Is it malaria?"

He shrugged and articulated through chewed bread. "With these symptoms, in Holland, I'd tell you to take codeine and aspirin for flu. Out here we say quinine and aspirin for malaria. We never really know what it is. But in both cases it works – usually – unless you die. But you won't. You're going to feel pretty drained for a while. Get out of this furnace. Go to the hills." His own advice seemed to irritate him more, he who could not escape the heat of duty.

"Kintamani?"

"That's a bit far. Up there you'd catch pneumonia and peg out, like as not. Somewhere like Ubud. There's an old government resthouse there, a *pasangrahan*; I sometimes send the fever cases there. Bit tatty but do you I should think." He looked at the plate hopefully, found it empty and shrugged again. The thermometer, held up to the light, seemed to bore him. "Avoid fat, no booze of course and don't forget your John Hancock if you pass your time the other way."

John Hancock? Ah, of course, Hancock and Goodyear.

"Could you possibly do me a great favour and tell my slave ... driver, Bagus, what's going on?

He grunted and seized the empty plate, heading, no doubt, for a refill. "And I'll leave my bill at the desk." It would,. I foresaw, be covered with crumbs and buttery fingermarks.

The next day we drove – no, in those days one still motored – up to Ubud through villages that all seemed asleep and turned blank walls and gateways to the road. The manager of the Bali Hotel, as I paid my bill, favoured me with his views on my – Fatimah's – motor car. He disapproved of it as being a two-seater, not a four, so that driver and passenger were obliged to share the same bench seat, suggesting imperfect racial segregation. For myself this was barely tolerable, for a female passenger it would be outrageous. As Bagus and I drove in this scandalous propinquity, occasional resting figures like public statuary might be glimpsed dozing under trees or beside baskets of cockerels set out to watch passers-by. We swooped along the smooth roads and warmth seeped from the wind that buffeted my arms and face.

Ubud was little more than a small village, a thing of a single street, a shabby palace and a market. The *pasangrahan* lay some small distance beyond, by the river. According to standard terms it might be used by any bona fide white visitor unless a Dutch colonial official required it on his tournée, in which case, it was to be instantly ceded.

"There," said Bagus pointing, "there the house of Walter Piss. We go visit him?"

"Certainly not." I was unforgiving. "I have not come here to spend my time with Dutchmen."

Bagus shrugged and drove on, turning almost immediately to pull up outside an old wood and bamboo house that quavered in the heat and stridulations of crickets. We got out and walked around, calling. Was there anyone? Hello? It was deserted. The guardian must be otherwise engaged. Never mind. I settled on the verandah and waited. Bagus arranged himself on the ground against a pillar and fell immediately and profoundly asleep, like a machine that had been switched off. After an hour or so, came a crunching of gravel from the back, at first tentative and then more insistent. I rose. The guardian should have a bit of my mind for abandoning his post. Already I was full of the white man's rage of the Indies. In my head, I rehearsed the list of instructions I should issue for my immediate comfort. Bath. Dinner. Gin. The path led me round the side of the house through a neglected garden of red lilies that swarmed with insects and between two raddled pavilions used for storage. There was a crouched figure in there performing some task of village idiocy, rootling in the shadows amongst the firewood and the old lamps.

"You!" I called. "Where have you been? Don't you know I've been waiting here for over an hour?"

The figure stood up, tall and slim. A ruefully grinning face appeared covered in cobwebs and dust. A white face, about the same age as my own, but in his case, very handsome with classical, even features beneath a shock of unkempt honey-blond hair and icy blue eyes that washed over you like a cold wave. He was dressed like a schoolboy on holiday, wearing a simple khaki shirt, open at the neck, and shorts with sandals scuffed onto very brown feet without socks.

"Terribly sorry," he blushed, "I'm afraid you have caught me. I'm trespassing." The voice was light, humorous, oddly accented. "You haven't perhaps seen a white cockatoo? She answers to the name of Ketut when not being naughty, which she clearly is today. Normally I wouldn't be offended if she went back to the wild – her choice – but I brought her so far from Nusa Penida and she'd be all one her own in Bali, you see. Oh sorry," he extended a dusty hand. "My name's Walter. Walter Spies."

I shook the hand. Then the penny dropped. "Oh my god, it's you. Walter Piss – Walter Spies. I should have guessed. I'm Rudolf Bonnet. Isn't *Ketut* a human name, fourth-born child and all that?"

"Yes, naturally," he ran his fingers through his hair, a characteristic gesture. "It's a sort of joke. Cockatoo is *kakak tua*, 'old elder sister or brother' so that leads to eldest child so ... er ... well ... it's a sort of joke," he ended lamely. "As for Piss, that's as close as Balinese can get to Spies. I've had to get used to it."

There is a problem with all this linguistic badinage. What language were we speaking? I, surely, was speaking Dutch, maybe Malay, because it is impossible to be rude in a language you speak really badly. But Walter's Dutch was abysmal. Like many Germans, he found it too close to Plattdeutsch to take it seriously as a language in its own right. His pronunciation was appalling and the vocabulary he just made up for himself out of Germanic roots. Yet he understood it perfectly, as I did German. Stupidly, it took us a while before we realised that there was absolutely no need for us to speak the same language while holding a conversation. He could speak German, I Dutch, and it worked perfectly well. Of course, with others we would sometimes speak English or Malay or Balinese. So we would flit in and out of languages, sometimes from sentence to sentence, sometimes from word to word, using whichever came first to the mind. So I've no idea what all this was in. Anyway, I don't really remember the words. I was staring at the mouth. There was the suggestion of a blond moustache as of one who did not take more than boyish pains over his appearance and barely washed behind his ears before running out to play in the sun every morning. The lips had a full, infinitely mobile quality that denied any possibility of meanness and fell easily into a smile. The teeth were unaffectedly white and even and doubtless overjoyed to be in that mouth. They embraced you in a laugh of such childlike innocence that you forgot to listen to what they were saying. As I think I said before, he was the most magical person I had ever …

A sudden flash of white and a squawk and a large bird was crabwalking up his shoulder and nuzzling his ear. Walter chuckled delightedly.

"May I introduce Ketut." We began strolling back towards the front of the house. He had a leisurely, elegant walk despite the sandals. He paused and inclined his ear to the bird and made a solemn face. "A little bird tells me that the guardian has gone off to his sister in Sanur and will be gone for at least a week. There is neither dinner nor fresh bedding to be had. You had better come and stay with me across the road." Walter, it seemed, in addition to everything else, spoke bird talk, a paraclete of parakeets. He nodded at snoring Bagus, mouth vulnerably open, oozing drool. "Is that your young man?"

"That's Bagus."

He smiled. "Hmm. Only comparatively." He did the bird-whispering act again. "Ketut says he'd better come too. Naturally. Oh, I hear you're a painter. Me too – in a small way of business."

5

I pushed the homemade mango marmalade back across the table and smeared the dollop from my plate onto the fresh-baked bread.

"The boys made it themselves, entirely without help," Walter twinkled, "the very best *oat cuisine*." There was no butter. Times were hard at Walter's.

"I simply cannot," I repeated with tears starting to my eyes, "stay here another day." It was one of those traumatic meals. At Walter's there would be lots of traumatic meals – mostly breakfasts. It was as if people lay awake at night rehearsing their lines for delivery at precisely the moment when drama is most intolerable. It was not material deprivation that was the issue. Walter's house was well enough, comfortable, indeed, it found many admirers and even imitators.

It was of original design, built of black wood, not *on* but *into* the landscape, a small, steep valley just above the joining of two rock-strewn rivers, Campuhan, a beautiful reserve of nature – mists and plants and dragonflies with rainbows on their wings. His nearest neighbour, across the water, was the old royal temple and among the rocks was a hollow where a primordial holy python lived. Such juxtapositions are untroubling to Balinese thought. Out among the water-smoothed stones lay a deep spot where he would encourage the boys to dive for the sheer pleasure of their screams of laughter and the beauty of their gleaming brown bodies, slicked and darkened by water. In the Balinese fashion, it was less a house than a series of interlinked buildings, with high, thatched roofs, at various levels, joined by paths and steps and even little bridges, constructed of a mix of delicate basketry, huge beams and ancient blocks of stone. Like a grand lady, it gleamed with subtle touches of gold at throat and ear but, in its flirtation with open space, it recalled childhood tree houses and "camps" constructed in the bamboo at the end the garden, a Peter Pan if not a Wendy house. Baskets of scented orchids hung down from the gables. Inside, it was dotted with local works of art, upholstered with vivid Sumba cloths in nursery colours and, of course, resonant with musical instruments, including a grand piano and a complete gamelan orchestra. There was nothing Walter could not get a tune out of. I have seen him play a teapot, blowing through the spout to coax well-formed notes through the manipulated lid. Walter was also a painter whose works found a steady market with the tourists and sometimes, over the years, one would be hanging in the hall but, he explained, he only ever painted to get rid of something within himself and when it was done, his only interest was to get it out of the house. It was some time before I saw any of his work. The whole house exuded melodrama, invited the suspension of disbelief – and encouraged damp. Mould blossomed on any exposed surface. My Johnny Hancock, long unneeded and unused, would be, by now, bright green inside its rusted-solid tin. My lower limbs sprouted not Nieuwenkampian moss but athlete's foot.

Then there were the animals. Cats, dogs, canaries are all well enough but Walter had never outgrown that stage where a little boy keeps frogs in his pockets and beetles in jam jars. Any receptacle placed on the dining table had to be carefully examined before being opened. There were stinging fish in the pond and baby crocodiles and a deer with a broken leg that cried pitifully night and day. His snakes – admittedly non-poisonous – favoured the darker corners of the bathrooms for their afternoon siestas. Worst by far were two snarling monkeys with great green teeth that consorted freely with their wild, loutish brothers, fifty of whom lived in a tree in the garden. Since my simian encounter in Columbo, I bore them instant ill will. Monkeys are far too close to humans to be endearing. They moved at pleasure between the house and the wild and made hay with everything that was not locked away. They smashed the china so that, for two weeks, we drank from tins and ate off enamel plates, and that only after having climbed on the roof to retrieve the spoons and forks. Positive as ever, Walter used the windfall of fresh material to tile one of the bathrooms in a mosaic made from the fragments. They licked the paint off one of my Italian canvases which loosened their bowels. ("Ha ha, moved by your art" – Walter) so that they fouled my bed and pillows. They tore up my few Balinese sketchings ("At least it was nothing important. Something they might have drawn themselves" – Walter) and drank a bottle of ink that they then vomited back up over my wardrobe ("What a pity it was *black* ink, so formal" – Walter). I could not persuade him that this was anything but funny. He leaped childishly around on the furniture, arms pendulous, screaming monkey noises back at them – Ooh ooh aah – until they all became hysterical. I suppose it was evidence that he would have made a wonderful father but I wanted to slap him and could not. It was, after all, his furniture. There was constantly some Balinese at the door trying to sell him some new, inconvenient, more dangerous, even more insanitary companion, captured in the fields or woods. He began to speak dreamily of the tigers that lived in the great western forest and his absolute need for one.

Then there was the sheer expense of being Walter's guest. He gave you everything he possessed: lodging, food, drink, laundry, transport, service. He placed at your disposal all his knowledge of Bali and his contacts from the lowest to the highest and money was never mentioned – except to point out that he didn't actually have any, not a sou, no coins, no notes, anywhere in the house. By that time, it had been established that you were in a kind of fraternal, primitive joint economy and to try to segregate his needs from your own would be to betray the friendship given so trustingly. The boys would ask what you wanted for dinner and, when you answered, they would hold out their hands and say "One ringgit maybe enough". Bagus had been sent back to Buleleng as an economy measure but the free use of Walter's car was at least as expensive and certainly more unpredictable. Petrol had to be brought by pony, at great cost, from Denpasar and, once the tank was filled, Walter always had household commissions in all directions that rapidly drained it again. The boys brought the laundry and Walter bewailed the fact that – though they were very good and faithful boys – he had no money to pay their wages. They turned their good and faithful brown eyes on you in disappointment and, before you knew what you were doing, you were patting their cheeks in compassion and bearing the costs of the entire household. It was an economy of frank enticement. And it was not just me. As I walked around the little town, people would ask, "You stay with

Tuan Walter?" and when I assented, they would press eggs and chickens and little presents of rice into my hands – refusing all payment. "Tell him from Ketut in the market" or "From Wayan at the temple".

Walter chuckled. "They call them *titipan*."

"Tittypans?"

"*Titipan*, something given by A to B so that he may pass it on to C. Up here we're all in the *titipan* business. A telegram came through the post office the other day from the bank in Batavia, asking when they might expect a deposit and making threats. In a small town, people hear these things."

I was appalled. "Walter, how can you live like that?" He shrugged and looked suddenly serious.

"In villages there is what the Javanese call *gotong-royong*. People help each other, exchange things without money. While I have never been rich, I think I should have been rather good at it. Towards the end of the Great War, I happened to be in Russia and to get back to Germany, I had to walk across quite a lot of it, through the Russian lines, across no-man's land and then through the German lines. I think many people tried to shoot me, some by accident, others deliberately. When I arrived, they arrested me as a spy and offered to shoot me more formally the next day before an invited audience. I was twenty-two years old and I worried about it all night, after all, I didn't have a thing to wear. I don't think I shall ever be truly afraid again, certainly not of debt collectors."

Then there was the matter of my first night in the house by the river. We dined by candlelight, *à deux*, in the beautiful cool of a tropical evening, looking down on the shimmering little river. It was a simple enough meal: local chicken – a gift of "Nyoman at the crossroads" – rice and a vegetable dish made of wild fern shoots, washed down with river-cooled beer and deftly served by Walter's smiling boys. The Balinese way of eating is for each person to go off with his banana leaf of food and eat alone. It is a fineable offence to talk to a man who is eating, so meals were always served in silence, the boys shocked and amused by the phenomenon of Western table conversation. There was some sort of a sweet, made from *marquisa* fruit from the garden, a new, palate-tingling taste and the table we sat at, three meters long, was a piece of eternity, the polished trunk of a huge forest giant, split lengthways and resting on massive supports. That table was always covered with work in process – diagrams of dances, a Balinese dictionary, collections of folktales or altar decorations – hobbies that had been set on the back burner or newly called back to life. That day, we talked mostly of Walter. I confess, I felt an insatiable curiosity.

"Walter," I remarked boldly, sipping coffee, "you have a strange accent, what is it?"

He smiled and swiftly intoned a potted history of his life, as he must have with so many visitors before.

"I grew up in Moscow. My father was German consul there but my first language was Russian. So when I speak German it is with a Russian accent and, when I speak English, a German accent. When I did something wrong, my father would beat me in German with a meter rule and then my mother would comfort me in Russian with soft hands. I suppose it left me with a deep suspicion of the fatherland and the metric system but a deep love of Mother Russia. During the Great War, as an enemy alien, I was interned in a camp in the Urals but I managed to turn the guards into my friends so that I painted and gave concerts and made a little extra money with piano lessons and had really a wonderful time, running wild in the mountains and learning some of the local languages and living with the peasants and writing down their music. Wait ..." He threw down his napkin as if tired of words, took my hand and led me up the little staircase to the music room, where the piano stood gleaming on its own plinth, a sort of stage. A full moon shone down melodramatically through the open doorway, a natural milky spotlight, and he milked it for effect, stretching his interlaced fingers and – I swear – flicking out the back of a non-existent tailcoat as he sat down. He began to stroke the keys, slowly and sensually, coaxing forth a dark, wild melody with deep runs and trills and a curious limping rhythm that somehow summoned the loping creatures of the night. I crept across to stand, transfixed, at the end of the keyboard. As he played he stared up at the huge moon, the same moon they have in the Urals. I have no idea how long it lasted. It seemed to be contained in a time of its own. His music grew faster and he bent over the keys and the pounding hands conjured up black pine forests and the howl of wolves in stark silhouette, leading to a crescendo of muted violence that then faded to a crystal tinkling swept away by the sound of the dry-season tropical river outside. He deliberately broke the mood with a cheap, cheery chord and turned towards me grinning. "Based on a couple of old tartar tunes the peasants play on the violin at their barn dances. I forget the rest."

I was beside myself with the romance of it all. A shooting star rocketed across the sky and showered down the perfume of frangipani blossom in the garden trees.

"You play beautifully," I gasped. "Did you have lessons?"

"Not really. Just a little, first with Rachmanninov, then from Arthur Schnabel. And now, Rudi ..." he yawned and fluttered blond lashes. He had called me Rudi. "... it is late. I'm afraid all the boys have gone to bed. It doesn't seem troubleworth disturbing them to make one up for you does it? Why not just share with me, like the Balinese do? Less fuss everywhere?"

I awoke with the anxious sense of puzzlement that comes from sleeping in a strange house. I felt a stir of breeze on my naked skin. I had not cleaned my teeth or applied the medication betwen my toes. The river sounds of flowing water and the wind in unknown trees came first, then memory of the night before pulled sleep away like a lifted blanket. I rose on one elbow to see Walter exposed in the terrible vulnerability of dreaming, arranged in one of those implausible sprawled poses favoured by that old fraud Gaugin. From his parted lips came an odd musical sound, not snoring exactly, more like the purring of a great cat. As I watched, he supinated brusquely and stretched in an even more feline manner, batting some imagined vexation from his face with one hand. His fingers fell warm and unheeding against my skinny thigh. I examined the body with forensic detachment, took inventory, as Jacob Vorderman had taught me. It was a good, sound basic design without the narcissistic finish of the athlete, but made for use, compact, strong, bearing no marks of dissipation or old injury, indeed, resolutely boyish. The chest was hairless, muscular, very trim, the stomach flat. Tufts of blond in the armpits and crotch like ermine edging. The genitals I had explored earlier and established their good working order. The legs were hard and slim, tapering away into darkness. It would give years of maintenance-free service and wear well – like solid mahogany furniture with real brass fittings, as opposed to the splitting and cracking of cheap veneer. With time it would even acquire a fine patina of wear that would only enhance its beauty and exude a sense of comfort and solidity and so increase rather than decrease in desirability. It would, I decided, do me very nicely. With shock, I realised that I was in love. I drew up my knees to think about that, horribly aware of my own scrawny form.

Normally, in such matters, I had found that there came a point of conscious choice. You approached the edge of – as it were – an emotional cliff, looked hesitatingly over the brink and made a choice of whether to jump or not. I had always been ruled by prudence and, even in the case of esculent Luigi, had turned back at the last moment from the dizzying view. But here, puzzlingly, I was to be offered no choice. I must have leapt for I had already fallen. So here it was then, that thing so much written and sung and, I supposed, painted about – love – and I sounded my own body and mind with fascination and trepidation. What I felt was a mixture of infinite joy and piercing sadness that curiously involved a mellow pain in my left side, so that I smiled even as tears coursed down my cheeks. Shakily, I climbed out of bed, careful not to wake the sleeping object of all my future affections and wrapped a towel hanging there around my thin waist as I groped for my glasses. The floors were reassuringly solid and cold underfoot, like reason. Somewhere out there, down there, was water.

I eased my way through the door, snagging the towel on one of the particularly bristling figures of folklore it bore in carved relief and fingered and toed my cautious way down a precipitous cement staircase with no bannisters, to regain the living room. Even then, it seemed an absurd architectural metaphor. Wooden masks of heroes and demons, arranged like trophy heads, smirked and snarled from the walls to mark my descent from felicity. The last in the series was a stupid and angry Dutch face, with glasses and moustache surmounting many chins. There was, if my memory served me well, a carafe of water on the table. I moved slowly forward, then tripped and fell, crashed into the corner and sent glass and carafe tumbling to the floor with outstretched, fumbling hand. I crouched and listened, cursing under my breath. In a flash a face appeared at the door, the boy Resem, clutching a lamp.

"*Apa*?" He rubbed his eyes and registered a strange very white white man, scuffling for a towel under the table. With the aplomb of a British butler he made it all right. "Oh. I think is monkey but only Tuan. If Tuan go back to his room I bring coffee." Then I saw the wheels of his brain slowly turn as he tried to work out where exactly my room was and then his eyes traced my guilty route, in reverse, back up the stairs and he grinned. "Oh. I bring for Tuan Walter also." Before I could say anything, he was gone. I knew the boys all slept in a great bed back there, entangled like pullovers in a draw – the Western bed a luxury that some Balinese adored and some disdained for a traditional, hard, woven mat, to them more comfortable. I heard whispering offstage followed by a belly laugh, more whispering and another laugh, the sort provoked by a Charlie Chaplin pratfall. They all knew then. I crept back, in shame, up the stairs.

Walter was already up and dripping water from wet hair, unselfconsciously naked. As I entered, he turned, smiled, dragged his fingers through his hair and knotted a towel into a sarong. Ready to go.

"Breakfast," he said with energy. "Downstairs. Take your time, Bonnetchen. Then I'll show you Bali." He ruffled my own hair in manly affection and pounded off down the stairs, intercepting Resem on the way. Greetings, giggles. I sighed like a shopgirl – he had called me Bonnetchen – as he rampaged through the house like a force of nature, stirring it into life, evoking happy shouts, screams of laughter and the rattle of pans. As if at his command, the sun rose in magnificence above the trees to reveal the valley slathered in a fog of whipped cream. A dragonfly as big as my hand perched on the windowsill and pumped up its red filigree wings in preparation for another day. This was how I wanted life to be.

An hour later we were fed and watered, the car had been brought round and a picnic hamper prepared. It was an odd-looking car, long snout, long boot and a little island in the middle for two passengers, rather like a motorboat intended for some inland regatta..

"My Willy's Overland Whippet," he announced proudly. "You pay $500 for one of these things straight from the works in Indianapolis, Indiana." Perhaps so. But I doubted that this one was a Whippet exactly as known to the citizens of Indianapolis, Indiana. While the main body was still black, as intended by the manufacturer, the mudguards had undergone radical piecemeal revision, each being a different shade of blue and of different shape. The perceptive observer would have noticed the same shades of blue in decorative use at various points about the house.

"Did *you* pay $500 for it?"

"No, of course not. People give me things," he explained vaguely. "This was Baron von Plessen's auto. We made a film together. You have not seen it?" He sulked. "It was a work of some artistic merit. One day I will tell you the story."

I walked round the vehicle suspiciously. Was it safe? "What happened to the mudguards?"

"In Balinese circumstances mudguards are not necessary. Generally, I only use it in the dry weather. The roof got lost in an accident involving a pig. It took me a little time to adjust to autos. When he gave it to me the Baron asked whether I could drive and I replied with complete honesty that I had no idea as I had never tried."

"Oh my God."

He laughed so that I was unsure whether he was joking. "It's all right, Bonnetchen. I am much better now. Nowadays I hardly ever kill anyone when we go out somewhere and I have learnt not to try to avoid the pigs but to run them down and offer compensation which is really much safer." At this point, the two domesticated monkeys came scampering round the side of the house and tried to insert themselves into the car, something they were normally permitted. They were detected and vigorously repelled and snarled at me as at the "other woman" who had ousted them from grace. Then the three boys came, lugging the heavy picnic hamper between them and looking sad-eyed at their abandonment. Walter sighed and opened the curved boot. Inside was a dickie or rumble or mother-in-law seat in scuffed leather.

"Alright," he said wearily. "The monkeys stay. You can come. But there is only room for two, You must toss to decide who stays to look after the house. Er ... have you got a coin, Bonnetchen?"

He tossed, they called, the loser, chubby little Oleg, got to keep my coin and whistled happily as he performed artful throws and catches with it up his back and over his head. The winners, Resem and Badog, tucked up their sarongs, leaped lithely in and gripped the back of the front seat like postillions, eyes wide with excitement. Universal smiles. I would learn that Walter always left everyone happy, wanting more. And he always managed to use someone else's coin yet leave them humbly grateful to be allowed to supply it.

We set off at a spanking pace. He had lied about the improvement in his driving. The key to his technique seemed to be that he must be, at all times, accelerating hard unless actually executing an emergency stop. The Whippet was a sporty roadster that incorporated several features considered advanced at that time, such as a pressurised lubrication system and brakes on all four wheels. They only exacerbated Walter's exuberant style that was in direct contrast to that of slow-revving Bagus. Its most important component was the horn that had grown hoarse from overuse. The boys, of course, loved it, secure in the immortality of youth and never having experienced anything faster than a horse. Every wild swerve and improvident bump elicited fresh squeals of delight. At one point we became airborne over a hump in the road and they begged Walter – please, please Tuan Walter – to reverse and do it again, which I forbade, becoming ever after grumpy Tuan Rudi, the spoilsport. Bridges were a particular source of exhilaration to them. On Bali, because all the rivers flow between north and south in deep valleys, so do most of the main roads. Going from east to west or west to east was always very difficult since so many rivers had to be bridged and only "we" Dutch had thought the investment worthwhile. Still, as an economy measure, bridges had been frugally constructed wide enough for one-way traffic only so that to approach them at full speed, klaxoning wildy, as Walter did, was to bet one's life at 50–50 odds. Fortunately, in those days, there was little motorised traffic outside the towns. People did not seem to have the pathological urge to move from place to place that grips us now. Mostly it was men carrying protesting pigs slung on poles and women, bare breasts haughtily aswing, living lessons in deportment, bearing great pyramidal towers of fruit to the temples, or, their essence having been extracted by the hungry gods, carrying them home again to the pigs.

"Think," urged Walter, "how life would be simpler if all Balinese gods did regular home visits."

We must have been speaking English that day as I remember several eclecticisms of his that were new to me at the time. The semantic field of automobiles was always particularly challenging to one who favoured speed over precision. Indeed, "speed", or "*Geschwindigkeit*", he called "quickety" and the speedometer became thereby the "quickety clock".

This freed up the word "speeds" to be used for "gears" and the "tyres", as I recall, were always referred to as "gummytyres". We bounced along on high leaf springs, the land becoming flatter, the fields larger. The ocean blazed deep blue on our left. Whenever we slowed the heat beat down on us flatly. A small town, more a large village, gathered itself about us.

"Sanur," explained Walter as we picked our way down a small track to the beach. "This is the best spot for a swim because the reef here keeps the surf and big waves out."

The sand was the purest gold, shaded above the high tide mark by coconut palms and swept by a stiff breeze. In the misty distance, the volcano, Gunung Agung, swirled in cloud. Outrigger canoes were drawn up, white, blue and red, their eye-decorated prows carved with the long snout of some great sea monster and, further up, some simple fishermen's huts. We had no idea then, of course, that this place would be our nemesis. The boys sprang out, looked at each other, shyly tucked their sarongs between their legs and up into the waist fastening, creating immediate swimming trunks, and rushed off whooping into the sea, diving and splashing. Walter looked around to ensure there were no women to shock and stripped boldly to the buff, token modesty being maintained by no more than a cupped left hand.

"Come on, Bonnetchen!"

He pounded down the beach, waded, dived and was soon sporting with the boys amidst screams of laughter. Some men came out from under an awning and held their hands over their eyes. I picked out the word "Walter" over the noise of the surf. Then, they too, were running laughing into the sea, slapping him on the back, hugging him. Soon fights had been arranged, one perched on the shoulders of his friend, jousting his opponent into the water with shoves and feints, Walter always on the winning side to cheers and shouts. Since I had no bathing dress, I rolled up the legs of my flannels and waded up to my ankles in the warm water of the shallows then sat on the sand and watched them at play. After ten minutes or so, they began to drift back to the shore, panting, tousled, bodies shimmering with golden flakes of mica. The younger men were sent off and came back with cigarettes, hand-rolled from a pinch of tobacco and a dry *nipa* palm leaf, and coconuts to be sliced open with long machetes. We sat, drank, sucked in the smoke that smelled of autumn bonfires and Walter was, as always, the centre of it all. A little boy waddled up, a single lock of hair left on his shaven head, and kissed his hand, was seized and dandled, ecstatic, on his knee. Walter fired off fluent Balinese, from its effect, clearly jokes, endearments and words of sincere affection. A man came up, pluming more bonfire smoke, gripping something wrapped in an old piece of red rag. Walter unwrapped, examined. It was two old plates. He held them out for me to look at.

"Chinese. Mid-eighteenth century. They turned up in the sand, uncovered after a big storm. See the way the pattern has been rubbed off one. You know about that historic wreck, the *Sri Kumala*, a quarter of a century back? It was cast up here and the wreck was looted by the locals, thus breaking an old treaty the southern rulers had signed with the Dutch and long forgotten. It was the excuse the Dutch had been waiting for to invade and all the massacres that followed. These are supposed to be from there but are far too old. Could be important. But actually the cloth they're wrapped in is more so, a genuine Indian *patola* – very rare – evidence of ancient Hindu links. Sanur's an odd place. Odd things happen here what with all the sorcery and Brahmanas." He turned and, from his gestures and faces, it was clear he was haggling gently, transforming it into a comic turn. He rolled his eyes, flapped his arms, gasped and clutched his head. They exhaled a chorused chuckle. Handshakes, hugs, smiles. The deal was done.

"But Walter," I objected, reasonably, "you don't have any money."

"Oh. That's all right." He looked astonished. "They'll trust me." He shrugged his clothes back on and we climbed back in the car, the plates rewrapped and stowed in the rear. The boys were some way off, carefully brushing the sand off their feet, one with the other. "Resem! Badog!" he called, like a man summoning a stubborn hound. He glowed with happiness. Then, he turned his big blue eyes on me and spoke very quietly.

"There are many ways, Bonnetchen, to divide up the peoples of this world but, for me, the big divide is between those who are gigglers and those who are not. Balinese are emphatically gigglers. Resem and Badog are gigglers. I am a giggler. You are not. It is perhaps my life mission to turn you into a giggler." In the dickie, the boys were peeling off their sarongs, wringing them out and spreading them to dry on the hot metalwork, mischievously laughing at the sensation of driving naked, though unobserved, through the middle of the village.

"Look at them, Bonnetchen." He nodded in the rear view mirror, in Walterese his "backlookglass". "Two beautiful, healthy young animals. Children of nature. Not an unkind or ungenerous impulse in them."

I looked. I saw two boys in their mid-teens, for whom life was a series of happy new experiences and joyful prospects, hair thick and wet, eyes wide with joy, teeth shining, skin flawless, leaning like brothers – but not like my dour brothers – with their elbows trustingly on each other's shoulders, knowing the world to be a fine place. They pulsed with life, two young lotus plants twirling up towards the sunlight of their full growth. If this had not been the first day of my new life with Walter, I should have been depressed by it, a sort of anti-*memento mori* from some painting, showing everything that I lacked in spontaneity, physical beauty and capacity for joy. Walter was suddenly fierce.

"You see why I live here. Bali is the only place I have known where it is possible for me to love humanity in general. I feel myself humbled and civilised by their goodness."

I thought I saw tears in his eyes and, indeed, felt them briefly in my own. Then, over his shoulder, I glimpsed something that distracted me.

It was one of the most beautiful images I had ever seen, something stepped straight from a painting. A young girl leaned against one of the palm trees, barebreasted, in a bright, flowery sarong, a gold necklace around her slim throat and red hibiscus plaited in her hair. The artist in me flared up, rearranged her in a lying posture, no wait, she was reaching up to pluck blossoms from a tree, no, some kind of fruit – memories of Eve, unspoilt, innocent – a passion fruit! She was perfect. I was shaking with artistic excitement. Over by the coconut palms, she thrust one leg forward and scanned the horizon. I pointed, stayed Walter's hand on the wheel.

"Stop! Walter, don't you see? My perfect model. The absolute essence of Bali. I must find out who she is. I must paint her to save my soul!"

He looked round in alarm, then rested his forearms on the wheel and laughed deep and hard, shoulders quivering, incapable of speech. "Bonnetchen! Ha ha. You can't ... Ha ha ... Don't you know ...?"

Over by the palm trees, the nymph leant back again languidly and raised one arm in a melodramatic pose that showed the profile of her full breasts to advantage. Walter patted my knee comfortingly.

"Poor Bonnetchen! Sometimes you talk like a romantic novel written for schoolgirls. You are not the only artist who lives here. Look, there is a Belgian painter who lives in Sanur, Le Mayeur. *You* might like his stuff, all pretty pastel shades and wobbly post-impressionist boobs. That is Ni Polok, his model. He never paints anything else, worse than Monet and those damned water lilies. Whenever I bring tourists here – er … visitors – he sends her down to the beach to lurk among the trees like the Loreleimaedchen and lure them back to the house where he sells them a painting of her. God knows he's got hundreds and they're spreading all over the world. You will have noticed that she is somewhat lacking in artlessness. She used to be a famous *legong* dancer before she got old."

"Old? But she can't be more than fifteen or sixteen."

He gunned the engine. "The career of a *legong* dancer extends from the falling out of her first teeth to the onset of menstruation. After that, the pretty ones get snapped up as concubines in the royal houses and the others are sent back to the fields. And you had better not cross Le Mayeur since he is *very* well connected. It is said that the local *controleur* was upset by the fact of a white man living openly with a native and tried to deport Le Mayeur. Le Mayeur wrote to his cousins, the Belgian royal family, who phoned up their cousins, the Dutch royal family, who gave the Governor-General a rocket who arranged for the *controleur* to be shifted to a hellhole in Timor. Since then, people don't cross him and you shouldn't either." He slapped the side of the car, shouted to the woman who laughed, waggled her backside coarsely at him and trudged off humming. In the back, the boys blushed and whispered.

We drove slowly along the coast, heading south, the road cutting inland to avoid bays and inlets but with occasional vouchsafed glimpses of sea and sand. Resem and Badog held up their sarongs like streamers, whooping into the hot wind, till they were dry, then slipped them back on, once more becoming perfectly behaved choirboys. Walter's eyes were busy in the sky. Suddenly Resem shouted and pointed and he let out a hunter's cry of triumph and veered off, bumping down a bank of razor grass towards the sea. A deep thrumming rang out through the undergrowth and then, all at once, a great beast reared up over the trees, black and red, with whiskers of white – a huge kite, treading the wind, its snout out to sea. When we ran out onto open beach, there were six men hanging on to it, chests heaving, muscles straining, holding on for dear life and giggling as one bounced along on his behind.

As everywhere, Walter was welcome here, an old friend, handshaking, patting shoulders, trading smile for smile. Immediately, one man made way for him on the rope and his shoulders tingled with its energy as it bucked and dived against them, his hair flying in the breeze, at once fitting into the team, knowing the right thing to do.

"Bonnetchen!" He gestured me over, put my hand on the rope, let me feel the surges of zithering power. "Kites are important here, a thing of men. They have heads and hearts. This is a *bebean*, a catfish kite, but there are other kinds. Did you know there is a special temple for kites? And kites have magical power. They join earth and heaven, stop disease and the mice that eat the rice. A man who flies a kite, like us, performs a public act."

As if sensing my disbeliever's touch, the kite folded immediately into a slow dive and the men began, as one, to run in the opposite direction, wailing, stumbling over each other and me until the behemoth skittered to the ground with a reasonably gentle thud and a crack of bamboo and we all fell over and lay there in a heap, laughing till our lungs ached.

"There you are," Walter stretched and turned his cheek back and forth against the damp sand, enjoying its cool abrasion. "We are winning, Bonnetchen. Little by little you are becoming human, a giggler, despite yourself. You see, you are beginning to enjoy your own stumblings. And now we must bring you closer to God."

We drove on, the car almost coasting on its own, engine hushed. Turtle Island lay out a small distance to one side with little boats plying back and forth. We stopped and ate in the shade of some trees. A poor family, burned black by the sun, broke off from work on their salt pans to watch us large-eyed. The boys happily ate rice from banana leaves, off to one side. Walter, of course, had thought to bring sweets for the thin, dirty children and cigarettes for the adults and was greeted like one of the deities that descend, at regular intervals, to dine at Balinese temples and dispense the small change of their blessings. We moved on again.

"This is a special place," said Walter.

"But you say that about everywhere!"

He looked surprised, then considered. "That's true. But then every place *is* special". He dug sand out of one ear pensively. "The Balinese have no history, Bonnetchen. Most peoples divide time into sacred time and everyday time. The Balinese live every day in sacred time so they go straight from family reminiscence to myth and myth soaks into the soil." We drove along the narrow peninsula towards Nusa Dua, a bare, arid contrast to the lushness we had just left, one of those geographical oddities that finds no human use. "This has always been a wild place," said Walter. "A sort of hunting reserve for the royal family, with a few fishermen here and there – criminals, runaways, even lepers at one stage. Oh and it is the very best place for snakes. There are more snakes here, and bigger ones, than anywhere else in Bali."

On all sides was rank vegetation, mangrove swamps, featureless mud. The road suddenly began to rise and we whined up a series of hairpin bends in low gear, nasty dry branches reaching out to touch and scratch us and then stopped.

We were on a narrow headland that rose towards the sky. I went to the edge and looked over. Several hundred feet down, huge waves crashed against the bare rock and dissolved in spray and thunder. Above us towered a temple in grey stone. "Uluwatu," said Walter. "Eleventh century, one of the most important temples guarding Bali – long before the Muslims drove the Hindus out of Java in the fourteenth century and they came to establish themselves here. Don't get me started on that. I hope you are not menstruating Bonnetchen? No? Not even manstruating, ha, ha? No? Then we can enter." The boys yawned, crouched down and began to play cards, plucked from God knows where, behind the car – they had seen enough temples in their young lives – while Walter led me up a long staircase and through gate after exuberant gate. An aged guardian of some sort shouted at us angrily, but when Walter turned and greeted him, he was suddenly all toothless smiles and *sembahs*, bowed, waved, urged us, agonised with love and respect, on through a portal flanked by ancient stone elephants till we were at the highest terrace, thrust out into the ocean like the prow of a ship with wind buffeting our faces. Walter ran his hand gently over the rough stone. "Coral, from the sea. Living rock. See all the little creatures compressed into it?" He closed his eyes and stared blindly out into the empty ocean, weathering himself in the elements. "What I said about myth ... When I come here, I do this and allow myself to sink into the earth – what you call letting moss grow up your legs. We are both painters, in our different ways, and know what a terrible instrument the eye can be. The whole history of the Enlightenment has been the conversion of everything else into something that we can see so that it can be measured so that we become eyewitnesses at some trial of Nature. To close the eyes wilfully is the only way to know the poetry of a place."

I shut my eyes, seeing only the pinkness of the sunlight glowing through the lids. I felt, rather than heard, the roaring of sea and wind. It was as if I could sense the swelling rise of the soil about me. Then, Walter tweaked my glasses off my nose and I smiled and opened my eyes, in soft rebuke, to see a hideous monkey clutching them and making off across the precipitous rocks.

"Stop him!" I shouted in terror. "Oh, I haven't got a spare pair and without them I'm as blind as a bat!" I lunged at the creature and it scampered away to a high point showing its teeth. To attempt to follow it would be suicide.

"Perhaps," suggested Walter sweetly, "you should forget your eyes, attune to your other senses and appreciate the poetry of the place."

"Oh for Christ's sake!" I looked for a branch to attack the monkey with.

"What is it with you and monkeys?" pondered Walter with irritating detachment. "Perhaps you are a reincarnation of the hideous demon, Rahwana, and doomed to wage eternal warfare on the troops of Hanuman, their general. One day I will write a piece," and then he saw my face, "no. Not perhaps the best moment, I see that. Bonnetchen, if you would like your glasses back, I would suggest you sit down perfectly still and make not a sound while I have a quick word with our friend." He stretched out his upper body low over the rocks and turned up his face to the creature. His mouth made lippy sucking motions and produced a series of fat plops and soft farts. The monkey, that had been subjecting the spectacles to an almost professional ophthalmic examination, looked up. Walter repeated the process, now blowing kisses and reached, with infinite slowness, into his pocket to bring out a sweet, rustled the paper wrapper seductively and held it out. The monkey looked down over the cliff, as if considering dumping the glasses over the edge and then thought better of it. Instead, it approached cautiously, held out the glasses with one hand and took the sweet with the other. Then, it scampered back to its perch and flashed new defiance with crunching teeth. I looked for a rock to throw but Walter was firm.

"There," he said, restoring the glasses and taking the rock gently, "we have made our barter. Even monkeys are reasonable when approached in a reasonable monkey way. It is not their fault. They are like the people of Denpasar. They have learned that when they behave badly towards visitors, they are rewarded. And now it is time for our siesta."

We trod fine, windblown sand underfoot as we made our way through blank sun to a clump of trees a few hundred meters off. Walter stretched out on the soft ground and placed a large, spotted handkerchief – surely a comic prop for some routine with villagers – over his face. Resem lay back against a tree in dappled shade and Badog curled up beside him and put his head in his lap which Resem softly explored, nail-clicking, for fleas. All three closed their eyes and were immediately – outrageously – fast asleep, leaving me abandoned, awake, helpless and hapless, by default on guard against monkey molestation. To pass the empty time, I might happily have sketched them but had neither paper nor charcoal. If I roused Walter – I knew – he would airily suggest I try sketching in the sand with a stick since the work of all artists is mere marks in sand, or some such nonsense. I tried to sleep too but first there was a twig digging into my back. Then, the grass itched against my neck. Then, marauding – possibly stinging – ants found me. I sat up again and contemplated their sleeping innocence with envy and resentment. I worried that this spot was a natural latrine for temple visitors. What was I sitting in? Every man, surely, peed *against* a tree such as was my backrest. What was that rustling in the undergrowth? Perhaps it was one of the huge snakes that Walter had spoken of or – even more sinister – a small but deadly scorpion. When they awoke smiling and refreshed an hour later, I was exhausted, anxious, almost tearful with reproach. The boys exchanged heavy downcast glances. Tuan Rudi was grumpy again.

We set off back down the hill, Walter having paused to take elaborate leave of the guardian. He had not started the engine, relying on gravity, and the magic of our silent motion excited the boys again as we gathered speed through crunching leaves and skidded gummytyres ever faster round the bends. As we descended, the sounds of sea and wind hushed and merged into the mechanical noise of crickets. Walter smirked.

"The crickets are a little behind the time today. Still, as the English say 'better stridulate than never'." He sniggered at his own joke and watched me in the backlookglass, while I remained stony-faced. We motored without motor for over a kilometer and then, as we crept to a halt, Walter cut in the engine with a jolt that smacked of the bite of sad reality. We headed north, along a road dotted with villages where dogs came out and barked at us, as a novelty, in the street. Each hamlet, it seemed, had some artistic speciality.

"That place is good for woodcarving. That for silverwork. There lives an old man who makes exquisite masks – you know, the ones on the stairs. There is a woman there who weaves fantastic *ikat* – the cushions on the sofa. That is a place for stonecarving. There is the best place for carved *kris* handles …"

I was still feeling peevish. "Buy a lot of *kris* handles, do you? Is there anything Balinese don't do?"

He relaxed. I was talking again. "Well, actually, yes. They don't paint – at least not in our sense. There's a tradition of temple painting where they do the gods in profile, as in the shadow plays, but no depiction of ordinary life. They are craftsmen rather than artists. Each man wants to paint just the same as everyone else and newness is seen as error. But I'm working to change all that." He slowed at a crossroads, waved to a little old man who danced on the spot in delight, and then accelerated away hard. I had been to enough dull courses on the true meaning of art to be able to pick a fight with anyone on that subject.

"What's the difference?" I enquired with saccharine curiousity, "between an artist and a craftsman, I mean?"

He considered. "For present purposes, an artist is someone who produces work that interests me, a craftsman someone who makes stuff the tourists buy."

I smiled even more sweetly as I slid the knife between his ribs. "Don't you sell your paintings to tourists?"

He looked over and laughed, not in the least put out. "I sell my paintings to art lovers who just happen to be here on a visit."

"I see." I grimaced in bitter triumph and then our eyes met in the mirror and, despite myself, the sudden warmth of complicity flashed between us so that we both burst out laughing. He slapped my knee in affection. I felt a wonderful unaccustomed glow around my heart, a heart that finally belonged to someone.

"And now," he said, "this is Peliatan, not far from home but a special place. And just for you Bonnetchen, the *legong*, dance of the virgins, said to be the product of the fevered dreams of a ruler about angels."

They had drawn up a red and black awning over part of the marketplace, shading it from the mellow sun of late afternoon. Under it, sat a group of some dozen men, straight-backed and bare-chested in matching red sarongs with headcloths teased up like flames. Around them stood a *gamelan* orchestra, percussion instruments gleaming with bronze and gold-leafed carvings, from which flowed a surprisingly gentle and complex melody, tinkling with sensuous variations and artful ornamentation, like a stream through a ricefield. It was subtle and immensely pleasing to the ear, full of soft modulations and warm accents. The musicians flashed eyes and teeth in greeting at Walter who made a deep, respectful *sembah* to the lead drummer and received a nodded invitation to be seated. Three little girls, tightly bound in irridescent green and gold cloth, like insects, with waving flowers of gold in their hair knelt to attention before the orchestra, faces whitened and rouged. Two were decorated with all manner of coloured stones and mirrors.

Little boys swarmed all over the car, exploring the possibilities of the horn as a supplementary *gamelan* instrument, Resem and Badog slapping them softly away. A large crowd had gathered but, it seemed, largely indifferent to the music which was – if I understood correctly – directed at the gods, for the women loudly bargained over fruit while the men sat engrossed in cockfights, card games or a primitive form of roulette run by a fat Chinese. For children, the frogs hopping between their feet from one culvert to another were an endless source of fascination. Mothers were breastfeeding or shouting at their offspring while bachelors were hotly eyeing girls or rubbing themselves against them in the crowd. I thought of those 18th-century aristocrats, in their boxes, gambling, chattering and trying to spit on the conductor's bald head as Mozart's *Magic Flute* played the music of genius beneath them. As if he had been waiting only for Walter, the drummer now paused, caught the eye of his troupe and led off with a series of smart taps as the players etched a new theme.

At that time, we had not yet suffered the lisping and syrupy cinematic performances of Shirley Temple but they were exactly what I feared in the Balinese *legong* dance we had come to see. I have always, from earliest childhood, detested little girls. Much may, no doubt, be read into that simple confession, explaining the course of my adult life, but it was always made absolutely plain to me that little girls had been put into the world solely to stop little boys having any fun, dividing them, undermining their friendships, manipulating and domesticating them till they were broken and reduced like stallions hitched to a milk cart. My own sisters were always bursting into tears, throwing tantrums, twisting my parents round their little fingers with cutesy wiles or screaming in their frilly frocks to get their own way which always involved me not getting mine. There is something particularly vile about the screams of little girls – that totally tuneless, high-pitched, almost whistle – that is insufferable, that unmasks them as inhuman creatures from another planet. And Walter had brought me here to watch little girls at their wiliest and it was all my own fault, thanks to my fit of artistic enthusiasm in Sanur. And then, after the introduction, it started.

"What," I asked, "is it about?"

Walter groaned and grimaced, grasped at the air as though trying to force it into solid form. "Oh god! Look Bonnetchen, the problem with understanding Balinese culture lies not in the answers but the questions. It may be hours before anyone lets on what story we are talking about and they are not here for a story but a performance. The thing is, most of the dialogue here is as unintelligible to them as it is to you. Think only of the form. It is oddly like the cinema, less movement than a series of static poses that they switch a couple of times a second."

I gave up.

The smallest girl, surely not more than eight or ten, took her place in the centre of the clearing and, as if electrified by a sudden chord from the orchestra, contracted her body into an intense pose – arms raised, knees flexed, hands spread and fingers curled backwards into claws. At a sign from the drum, she careered rapidly, whole body trembling, round the circle of onlookers, fingers aflutter, eyes flashing back and forth in perfect discipline. Her face fixed in an empty stare, she came to rest and contorted her body into jagged patterns of physical counterpoint, then scooped up two closed fans lying on the ground and danced, her whole body transformed into angular geometry. The other two were suddenly animated by the music, snapped into rhythmic harmony with her – fingers, eyes and feet blazing in the gathering darkness. Then the fans were handed to the two main dancers who flipped them open and transitioned into a dance *à deux* as the musicians crashed into a thundering new theme, their hands a blur but their faces totally calm and remote, the rest of their bodies detached. A wall of sound buffeted our faces, like the wind at Uluwatu, the two sides of the orchestra resonating against each other, the air itself become an electrified force that raised our hair and seemed to draw sparks from our flesh. Former performers in the audience fell silent. Eyes blank, they undulated their shoulders in sympathy as their bodies resonated to the remembered motions literally drummed into them in childhood. The two dancers snapped necks and eyes back and forth, fans an invisible blur, approached their faces to each other, shuddered their shoulders. They swooped and dived, limbs in constant zig-zagging motion and perfect synchronicity, yet remaining, themselves, cool, remote, perfectly adult. I was transported, expunged of gross matter, swallowed into the golden shower of music and movement.

Walter smiled. "You see. Bonnetchen. The Balinese have no word for 'artist'. These are farm girls. Those musicians there are just illiterate farm boys. They come every night and practise after hours of driving a buffalo through the mud or ripping out weeds with bent backs. In the old days, aristocrats studied music but less now than before. The point is, when they play together, distinctions of caste are suspended. Lord and labourer sit side by side and both are told what to do by a penniless drummer. What you see here is a thousand little details, endlessly perfected over hundreds of hours of repetition so that whole thing can seem effortless and unstudied. Art here is a way of life, a form of communal understanding – not just for madmen like me and you – a means through which the whole hamlet expresses and feels itself."

My face, I knew, was white and drained. I had seen, perhaps, too much at one sitting, a sort of visual and conceptual indigestion. His hand was gentle on my arm.

"Enough for now. You've had a long day. You're watching as if we were in a Western theatre and that's not the way. Time we left."

We walked back to the car, the music still zithering in my ears. Resem and Badog tumbled with bony adolescence into the back. A man in some sort of tinsely theatrical costume, clearly one of the actors out of role, approached and pressed a package, wrapped in banana leaves, into Walter's hands.

"Spit-roast pig." He waggled his eyebrows. "How very kind. Our dinner. And now home with quickety."

"With quickety?" Already I was dozing.

"With the allgreatest quickety."

* * *

I slipped a long shirt over my bare and tingling body and tip-toed from my room, out into the warm night, the air like velvet on my face, all my senses sharpened, slipping into the skin of Luigi, renowned landing lizard and great deflowerer of virgins. My heart pounded and I felt as if I had been long marinated in some sweet southern wine. My whole body throbbed with incipient tumescence as I slithered with bare feet – "chicken feet" in Malay – over the dusty concrete paths and touchtoed silently down the steps outside the boys' hut and, there, paused to listen. From inside came a faint but reassuring snoring. Then through the arched doorway of the living room, carefully across the floor, avoiding, this time, the sharp table edge, and up the stairs with mounting excitement and proud erection, hugging the wall, shirt carelessly snagged by the fangs of a carved monster and to the door of Walter's room. That door, you will recall, had been carved, like many of the other doors of the house, by a master of the art, this one with a representation of the bodiless demon, Kala Rahu, eating the moon and so causing an eclipse, rendered merely temporary by the monster's absence of body and digestive organs. Much later, a German writer would visit Walter and spend a morning going round the house asking the boys to tell him the tales of legend and folklore engrossed on each door. He wrote them down, added a few quick Beardsleyesque sketches, banged it all together as a book, and – behold

– become an acknowledged world traveller and expert on the Balinese – enjoyed a bestseller. Yes, I am delaying opening that door, for I know all too well what lies beyond. The Balinese do not make complicated door fastenings, a simple hasp and loop, the flap pushed open to reveal a room bathed in bright moonlight, the great bed stark in the midst of it, and there in the bed … the mosquito net pushed up – because of the altitude there are seldom mosquitoes in Ubud, hence my being sent here by Dr Stove in Denpasar. There in the bed … designed by Walter, unhappily built in and so a refuge for cockroaches, scorpions and other undesirable experiences – I never would put my hand in any cupboard of that house without checking first for infestation. There in the bed, the sheets thrown off from heat, not one form but two. One Walter, quite naked – I had time to note the scooped pelvis and finely corded thighs – the other a young, slender, brown body preserving its modesty in a sarong, one arm around Walter, the face buried in the pillow and obscured by the mass of tousled, black hair. I stopped dead.

It must, surely, be one of the boys – Badog or Resem – Oleg would be too chubby and too young. I was embarrassed, an intruder, but could not tear my eyes away. Perhaps this was not a sexual propinquity, mere Balinese comradely affection, like Resem with his head in Badog's lap at Uluwatu, or had it been the other way round? But then I thought back to Walter's loud announcement to the boys at dinner – we ate most practically off banana leaves that were then dropped in the river – that they should make up the bed in the room at the back – *my* room – and ensure I had towels. It was not, as I had assumed, the boys being thrown off our trail, it was the hint being dropped – to them – that Walter was now available for nighttime visitation. Which one had been in the room? I could not now remember. They stirred in sleep as if feeling the weight of my gaze but perhaps they were simply lost in fevered dreams of angels. I moved, as in a dream myself, back past the eclipse, back to the landing, sat on the top step with my knees about my ears, my head in my hands and my future plans in ruins. My erection shrivelled and tried, hooded with shame, to creep back inside me to die. How had I dared to imagine that this was it, my spiritual soulmate finally found, my lifetime destiny finally made clear? My night with Walter had been no more than my free welcoming cocktail at the Bali Hotel, the basket of complimentary fruit about to putrefy if not swiftly bestowed, the chocolate placed, with corporate insincerity, on my pillow. Walter had said that in Bali he loved humanity in general which meant, I now saw, that he was in love with no one in particular.

6

This was my sixth day at Walter's place. We had roared all over the island in the Whippet. I had seen palaces and temples in the northern style, the archaic style, the water style. I had seen antiquities – confidently appraised as pre-Hindu, early Hindu and Buddhist. I had seen temple festivals and tooth-filing and naming ceremonies. I had seen warrior dances and sacred drama and masked dances – women dressed as men, men as women. Yesterday, Walter had needed to go down to Denpasar and I had refused the proffered generous offer of a ride fuelled by the petrol I had paid for, preferring a quiet day at home – that is at Walter's place.

Badog and Oleg and the short dark woman, Mas, who cooked and performed other kitchen mysteries had gone with Walter and the house was limpidly calm in their wake. In the early morning, Mas had pottered about disposing little trays of flowers, joss sticks and other offerings at doorways and other strategic points to ensure safety from demonic molestation. The air was heavy with the scent. Pigeons fluttered and cooed on the roof. The Balinese set little tubes of bamboo under their wings so that, as they fly the birds play a sort of susurrating music. Resem had brought me – unrequested – a cup of coffee on an exquisitely woven tray. Milk was too complicated in that house so we all drank our coffee black but, in the corner of the tray, he had set a perfect, long-stamened hibiscus blossom, freshly plucked. Another was tucked behind his ear. I sat and sipped and watched the dust motes dance in the air and savoured comforting warmth and straw and wood smells from the building and rested my eyes on the muted gold of ancient carvings and soft-hued cloths. Faint sounds of village life filtered in from outside, shouts and laughter and the happy cries of children or the clop of horses' hooves on the road all steeped in the cleansing rush of the river. The evil monkeys had been lured away by their wild comrades on some mischievous expedition into the fields and none of them had been seen for days. Later this morning, when I was soothed and steadied, I must, I knew, get down to drawing. I had taken in so much that was new and produced, as I saw from flipping through my sketchbook, virtually nothing – a few outlines of ornate temple gateways, the odd bare-breasted female study – mere doodles that could be worked later into some bigger project. I was bloated and distended with novelty and too many emotions.

Outside reality burst in as the clatter of boots on the steps and a rapping at the door and a Dutch voice calling whether anyone was at home. Clearly Mas' offerings did not work against Dutchmen. I thought at once of bailiffs. Resem appeared and hovered nervously, I looking at him, he at me, as if to say that Dutchmen must be my business. Sighing, I went to the door where stood a short fat man, red-faced and sweating into his moustache. I recognised Smit, the *controleur* of Gianyar. My face was the only licence he needed to push his way in.

"Bonnet, I think. Wondered where you'd got to. Thought to find you at the resthouse. We don't too much like our nationals coming here and getting lost. Makes paperwork if nothing else."

Walter had adopted the Balinese practice of removing shoes at the door. None of that for Smit. He stamped in roughshod, hobnails ploughing into the floor like a tank crossing a field, and sat down uninvited in a creaking rattan chair, throwing his hat onto the table and revealing cropped, grey hair. The hat had left a red line all the way round his head, making him ridiculous.

"Coffee!" he barked at Resem who looked at me. As resident European, therefore substitute householder, I shrugged weak permission and he bustled off to the kitchen. Smit slid a packet of Thomas Bear's Elephant cigarettes out of his side pocket and lit one, no pretence of social manners, dropping the expired match on the floor. "No Walter?" he asked.

"You just missed him. He's gone to Denpasar." I tried not to sound pleased at his inconvenience but then it struck me that if he had been at the resthouse, he would have heard the car just leaving and known he was not here. He reached for my sketchbook, without asking leave, and flicked through, pausing and puckering his lips ruminatively at the bare breasts.

"That reminds me," he smirked. "We had a complaint about you." Resem glided in bearing coffee without benefit of artful tray or hibiscus flowers and set it down.

"Me? Are you sure?" I was genuinely shocked. Who could have complained? No one even knew I was here.

He smiled happily, set down his cigarette, sipped coffee, making me wait, swallowed and burnt himself, not having waited long enough. "Damn and blast!" He spat back hot coffee through scorched lips. "It seems there was some incident involving a half-caste, man called Niemeyer. Seems you knocked up his daughter on the boat on the way over." He leered. "Well, he's made a complaint, accusing you of moral degeneracy." He shook his head sadly and smiled on. "This is not Holland you know. Here we have a duty of care, have to protect the natives from bad influences." He looked down at the sketch as if it provided clinching evidence of bad influence.

"Niemeyer? But that was nothing to do with me. I don't ... didn't. I suggest you look elsewhere for the penetrator ... the perpetrator." I blushed.

He blew slow smoke. "Thing is, a complaint's been made and it stays on your file. Now Niemeyer, being Eurasian, is not, strictly speaking, a native and I'd be the last to begrudge a young man the right to give his tubes the odd blow through, just for his health's sake if nothing else. Nothing wrong with a bit of brown. Stimulates the appetite. We all like a bit now and then. We don't ask you to be a saint, just to show a little discretion, old man, keep up a bit of front, if you see what I mean. If you can't control which way you point that thing, I suggest you get yourself a Johnny Hancock." I was back with my father on the docks, engaged in embarrassing intimacy, or at school learning about rutting rabbits. At any moment, he would move to the blackboard and draw diagrams. His wife, I knew, was an aridly Christian creature. I wondered how she would take his advice.

"Is that what *you* do?" I snapped. "Thank you," I said stiffly, "I have already made all necessary arrangements."

He got up and began to inspect the furniture and fittings like an impertinent prospective tenant, then went and stood on the terrace, looking down at the river, thrust his hand deep into his pocket and juggled his balls as one might a handful of loose change.

"You know why this house is here, don't you? It's not for the view or the peace and quiet. They gave Walter this land because it's near the graveyard and in the river valley, both areas for demons, witches, that sort of thing. Makes you wonder just what they think of him, doesn't it? It's the sort of place they chase off lepers to live in. No Balinese would ever live here at any price. Be scared to death and get ill just from the worry, like as not. Seen it happen loads of times. How does he get his boys to stay, I wonder? What is it he's got?" I thought maybe I knew precisely what it was that he had but wasn't about to tell Smit. He returned to the table and drained the now-cooled coffee and turned on his heels with a smug driven-by-duty look on his face. As he reached the door, he turned.

"Of course, it cuts both ways," he remarked as if the thought had just struck him. "With your record, I mean. Records out here often get lost. I often wonder exactly what goes on this household." He waved his hat around the room. "As a loyal Dutchman, I'm sure you'll let me know of anything untoward." He did a bit more of the ball juggling and clapped his hat on his shaven head. I shook his proffered hand with deep reluctance and his feet clumped up the steps, leaving me feeling defiled and demeaned.

Resem returned to clear the cups with deft, coltish motions. I was aware of the exaggerated tilt of his thigh, the extraordinary length and thickness of his eyelashes.

"Resem is a dancer?" I asked.

He smiled with downcast eyes. "Before. Now I am too old." Bali, it seemed, was full of elderly youth. I offered him one of Walter's cigarettes, a Mascot No.7, from the elegant sandalwood box on the table. He hesitated, then accepted, received the light with grace. I did not smoke myself, but took one and lit it and mimed smoking for companionship's sake.

"Has Tuan Walter ever painted Resem?"

He exhaled through dilated nostrils and looked at his cigarette in appreciation. "He does not paint people, only places, fields, volcanoes. Sometimes there are people there but not real people, people from Tuan

Walter's head only."

"How would it be if I drew Resem's portrait?"

He was aghast, hand to bare chest in a gesture from the silent films. "Why would Tuan Rudi want to draw me? I am ugly." He held out his forearm in proof. "I am dark."

A simple, flat statement. This was no coyness on his part. He genuinely did not know he was beautiful. Now it was I who was aghast. I carried a bamboo chair out onto the terrace, arranged it in the light, dragged over one of the slender, fluted, but solid wood Nias stools for myself. I arranged him in the chair, one arm behind his head, one leg drawn up, looking down at his own knee.

"Loosen the sarong a little." It sagged sufficiently to show strands of incredibly shiny, black, pubic hair below the navel. I settled, my pad on my knee and drew a few swift, defining strokes with dark pastel fixing the basic contours. I formed the elfin face, softened the chin with a rubbing finger, placed the huge eyes, gave them direction, caressed the curved neck, the soft, full lips with a suggestion of pink tongue, the lift of one shoulder. The chest was strong muscles on light bones.

"Tuan Walter," I said. "Is he good to you? If you smoke please move nothing but your arm. Don't change your expression."

He stole a swift drag. "Tuan Walter is very kind. He takes us with him when he travels. He never beats us. He is teaching us to read and write because the Dutch do not allow us to go to school. He is funny. He makes us laugh."

I began to shadow the neck, bring out the cartilage of the nose, the provocative, bobbing Adam's apple. The hair was a tangle of blue highlights and deepest black.

"Does he play with you?"

He paused on the way to another drag and looked cautiously at me. "How do you mean?" *Main-main* is "to play around", "to engage in social chit-chat". *Main* is "to play a game or instrument" but also "to have sex". I opened my eyes wide with innocence and coaxed a slight puffiness from under his own in dark red. My hand was shaking.

"Tuan Walter is a friendly man," I said. "He likes to play in all sorts of ways. Sometimes he plays at night."

He looked up sharply, then remembered he was not supposed to move and looked down. I raised the cheekbones, curved the upper lip with its hint of a moustache.

"Sometimes," he said carefully, after a short silence, "he asks if we would like to play any game with him and then we must tell him what game." He stole a glance at me through lowered lashes. I shaped the tendons in his neck and stroked them into a blur.

"There is no harm in that," I remarked casually. "In Bali, I have heard that, before they are married, friends often play games together." I slipped off my glasses and held up the portrait. He cried out in delight, stubbed out the cigarette and stood up to touch it. As the loose sarong dropped, I saw that he had risen in every sense.

I shall not detail further our shameful activities of that late morning except to say that it was then and there that I convincingly entered Bali and it me, that I drank its very essence and I understood Walter's engagement with the whole island. Resem incarnated for me the whole of that ancient culture. As we bathed together and Resem gently washed my back, it was not a personal act. It was the whole of Bali cleansing me in holy water, a baptism. As Resem curled up soft and warm on my bony lap, the last afterglow of our lust crushed out, and rested his head against my chest, I felt … what? Gratitude, affection, compassion, an urge to protect, the feeling that human kindness and simplicity were raising my estimation of what a person should be, were making me a better man. We agreed at once that what had happened should remain a secret between us. Walter might be angry, would certainly be offended. We ruthlessly expunged all signs of our debauch. I picked up the crushed hibiscus, trodden underfoot in our passion, and refused to see it as a too-obvious painterly symbol. The furniture was rearranged and polished, the floor washed, the tools of my art hidden and when the car finally returned at dusk I was sitting innocently at the table reading Nieuwenkamp's book as Resem bustled far away in the kitchen.

Walter burst in with his arms full of parcels, like a dog bringing a stick. On his head, he was wearing a navy brown beret edged with leather, perched aslant over one ear. It looked silly, the mark of urban bohemian affectation or a Garbo fan.

"Why," I asked cattily, "are you dressed as an artist?"

He adjusted it, with fake pride, into a sort of halo and posed in the mirror. "Do you like it? I was at Lee King's, you know the big shop by the market, and I saw it. It spoke to me."

I indicated the heap of parcels. "For a man who left here with no money, a lot of things spoke to you. It must have been very noisy in that shop."

"Yes ... well ... egg cups, a toast rack. Whenever I have British guests they do so go on about breakfast. Anyway, the boys will love these odds and ends for the morning. Lee King's does credit." He came and perched at the end of the table. "So. What did you get up to while I was away?" He stared me in the face and I saw, as in slow motion, how a slightly puzzled expression came into his eyes as he looked around the room and then his jaw dropped in delight and he pointed and laughed. "You had sex with Resem! Ha ha ha. Good isn't he? A sweet, affectionate lad."

I blushed. Blood roared in my ears.

"No ... yes ... how the hell? Aren't you upset?"

He looked at me in genuine surprise. "Why on earth should I be upset?" He touched my hand, a joke slap.

"I thought you might be – sniff – jealous."

"Why jealous? I think it is lovely when two people make each other happy. Better a blunt knife than a fork with no prongs."

"What?"

"It is a saying in the Urals." As if on cue Resem could be heard singing, with a soaring voice, in the kitchen. "Sex is magic because it conjures up solid happiness out of thin air. The only reason I would be upset would be if you were not nice to him and I know you wouldn't do that. What did you give him?"

I bristled. "Give him? Nothing. It was not," I said primly, "a commercial transaction."

He shook his head sadly. "Oh Bonnetchen. Sometimes you are so stupid. When a man gives his wife a bunch of flowers or a bottle of perfume does that make it a commercial transaction? Quite the reverse." He dug in the pile on the table and pulled out a flat, brown-wrapped package. "He is a poor young man who has given you everything he had to give, now you must give something back. Here is a nice new sarong. I bought it for myself but one of the good things about a sarong is that it fits anyone. Don't do it in front of the other boys – who all know by now by the way – he would be embarrassed. When he is alone, give him this, say something nice and – for God's sake Bonnetchen – smile! Then he will know you genuinely like him and respect him and you will be real friends. There is another advantage to giving Balinese cloth. Though the Balinese are scrupulously clean about their bodies, they never wash their clothes. Those gold-leaf costumes of the dancers for example, *prada*, can't ever be got near water, though they get soaked in sweat at every performance. You mustn't, of course, ever mention it but a new sarong, from time to time, sweetens them up in every way."

I was touched. Walter was not concerned that others were fishing his pool or that Resem might prefer me to him. He just wanted everyone to be happy and feel good about themselves. There were tears in my eyes.

I said grudgingly, "I like the hat." I shuffled my feet under the table. "It suits you."

* * *

"The Lord giveth," said Walter, waving a brown official envelope triumphantly over the new toastrack, "and the Lord taketh away." It had been a special breakfast, fuelled with treats from the city, oranges, cheese, relatively new newspapers, even butter from a tin made irresistible to the customer by images of Dutch milkmaids in clogs. Walter always believed that as long as he had the luxuries, the necessities would take care of themselves. "You did not tell me Smit had called. Perhaps your mind was distracted by other things."

"Perhaps. But I don't think he's any friend of yours."

My first thought about such an envelope was "bailiffs" but then even Walter would have been less cheery. Mas came in with fresh coffee, displaying in smiles the gold incisor that must be the origin of her name.

"Well, he's done me a kindness. He sent this across from the resthouse. You are looking at an official state artist of the Dutch East Indies administration." He poured for both of us.

"You must have known. Psychic. And that, surely, is why you bought the beret. Isn't that part of the uniform? But you forget, I have still not seen any of your work. You have seen all of mine." I sounded like a disappointed schoolboy behind the bicycle sheds.

He made his crooked face. "You would not like it. I have told you that I paint to rid myself of bad things inside me, like er, fallthrough …" Fallthrough? He distractedly mimed face and stomach pain, crouched like a man relieving himself, blew a raspberry. Oh, diarrhoea. "… and then I get it out of the house. I have several commissions waiting but I hate to paint for money. That is the difficulty here. The worst is when I have spent the money and still not done the painting, then I am like a man in chains, walking around, hearing them rattle."

He raised his arms to demonstrate his shackles and groaned with pain, then passed me the letter. It was from Dr Stutterheim, the famous archaeologist and head of the Archaeology Section of the Antiquities Service. Walter was to paint a whole series of twelve pictures of past life in the Indies for an official publication. At 800 guilders a picture, it was a life-saver.

"Walter!" I said. "You'd be crazy not to do this. Think of the money in terms of berets or toastracks. And think of the fun you can have. You could put Smit's face in it and give it to a monkey or a cannibal. You could make us both kings. Resem," I said tenderly, "could appear as some great hero."

He brightened. "I could put the ladies in breastholders and the men in sportsupporters and who is to say the builders of Borodur were not covered in tattoos?" Then a sideways leap, a suddenly serious voice. "I see Badog has a new cloth and I hear you have been sketching him, too. Is everything all right there?" I blushed. It was true. I had been making him a model by slow steps.

"Resem is happy," I said. "Badog is happy." It was all he wanted to hear but I could not leave it there. "The problem is Oleg. The others tell me he, too, is eager to be stretched – sketched – but …"

He held up a hand. "I don't want to know. You must work it out amongst yourselves. Has it occurred to you that you might make fewer moral considerations if Oleg were not short and fat? But I don't want to know."

It had not occurred to me. Now it did. I felt ashamed. Why was I always feeling ashamed? Walter ducked behind a newspaper and lobbed out wisdoms like grenades. The headline read "New planet discovered and named Pluto."

"You see, Bonnetchen? Life is not about rules. Everything lies in the circumstances. The only thing is that I cannot have rows in my house. No breaking of glasses and banging of saucepans. It was like that when I lived with Murnau. I could not stand it again."

I gaped. "Murnau, the film director? The man who made *Nosferatu*? Tell me."

Walter sighed and laid down the paper.

"His real name was Plumpe and even after he changed it, he was always really Plumpe. He was a Plumpe. It was in Berlin. I was young, knew no one. He was older and, I thought, wiser. But, after a while, he became possessive, aggressive, obsessive, excessive and he drank. I ended up looking after him in a sanatorium and he would not allow me out of the grounds. When I ran away from Europe, I ran away from Plumpe. At that age nothing is really bad for you. You learn. From Plumpe, I learnt about rows and about films. You remember all those shadows in *Nosferatu*?" I nodded. People always commented on the way that the creature was seen more through its shadow than reality. "That was me. I was already keen on the Indies and had bought a couple of shadow puppets in Rotterdam when I had an exhibition of my paintings. We spent an afternoon playing with them." He shrugged. "The rest is cinema. And now," he stood up purposefully, "come with me. We have work to do. Oh. And what I said about not wanting to know. I was lying. You know I love to gossip. The great fault of the Balinese is that they are so terribly discreet."

We walked out of the house and up the steps to the side of the road, shaded by fruiting trees and turned towards the centre. A panorama of rich ricefields stretched out, with leaves hung out over them like washing to scare away birds. Everywhere was the happy, comforting sound of running water. On either side of the road were deep gutters, each house with its own little bridge, clear water tumbling underneath. A fat child was driving a flock of fat ducks out to the flooded fields. We walked in dappled sunshine and shadow and, of course, everywhere Walter was greeted and waved to with flashing smiles. Shortly, we came to the *puri*, the palace, a fresh-looking building in stone, completely rebuilt since the great earthquake of 1917.

"You will notice the stonecarving by I Gusti Nyoman Lempad," he instructed. "He did my doors and I can claim some small credit for his development from simple builder to artist." Somewhere nearby odd *gamelan* instruments were practising with drum thuds and occasional crashes. "Children," said Walter. "As soon as they can walk they sit on their father's laps as they play so that the music seeps into their bones and soon they are exploring music for themselves."

A tiny, totally naked tot, guarded by a wizened crone, crouched in the dust outside the *puri* gate, playing hysterically with a small, sand-coloured puppy that was dancing around the child, occasionally darting in to nip its toes and provoke screams of delighted laughter. To my surprise, Walter, ignored the woman, went down on his knees and spoke lowly to the child that then got up with great dignity and waddled inside. It must have discharged its mission satisfactorily, for a small sharp-eyed man of middle age came out and greeted Walter warmly. I was pointed at, looked up and down, discussed at length and equally lengthily ignored. Finally Walter turned to me.

"The big boss, Cokorda Gede Raka Sukawati, is away so we get to see his little brother Cokorda Gede Agung Sukawati."

The names swum in my head.

"I thought Balinese only used the names of their birth order followed by a nickname?"

He smiled. "Normally they do but some of the nobles have titles long enough to hang a week's washing on. Agung is actually a better option. He's much more interested in the visual arts, Raka plays the violin and the flute so goes for music, but you can never be sure how Agung wants you to behave. Being young, sometimes he's all modern, drinking gin and listening to jazz records. Sometimes, he's all traditional Balinese and will talk to you in low Balinese and you have to talk back in special high, palace Balinese which is a pain since you have to refer to him as Your Feet."

"Your Feet?"

"Yes, the idea seems to be that he is so above you that the only part of him you dare to address is his feet."

"Oh God."

"Don't worry, Bonnetchen. Just follow my lead."

The child crouched down and laid a turd. The puppy rushed up and ate it, then licked the child's behind. A message of hope to Holland's housewives.

We set off in pursuit of our guide, who strode off through a maze of flagged courts at various levels, gateways and dark passages, none very grand but impressive by sheer weight of numbers. We were thus treated to a cross-section survey of palace activities. Women were cracking nuts, folding clothes, picking bugs out of rice and each others' hair while men were caressing fighting cocks, mending shoes and tormenting otherwise tranquil children. People looked up as we passed. Many greeted Walter by name. Finally, we were left on a low verandah, our shoes were pointed at and our guarantor disappeared for a considerable time. On top of a wall, a row of torch batteries were warming in the sun to coax a little more life out of them. We waited in unshod patience, watching a child playing with a bizarre toy, that I took, at first, to be a model aeroplane.

"They trap them, the big red dragonflies, with a sort of resin on the end of a reed. One day, I must do some work on them. I suppose it is cruel but when they tire of them, they eat them. Also bumblebees. Did you know Oleg means bumblebee, by the way? There is even a dance ..." We were waved in and I followed closely on Walter's heels.

It was a moderate-sized room, with a floor of cool multi-coloured chequered tiles that would have driven Escher mad, and a raised dais at the far end, covered in carpet, on which perched three heavy chairs of antique form. The walls were much mirrored and a sort of faux fireplace had been constructed to one side as if in emulation of Dutch interior design. Even in the sweaty Indies, the Dutch needed fireplaces so they knew how to arrange a room. On it stood two fussy clocks, swarming with cherubs, that disagreed completely about the time. A large and offensive chandelier hung from the centre boss of the ceiling where lizards slalomed around it and the still air exuded a smell of damp and mould. In the centre chair sat a chubby, dapper figure, short of stature, dark of hue and dressed in floppy shorts and a bush shirt tightly unbuttoned to mid-chest. Unlike most Balinese, when confronted with a chair he sat in it after the Western fashion, not cross-legged *on* it, after the Balinese. Walter strode across the room with me in tow.

"Hi Walter!" Modern, today then, very. No feet. "Come in out of the hot sunnyshine." He turned to me. "Walter," he said, "has been learning me English. It is better that we speak English because the palace language is very complicated. If you use the wrong word we can all end up having to be cleansed by the priests and that is expensive and they are such a bore. Of course, there is no problem if a madman or a child does it, so we have agreed that officially Walter is an imbecile child and he does that well. But the whole business is better avoided."

"Hallo Agung!" Walter bowed low as he *sembahed* high. I emulated. "May I introduce my dear friend, Rudolf Bonnet? Mr Bonnet is one of the foremost painters of Holland." It was the only compliment on my artistic talents I had ever heard from Walter's lips.

"What brings you to Ubud, Mr Bonnet? I have heard much about you." What had he heard? He was about twenty years old, sleek black hair, the chest and legs hairless. He looked like a smoother relative of Oleg.

"From afar, I have read strange stories of the richness of your island and the beauty and artistic talent of your people and, come to see them for myself, I find them no exaggeration but rather understated." Why the hell was I talking like this? Did he even understand me? But as I laid it on good and thick, I realised it was really nothing but the truth. The Cokorda smiled and made a gesture of the dance, parting both hands away and up from the body, as though towards the chairs but Walter perched one buttock, instead, on the edge of the dais, so that we were obliged to engage in an uncomfortable sideways-on, looking-up conversation. The famed, honorific feet, at which we now sat, were, I was obliged to notice, shod in highly polished schoolboy shoes. In the Indies, who you are and where you are, are indicated not by what you tie around your neck but what you put on your feet.

"Understated? I sometimes feel, Mr Bonnet, that you Dutch are rather ashamed of having colonised us, with all our great earth and water, when your own country is hardly bigger than a noodle stall. It is so. I have seen it on a map. Some refreshment, perhaps?" The Cokorda raised a bored eyebrow and an aged servant hitched up his sarong and shuffled effortfully from the door on his knees.

"No thank you," Walter replied. Agung waved the servant away and he sighed and shuffled all the way back, still kneeling.

"Do you have an automobile, Mr Bonnet?"

"No, I'm afraid not."

"A pity. I should like to have an automobile but my brother is in dispute with the *controleur*. He will only allow what he considers the main rajahs to have an automobile with a golden parasol on the engine-cooler lid." The what? Ah, a Walterism for the radiator cap. "My brother considers any automobile without such a parasol an affront." He lapsed into silence and brooded.

"The Cokorda," Walter said to me waggishly, "is my boss."

Agung giggled. "It is true, Mr Bonnet, though he was actually engaged by my elder brother. I have many brothers." He made a face to show that each and every one of them was a burden to him. "My father had forty-six wives and thirty-five concubines but I only have one. That is the modern way. As a member of the nobility, I was permitted by your countrymen to go to school in Denpasar. I lodged opposite the gates of the Bali Hotel which was good for my English. Every day, I would hear these white people talking about art, art, art and where they could buy it and the high prices they would pay. I had no idea what art was. I looked it up in the Dutch dictionary but had no idea what *kunst* was either. The more people tried to explain, the less I grasped it, but since there was so much money in it we knew we must find out. My brother and I were on a visit to our dear cousin in Yogya, in Java, where Walter directed the Sultan's orchestra and at dinner, one night, we were seated side by side and he talked much about art. It seemed that Java had already got it so we knew that Bali must have it too, so we hired him to teach our young people to have it. Our cousin was very angry that we took him away. Only Walter had been able to teach the palace musicians the foxtrot and the Dutch national anthem and the difference between the two, which pleased the Resident very much." A frown crossed his serene features. "That was some years ago now and still I ask Walter, 'Where is the art? Do we have it yet? When is it coming?'"

Walter, glowing with confidence, was not in the least put out.

"Agung, as I keep explaining, art is not just a thing, it is above all a state of mind. Already we have made great progress and soon there will be more. That is why I have brought Mr Bonnet here to help me with this matter. I have been requested by the government to produce a series of official paintings showing the history of the Indies in which Bali, I shall insist, must have its place. This will take much of my time but, of course, for government, I cannot refuse. As Holland's greatest living painter, it is our huge privilege to have Mr Bonnet here to teach the young artists in my place. Success will surely follow." I stared at him in horror. He winked. "It is extraordinary that he should be here at this moment. I see in it the nothing less than the work of destiny."

The idea dropped into my mind like a stone down a well. So there it was, the work of destiny, an act of Bali itself. I was hopelessly seduced by the idea. that Bali had somehow chosen me. I felt myself, astonished, surrendering to the conceit. There is nothing worse than to be free. The Cokorda expressed delight and clapped his little hands together. By now, I suspected, he must have despaired of ever turning Walter into a mere employee.

"Wonderful! Wonderful! You know that in order to attract Walter here we had to promise him a place in the palace with food, free canvas and paint – oh – and he was most insistent that all the men he might want to paint should be willing to pose for him." No fool then. He knew. "We might be able to offer you to share the same inducements." He studied me with an excessive and deliberate – as it seemed to me – very Balinese innocence. "Do you like to paint Balinese men, Mr Bonnet, or women, or do you like mountains and fields? But then, perhaps, it was just the free paint that attracted Walter to us and he didn't find any of us pretty at all." He giggled, I blushed. What was he really saying? What did he know? What had he heard? Had the boys gossiped? Had Smit mentioned my naked breasts? I left with a sense of having met someone who was either infinitely simple or profoundly subtle but then, that was the way I was beginning to feel about Walter too. On our way to the palace, he had pointed out to me the little zig-zag gates that Balinese build at the entrance to their compounds. It seems that demons and other hostile beings are so stupid that they can only move in straight lines and so are totally flummoxed by them. Walter, then, on present evidence, was no demon. We walked back towards the door and turned to bow before going through it. "A very good bye," called the Cokorda. Walter bowed, *sembahed* and whispered. "They also promised me a small salary that never quite turns up. Good luck with that Bonnetchen."

* * *

"I simply cannot," I said in tearful emotional outburst, "stay here another day." Perhaps I had been too greatly exposed to theatre since my arrival in Bali.

It was not the animals, though the day-long screeching of the parakeet, that so delighted Walter, grated on my nerves. The sickly deer had been despatched by a hard-hearted villager and turned into several meals for us and credit with the meat-hungry neighbours. The monkeys had reverted fully to the wild and last been seen heading west towards the Great Forest. Recently, Walter's interest had turned, thankfully, towards insects that were captured and contained within glass jars and thus impinged less on our social lives.

It was not the boys. The foreseen complications and jealousies had not materialised. We all remained the most affectionate friends. The neatly segregated relationships with which I had grown up did not seem to apply here. Friend, lover, master, servant were a beast divided up into quite different cuts.

It was not the relationship between Walter and me – well, not *just* that. I had accepted that we were two Thomas Mann characters, from different novels, wandered into the same plot, both embodiments of the cold north, looking for our warm south and naturally not finding it in each other. It was sad – even comic – rather than tragic. There might not be love but there was much more than cold indifference.

It was, rather, the Countess that sharpened the problem to the point where action was required. The announcement of her arrival was brought by one of the boy from the post office, a gangling, permanently exhausted youth, armed with a bicycle and a peaked cap into which messages were tucked.

"What's a *Gräfin*?" he asked as he handed one over.

"Sort of like a Cokorda's wife," Walter explained, thumbing the envelope open and reading.

"Well. You've got one coming."

"So I see."

It was unfortunate that this was the precise moment when her honking car – or rather Fatimah's – drew up outside with smiling

Bagus at the wheel and a hatchet-faced woman of a certain age, grimly hatpinned in tweed and feathers despite the heat, beside him. She had been sent by Walter's mother, a deluded goose of a woman whom he quite naturally adored, one excessively in awe of empty titles, and bore a letter of introduction from her like a warrant to distrain upon his goods. Walter was there, up the steps, car door open, hand extended, bowing and heelclicking – *gnädige Dame* – then, God save us, handkissing. She was tall, aridly thin, with eyes the colour of sloe gin and a charmlessness reminiscent of my own. Bagus leapt from the vehicle in a nice new shirt, green as peppermint, and rushed up to me, then paused – stranded between two gesture systems – as we half handshook, half bowed, dithered, patted each other shyly on the upper arm and circled like two boxers in the early stages of a fight.

"You have found Tuan Piss."

"Yes, I have found him." The boys emerged and fell upon Bagus in loud and joyful greeting – no dithering there despite alleged differences of caste – and whisked him off to the kitchen with the telegraph boy and his bicycle, for group refreshment, while the Countess, arm interlinked with Walter's, moved into occupation of the house like an invading army. I was left, as at Uluwatu, quite alone and unheeded before a heap of luggage strapped to the hot car, in the stench of petrol and rubber. Well, I was not going to be taken advantage of. I selected the smallest hatbox, just to show willing, and carried it down to the main house and the sitting room.

"Affairs in Germany are quite terrible," she was braying. "Many persons of quality have been reduced to labour, the middle classes have abandoned all pretence at respectability and the poor are suffering of course – but then they are used to it." Walter was not really interested in Germany except inasmuch as it directly affected his family. It was too remote. What had it to do with us here? And then, being a fundamentally decent man, he was bored by the generality of politics. "Oh," she caught sight of me, "be careful with that, whoever you are. You look clumsy and I see you cannot be trusted. It is fragile and quite irreplaceable. Bring it here at once."

The words "please" and "thank you" were clearly unknown to her in any language. Grinding my teeth, I crossed the room and plonked it down beside her, on the floor. Over the back of the chair was a foxfur stole – a horrible thing – with paws, tail, head and eyes, looking as if the unfortunate creature had fallen under a rigorous steamroller, a most inappropriate garment. The boys, I foresaw, would be nervous around it. I half wished the monkeys would return. They would have known what to make of it. Nevertheless, I extended a hand in greeting.

"Bonnetchen ... er Bonnet, Rudolf Bonnet. A guest here – like yourself."

She pursed her lips sceptically, averted her gaze and, ignoring my own hand, extended her own, wrist cocked, for kissing. I seized it, twisted firmly and shook it hard, feeling her shoulders bounce gratifyingly against the hard chair back and experiencing the sort of greedy pleasure that would come to a Lutheran publicly disdaining to slobber over a Pope's ring.

"Rudi," drawled Walter in an unknown languid voice. "Would you be an angel and go to the kitchen and ask the boys to fetch the Countess some tea? They seem to have quite forgotten us." So, then, I was Rudi again and a sort of unpaid butler and Walter, the chamaeleon, was already colouring himself into an aristocratic accessory.

As if I were not there, as if I were a native who did not speak German, she turned to smirking Walter and said, "What a funny little man. He reminds me of poor Herr Hitler. You know they wouldn't let the dreadful booby take his seat in Parliament because he was still an Austrian. The only good thing about him is that he would get all those work-shy men – I can't think why they call them the *working* class – into the army. The lower orders always look so much tidier in uniform." And Walter smirked and nodded.

Over the course of the next week that smirk would set into an ever more desperate wild-eyed rictus. First there was the problem with the steps. Why were they so steep? Why were the bedrooms near the noise of the kitchen? The architect was a fool. Why was the river so loud at night? It seemed that my own room was the only one that was even tolerable, so I found myself moved out.

"You will understand, Bonnetchen. She will not," soothed Walter. Then there were all these Balinese who came to the house. Why were they always sitting about? Some even sat on the furniture not the floor and drank from our cups. They weren't clean. It wasn't safe. And why were they always dancing for so long and talking a foreign language? Why were they always grovelling to their gods?

"You might as well ask," countered Walter mildly, "why they work their poor gods so hard, dragging them down to ceremonies all over the island. They barely get a day off."

Very well. But why was there no hot water for bathing? Why did we eat rice and not proper tinned potatoes? Why was there no wine? Then came the matter of lamps.

The Western nations have served the Balinese very ill in their classification of volatile hydrocarbons. Gas and gasoline, petrol and petrole, benzine, kerosene, paraffin and oil jostle each other and dispute an over-populated semantic field. A major source of mortality is the use of petrol in oil lamps, which, of course, despite their name, habitually burn paraffin, by confused servants who thus convert them into firebombs. At Campuhan, Walter wisely opted for the standard golden glow of old, sooty-wicked oil lamps by which to engage in music or conversation after nightfall. The Countess yearned for modern petrol lamps that blazed with pure white light so that she could paint publicly, in the midst of the living room, and interrogate Walter on matters of style and technique. Which was better, dark or light background? What was the colour of a Balinese sky? Even I found her daubings of geese and ducks horribly sickly. Having been refused her lamps, she travelled to town on her own initiative and my petrol and bought a vast array of luxuries on Walter's account at Lee King's. Since the result of the economic crash had been to actually cheapen goods from the local market but drive the price of imports through the roof, it was not the moment to buy tins of cheese, let alone foie gras, as she did. Moreover, acts of wild prodigality were strictly Walter's domain. She then went further and persuaded the manager of the Bali Hotel to "lend Walter" a petrol lamp *for a few months* that she bore back in triumph. Walter was silently furious, Resem noisily ecstatic at the new toy that glowed with the wonder of the latest gas-mantles. Sensing the inevitable storm, I took the opportunity to cadge a lift on the KMP charabanc from Buleleng that occasionally made a deferential detour to give the Cokorda a ride into Denpasar. As honoured front-seat passenger, social elevation marked by a high cushion under his behind, he was permitted to ring, without let or hindrance, the brass bell that substituted for a hooter.

I spent an agreeable day pottering in the unaccustomed Western atmosphere of the Little Harmonie club for Dutch residents, reading fresh newspapers beneath the fans, strolling in the library, gossiping with gin-soaked old Indies hands in the pillared bar. I would stay the night there, head back tomorrow. Throughout late afternoon, more and more drifted in, rehearsed ancient wrongs, news, jokes. "Just got back from Semarang. Do you know it? Pig of a town. We went to the club there, all falling down. In the dining room, we said to the secretary, 'Put us near the hole in the carpet so we can see the floor show!'"

Then, as the evening set in, the mosquitoes took to the air, the night-smelling flowers gave out their scent and the rosy sky faded to black, I decided, with a faint tingle of excitement, to take my habitual stroll to the *lapangan kota*. In the Indies, every town centres on its "town field", a grassy, green space handy for parading troops, loyal schoolchildren and, as my countrymen were finding to their increasing annoyance, protestors in favour of independence. That in Denpasar was conveniently near the Bali Hotel and a place rich in memory. When invading Dutch troops had arrived, some fifteen years before, the ruling house had accepted the futility of military resistance and embraced the spiritual path of *puputan*. The palace and its retainers and followers – men, women and children – had dressed in pure white, put on their finest jewels, and marched into the Dutch guns, completing their own extinction, where necessary, by suicide. The troops – mainly Christian Moluccans – had been briefly shocked, then turned to the workaday business of looting the bodies. The world's journalists had not been impressed. Universal condemnation had ensued and, as a result, Bali was now handled with kid gloves with even missionaries forbidden to disturb the *status quo*.

Curiously, the spot was not regarded with any particular awe. Like most others of its kind, this town field was the place of forbidden nocturnal activities, the tail to the coin of Dutch rule, a little square of moral extraterritoriality. One end was conveniently obscured by a clump of spindly trees with a building probably originally intended as some sort of a sports pavilion that was edged round with a low brick wall now providing seats for those that congregated there. People who rested there during the day usually chewed *betel* and spat its blood-red juice in all directions so that it looked as if some foul murder had been perpetrated on the spot. This evening, someone had hung up a flickering lamp and around it was the usual mix, like a crowd scene from *La Bohème*. There were exhausted rickshaw drivers, lolling, smoking lontar-leaf roll-ups, in the seats normally occupied by passengers, feet up on the handlebars. Eight or nine, gloriously overdressed ladies of the night were gossiping in throaty voices that alone showed they were really gentlemen of the night. The Southeast Asian mind naturally equates sexual deviance with transvestism. In some parts of the Indies, Walter would tell you, such persons had important ritual, sacerdotal functions but, on Bali, where women danced as men and boys as girls, it was simply for recreation. I avoided them. For myself, women's dress was simply the wrong packaging for what I desired. Moreover, beneath the frills and fripperies of these *bancis* lurked strong male muscles and a temperamental sensitivity, bred of persecution, that made them irascible companions. A few lads, potential customers, were smoking and joking with the "girls", for men sleeping with them are regarded as sexually normal. Others, even younger, with bright eyes but no money were hovering sniffing in the heady incense of sexual heat. Cheap rice spirit was being handed round. A couple of older men, possibly pimps, voyeurs, fixers in general, played cards off to one side and added dignity to the scene. A sharp-featured young man in Western dress was wrestling with the dial of a whistling and thrumming wireless whose back lay open to accommodate supplementary wiring leading to a large acid battery in one corner.

"May I," I asked quietly, "sit down?"

Conversation died like the slammed lid of a trunk but, even in surprise, they were courteous, wiped off the wall, gestured in invitation. The young man clicked off the raddled wireless and wiped his hand on the seat of his trousers before presenting it for shaking. He was in his mid-twenties, slim, dark.

"The booster station must be down. Signals can't get over the mountains. My name is Dion." Good Malay but with throaty Javanese vowels.

"Rudi. What were you listening to?"

He hesitated. "Oh, a political thing from Batavia. It is of no significance." His eyes narrowed. "Where are you from? What is your work?"

"From Ubud. A painter."

A broad grin spread over his face. "Oooh. You are Tuan Piss."

"No. My name is Rudi."

"Then you are Tuan Piss's little brother."

I shrugged. "If you like."

"What are you after, Tuan Rudi? Perhaps I can help you find it." The eyes flashed in the lamplight.

"Just walking, 'eating the wind'. It is very hot tonight." I passed cigarettes. Walter had taught me to always carry them as the small change of sociability. I had ended up smoking them myself. A few accepted, *sembahed* thanks, pretended not to be listening.

"Perhaps," he suggested coyly, striking a match, "you are butterfly hunting? Here there are very lovely butterflies." He gestured widely. *Kupu-kupu malam*, "butterflies of the night", "moths", is a flowery, lepidopterous term for prostitutes. "And where is Tuan Rudi's wife?" He wore a wedding ring but it would mean nothing.

"Sleeping." It made no sense to talk of being unmarried in the Indies, for here only the criminally insane were unwed. In a land where everyone had to marry, like it or not, they would all know about the welcome relief of sleeping wives. "And *your* wife?"

"Sleeping too – in Semarang."

Pig of a town, apparently, Semarang.

"A beautiful city, Semarang. You are Javanese?" I liked him, a cool, intelligent young man. Possibly a school teacher?

"Of course." He eyed me with superior knowledge. "You do not recognise me." There was something nagging at the back of my mind. This afternoon. "I served you your coffee at the Little Harmonie. I work there. I noticed you." He eyed me closely. "You like Javanese coffee. Do you perhaps like chocolate?"

I smiled. "They say that once you have tried chocolate, plain white milk never tastes good again."

"I have heard that too. But for some it is the other way round. After so much chocolate, a little milk can be an interesting change. Myself, I like to drink beer but I cannot afford it."

"They sell beer at the Little Harmonie. Perhaps you would like to take a glass there with me?" The heat was rising between us. He leaned back and took a good look, making up his mind whether I could be trusted, was worth the risk. He had a sweet, little nose.

"It would be difficult for us to drink there together. The head waiter watches me all the time, always criticises me. People would not understand ... unless ... I think you have a room on the ground floor?" I nodded. "Perhaps you might order some beer, take it to your room, leave the window open and I could join you to talk some more. But perhaps that would disturb your wife."

"My wife sleeps elsewhere. She sleeps very soundly. That would be nice. I should like that." We shook hands. My palms were clammy. Our eyes locked. I stood. My enthusiasm must have been clear to all.

"Perhaps you should take a pony cart back. Nyoman over there is very good." Nyoman, little and happily buck-toothed, was beckoned over, whipped up his steed, eager to get a final fare. "I shall follow behind." Spreading the benefit around. Looking after his friends. *Gotong-royong*. Walter would approve. That was fine.

Forty minutes later, a lithe figure slipped through the window. I poured beer. There was nowhere to sit but the bed. He drank, held it in his mouth, savoured, a real treat.

"Aaah!" He leaned forward and stroked my arm experimentally. "Dutchmen are hairy. Like monkeys." It was a clear signal. I stood, boldly lifted him against me, unbottoned gently, flattened my hands against his firm waist. He broke contact and bent away blushing.

"I am sorry. I am *malu*." Shy, ashamed.

"There is no need, Dion. We are both men. We both know what men look like and that these things happen. Take your time. There is no hurry."

"No. It's not that. Look, I am poor. I am ashamed because I have holes in my underwear." There was rage blazing in his eyes.

"Oh, Dion." Now *I* felt a rush of embarrassment, anger at the world for making this proud creature ashamed, for dashing this tender moment to the ground. I turned off the lights, drew back the curtain so that we stood in pale, forgiving moonlight. Our embrace was warm, gentle, surprisingly tentative. Our bodies were both shaking, despite the heat.

We lay down. He stretched out like a beached starfish on the musically creaky bed, closed his eyes and suffered me to stroke and nibble and lick, all the strain disappearing from his face. I loved having the run of him, having someone to be kind to. He was deeply beautiful.

"Mmm, chocolate," I whispered. He giggled.

"I am not a *bencong*," he said firmly. "You cannot use me like a woman." I stroked the hair, pressed my lips to the strong neck, breathed in the musky smell of him. Walter had said something about ignoring the eyes.

"It does not matter." I slipped an arm lightly around his waist, feeling warm, heart-beating humanity. "Like this is fine. As long as we can be together. If we just sleep like this, I am happy, Dion."

He rose and laughed, rolled over on top of me.

"You are a nice man, I think. But just to sleep, I feel, would be a waste. I do not often get the opportunity to do this. We can do better than sleeping." He rubbed his nose against my cheek, inhaling, in that most delightful of gestures, an Asian kiss, then bent more prosaically to his purpose. Sadly, in that moment, as we wrung resonant music from the bedsprings, I realised that what I really wanted, far more than anything else, was to draw him just as he was at that second. That would be true intimacy. That would be possession.

I woke to arrogant pre-dawn cockerels – rose with the cock – feeling oddly worn. Dion was already dressed, heading for the window, diurnal heat. It was an awkward moment. I thought of just letting him go, then – ashamed – propped myself up on the pillows. It was the right thing to do. It was what Walter would have done. Walter always found it easy to do the right thing, a man of easy virtue.

"Dion needs money?" I whispered.

He looked at me evenly. "I have work. I did not ask you for money."

"No. You did not ask but friends should help each other. That underwear business. It is not right that you should be ashamed. If I gave you some money for new underwear, you could come and show me what you had bought the next time I am here. I should like that very much. It would be the act of a friend. *Gotong-royong*."

Twenty minutes later, he was coolly serving me coffee in the dining room, scrubbed, immaculate, hair still wet from washing clinging to the nape of his brown neck. Outside, people were sweeping, sprinkling water, beating carpets. I was the only one that knew what he wore under that uniform. The thought inflamed me.

"Good morning, Tuan Rudi. Did you sleep well? I have only coffee here but I remember that you love our hot chocolate. May I get you some?"

"Indeed, Dion. I can't get the taste of your hot chocolate out of my mouth. It will inhabit my dreams for ever. I should be delighted to have more."

We looked at each other with unwilling amusement – I would dare to say – genuine liking. Our nocturnal secret was transforming the normal forms of social life, revealing them as no more than absurd stage flats that could be knocked down at any moment we chose. The stern head-waiter looked on with surprise and approval. The clients liked a bit of cheery chat. The boy was finally learning how to behave with the guests, learning to know his place.

***

I walked back into Campuhan in sizzling early-afternoon heat to find the Countess's luggage arranged in a neat stack in the entrance – though with the smallest and most fragile cases at the bottom and a huge trunk balanced on top. It was as if someone had piled up all the irrefutable arguments as to why she should leave. Yet instead of the debris of a shattering confrontation, the house seemed to be full of rainbows and sunbeams. Tuan Walter, the boys – welcoming with smiles – declared to be absent. A mountain man had called in on his way to consult a famous village healer, a *balian*, just up the road and Walter had gone along to investigate, document, help out. The Countess, herself, could be heard tra-lah-lahing offstage, something, appropriately, from *The Merry Widow* and when she entered, it was as one transformed, hair let down, a frock of light, frilly stuff, what looked like makeup on her gritty features.

"Mr Bonnet," she actually smiled, "I hope you had an enjoyable stay in Denpasar. As you will have noticed, I myself am bound in that direction."

"What happened?" I was cautious, suspicious.

She swirled round girlishly. "Walter simply explained that he could put me up no longer, that he needed the space, that I must return to the Bali Hotel." This was deeply unbelievable.

"And you were not ... displeased?"

"Oh no. Well, perhaps a little at first. But he put it all so charmingly that now I can only agree."

I had still failed to make all this fit the world as I understood it. "How *exactly* did he put it?"

"Well, we had a delightful dinner for once, chicken with fern shoots and then a dessert of some fruit from the garden. We even had wine. Walter said he needed it to help him do something he didn't want to. Then he explained everything." I listened attentively, not greatly liking all this. "The boys had all disappeared and he served me with his own hands. Then he played the piano, just for me, something special he wrote from Russia that he never plays to anyone else. That made him sad and made me want to comfort him." I saw only too well where all this was going. I was frankly shocked. "It is a pity he had to leave on an errand of mercy. I would have wished to say thank you properly. I wonder ..." she proffered an envelope "if you might give him this. I have to go. Walter arranged a lift in the charabanc." I was everyone's postman these days.

Walter returned schoolboyishly sheepish, neck craned round the door edge, hat in hand, as I was eating my tea. He moved into the room like a mouse scuttling from cover to cover.

"It's all right," I said, "she's gone." Then ... "Oh Walter, how could you? How could you take advantage of an old woman like that when you were showing her the door?" He did me the honour of not pretending he did not know what I was talking about. He sat and sighed and looked, himself, puzzled.

"I did not show her the door. I showed her all the doors. She was breaking my feet, a milestone around my neck. I had the nose full of her. It was a pure *boffe de politesse*. I wanted her to go away happy and it is easier than talking, so I pulled out all the socks. She is not old. Fifty is not old. Ruined grapes may yet be good raisins."

"Is that perhaps the way they put it in the Urals? Very well, elderly. But Walter. A woman, an elderly woman, an elderly nasty woman. Walter, you are such a tart."

He called through the doorway for tea, turned, shrugged.

"As to that, I can say various things. We are all tarts at one time or another but the important thing is to not be a tart who is only paid the wages of a respectable woman. Did I take advantage of her or she of me? She was, as you say, nasty." I thought of Dion. Had I been compassionate or predatory? Was it not a free trade between equals? But then the underwear stood up and argued against that. Had we been equals? Perhaps where there was such disparity of wealth and power, choices were never free which was why most women ended up married to men. I shook my head. Life was too complicated. He was saying, "I have studied musical counterpoint which gives a man a firm grasp of sexual fundamentals. Then, you must recall that, in my youth, in Berlin, I was a professional dancing teacher, paid by the hour. Often, ladies of a certain age would pay extra for supplementary dances of a special nature. What I mean—"

"Yes," I interrupted. "I see just what you mean." And I could see it all, Walter joking his way through the whole thing, making it unreal. "Young man," she would have said, "I cannot give you my heart." "Madam, my aspiration did not rise so high as the heart." She, of course, would understand nothing.

Resem brought tea, bread, jam, in little dishes. He, too, seemed lightened by the departure. We paused as he set it out, taking trouble to create a balanced composition and lay the knives at complementary but opposed angles. I wondered whether she had had the decency to tip the boys.

"Well ... then there is the fact that, as a painter, I construct from the imagination whereas you seek to depict, naturalistically what is before you. All cats are black in the dark. To me in bright sunlight also. And ..." he sighed, smirked and ran his hands through his hair, "it worked. I played my trump card. She has gone. There was no row. Everybody is happy, except, it seems, you."

I handed him her envelope. *My* trump card. Perhaps it was an embarrassingly passionate declaration, perhaps tearful, tedious reproach. I hoped so. I felt he was getting away too lightly, as he had all his life.

"But how, Walter, can you condemn the Balinese for prostituting themselves in the tourist trade with their carving and painting when you do the same with the gifts that God gave you? With your very body which is worse."

He gave a hoot of triumph and waved a cheque at me.

"You see! Happy!" He looked abruptly sad. "But this is a German cheque, worthless." He looked more closely and got cross. "Given that it can never be cashed, I really think she might have been more generous." It was all at once all too much, a sudden truth became clear to me.

" I simply cannot," I said bitterly over the too-sweet marmalade, "spend another day in this house."

I don't know quite what I expected from Walter – tears, apologies, requests on bended knee to stay, at least a sharp intake of breath. All I got was a distracted, "I'm sure you know best, Bonnetchen. If I were you I'd take up the Cokorda's offer, move into the old water-palace. It's a perfectly good spot. I lived there for ages before coming here. Then you can always drop by. I need the room anyway for Conrad."

I was stunned, staggered. "Who is Conrad?"

"Oh, haven't I mentioned him? My cousin. He lives here. Didn't you know? Oh, you will like Conrad."

* * *

And so I ended up at the water-palace without so much as a valedictory *boffe de politesse*. It was not a great change, just a couple of hundred meters down the road, within the chatter and children's noise of such a lesser palace but withdrawn, off to one side, the haunt of Walter's giant red dragonflies. In previous times it had been the secluded spot where the more libidinous rulers had staged their amorous liaisons and so was richly provided with private exits. Here also, the more studious had decrypted the intricacies of ancient literature as scratched on *lontar* leaves so that tranquillity was an entrenched habit with the force of law. The ancient pavilion had long succumbed to the climate and the ravages of insects but, on the original plinth amidst the waters, they had built a simple but elegant, one-floored structure of grass and bamboo that breathed in light and air and met all my needs. Walter's hand was to be seen in many of the details, the raised dais that housed a huge sofa by day, become a bed by night, the care with which simple but solid furniture had been selected and arranged. Whereas I had previously suffered invasion by monkeys, it was now ducks and their pursuing little guardians who might burst in at any moment while the Cokorda was mostly busy or elsewhere and left me in peace. The pert domestic boys of Walter's establishment had been replaced by Putu, a mature palace retainer of indeterminate age, who damped down my passions to the slow smoulder conducive to labour. And Walter and I visited each other daily. On most evenings, I would collect a dish of vegetables and rice from the palace kitchens and take it along to a sort of joint picnic on the great table of his house.

A focus of my activities was the *balai*, the freestanding shady pavilion of the palace where meetings might be held, or the *gamelan* orchestra or the dancers practice, for it was here that my chicks collected. The spot was chosen deliberately, for painting was held to be the lowest of the arts in Bali and this must change by association. Music, dance, carving all had their important place in social and religious life but painting was only occasionally required for temple calendars or ceremonial beds or whatever, and then, in accordance with Balinese ideas, it was never a matter of individual creativity but of a group of male friends sitting around, each chatting and joking and contributing to the general image according to established rules and norms. As in everything else, it was the ancient tales of the Indian Hindu corpus that were the main subject matter to be drawn and drawn upon. My chicks, all boys in their mid or late teens, had been selected by Cokorda Agung and assigned to Walter for artistic instruction. Some had been chosen for their obvious artistic talent and desire to learn, others in the serious hope that painting might provide a remedy for their inherent laziness and fecklessness – all Walter's favourites these – and the rest because they were simply palace "extras", as Walter cineastically termed them, and had no better way to pass their time. All had in common that, unlike ninety per cent of the Balinese population, they had affectations of high caste and nobility – a sop to the Dutch who restricted education to the aristocracy lest it inflame social unrest. So there was Anak Agung Gede Sobrat sucking his paint brush next to his cousin, pencil-sharpening Anak Agung Gede Meregel while Ida Bagus Made Nadera practised a conjuring trick whereby he made his rubber disappear from one hand to the other.

On that first morning, they all sat, cross-legged and straight-backed but grinning, in two neat lines, sarongs tucked up into the sort of giant nappy worn for dirty work, all teeth and sticking-out ears. On their laps rested the pads of precious smooth paper that would revolutionise Balinese painting. Walter crouched down, fixed them in the eye and grinned right back, instantly becoming one of them and certainly the most mischievous. They glowed in his presence. It was clear that they adored him. It was also clear that our methods would be totally opposed. In retrospect, I realise that, by Balinese standards, he was probably an excellent teacher since, on that island, knowledge is not simply poured, by the bucketful, from the full head of the teacher into the empty head of the student. It is not even freely given. It must be first made mysterious and then coaxed, little by little, in return for favours or service, into the light. At any moment knowledge may be unmasked as only preliminary or downright false and there is always another stage beyond, which the student may never reach, since the final transfer may never be made. Small wonder then that a *guru*, a teacher, is an honoured, almost divine, being for whom a student becomes a sort of willing slave. Walter loved being one.

Drawing inspiration from the beret clutched in his hands, he launched into a rambling and befogged explanation of his dilemma, turning it into a dramatic performance with slow and exaggerated gestures. He had been brought from afar to teach them what was art. Yet that is what he, himself, had come to Bali to learn from them and was only beginning, even now, to discover. For, in truth, there was no thing called art – it was like those indefinable Balinese words *sakti* and *guna* that they understood only through encounters in life – there were merely artists, and the secret they were all seeking lay not outside themselves but within, for they all grew to the recognition of it in their own works. And no art was good, none was bad. It required great effort to understand these things, yet effort brought no necessary reward for they must paint not from their heads and eyes but their hearts and livers, which alone brought wisdom. And learning to make real art often involved forgetting everything that one knew, for the work of the artist was to create his own world.

They sat and frowned and understood not a word in all these twisted thoughts whose unintelligibility merely proved to them that there was something indeed worth knowing here. He put his beret on his head. He would leave them now to Tuan Rudi – one of the greatest artists in the whole of Holland, home of painting – since he had been called to make art for the government and the great white queen and such a call could not be ignored, though he loved them dearly in his liver. In this his royal art he would seek to explain the soul of Bali to the Dutch and Bali's own art, of which it had yet to become aware, for only when its roots and origins were secure and it was truly Balinese, could it safely evolve and move forward to embrace the art of the world.

Walter withdrew, throwing me an unhelpful wink like a lifebuoy to a man in the middle of an ocean storm surrounded by sharks, and it was left to me to look at those rows of confused and trusting brown eyes, several glistening with manly tears at alleged parting – though Walter was only going a hundred meters up the road. I felt horribly the responsibility of forming pliant young minds, not knowing where to even start. Balinese, I knew, learned best by constant repetition and imitation of a master. Everywhere, you would see children, racked on the bodies of their dancing teachers as they led their muscles through the motions of their own. I could see on the pads in the laps of some that they were had even been encouraged to experiment in oils which was both absurdly costly and incorrect, since technique is best learned, first through drawing, second through watercolour and only, at a late stage, through the medium of oils. Only when one had truly mastered rule and method might one throw it away like Michelangelo on the Sistine ceiling.

"What Tuan Walter means is that we must begin at the beginning and slowly become masters of drawing what we really see, the shock of the real. I shall teach you the secrets of the West. I shall explain the tricks of perspective – how to show things far away and close – about light and shadow to give depth within a flat piece of paper and about the human body, for you must understand your own bodies to be able to paint them. You must put away the ideas from the *wayang kulit*, the shadow plays, where people move their limbs only from left to right and up and down." I flapped my arms stiffly like old men do their walking sticks and they laughed. I had them. I must draw a line under Walter before I lost them again. "It is no longer good enough to just put the gods at the top of your pictures and the demons at the bottom. There must be style, composition. It will be a long journey but we shall make it together. So, for next week,

I want you to do something at once very simple and very complicated. Look at your own hands which move as puppets do not. Really look at your hands and how they move. Really see them. Then, with your right hand, draw your left. That is all." In Walter's house I had seen an extraordinary fragment of a Batak woodcarving, showing the interlocked hands of a priest. Already my mind was constructing paths leading them from graphic to plastic.

They sat there in silence, staring wonderingly at their hands, perhaps defamiliarising them into the alien pseudopods of strange sea-creatures. Balinese children are the only children in the world who can bend their fingertips back to almost touch their wrists. Then the little one with the surprisingly developed torso for his height, raised and fluttered a very human hand. The hair in his armpits was provokingly black and curly, the voice alarmingly deep.

"Please Guru Rudi. Does that mean you will tell us what is right and wrong, good and bad? Guru Walter always got angry when we asked him that." They nodded. Yes. Yes.

I smiled soothingly. "In time. In time I will teach you what is right and what is wrong, what is good and what is bad." I would too. They all sighed with relief and began chattering happily. I could see that having Walter as one's teacher might be hard work.

**

No one ever saw Walter put brush to canvas but, over the years, we all got to know the signs. He would go broody, like an old hen, silent and withdrawn. He would sigh and groan for no apparent reason, look infinitely glum, shift his limbs as if there was no position that brought him comfort. Then, one day, he would clap on his head the old half-calabash hat he always wore to paint and stump woefully down the steps that led to his studio at the rear. He might be gone just a few days or it might take months and he would withdraw from society as completely as the ancient monks whose cells he had explored in the Elephant Cave with Stutterheim. Only Badog was allowed to disturb him with food and drink. Then, one day, he would be back, purged, drained, but smiling like a man whose fever has just broken, and with a new addition to the family.

Just inside the doorway of Walter's living room was a space flooded with light reflected down from the open eaves. It was here, on a sere ledge of hardwood, that he displayed small gee-gaws, carved *kris* handles, amulets, betel-boxes and the like. It was here, too, that his new paintings were publicly auditioned. The first surprise is that they were so small. When you saw photographs of them, as I had, you thought they would be the size of those enormous Douanier Rousseau canvases that had been his jungly inspiration. And they always seemed to be getting smaller. It was, I suspect, less the difficulty and expense of securing supplies of proper canvas and oils in the Indies than the discovery that he got much the same price for small as for large paintings. His own explanation was, of course, less succinct. "When you are painting the Balinese landscape, Bonnetchen, everything is small."

It is no exaggeration to say that I had lived in fear of this moment. Artists regard their own works much as mothers do their children and for the same reasons. Conceived in the madness of passion, torn from their bodies in agony, even the dullest, most indifferent progeny are regarded as exceptional and uniquely flawless. His dismissal of my own work might be seen as a running joke, an ungainly pose calculated to avoid sentimentality and hiding a deeper respect. But it rankled. From what I had seen of his earlier work, the archived photographs in his studio, I knew I should not like it. Derivative of Chagall and Rousseau, with its multiple horizons, depiction of the same scene at different hours of the day, contempt for perspective, hysterical use of colour, repetition of the same motifs within the frame – it all showed a talent of substance but one that had lost its direction and was drowning in a mass of modern whipped cream. Unlike Walter, I could not be brutally frank. Like most artists I was schooled in articulate insincerity.

It was a shock and a relief that I liked it. "Holy forest near Sangsit" took my breath away. The subject matter was simple enough, the stand of ancient nutmeg trees up in Mengwi, light flooding through their leaves and trickling down their great, close-packed trunks, with the hoary Bukit Sari temple crouching in their midst. I had not, at that time, visited the forest and the reason why was also included in the painting. In the foreground hunkered a Balinese peasant, back to the viewer, the horizontality of his great hat cutting through the soaring verticality of the trees. One arm was casually stretched forward to feed or otherwise engage one of the particularly nasty monkeys that live there. Popular fancy connected them doubtfully to the army of the monkey general Hanuman of the Ramayana legends. But it was the style that was so unexpected – gently naturalistic, unforced, coherent, no part of the painting shouting for disproportionate attention and arguing with the rest. It seemed to have emerged whole, assured, a calm assertion in oils. I recognised, sadly a larger talent than my own but one that would never be great because *he* possessed *it* not the other way around. Later, when my chicks came to see the picture and have Walter explain it to them, they would offend him by crying out in sincere admiration, "Beh! Wonderful. Just like a Japanese photograph!"

Walter looked at it with paternal content, not overweening pride. A satisfactory painting, his face seemed to say, but at least done, finished, laid to rest, signed and simply framed in black by the little old man who had built the cupboards.

"Where did you get the idea?"

He made a face. "Works of art are like sausages. It is always best not to enquire too closely where the ingredients came from." He grinned. It was, I could tell, a line he had used before. Then, more kindly, "Inspired by yourself Bonnetchen." He laid an arm securely round my shoulder.

"It's wonderful, Walter. Is it really for me?" I was entranced. I would hang it across from the bed. It would be the first thing I saw every morning. He barked an expectorant laugh rather like one of the monkeys.

"*For?* Yes, in one sense. Dedicated to, inspired by … 'for' like that. But it is already sold, I'm afraid. It goes to mend the car. I have to go to the big garage in Denpasar. Nothing works on that car. No steering, no horn. Now, the brokes are break and I am broken."

I thought about that. "You mean the brakes are broken and you are broke?"

He laughed and slapped me in comradely fashion. "Possibly."

"How are you getting there?"

He looked at me as if I was mad. "Driving of course. Do you want a lift?"

"Er … no thank you."

He paused and considered, lip-puckering. "Anyway. If I gave you one of mine, you would give me one of yours and then I would have to say I liked it." He threw his arms apart and shrugged. "Where would it all end?" Already he was walking away.

7

The filmmakers came with the rains and three grey truckloads of equipment. They even brought their own Javanese cook. Whenever I think of that time, I see splashing mud and money. In overall charge, as the source of the funding, was Baron Viktor von Plessen, adventurer, hunter, painter, cineast – owner of an ancestral estate in Holstein and a pencil moustache. Everything apart from the moustache was big and he stood habitually in the pose of eighteenth-century swagger portraits with one leg thrust out and hands in his pockets. A few years back he had lived in Bali and, curiously, it was an interest in the birds of Nusa Penida that had brought him and Walter together. Once they had billed and cooed over their ornithological collection, argued pigeon classification and fallen out over the calls of the native Balinese duck, they realised that they both knew Murnau, Walter's old friend from the UFA studios in Berlin and, of course, Walter's earlier film, *Goona-Goona*.

By some strange irony, von Plessen, fresh from a European visit, was the only one of us that had actually seen it. Walter had worked with Andre Roosevelt, a vast, shuffling wreck of a man who somehow had, with a camera, the empathy that Walter had with musical instruments. The actual shooting had to be fitted into the ever-shorter periods of lucidity when Roosevelt was not incapacitated either by drunkenness or resultant hangover and it glorified in the standard bare-breasted charms of Balinese womanhood and sexual allure. The story was about the chemically enhanced love between a handsome prince and a servant girl and it had to be stringently re-edited to meet American censorship laws. The resulting version, dehydrated and flavourless, was appropriately dubbed *Love Powder*. Walter had adored the whole process, shamelessly prancing around the set with a megaphone, directing, changing the script, rehearsing the actors until the real director, Armand Denis, threatened to leave in a huff. But ultimately, there was little they could do since Walter was the only one who could communicate with the performers. I would see it in the Italian theatre in Denpasar later that year and it would go on to be a worldwide hit, not least in the Indies pavilion at the Paris World Fair of 1931. *Goona-goona* became, briefly, a term for illicit sex amongst the glitterati of New York and, of the foreigners I subsequently met in Bali, I think at least half had been first attracted to the place by that film. All this may well not have been poor Walter's fault. He certainly made no money out of it. Much of the original footage was lost in a fire (alcohol-fuelled?) during processing in Surabaya and clumsily re-shot in a great rush without him.

Film people are loud, opinionated and eat and drink all the time, a little like armies. The process of the making of *Island of Demons*, barely three months in all, seems now like a protracted barroom brawl. Many of the duties were fluid and discharged by the ubiquitous and darkly sardonic Dr Dahlsheim. Having worked principally in Africa, he was convinced that every river must conceal a hundred forms of sudden death, that the soil must boil with lethal parasites that sought only to bore through the soles of his feet to destroy him and that every form of kindness or beauty was a snare masking savagery and hostility. In theory, there was a director, producer, cameraman, soundman, scriptman; then all the assistants: director, producer, cameraman, etc. doubled up over again. I asked Walter what an assistant producer did. "Usually sleeps with the producer," he replied cheerily. They were all crammed into the rain-soaked house in Campuhan, sitting endlessly hunched over the forest giant table that swarmed with papers, photographs, bottles and ashtrays, all waving fists and shouting to get their way or sulking because they hadn't. Oddly, Walter told me this insensitivity to noise was a common feature of technicians who had learned their trade in the "silent" movies.

The film was very much Walter's child and dealt with the primordial battle of good versus evil. Beautiful Balinese farmers dwell beatifically in a sunlit natural paradise of hard work but plenty. But their happiness enrages an embittered old witch who jealously uses her magic to create an epidemic bringing death and misery. Only complex public ceremonies and the ancient wisdom of the priests can cleanse the island and bring an end – possibly, it is intimated, only temporary – to evil and a return to the goodness of the life in harmony with nature that is Man's true goal and right. The actors, of course, were not actors at all but ordinary Balinese who had garnered a little acting experience from their own ritual drama at the village level. The old witch was a widow from just down the road who was not considered immune from such allegations in real life and had what Walter termed a "good" face, i.e. one full of character, framed in wild, grey hair and as scored with ruts and ravines as a relief map of the island. The young lovers, Wayan and Sari, retired dancers, on whose beautiful shoulders all this hung, exuded a breathtaking purity that somehow redeemed the whole of flawed humanity, provoking awe rather than lust. The formal movements of the eyes are an important element of Balinese dance, at least as central as those of the feet, and Walter was able to use their schooled control of them to great effect in the film. All this to the new thing of a soundtrack incorporating not just the incidental music of the gifted Wolfgang Zeller but Balinese *gamelan* and the genuine sounds of redeeming nature in the Indies – the wind in the bamboo, running water, etc. The world was briefly in a period that was language-poor, where barking speech had been displaced by music and gesture. We had no inkling of the deluge of words that was shortly to knock us all off our feet. *Island of Demons* would be marketed in Germany with a poster of a bare-breasted, grinning woman with tropic fruit plonked on her head.

Much of the shooting took place at night, using the new high speed films that had just come on the market and stretching them to their limit. Hans Scheib puffed endlessly on cheroots, despite the lethal inflammability of film in those days, and coaxed magic out his lenses and apertures while swearing relentlessly in Bavarian dialect. Walter organised flickering oil lamps and torches, smoke that lay around the feet of the actors and – of course – elaborate *Nosferatu* shadows to add drama and foreboding. The rain, at this stage, was only intermittent so rarely interrupted the schedule but hauling equipment through the muddy roads was a nightmare. "Like a re-enactment of the Somme offensive," puffed von Plessen, cinematographically punctuating out heat and palm trees to see only the desired muck and water that he could use in such a scene. "We should have armed guards," opined Dahlsheim, "like in

Africa." Transport was the responsibility of a big, raw-boned young man with a mop of thick blond hair and endless good-nature. It was at least a week into the shooting before I realised that this was Conrad, Walter's young cousin – come, confusingly, with the crew from Java and found employment out of such almost-nepotism – for I heard them call each other Walja and Kosja and knew that Russian diminutives of affection were obligatory in that family.

The highpoint of the film and the big set piece of the whole shooting schedule was the magnificent *kecak* dance. It came two months in, when everyone was already exhausted and homesick for potatoes and cabbage, when camera shutters had begun to stick, mould to sprout in camera gates and when no word had yet come back from Java confirming the integrity, or even arrival, of shot footage, so that Walter and Viktor were prone to squabble over the enormous unpaid bill at Campuhan that had exhausted Walter's always limited liquidity. The two had much the same lack of respect for the processes of normal accountancy. There was crazy talk of Walter's taking time off from the film to paint another historical picture for Stutterheim just to keep the crew fed and watered. They were all a little mad by now and I really did not know what I was doing struggling off with them, one late afternoon, into the fat, hot rain towards the village of Bedulu where the crucial scene was to be shot. It was probably the romance of the silver screen that had seduced me, though, as it turned out, there were other seductions enough.

The Overland Whippet had previously belonged to von Plessen, made over to Walter in exchange for two of his paintings, and he now resumed unspoken ownership, uncontested by Walter since he also paid for all very necessary repairs and a new set of tyres. Von Plessen and Conrad, at the wheel, sat at the front in steaming raincoats, Walter and I behind, the light car skittering across the slick surface as the trucks grumbled up behind. All went well till we were about three miles from our goal. At the base of a steep incline, torrential rain had washed the light surface dressing off the rock base of the road and coagulated into a thick paste in which the tyres would not grip. Planks, vegetation torn from the roadside and flung under the spinning wheels, brute manpower, all to no avail, they all – naturally – opted to stand in the rain and squabble. Von Plessen raged and stamped, made as if to lay about him with his directorial megaphone, was offered defiance by the rest and caved in.

"Walter, this is crazy. We can't work in this." He was shouting to be heard above the drumming of water on the canvas of the trucks.

"Viktor. I assure you. The rain will stop soon. We must go on. This is the only night we can do this for the next two weeks."

"How do you know? You can't tell the weather. No one can."

Walter smiled. "It's not just a matter of weather. There are good days and bad days, the phases of the moon, the intermeshing of the different Balinese calendars. I consulted a priest."

Von Plessen stepped back, genuinely astonished. "Our filming schedule is being decided by a fucking priest?"

"We must keep moving at all costs," opined Dahlsheim, nervously. "To stay here longer is to invite attack from the natives. I am sure I saw movement in those bushes."

Walter turned and shouted to Conrad in Russian and precluded further argument by seizing a camera tripod and splashing off on foot. Conrad, grinned and reached back to grab the main camera body from the floor of a truck and raced after. A cameraman will sooner let you lay hands on his wife than his equipment so Scheib was soon off in hot pursuit with the reserve film stock in his arms, uttering *Scheissing*-great Bavarian *Arschloching*-oaths, certain words coming through loud and clear like the taste of venison in curry. To a film crew, the main camera is as the battle standard to a Roman legion, so they followed too. An exhausting hour later, we were setting up with hands trembling from fatigue as the rain died off into ethereal and photogenic steam. Bamboo platforms had been set up to allow more dramatic angles. With only two cameras, they would have to be rushed from location to location during the performance and edited into coherence later.

The dance was to be performed and filmed in the space before the old temple and was very much Walter's big scene. For weeks he had been coming here alone or in the company of Katharane Mershon, a big-boned modernist dancer from Sanur. There were two versions of the full-lipped life she led with her sparrowlike husband Jack and their reasons for living there. The first had it that they were good, simple folk, moved by the plight of the inhabitants of heat-soaked Sanur into establishing a free clinic where locals might be treated for the many minor ailments to which the climate there disposed them. The other had it that they had there adopted a beautiful and pliant Balinese youth whom they serially and jointly debauched with almost forensic deliberation, paying his mother a dollar a month for the privilege. Probably both were true.

Walter was crouching down with his arm around a spectacularly muscled, loinclothed man in his early thirties who was leaning affectionately against him. My jaw dropped. Behind crowded a whole army of pared athletes all naked but for a little strip of the Javanese *batik* cloth. Walter turned to me. "My friend Limbak," he introduced loudly in Malay and glowed with paternal pride. Balinese theatre uses the technique of a narrator addressing low characters who are there just to provide someone to be talked to. This, I foresaw, was to be my part. "The greatest *baris* dancer on the island." Limbak blushed. I knew the *baris*, a demanding military dance that came in a hundred different variants. In Sanur, it was said, they had a form where the men dressed up with glasses, stuck their teeth out and imitated Chinese; elsewhere women imitated men. "But we've moved him on a notch or two. Wait till you see."

Von Plessen was hovering, rudely overshadowing, nervously puffing. "Christ, Walter. All these people. At the rehearsal we had a dozen. I thought you hated Wagner. Next thing you'll be using fucking dwarves with tuned anvils. Wait, of course." He clapped his hand nastily to his forehead. "That's the iron *gamelan* of the Bali Aga you were telling us all about at such length the other day." Even more nastily. "How much is this costing us? Can't we cut it down?" Walter ignored him.

"Limbak had been experimenting, trying to come up with a new *baris*. He was trying to get his hands on rifles to incorporate military drill into the dance. Of course, the Dutch didn't understand that and he ended up in jail."

"Are we paying by the hour, or by results? Can't we get them moving, for the love of God? If the priest got it wrong can we get a refund?"

Walter dug serenely in his bag, slowly passed out packets of cigarettes and matches – gently with both hands – smiles, pats, greetings, little jokes. "That *baris* would have been a sensation and knocked the socks off his rivals in the other half of the village – wearing socks was part of the outfit by the way – but we've come up with something better."

The men at the back were putting their arms on the shoulders of those in front, swaying and giggling like schoolboys, tentatively groaning out a sort of deep yo-heave-ho melody. They were excited, tingling. It was infectious.

"Just tell me this is all flat rate and no extra payments for reshoots."

Walter switched to German for the crew. "We've taken Pak Limbak's *baris* and grafted it onto the *kecak*, the old monkey dance used for exorcising evil. In the original version, it's not much performed, just a very minor element of the whole programme. The demon king Ravana has carried off Sita, wife of Rama, and ravished her. Ravishing strictly offstage. Rama gets Hanuman, the monkey general, to use his troops to fight the demons. Halfway through the dance, half these lads turn into monkeys and, for a month now, they've drilled themselves into a real monkey army. Everyone should just relax. They know exactly what they're doing. There's coffee coming and nothing more to be done till it's really dark. That's in ten minutes." The reliability of the equatorial nightfall.

"Do we have to pay for the coffee?"

Something in Walter snapped. He looked up at von Plessen and spoke very quietly. "Viktor. Limbak is here because he's my friend. The others are here because they're *his* friends, because they want to try something new, because they've never done this before. All we've paid for is a few pieces of cheap cloth. What we will get is something you could not buy anywhere else in the world for any amount of gold, a Balinese dream that has never been dreamed before. Now please go and sit over there and we will run through everything with the cameramen before we start."

He went like a lamb.

The night came, as ever, suddenly, as if someone in Lighting had thrown a great celestial switch. No messing about with twilight in these latitudes. Walter did a final check, lit the lamps and signalled to Limbak. The men arranged themselves, six rows deep, in concentric circles around an ugly, fat trivet of a candelabra and Walter retired to his elevated platform like a *pedanda* priest at a cremation. "Faces, faces!" Walter urged the cameramen. "Focus on faces, we do no want to shoot them or ourselves – ha, ha – in the feet." From up there, the men looked like the petals of a beautiful flower whose centre was light. Scheibe could be heard dimly chanting his mantra of *Sheissing-*, *Arschloching-*, *Huring-*. It occurred to me charitably that it might be part of a professional technique by which he maintained the cranking of his camera at a constant speed.

A brief moment of silence – deafening and uncanny – for nothing is rarer and more unnatural on Bali than total silence. Then, at a sign from Limbak, the men rose and sank as one with the hiss of a great serpent, then intoned a monotonous melody I recognised from the *gamelan*, raised it up, pressed it back down into the earth, their voice imitating the instruments of the orchestra. Already a light sweat slicked their swaying bodies, their eyes gleamed, half-closed, as the tune hammered out relentlessly, over and over again. The swaying grew hypnotically in intensity until, in perfect unison, they flung themselves backwards into their companions' laps – the flower opening, then closing, then opening again. The bodies rose and fell, floated forward and back, a shrill solo voice emerged then plunged under a mass chant of monkey language. "Chak-a-chak-chak, chak-chak-chak-chak." The sound swelled, dimmed, was flung back from side to side in deafening insistence, the hands shot up and fluttered like the tendrils of sea anemones, dived again in and out of the flickering surf of torchlight. The pounding beat was cross-cut by the waves of inhuman cries and I felt myself begin to shake, the hair lifting from the back of my neck, being dragged down to some animal plane of horror and fear where language did not yet exist.

I have no idea how long the performance lasted. I drifted in and out of the consciousness of heat, sound, light and dark, throbbing male flesh, breathed it in, wiped it dripping from my eyes. From subsequent experience, it was perhaps a little over half an hour. At some point, individual characters emerged. At some point, I recall Limbak in the classic high pose of *baris*, knees flexed, arms high, fingers fluttering and eyes distended in apoplectic fixity as the rhythm pounded on and the monkey-chattering crackled across it. I could feel their deep staccato shouts through the soles of my feet. The story was told in wailing language far beyond me in layer on superimposed layer. I recall the monkey chorus replaced by the same cadence expressed in perfect handclaps, then the parting of the singers into two crescents, wrestling monkeys and demons that overshadowed and intimidated each other till the demons rose and swelled and drove their adversaries out into the echoing night, their cries growing fainter and fainter until the only sound was the soft beating of the lamps' flames like neglected sails in the wind.

Walter was down from the platform and rushed out into the dark reappearing, hugging dazed, prostrate Limbak, sweat coursing down his face and chest, loincloth sopping wet, leading him back into the light as though for an encore, pouring delight and congratulation into him, sitting him down, mute, kneeling at his feet and clasping his hands in rapture. I sat quietly in my corner since it would be impossible for me to embrace those glowing, saturated athletes with even a pretence of merely platonic glee. Von Plessen and the crew applauded wildy, all except Scheib who, professional that he was, was already checking the camera gate for any *Scheissing-* , *Ficking-*, *Arschloching*-problem.

None of us knew, that night, just what it was that we had given birth to. I have seen it so often since for, from that moment, the Balinese took up the *kecak*, nurtured it, made it wholly their own. Never have native and foreign minds meshed and fused so completely. The new version was a sensation and swarmed over the island like the monkeys it contained. They perform it now at distant Uluwatu for the tourists, as the chewing baboons look on impassively at this impertinent attempt to recount simian history. If you have not seen *kecak*, you have not seen Bali. And of course, it lives and breathes and changes. I once witnessed a version incorporating a black American tap-dancer, the "chak-a-chak" hammered out by his own fervent heels, the face not a bad approximation of goggle-eyed *baris*. Yet, not so long ago, I saw it described as "the epitome of immemorial Balinese culture, reaching back into the mists of time and unchanged for thousands of years". Margaret Mead was less kind about its inautheticity. "*Kecak*?" she once said. "Walter's *kecak*? I think you mean ketchup."

8

It was Walter who brought surfing to Bali, even if we did not, then, know the word. After the completion of the film, the "wrap" as it was called, the crew were understandably in high spirits. It was initially unfortunate that an evening stroll down the main street of Ubud, with drink taken, coincided with the heaviest downpour of the year. One moment, the air was clear and Walter was progressing, handshaking and greeting down the road. The next, the heavens opened and vomited bucketfuls down on their heads. The locals squealed and ran, Walter looked up and laughed. Then a stack of broad planks stacked at the roadside caught his eye. The normally tranquil streams that edge the road, used for washing and other domestic purposes, were now raging torrents, a meter deep, whirling away all the accumulated rubbish of the year, scouring out their beds and racing down the hill to rejoin the river. With a "Beh!", Walter seized a plank, flung himself face down on it in the flow and cascaded down the stream, whooping and cheering, as cowboys are supposed to ride bucking broncos. Conrad and von Plessen roared and hallooed, similarly took to the waves and shot along the street, ducking under the little bridges leading to each house, helpless with laughter. I withdrew under the eaves of a house and wiped my glasses. The Balinese came out and looked, pointed wonderingly. Soon all the young bloods in town were riding the thundering streams, racing Walter and each other, with the older and more dignified doubled over with laughter, cheering them on. Several came to grief, heads were split, clothes were shredded, money was gambled and technique evolved rapidly. The lads were all sure-footed farmers, used to teetering along the tiny raised paths of the paddy fields like tightrope walkers and they clamped their feet to the boards like suckers. As the water level continued to rise, it proved possible to leap over the little bridges to rejoin one's board over the other side, to control the speed of the plank by the angle of its inclination, to execute elegant dancerish motions. Soon the whole town was lining the ditches, clapping, laughing, jeering foes, cheering heroes. I don't think it ever happened again. Conditions were, somehow, never quite right for it and, in a few years, Bob Koke would bring Hawaiian surfing to Kuta Beach and proclaim it as something new. The Balinese had always turned their backs to the sea, fixing their gaze on their holy mountain, after all the sea was for disease, dirt and death. Yet perhaps, here, a seed had been planted. A murky, rainy day had become a festival. Walter gave them that.

And then he disappeared, Conrad along with him. The boys opened their eyes in pretty innocence and shrugged. They did not know. Maybe *jalan-jalan*, travelling. I set about my duties as an art instructor, teaching my chicks – *his* chicks really – Western perspective. Many had brought other skills with them from which they had to be laboriously weaned. Little Sobrat had been apprenticed as a maker of puppets for the shadow theatre, cutting the filigreed shapes from thick buffalo hide, colouring and gilding them. He had lived, till now, in a flat world.

"You do not," I urged, "really look at each others' bodies as I do. Look at the way you paint them. They are tubes attached to a *salak* fruit. Who has the best thighs amongst you?"

They tittered and blushed. They did not notice such things.

"Nonsense," I thundered. "In the West, artists are dispassionate students of the human body. When they want to know how to paint the human form, they must first learn how it works. They are like doctors. In the past, they studied with doctors. Now, who is to be our model." There is always someone ready to betray his friend.

"Please, Tuan," called out a pale boy at the back, pointing. "Togog has a rickshaw driver's legs." Cheers as he was pushed to the front, made to hitch up his sarong and sit, face blazing, on a stool.

"Now," I resumed, magisterially stroking caramel thigh, "see how many contours and textures are here in this fine thigh." More cheers. "Here," I gripped without pity, "is the Vastus Lateralis. Here the Vastus Medialis. Here," I sculpted with cupped hands, "the Biceps Femoris." I tweaked. Togog yelped, to the joy of his comrades. "Note that muscles slide over the top of each other; they shorten and thicken. Skin stretches and changes its texture." I palpated, a stern-faced connoisseur of thighs. "Every thigh is a conversation of skin and bone and muscle. I never want to see your pictures full of tubes again." I sent Togog back to his place, barely resisting the urge to give him a pat on his pert little Gluteus Maximus.

* * *

It was Steinway and Co. of Hamburg and New York, manufacturers of grand pianos by appointment to the royal houses of Europe, that brought Miguel and Rosa Covarrubias to Campuhan. Already a gifted caricaturist and graphic illustrator, Miguel had just won a prize from the eponymous company for his fashionable illustrations of Gershwin's *An American in Paris*, all leaning Eiffel towers and scribbly poodles, images of the jazz age. It is a sad truth that artists always make most money from their worst work – my own bare breasts for example – and Miguel would do very nicely from a series of caricatures called *Impossible Interviews* drawing two totally opposed characters in juxtaposition, the most famous being "Clark Gable meets the Prince of Wales". He had done less well with a set of studies of the blacks of Harlem – the New York version, not the Dutch – that were part of an early foray into anthropological caricature. It was not that anthropological caricature was condemned as racist, simply that it was seen as too commonplace. Rosa was a famous modernist dancer and much photographed, in her own right, in the glossy magazines. Only South Americans were supposed to be able to dance in those days, so she had changed her stage name from domestic Rosa Cowen to exotic Rosa Rosaldo which fitted her lustrous dark eyes and thick black hair, pulled back now in the inevitable pony tail that is the mark of the out-of-costume hoofer. Both darkly handsome, both small people, though he Mexican and she American, the Covarrubiases were a well-matched couple and similarly inspired by Krause's erotic photographs with an interest in all things Balinese. Bali was to be their honeymoon, their little earthly Paradise, steeped in sex and self-discovery. And it was on the cramped steamer from Surabaya to Singharaja, as they sat maritally glued together at the rail, searching for things in nature that reflected the heat of their craving, that they encountered a fascinating golden young man to whom they already carried, in Miguel's jacket pocket, a letter of introduction from Andre Roosevelt – Walter.

They were all in Campuhan, whisky in their glasses, Rosa breathing a thread of smoke from an ivory cigarette-holder and gripping the hand of Miguel on the sofa in the same newly married passion. Probably in their mid-twenties but somehow young for their age, he in a lightweight tropical suit, she in an elegant shift of thin grey silk. He offered round a slim cigarette case in white gold and ebony, flared a matching lighter. Smoking was still an act to be performed with elegance in those days.

"Why did you not tell the boys?" I was saying. "Nobody knew where you were. Nobody knew what to do." Even to myself I sounded like a brittle, hysterical wife. Walter soothed. The Covarrubiases smiled wanly. Perhaps their first row lay still before them. As for two men in a clearly domestic tiff ... well, they had both worked in the theatre, she as a performer, he as a set designer. Such scenes neither surprised nor shocked them.

"But that would have destroyed the beauty of the moment – to just walk off because I felt like it, to be free. That's the greatest feeling on earth, Bonnetchen, to be totally free. Besides, I didn't really know where I was going or for how long. The telegramme merely said a concert tour, as an accompanist, in Java. As it turned out, with that violin prodigy, Fritz Hinze, horrid brat. He scraped the strings and I banged the ivories, Mozart suffered and everybody clapped. The old ladies loved him. Fantastic for a boy of that age, they said and pinched his cheeks ... Quite true. But I suspect he will still be fantastic for a boy of that age in twenty years time. If you read the reviews closely, I had the better of the encounter. As it turned out it was just a few weeks but I brought something back that will knock your socks off." Since *kecak* he was keen on the knocking off of socks. He led me back up to the new music room. The Covarrubiases followed, still stickily linked, and paused on the landing to snatch a very wet kiss with maximum adhesion.

"Mrs Covarrubias!"

"Mr Covarrubias!"

"Oh my God," whispered Walter. "Newlyweds. I suppose it's a complicated name and they have to practise but can't they stop gumsucking?"

"That's a very nasty word."

He smiled, as though at a compliment. "Isn't it?"

The boys had already lit the lamps and muted them to a golden glow. New people inevitably meant music. There was the *gamelan* orchestra, used by the local group, sitting like a jury, there the Steinway grand, there – oh my God – *another* Steinway grand.

"But Walter, how can you possibly …? What on earth do you want with …?" Smirking he slid behind it and banged down on the keys. The sound was weird, uncanny. It was like biting into a cake that turned out to be made of corned beef and cheese instead of the expected chromatic sweetness. And then a haunting melody trickled out from between his fingers, a tune from the Balinese shadow theatre, limpid and inchoate. After a dozen or so bars, he jumped up and clapped his hands with delight.

"Tuned to the *gamelan* scale. You can play Balinese music directly on it. I found it in the old concert hall in Semarang – pig of a town Semarang – totally out of tune, full of dead lizards and birds' nests and so on and somehow gave a recital on it that was so bad it convinced them it was beyond saving. So I got it absurdly cheap, had it repaired and retuned – you know the Javanese can do anything – and here it is. You will note," he stroked his hand over its top, "the special American satinwood finish. You might say …" he twinkled leeringly, always a sign that a terrible joke was coming, "you might say I got it for a song." He laughed at his own joke. The Covarrubiases put their heads together and whispered, puzzled. "Anyway, it was what you might call a" – leeringly – "sound investment."

"Stop it Walter." The money from the film, the concert tour, I was sure it had already gone and not to pay the teetering bill at Lee King's. Not, strictly speaking, my business but still …

"That music. It was beautiful." Miguel's English was soft, the "r"s a little rolled, the sibilants with a rustle as of Mexican brushwood. They had perched on two of Walter's elegant Nias stools and were peering down into the river, sharing a cigarette by passing it back and forth as Western schoolboys and Balinese men do, Rosa showing a lot of coffee-coloured leg. As a dancer, she had a very Balinese sense of her own body as a separate instrument with which she was not emotionally involved. Legend had it that an anthropophagous giant, specialising in the eating of *legong* dancers, had once lived in a hollow down there. Locals pointed out a big, pierced rock, way out in the stream, as the place where he had ground chilli for his fried rice. In Bali it is unthinkable for even a cannibal not to eat rice. The imagination always has its boundaries. "I should like to hear more, if that is possible."

Walter moved back and resumed, doing a little dance with his shoulders as he played. The melody was like a fish in the water. The stars were very bright tonight.

"We came here to look for something," said Rosa tiredly.

"We had had enough of New York." They spoke antiphonally, like the two sides of a *gamelan*, passing back the cigarette after each line.

"Miguel could not stand it any more, the noise, the shallow people, the empty rush for material possessions."

"It is different in Mexico. Time is slower. We thought it might be different here."

"Miguel and I wanted to look for another way, a place where perhaps things are simpler, where people are different ... better." Her voice was flat, monotonous.

"We saw pictures. There was a film. We met Andre Roosevelt at our wedding in the house of another illustrator and he spoke of you. Bali seemed to us special." He shrugged. "Perhaps we were foolish. Perhaps I am speaking total nonsense." Walter turned from the keyboard and smiled, pushed his hair back from his forehead.

"You are. But you speak it very well. Bali is not special. Bali is magical! It is an island. All islands are magic because they are complete worlds with their own sea, sky and land, a separate reality. Islands are the stuff of our dreams, the only place they can live in the modern world. And Bali is also a special island with volcanoes, forests, lakes, rivers, ancient ruins too. Islands are the universe in miniature but separate, subject to their own laws, places where the rules of the mainland have no force. People here live in harmony with nature which is why their culture weighs so lightly upon them whereas ours crushes us under its wheels and squeezes the lifeblood out of us like a great machine. Here people work together to make beauty which is at the centre of all. All the priests, musicians, dancers, artists are part of life, grow their own food with their own hands, feed their children and loved ones with the fruit of the fields that surround them. I have looked all my life for a place where I would know how to just *be*. Bali is that place. It has driven me sane."

I was astonished. I had never heard Walter speak out a coherent credo with so much calm assurance. Rosa's face glowed.

"You mean ..." She sat erect, fists clenched and looked round in rapture at Miguel. "... the people here ... they are natural socialists?"

"Er ..." I had sat quietly. I had been good. I had not dashed any cold water on all of this. Now I looked at him seated at his second Steinway grand with its American satinwood finish and said, "And you, yourself, Walter. Do you live in simple harmony with nature?"

He turned and grinned with crushing insincerity. "Me? Me? I am so in harmony with nature, dear Bonnetchen, that, at the full moon, I almost feel myself begin to menstruate."

***

"This is downright embarrassing." No one heard me above the din. We were racketing through the countryside in the Overland Whippet, myself in the dicky, Badog up front with Walter and navigating with that intuitive map Balinese carry always in their head, revolving around the direction of Gunung Agung, the mountain seat of the gods. It was never "turn left" but "go west". Walter did not seem bothered by the deafening noise that came from the rear and our having lost the silencer on a rock several miles back or, as Walter put it: "the knockpot has fallen from the outpuffpipe". "Never mind," he had dismissed my protests with airy frivolity, "the more noise at a Balinese wedding, the better they like it."

The wedding was Badog's, polishing his teeth and combing his hair there in the backviewglass, but Walter had, as ever, anticipated matters. There are a number of ways you can get married in Bali. One is for parents to arrange the whole thing, with or without the use of a matchmaker. But far more common is kidnapping. This is not as bad as it sounds. Often it is a sort of elopement, both families and the couple are in full agreement and the act of violence is simply an administrative shortcut that saves everyone a lot of bother. The girl arranges to be at a certain time at a certain place so she can be conveniently carried off by the groom and his friends. The bride's family have to storm around and summon the whole village and make a great fuss and search futilely for their daughter and then the boy's family turn up to pay a fine and make amends and the whole thing is regularised. But the Balinese, like Walter, love an adventure and a bit of melodrama and every bride and groom anticipates this day with trembling excitement. To be carried off in a motorcar was the very greatest chic and by two white men to boot would make her the envy of her friends.

Badog, oiled, perfumed, freshly coiffed, let out a shout and stood and waved joyously. There was his beloved, sitting by the roadside, hot and peeved. It seemed we were late. She was very young. There was no denying she was beautiful, flawless skin, supple body, perfectly symmetrical face with bee-stung lips and elfin ears pierced with gold. When she saw us, or rather Badog, her anger evaporated and, intimidated, she turned all coy, simpering and giggling, blushing and waggling about in cutesy movements from the *legong* dance as she was introduced. Ayu was her name. Then Badog grabbed her.

I had always regarded as overblown those representations of flailing limbs and physical confusion seen in the various classical versions of the *Rape of the Sabine Women*. Now I was to learn my error. A Balinese bride makes it a point of honour to put up a good fight and Ayu struck out soundly with fists and nails. She was a good strong girl, muscles honed by years of physical labour and two effete Westerners were no match for her. Badog had seized her from behind but could do nothing to restrain her kicking feet and windmilling arms. An old man in the field behind paused from poking in the mud and watched, then made a gesture rather like Fatimah's shaking of the bottle and cackled obscenely. I danced around the edge like a flyweight, seeking to grab her hands but, whenever I did so, encountered only a sizzling bare breast. "Oh sorry!" She swung a great slap, saw that it was about to connect to her beloved Badog and clouted me with it instead. "Oh my God!" Then, good streetfighter that she was, she lunged forward and kneed Walter hard between the legs and he went down. "Jesus! I should have brought Conrad. Normal men have more experience of hitting women." The old man in the field was beside himself with glee, slapping his scrawny old thighs. I wondered whether I should ask him to come and help.

Walter was up again and limping to the boot of the Overland Whippet, then back with a blanket.

"Capturing women," he gasped, "must be much like catching wild baboons" and threw it over her head. "This always calms them down." The effect was indeed remarkable. Ayu let out a scream that would have etched glass and lashed out blindly in all directions, lost her balance, grabbed at anything within range and tumbled into the flooded field, taking Walter with her. The old man was less happy about that. There were germinating rice seeds in there and women were not supposed to have any contact with the fields at that stage.

It was at this moment that the KPM charabanc chose to round the corner – Cokorda Agung, my employer and landlord, in modern dress industriously ringing the bell – and packed with white tourists. It slowed, as though to afford them a better view of Ayu's rucked up skirt, smooth, golden thighs and bare breasts, my red, obviously just-slapped face – her handprint clear upon it – as the Cokorda raised his hat with the other hand.

"Good afternoon, Mr Bonnet."

"Good afternoon, Cokorda."

The faces of the white women showed shock and the righteous disapproval that goes with marriage documents, those of the men – I am quite certain – nothing but the greatest envy. The vehicle drove on and disappeared as if the violent abduction of women were an everyday event – which it was. Walter's head reappeared from under the blanket. "Quick Bonnetchen. Get her legs."

By now Ayu must have felt she had done enough to fulfil the requirements of a chaste and dutiful bride and allowed herself to be conveyed to the car and the firm, manly grip of Badog who seemed absurdly invigourated by the whole thing. Walter started the engine and we drove off with a wedding train of loud detonations, Ayu lapsing into further coy gigglings. The old man waved his hat and cheered, rotating his dessicated groin.

A couple of miles further on was the marital hideout, the house of a complaisant friend who had prepared a love-nest where their tryst would be consummated and where they would await forgiveness. The neighbours had come out to watch their arrival and, as Ayu was led from the car, the women's smiling faces spoke of the memory of first tender love, the men's hot eyes of anticipated sex.

"There have to be special offerings formally laid out and Badog has to get through the necessary consummation before they wilt. Rather a nice touch that. Poetic." We left them, standing in the doorway, he, aflame, absolutely no sign of premature wilting, rubbing his cheek against hers in ecstasy and gasping out his thanks.

"Time for us to be off. No need to rub the groom for good luck. Look at them Bonnetchen," sighed Walter settling behind the wheel, delighted, like a gossipy old auntie. "So young and beautiful and they can't keep their hands off each other. They have become totally 'co-varrubious'. Their babies will be beautiful whereas people like us can only make dry art. But enough of serious matters." He scowled like a boy being made to eat his greens. "We deserve some fun. Let's go to a cremation. Back to the house for an early night and to lick our wounds and then, first thing tomorrow, we head for the coast."

* * *

Rosa and Miguel had first established themselves at the Bali Hotel, Campuhan being too far out for their cosmopolitan tastes. In those days, the groups of musicians and dancers who performed for tourists were chosen from the best traditional artistes and no one saw any harm in it. With the decline of aristocratic subsidies to such groups, it seemed natural that tourists were to be the new sponsors of art and support traditional values. We had not yet seen the prostitution and debasement that too much easy money, uncoupled from good taste, can bring. The leader of the Bali Hotel group was Gusti Alit Oka from Belaluan, one of the foremost musicians and woodworkers of his day. He was in the habit of introducing himself as "an aristocrat by birth, a carpenter by trade and a musician by choice". From the regular Friday-night performances, Rosa, Miguel and Oka had become firm friends. It so happened that he had a building to let, a rudimentary garage, and they had bought a dilapidated Chevrolet. In an odd sort of logic, they ended up borrowing some cheap furniture and living in the garage in Belaluan, with the Chevy parked out front, and from there, in his company, they executed Walteresque sorties to the ceremonies, musical performances and monuments that attracted them. It was no surprise they were here, holding hands, as we drove up at Krobokan, turning all heads with our multiple detonations. Walter dug in the back for notepad and camera and we joined a milling mass of people around what I recognised as the Pura Dalem, the temple of the dead. Somewhere, a *gamelan* orchestra was playing.

"You are very beautiful," an old man was saying to Rosa flirtatiously. "You could be Balinese. Even you," addressing Miguel, rapidly darkening under the Balinese sun, "could easily pass for one of us." I saw Walter pout. Blond and blue-eyed, *he* would never be Balinese even after all his years of effort and study to acculturate. The beautiful are unused to such slights. The rest of us hardly notice them. I thought of Manet's *The Execution of the Emperor Maximilian*, the aristocratic imperialist shot by the natives he tried so hard to identify with and the body stuffed by a local embalmer. Since there was no indigenous demand for glass eyes of the piercing blue shade of Maximilian's, they substituted brown. He had finally been made to look like a local.

Walter waved and mouthed a cursory hallo. "Excuse me, I must do some 'hallo darlings'." A term, no doubt, from the backstage of the theatre. He moved off and could be seen crouching and *sembahing* to various groups of old men, getting his head modestly down below theirs, lots of nodding, touching of shoulders.

The Covarrubiases were loaded up with full fieldwork kit, cameras slung around their necks, pockets bristling with pencils, pads clutched in their hands, both for sketching and the taking of notes. Rosa was dressed, as though for horse-riding, in khaki slacks and boots, Miguel in open-necked shirt and trousers that matched hers. Behind them lurked Oka. We greeted.

"Welcome, Mr Bonnet. I hear good things about your teaching our painters in Western techniques."

"What's this?" Rosa asked sharply.

"Some classes in perspective, shadow, Western media, that sort of thing," I said modestly, "for the lads in Ubud."

She flashed the whites of her eyes contemptuously as in the dance movement the Balinese call *nyegut*. "But our role here should be merely that of humble amanuenses of the Balinese, to record without changing."

She was beginning to irritate me.

"Then all we would need to do is just teach the Balinese to write – which by the way they already know how to do."

She took out a cigarette. Miguel lit it for her and then sat down and began to draw with firm, bold strokes. "A change in the way that oral cultures record themselves can have terrible consequences for the peasants and the value attributed to indigenous forms."

I pointed to the camera she was bouncing off firm breasts. "That, for example …"

"My pictures are purely for our own record, not to be allowed to pollute the spring from which we drink. Traditional artists should remain anonymous and part of the collectivity."

"But that's nonsense," I cried. "Everyone here knows who is the best carver or dancer or painter around. They become famous and people recognise their work." Miguel looked up.

"The important thing," he pronounced, "is that they work collectively, for goals defined jointly and in agreed ways. All the rest can change without disrupting the social order and introducing the false god of Western individualism. We learned that in Mexico during the Revolution."

I decided to change the subject lest I be instructed on Mexico during the Revolution. "Whom is this cremation for?"

Miguel flicked open a smaller notepad and read out a name that meant nothing to me. "Royal house of Klungkung, related to kings of Gelgel," he explained with a shrug. Rosa leapt in.

"But, of course, the really important thing is that it allows two hundred and fifty poor peasants to free the souls of *their* dead and finally liberate them by attaching them to the burning of feudal aristocrats. Their corpses become," Rosa said with relish, "beasts of burden for the poor."

Miguel smiled and held up his drawing. It showed an emaciated Balinese artist siting crosslegged before an easel, loinclothed and bare chested, with sticking-out ears and tufted hair. In his hand he held a paintbrush and his head was rammed through the hole in a Western painter's pallette – actually only big enough to take his neck – to his evident distress. Holding the pallette, was a snarling caricature of me, immediately recognisable, though prefiguring Heinrich Himmler in its skinny body, wire-rimmed glasses and dead eyes. The whole thing seemed to have been done in a dozen damning slashes of the pencil. Fortunately, at this moment, Walter reappeared and appraised.

"Yes," he smiled. "Very nice. I like the way you have decomposed him into triangles and squares like the Cubists. Stylish. But, like all portraitists, you have flattered the sitter." Covered by the drawing, he whispered, "Take your revenge by taking their picture." He pushed the Leica into my hands.

"What? How? I wonder," I smirked, "if I might take your picture. This is after all your honeymoon and you have taken so many pictures of others." I dropped the front of the case.

"Perhaps," said Miguel, "it would be better sitting down." He looked around vainly for somewhere to sit.

"No, no," said Walter. "Like that is fine, you two together, the festival as background." I was used to the apparatus and swiftly set aperture, speed, focus – click. Miguel looked annoyed.

"And now," Walter smiled, "we must take a quick walk round to see where we are." He seized me by the arm and led me away.

"What was that," I whispered, "about the photograph?"

Walter paused at a stall and bought two glasses of *tuak*, palm wine, pushed one across to me.

"Try this. Totally pure, from the sap of the coconut palm. It's been filtered through the entire length of a treetrunk." We sipped soapy, skimmed milk with a taste of mould. "I noticed, in all the pictures they showed me, that Miguel is always shown sitting down. Now, he has a nice face," he explained, swallowing, "but the most enormous arse, childbearing hips, female from the waist down – very un-Balinese." Ah, so that was it. "As a caricaturist he's obviously aware of it. In fact, he's very touchy about it so he always likes to be photographed sitting down, which lessens the impact." He laughed. "And remember," he quoted solemnly, "men seldom make passes at boys with fat arses." Wait. No. That can't be right. It would be years before Dorothy Parker would not say that. Instead, "And now, this is your first cremation. Let me give you the tour."

This event had been planned for years and represented the spending of tens of thousands of dollars by a people who normally calculated in fractions of a cent, the economies of years blown away in a few heady hours. The Dutch administration had tried in vain to legislate against such un-Calvinistic excess, the Balinese simply side-stepped the regulations, exchanging goods and service amongst themselves, pointing out that no money had actually changed hands. Excess was what it was all about.

"When you die," explained Walter, "you normally get buried unless you're a Brahmana, when you get burned straight away. When the time is right, the families, go to the graveyard and dig up the bones again and they're put in those towers there." I turned in astonishment. Swaying towards us, in a cloud of dust, was the Manhattan skyline in motion, uncountable towers of bamboo and wood, covered in cloth, coloured ornaments, tinsel, dangling fragments of mirrors flashing in the sun, roofs like Chinese pagodas, images of fanged monsters. Each was carried on the shoulders of dozens of straining men, not content to simply bear such a weight but running, turning twisting, this way and that, laughing and shouting, with marching *gamelans* delivering bursts of music like machine-gun fire. "It confuses the spirits," said Walter. High up were what I already recognised as *pedanda* priests hanging on for dear life, sprinkling holy water or making the arcane gestures known as *mudras* but that was the only dignified element in the proceedings. Baskets of rotten offerings were carted to the cemetery by the women, pursued by packs of hungry dogs. As bodies were unloaded, there were fights and attempts to carry them off, jostling, shouting. Breughel would have been at home. "The whole affair," said Walter, without irony, "is governed by the strictest regulations down to the smallest details." The decayed offerings, the sweat of the men and incense, the smell of trampled grass, the clinging stench of human decay combined into a miasma I shall never forget. "The old bodies are fine – just bone – as are fresh ones, but a lot here are at that awkward intermediate stage."

Walter was snapping away happily, working hard to avoid getting steatopygious Miguel or Rosa in shot, though, apart from clothes – as he well knew – they might have passed for Balinese. The men were manhandling, in every sense, the human remains into the great sarcophagi of hollow tree trunks, shaped like bulls, lions, fish, sea-monsters. Strings of Chinese *kepengs* were flung on the body, water, silks, more water, the music swelled. Then came one of those unfortunate pauses that occur in the rites of men as if an actor had missed his cue. "No cause for alarm," assured Walter. "They're starting the fire." I had an image of priests offstage, groping embarrassed in their robes, turning on each other, cursing that they had all forgotten the matches. Walter read my mind. "It has to be kindled by the sun or friction, the only pure fire. Sometimes takes a while." The crowds passed the time by shinning up the towers and plundering them, whooping, for trinkets and mirrors. Then, the flames were there, licking about the pyre, belching foul smoke, spreading to the other pyres, as if wildfire, and then the towers. The heat, added to that of the sun, was unbearable, beating at us from all sides. Sparks were flying high into the air, coming down on our clothes and hair. Somewhere, there were fireworks or maybe it was exploding bamboo. Soon, men were poking at the corpses with long poles as in a vision of Hell, laughing, cracking the resistant skulls and bad jokes I could not follow, calling out on the dead to burn faster. Everywhere was the crash of collapsing towers and coffins as their supports burned away and bamboo, smoking flesh and sizzling fat tipped into the eager flames. "Oh my God ... I must ... I have to ..." I fled to the entrance, crouched against a tree, breathed in deeply the breeze from the sea. A terrible tremor like *rigor mortis* passed through my entire body and I collapsed, shaking. Then Walter was there with life-saving unholy water, talking and gesturing over one shoulder to Miguel. "... marvellous display of artistic exuberance ... affirmation of life in the treatment of death ... drink this Bonnetchen. I shall tell everyone you went into a holy trance," as Rosa said in his other ear, "... rejection of crass materialism and declaration of human equality in the face of mortality ..."

"... affirmation of social hierarchy and shared values ..."

"... the revolutionary burning down of futile social distinctions ..."

Miguel lit a cigarette, inhaled smoke, blew it out gratefully through his nostrils, tongued away tobacco scraps. "Actually," he said – making me a friend for life – "it all reminded me most unpleasantly of a barbecue I once enjoyed in Texas."

We sat and gathered strength, rested in the shade, watched as the fires died down and families gathered to begin poking around in the ashes for undigested scraps of their loved ones. At a certain point, little boys were given licence to start fishing in the cinders for red-hot *kepengs* that they then threw joyfully at each other without parental rebuke. The dogs munched on. Something for everyone. The sun edged down towards the horizon.

Miguel looked around in deep content. "I should like to write it all down, everything that we can discover about these wonderful people. I should like to understand. The problem for me, as someone who grew up in Mexico, where we have all sorts of crazy festivals for the dead, is not to try to explain why the Balinese do the same. It's to try to understand why people in the West don't."

Walter perked up. "You mean *we* should be the focus of all those anthropologists, as the deviants in the world, not exotic peoples? I like that." He chuckled. "I shall await a team from the faculty at Leiden. I'm sure they would find me fascinating."

"What happens now, Walter?" I was still more interested in the Balinese than in us.

"The ashes are put in a coconut, wrapped in white cloth and ultimately taken to be cast in the sea, final dissolution of the flesh, then everybody bathes to wash away pollution."

"And the soul of a dead person?" I asked.

Walter frowned. "As you would expect, there's some disagreement but most people say it first goes off to Heaven or Hell and then comes back. If it was good in this life, it may go up in caste, if bad it may come back as an animal, but those are only theoretical positions. Most people are neither that bad nor that good. In practice, you return as a new member of your own family. After the birth of a baby, you go along to your local diviner and find out who it is that's come back."

"And Heaven," I asked. "What's that like?"

He looked astonished. "Heaven? But it's just like Bali, just like this – what else? – exactly like this. Only, in Heaven, of course, there are no Dutchmen."

* * *

"So Badog has gone for good then?"

At the forest-giant table, through a magnifying glass, Walter was examining the huge, red dragonflies in a killing jar converted from one made originally for the preservation of fruit.

"Oh yes. This was just a temporary thing for him." He removed one with long tongs, pinned it to a sheet, crucified it. Later, he would paint it and send the picture to the botanical garden at Bogor. "He has spread his wings. From somewhere he found money to pay for the ceremony. From somewhere, he found money for another field. So he and Ayu are growing rice and making more Balinese – things good in themselves, as I am sure you will agree." I had little doubt that Walter was that "somewhere".

"So you have just Resem and Oleg now?"

He looked shifty, held the lens up to his face, became, himself, a sea creature glimpsed in the depths. "Oh no. Now we have also Alit, Badog's cousin." He tonged out another specimen, saw that it had lost a wing, discarded its imperfection. "Would you like to meet him?" He turned and called through the doorway for tea. After a few minutes of saucepan noise he came, smiling and traytinkling. Very tall for a Balinese, broad-shouldered, the face of a happy angel but with a slight moustache that gave his upper lip a derisory curl and made him look unshaven therefore seedy, therefore slightly … soiled. Alit means "small". We were introduced. Giggling, he engaged in the unfamiliar gesture of handshaking. His long-fingered touch was warm and velvety. I slumped over the table.

"You know, to tell you the truth Walter, I'd rather hoped he might be ugly. It would make coming here more restful."

Walter frowned. "What on earth for? To be surrounded by beauty lifts me. Anyway, it is hard work to find an ugly Balinese. Yes, we have Oleg but that was mere chance, ugliness is something he has discovered for himself and grown into and you, yourself, have done very well with Putu at the palace, a very plain man." He surgically skewered a calopteryx water-nymph with a long pin. "I expect you will have a hang to sketch him. As Badog's cousin, Badog naturally explained the nature of his duties to him." Sex was simply unproblematic for Walter. He had always found it easily, bestowed it with grace, enjoyed it rather as one might this cup of tea, without fear or passion. To him it was not the fall of the Roman Empire or the humiliation of sin or self-degradation or even the strutting measure of one's worth in the world. It was just sex. I determined that I would not sketch Alit. Since coming to the Indies I had been like a boy in a pastry shop with eyes agog, greedy mouth and hands permanently sticky. That was not what life was for. I changed the subject.

"Where is Conrad?"

Walter sighed and lay down his lens. "Conrad has gone to take Rosa and Miguel to Pulaki, over in the West. Rosa became over-excited on hearing the news of the Japanese invasion of Manchuria on the wireless. Apparently it is the beginning of Armageddon, a new world war." He made the sceptical face that was his habitual response to politics. "When I told her I had no idea where Manchuria even was she accused me of burying my head in the sand. So I suggested she should go and bury hers. The sand in Pulaki is volcanic and black and the hot waters are healing. They go by outrigger from Bedugul and camp on the beach. It is Conrad's allfavourite place. There are tigers there. Like many young men, he likes to shoot things. I went there before with a visitor who shot things but he got carried away and shot the canoe, several times, and so we fell out in both senses." He lay down the lens with a sigh and pushed the clutter away. "What the hell. Shall we go? We could drive there and join them. It would be a nice outing for Alit."

As I was passing through the door, on my way home to collect my overnight survival kit, something caught my eye, fixed above the opening. "What's this? A new painting?" When had he done this? When Walter was at a painting the whole of Ubud knew about it. It was an act that required groans and lamentation and involved and defiled the whole community like a woman giving birth to twins.

He came and stood behind me. "There is a new dance called Oleg, invented by Nyoman Kaler. It shows the mating of two Balinese bumblebees. You know they have a particular kind of motion?" He swayed from side to side like a seagull in a gale. "Young Sobrat has painted it. I think it shows great promise. I showed them how to use watercolour but they always make a total *gouache* of it." He waited for laughter. None came. "So now we have not just a member of the household called Oleg. We have a dance and a painting."

I was not surprised that he liked it. It owed much to his own technique, richly jewelled and coloured, crowded with figures. So. Although it was me that took them labouriously through their exercises, it was Walter's style that they copied and his approbation alone that they sought. Balinese pupils remain fiercely loyal. The relation between a teacher and pupil is so close that a student may not marry his *guru*'s daughter. It would be a sort of incest against his spiritual father. I had not, until then, visited the west of the island. It would take us all day to reach it for roads from west to east were always lacking. It was all hotter, drier, emptier than the east, with no refreshment in the winds, the soil thin and baked to hot aridity, the vegetation mostly waxy-leafed scrub whose roots clutched at the earth. Forests here were not to be confused with the mossy, orchid-dotted steambaths nesting in the armpit-like valleys of the other side. For here there was none of the copious water that allowed the Balinese to indulge their taste for irrigation and the whole region had been neglected by the Dutch, themselves a canal-loving people, who had seen in the south Balinese obsession with channelling water a kindred mark of civilisation.

"There is," commented Walter, "a very fine temple, linked to the monk Niraratha who came from Java in the sixteenth century to a large town that stood here. Worried for their security the head of the town asked for it to be shifted to another state of reality by the saint and so it was. The town exists but is invisible, the people, *gamang*, exist but cannot be seen except by dogs. There are, of course, holy monkeys."

"No," I snapped. "No more monkeys."

We stopped along the way at a market instead, bought green coconuts and little banana-leaf packages of fried rice as a madman made faces and naked children screamed and ran away. Woven mats and great red pots were stacked by the roadside, being offered for sale. Alit was bravely nervous, like all Balinese away from home – this was, after all, a place of magic – and gripped the amulet that hung around his neck. We drove on. It was not until nearly sunset that the road skirted the sea and Alit let out a great cry and then gobbled Balinese hysterically. Walter stopped the car and turned to me in surprise.

"The sea," he said, oddly moved. "This is the first time Alit has seen the sea. His family had some sort of old feud with the Brahmanas of Sanur so they could not go there. Come on Alit. I will introduce you." They ran off, like little boys, Alit bending down cautiously at first towards the unquiet water, then paddling in the waves, then running back in delicious, giggling terror as they rushed in for him and collapsed between his toes. They returned, grinning, glowing, Walter yanking resisting socks over wet feet, suddenly tired. "After a certain age, Bonnetchen, there are no new experiences, you become dead, wooden. Everything is old. Even such a magical thing as the sea loses its power to amaze. Your senses are tired and you have to get your excitement from others, younger people, more generous and resonant instruments. You become a vampire, like Nosferatu."

We drove on. The road became a path, floured with salt and pepper sand, running down to the beach amongst bamboos and other plants of unknown name. There in the distant dusk, gleamed a fire. We parked the car, collected our gear and stumbled through ankle-deep softness down towards the retreating waterline where the sand was firmer underfoot. Alit flirted with the edges of the waves and, as we trudged, the sound of distant music emerged and gelled.

There was a group of about a dozen, gathered round a fire as in emulation of Walter's *kecak* dance. Rosa and Miguel, holding hands and seated on a picnic hamper, the sprawling form of Conrad, the two gnarled sailors that had brought them in their outrigger and a mix of other men from the nearby village. Other boats, blue, red and white, with the long snout of the elephantine sea monster, were drawn up on the sand. The music was from a flute and Jew's harp, a *genggong*, being played by two of the villagers and they flashed recognition to Walter with their eyes while the rest rose and greeted more formally. A container of *brem*, distilled rice spirit, was circulating and promptly offered. Walter took a token pull and passed it to me, doubtless expecting a gratifying coughing fit, forgetting I had been raised on Dutch gin, and made a face at an astonished little boy, sitting on his father's lap, his hand resting on his shoulder in gentle love. When had my own father ever held me like that? I felt suddenly, absurdly tearful and coughed in dissimulation. Remains of roasted fish were lying by the fire and a fresh supply was wrapped in banana leaves and poked into the ashes for us.

Conrad was lying back and had a great idiotic smile on his face. He was always happiest on a beach. In later times, he would have become one of the laidback but taciturn surfers of Kuta in grossly flowery shorts, or more likely, one of those intrepid giants who rode fat waves straight at the sheer cliffs of Uluwatu. His great hairy chest was a thing of wonder to Balinese, the attribute of a demon rather than a human. This did not preclude a certain success with the ladies – when I was out with him, people of both sexes would ask permission to touch it – but his tastes lay, I gathered, towards the rosy-cheeked-poetic-damsel sort of Dutchwoman. The men laid down their instruments to cheers and applause and smiled modestly.

"Now we have played for you," one said, "it is now your turn to sing for us." Such a simple and reasonable proposition caused mayhem amongst the whites.

"The only song I could possibly sing is of a darkeyed beauty from Guadalahara," proposed Miguel, diffidently.

Rosa, not from Guadalahara and jealous by reflex, pouted. "I could do a number I used to do in the Ziegfield Follies but it's kinda raunchy."

"At school, as a soprano," Conrad blushed, "I performed a version of Schubert's Trout but the words I have now forgotten. I could hum though." Walter looked at me.

"The only songs I know are hymns," I stammered. "Plain, Protestant hymns. I'm afraid I have no voice, I cannot sing."

"Wonderful," Walter headshaking. "You see how far we have allowed ourselves to be distanced from even the simplest social accomplishments? To say you cannot sing, or dance, is meaningless to a Balinese. It is like saying you cannot speak or walk or do not know how to breathe. In such circumstances, there is only one song to sing, that old English tune 'Old MacDonald had a farm', translated into Malay for our friends here and allowing them to join in with the animal noises." He gave swift instruction.

> "Tuan MacDonal ada kebun, ee-ay-ee-ay-oh,
> Dan di kebunnya ada babi ..."

It was a fantastic success. Our voices were terrible but the range demanded is not large and, in such circumstances, volume will easily substitute for quality. Walter teased the Balinese mercilessly, hesitating over the choice of animal, pointing suddenly at individuals who had to leap in with the appropriate noise, picking impossible, silent animals such as the tortoise to screams of laughter, reserving pig noises for the little boy. True, local zoological knowledge meant that the inventory of Tuan MacDonald's farm had to include, besides the more conventional domesticated beasts, goats, monkeys and bullfrogs but I have always been very surprised that no new Balinese art form ever emerged based on it as introduced to them that night. They were reduced to hysteria. We all were.

The villagers finally rose, stretched, shouldered their goods and children and strode off into the clicking, head-high bamboo with many warm farewells and a few residual animal calls. Did we not wish to spend the night in their village? No need. But were we not afraid? Here there were wild beasts, birds, worst of all witches. Thank you. Here would be fine. Rosa and Miguel had the tent. Conrad had his rifle. If the worst came to the worst Bonnetchen could sing and frighten anything away. Might we sleep in their boats if need be? Of course but perhaps the village …?

"Tea," said Walter in the silence of their departure, suddenly a solicitous butler. "Let us all have a cup of tea before bed." He set a saucepan in the glowing embers and lit a cigarette, even remembered courteously to set a cup for Alit. "Which kind would you like? We have camomile, jasmine or Indian." He disposed little envelopes pedantically along one knee.

"Indian," said Miguel, laughing. "Real tea, proper tea."

Walter twinkled. "Ah no. I think you should have jasmine. More suitable."

Miguel frowned. "How so? Why not proper tea? The tea I have always drunk at your house."

"Because, dear Miguel," he paused for effect, "as you are always pointing out to us, proper tea is theft."

We slept distributed among the boats and awoke with the dawn, stiff, cold hungry and then Alit was there with a warm smile and hot coffee. In daylight, the beach was a shocking sight, its smooth surface ploughed up and scored by the visits of a dozen different creatures. Walter was down on his knees.

"Look, the tracks of cranes. And here, a bear. And this is a turtle."

"What are those?" I pointed to deep ruts.

"Oh that's a crocodile's tail, a big one by the look of it." It came out of the sea, circled the Covarrubiuses tent, returned.

"And that?"

He scuffed it out with his feet. "Best not to mention that, I think. It's just a tiger."

We spent a day of sheer delight. Conrad swam and lazed and taught me to catch crabs – as the locals did – with a flower tied to the end of a piece of string. The fishermen loaded us into their boat and dragged us, bare feet crushing the razor-sharp coral, over the reef and handed us a biscuit tin with glass set in the bottom that allowed us to see to the very bottom and look, godlike, down into a watery world of sea urchins, bright fish, sea snakes and extraordinary reefs. Alit was almost hysterical with excitement at this new world. Walter and Conrad retired to one end of the beach to draw the inhabitants of a rockpool before their fugitive colours fled. Rosa and Miguel withdrew for a Mexican siesta. And I was left alone with my sketch pad and Alit, now the blasé sea-dog, legs spattered with sand, shoulders dusted with mica crystals, radiating happiness. He had tucked an orchidaceous red flower behind his ear, the same kind I had just used to catch crabs. Alit leaned back against a boat and stared out to sea. I *would* sketch him. I had to as the deference art owed to beauty. I raised my charcoal and pointed at the pad.

"Can I?"

He nodded. "Can!" He was an instinctive model, knowing not to move or change his expression as we talked. "Tuan Rudi, how big is the sea?"

"Well. The sea you see here is so big it goes all round the world and comes back to Sanur on the other side. If you want to go to Holland, you can sail in one of the big ships for three weeks without stopping." I captured the swoop of the back with two quick strokes. As good as Miguel.

"Beh! So far."

"And it is very deep. In some places it is as deep as the distance from Ubud to Denpasar."

"Beh! It is good to work for Tuan Walter. I learn many things."

"What did Badog tell you about Tuan Walter?" The angle of the neck was not quite right. It was artfully curved not straight. I adjusted and curled the tip of my charcoal around the tenderest part of his throat.

"He told me Tuan Walter was a good man and very kind, that he would look after me." The stomach was scooped, concave, the hipbones very pronounced, *art nouveau* hipbones.

"What else?" The arms were cocked at an odd angle, very Balinese, like the wings of a little bird.

"He said he would never beat me." I was shocked. How could anyone raise a hand against tender young Alit?

"Did he say you should play with Tuan Walter?"

"Oh yes!" He nodded, then remembered and froze. "He explained that Tuan Walter was a musician. So now, when the *gamelan* orchestra come to the house to practise, I play the *gender*, as I did at home, while he usually plays the *gangsa*."

I shook my head. "No, I mean. Did he say you should play with him at night?" One leg was bent. The muscles about the kneecap were difficult. I fudged, as so often, left them plunged in shadow where there could be no shadow.

"He explained that Tuan Walter was sometimes lonely for he knew very few women and so I might help him as a friend, if I wanted." I etched in the features of the face, shaded by long, black hair.

"How would you help him?"

He smiled. "Help him the way boys help each other. I don't think I should say. I am shy." He blushed in proof.

"I am like his little brother," I was relentlessly matter-of-fact, working on his hard, lean chest. "I too have helped him at times. Tell me."

"Really?" He was genuinely surprised. "But you are so old. Badog said that if I did not wish to, it was easy. I should look deep in his eyes and whisper that I could not, since I loved him and respected him too much, like a father. I could not get hard because I was ashamed. Then he would not insist and he would not be angry. Tuan Walter never gets angry like the other Dutchmen. Or, if he tried to use me as a woman, I should say that I was not a transvestite. Or if he wanted to use my mouth, I should say that it was against the ancient custom of Bali, that things of the above did not belong with things of below, that shoes did not belong on one's head, that rivers did not flow to the top of mountains, it was a pollution, *sebel*, then he would stop. The best way, at such times, was just to take him in my hand and be very eager and suck his face very hard, as the white men do – he showed me – and groan and the water would quickly come out and he would turn over and sleep. Then, the next day, he would buy me a new cloth and be very friendly." I shaded in the shadows under his arms.

"That cloth you are wearing," I remarked. "It looks new."

He laughed, quite unoffended and touched my arm softly to acknowledge a naughty joke. "From my mother, for my new job. You must understand that a new cloth is a big thing for us. We are very poor. This is the first time in my life I have eaten rice every day. Usually, at home, we eat manioc like the pigs." I felt the familiar gush of shame. Why was it my job to feel guilty about everything? He worked, after all, for Walter but I knew that in Walter's Bali Paradise there was no real want and certainly no guilt.

A group of fishermen emerged from the waving bamboo and pottered around doing nautical things, mostly just pulling on bits of their boats to test their security. One, with a lazy eye, came and stood behind me, watching me work.

"There's something wrong with that knee," he pointed. "You've got it wrong. It doesn't match the other one." Then: "That man with the hairy chest, Tuan Walter's little brother, I told my wife about it. Do you suppose he'd mind if I had a feel? She wants to know." I watched him wander over, get very excited over Walter's drawing. Of course, a fish – much more interesting than village boys. I saw them talking, then he reached out to touch Conrad's chest and started back as though from an electric shock and they all laughed. They began talking about the fish, the man making swimming motions with his hands and pointing to the sky and Walter stopped drawing and made notes. My own sketch was finished. On an impulse, I tore it from the pad and gave it to Alit.

"Send it to your mother," I said. "Show her how handsome her son looks in his new cloth." Alit, delighted, *sembahed* thanks. Miguel appeared from nowhere, eye-rubbing, lip-smacking, looked it over.

"Something badly wrong with that knee," he said. "Difficult things knees, though not as difficult as hands." Then, frowning, "Has anyone got any news about Manchuria? Rosa keeps going on about it."

The news from Manchuria was not good, Japanese massacring civilians, looting and the like. The Balinese shrugged. After all, the Dutch had done the same to them just a few years ago. They were a forgiving people. Walter skipped past it all unseen and homed in what was really outraging him, the Paris Exhibition, a competitive bit of chest-beating by the Western powers, going on in France at that moment. The Dutch had centred their pavilion around the Indies and the Indies around Bali and Bali around dancing. The whole collection of Western colonies was become what Rosa called "one big musical number" all-singing, all-dancing like the Follies. What upset Walter was that the Dutch had not asked him to do the murals, on which he had set his heart, choosing, instead, a very jobbing artist, Charles Sayers, the man who had so unsuccessfully hunted tigers in Pulaki.

"How could they ask you? You still have not finished those historical pictures for Stutterheim. Don't you see? They were a sort of interview for the big commission."

He groaned at the mention of Stutterheim. It was a recognisable symptom, premonitory sign of the gestation of the next historical painting, its first foetal kick. Delivery would be many weeks off and then it would be rushed from the house like something stillborn, being – as it would – very un-Walterlike, full of figures dutifully about variations on a single theme, rather like one of Sobrat's busy little paintings. When the time came, I must remember to make the comparison. No one here would mention my own quiet successes of the year, with exhibitions in Bandung and Yogya and no shortage of buyers amongst the steadier Dutch citizens.

"Yes but Sayers!" Walter tore at his hair, then smoothed it back into place. "A man doesn't mind losing a beauty contest but not to a warthog."

Later, there was still worse news, as the Japanese bombed the undefended cities of distant Manchuria to the sound of Rosa's protests, the Dutch pavilion caught fire and all the finest Balinese antiquities, borrowed from the Batavian Society, went up in flames. Fortunately, none of the little *legong* dancers from Peliatan, accompanied by Cokorda

Raka, had been hurt, yet Walter raged and stormed over the dinner table.

"The folly. The stupidity. Why weren't the Balinese antiquities locked up in a fireproof safe at night as was promised? Irreplaceable treasures so lightly puffed away. Cokorda Raka will say nothing, being in the pocket of the Dutch, but others here will never trust us again."

"Well," I comforted, "at least one good thing came out of it. It says Sayers' murals went up in smoke too."

He stopped shouting and brightened. "Yes. There is that."

He was really only half listening, being, as always, distracted by the wealth of insect life around the lamps and the occasional bat veering in, open-mouthed, to suck them up. We were seated at a table, littered with bottles and cigarette packets – God how we all smoked in those days – on the terrace of the Bali Hotel, the tropical night pulled down around us like a damp blanket. Outside, rain was lashing down so that the tables nearest the rail had cleared themselves, with squeals, as the monsoon crashed in. It was a mark of our not being tourists that we had chosen more advisedly and stayed in place and we were nominally here to say final farewells to Miguel and Rosa, dressed in matching grey silk, their visit stretched from an intended three to nine months. Under the table they would be gripping hands. They were leaving, having sworn great oaths to return. Miguel was "definitely going to do a book" on Bali. We nodded, smiled. We had heard it all so often from others before, said it ourselves, like as not. On the other side of the table were Dr Roelof Goris of the antiquities service who *had* at least written a tourist guide using Walter's photographs. Being both an alcoholic and "of the faith" he was here for a little recreation from puritanical Java. Next to him that night, if I recall aright, sat an odd couple, one thickening into middle age with one of those square faces and excessively even teeth that only Americans can have, the other unfleshed like an emaciated whippet. The Covarrubiases knew them, naturally from the States. The first was Templeton Crocker, Hawaiianly floral-shirted, eccentric American millionaire, whom the San Francisco newspapers habitually termed "sensitive", fearing litigational retribution for more precise use of adjectives. His yacht, the *Zaca*, had called in at Buleleng and dropped him off on the way to collect birds in the South Seas. Temp would rejoin it at Benoa, having spent a couple of days with Walter stalking the rare Balinese mynah. A master of the arts of leisure, his greatest pride was to have written the libretto for a Chinese opera, "The Land of Happiness", actually vanity-staged in Monte Carlo and – less surprisingly – in his fief of San Francisco and he had played us generous excerpts the previous night. It had been a terrible evening, not least because he attempted the female roles himself in a broken falsetto and torn French. In those days the American upper classes only spoke foreign languages badly lest they be mistaken for immigrants. At his side, was Hubert Stowitts, former track athlete, choreographer, costume- and set-designer who had been enthusiastically involved in the staging of the opera and now described himself as an "anthropological explorer of native sexuality" and artist. As might be imagined for one so creatively engaged, his life had not been without incident though his artistic output was limited to undulant male nudes in bright colours. Both he and Rosa had been snapped naked by the same society photographer, she as a water-nymph, he a rampant Spartan warrior. His gifts had first come into their own when, as a dancer, touring South America in the company of Isadora Duncan and the aging Pavlova ("plucked her brows and her fanny nightly my dears") the company's props and sets had gone astray. Hub had sensationally improvised both overnight and been judged dispensable again only when, on the evening of the world premier of *Scheherezade*, he had tired of the dull choreography they had all painstakingly rehearsed and instead performed, *extempore*, one of his own devising and centred on himself – to the dismay of the rest of the wrongfooted onstage company. Subsequently, he had starred in a film with Garbo and had ambitions to "probe" India, having himself once been repeatedly and memorably enjoyed by a huge Lascar on the docks of San Francisco in his student days. This all related in dance and an actorially projected voice – fortunately in English – in the dining room of the hotel on whose porch we now sat, unsurprisingly, alone. We would soon be asked to leave but this had been delayed by the ordering of several bottles of unbelievably expensive champagne that had now lulled Hub to a state of sleepy non-communication.

"You have no one to blame, Walter, but yourself," said Goris. "The government have repeatedly asked you to co-operate with them in the founding of a Balinese museum and you have never taken up the offer. It is the only way to place the Balinese heritage in a place of security."

"You should do it Walt," declared Temp in a hicksville voice he used for comic effect but that seemed to be taking him over. "Museums are great. I got me one, the California Heestorical Society. Got it real cheap."

Walter groaned again. "Do you see me as the director of a museum, in a tie, filling in forms? It has anyway been my experience that museum directors are pompous fools or rogues, sometimes both, who only love the sound of their own voice."

"I can't argue with that," said Temp. "Yup, we get through 'em by the dozen. All total assholes." He gestured for more drink. It was naturally understood that the whole evening was on him.

"It could be arranged," urged Goris. "A purely administrative official could be appointed who would take all the humdrum daily work off your hands – like Bonnet here with your teaching – yours would be a purely inspirational role."

"But museums are fearful places, full of the corpses of objects, cutting them off from life, a dead hand that would stifle the Balinese imagination. The greatest contributor to the Balinese creative spirit is the white ant, chewing away at dead wood and ensuring everything must be constantly renewed."

I intervened. "Look Walter. You can't have it both ways. Either Bali is a dying culture whose ancient treasures are being frittered away, or it is creative and vibrant and must resist ossification. Actually," I said, suddenly inspired and surprising myself, "you *can* have it both ways. Have a museum for the best of the past linked to a shop where visitors can buy the best contemporary art. Then you couple the two together. They fertilise each other."

"Yes!" interjected Miguel. "And the artists can work in a sort of collective – call it a club to slip it past the Dutch – to maintain standards and ensure the true communal nature of peasant art. Walter, you must do it. For the people."

"Clubs are great Walt. I got me one downtown called the Bohemian Club. I get together there with the boys. Why!" Temp clapped Hub affectionately on the shoulder. "That's where Hub here got started with the dancing in a private room when he was still just a kid." They stared at each other in misty nostalgia. "No one would have guessed back then that you would design costumes, seeing as how you didn't hardly wear one." There was, I understood, a Mrs Crocker, a serviceable sugar heiress, acquired, wed and swiftly archived in a white-painted house somewhere. Walter groaned again like an old bear beset on all sides by snapping dogs.

"But then we would be just like those terrible art circles in Java, full of old women who only like pretty trash done in pastels and ignore the natives except as models. You see them – they go to those exhibitions and talk about the frames." The people who had bought my paintings.

"Why couldn't you have Balinese, natives, on the committee, like we do in Mexico, like in the villages here?" This from Rosa, who, as far as I knew, had never set foot in Mexico.

Walter held up his hands in surrender. "All right, all right. I'll think about it. Goris, tell them I'll think about it. No more. A dog that has been bitten by a snake always fears sausages."

"What?"

"It is a saying of the Urals."

"A toast to that!" boomed Temp dispensing more champagne. He rose to his feet with great dignity. "Sir, may Dame Fortune smile on you and your endeavours and fulfil all your aspirations – jest lahk a slapped whore." We raised our glasses and toasted.

"And now," sipping Hub growled huskily, suddenly revived, sharp-toothed and dangerously bright-eyed though unsteady. "Where do we go in this town for a little ... fun?"

Fun, I could foresee, would involve wilful destruction of property, injudicious violence given and received, the plumbing of depths, possibly consorting with monkeys. Ah no. Denpasar had not been constructed with fun in mind.

"I must be off," I announced. "A meeting at the Little Harmonie club."

"Clubs are great," announced Temp. "I got ..." He frowned. Wait. "Aw sheet!" He had already said that. Walter smiled knowingly, looking – it seemed – through me.

"Don't drink too much. You know it disagrees with you." He drained his glass and Hub did the same and lobbed his off into the shrubbery where it, disappointingly, did not smash.

"Oh no. There will be no drinking. I shall stick to a good dose of their nice hot chocolate." But when I arrived Dion was not to be seen.

The head waiter was weary, had had a long day, irritably shaking his dead to dispense tired dandruff in all directions.

"He has gone. Disappeared." Wiping smeary glasses on a frayed cloth. "No I don't know where. It is just as well. The police were here asking questions. Politics."

As I trudged to my lonely bed, I heard a sudden girlish shriek and what could only be loud American fraternity baying from the *lapangan kota.* followed by the crash of splintering wood and a blast of *Madame Butterfly* in chorus. Fun, for those that liked that sort of thing, had clearly begun.

* * *

Goris had exceeded his brief. The museum was now considered a *fait accompli* and Walter was summoned to numerous meetings with the Resident in Singharaja. Every day brought official letters rattling through the door, the small arms fire of bureaucracy. It seemed that the Governor General in distant Batavia had taken it into his head that a Balinese museum was indispensable to Holland's chosen role as protector of the Balinese way of life and planned a visit, whose highlight was to be the opening of the completed institution, in just one year. The Governor General was a man with a whim of iron. Ancient plans were hastily disinterred, funding conjured from thin air. Walter groaned. The letters started having footnotes and appendices, projections, evaluations and estimates. Naturally, each contradicted the one that had gone before. Walter groaned yet louder and disappeared from the world to paint a picture.

The Balinese are one of the most organised peoples in the world. Every adult male is a member of all sorts of groups, in the hamlet, for the organisation of water distribution, for music and temple matters, even for kite-flying. These groups are run by committees, elected officials, little democracies that need no outside interference. Our artists' organisation fitted right in. At the top, of course, had to be Agung Raka, as titular head though it was recognised he would do nothing. Cokorda Agung would do all the real work. Correspondingly, Walter would be the senior white member though I would undertake most of his duties. Balinese participation was assured by the appointment to the main committee of Gusti Nyoman Lempad as the oldest artist. Amongst a people of determinedly sunny disposition, he was that rarest of things: a genuine Balinese curmudgeon. Then there had to be heads for different regions, Cokorda Rai from Peliatan for example, different skills – painters, weavers, silversmiths, sculptors, in all, some hundred and fifty members and the whole thing was so complex that it could never work so, in a very Balinese fashion, the actual formal structure would be simply ignored. Everyone had to come to the house of Raka, as titular head, but, once there, all this hierarchy would be in abeyance. But rules of hospitality, of course, must he maintained, so all were served glasses of diluted pink squash of vengeful sweetness. It took some time for everyone to understand how the whole thing worked. Finished works would be submitted for discussion every Saturday at the palace. The committee would look at them and there would be an open debate about their merits. They might be accepted or rejected by the organisation. If accepted, they would be sold at a good price through the museum shop or the dealerships and exhibitions with which the group had links. These extended as far as my old friend, Vorderman, the Amsterdam dealer. It required a lot of trust for such poor men to allow foreigners they did not even know to carry away and hold their creations, for months or even years, without payment. Only when money began to flow back to the artists in a steadily increasing trickle, did the message spread that this was a worthwhile thing.

At first, everyone was shy of criticising the works of others, simply murmuring, "Very nice" with downcast eyes, for the Balinese are a desperately polite people. It was Walter who decided he must make them see that criticism could be constructive. He pulled something coyly out of his bag, no doubt a new painting none of us had yet seen.

"Even the teachers among us must be subject to criticism. We can learn from you as you from us." He looked to me for support and I nodded enthusiastically. I thought this was extraordinarily brave of him, submitting his own work and urging them to comment, pointing out his own shortcomings to get them started. He propped it up on an easel and stood back. Too late, I recognised my sketch of Alit on the beach.

"But how did you …? Where did you …?"

"Now you will note," intoned Walter smoothly, "that the artist has tried to be modern. It is a drawing of a single, real person – not a mythological being – and I'm sure you all recognise the subject." Murmurs of "Alit". "Quite so. So it attains at least the lowest kind of resemblance. But what else do we see here?"

"There is a lack of animation," declared busy little Sobrat, standing and reknotting his sarong. "It is a picture of a boy just sitting. And just one boy. It is not *ramai*. It is lonely. Why should anyone want to buy a picture of a boy just sitting?"

"The knee's wrong," grumbled Gusti Nyoman, pointing and laughing. "It's terrible. Alit's not a cripple." This from a man who had never got beyond the conventions of temple painting and was obsessed with figures that moved like puppets in three-quarters profile.

"Yes and see," offered a man from the floor who himself carved nothing but the most execrable wooden frogs, "how badly he has tried to cover it up by putting that big shadow where no shadow could be. See where the light is coming from. It is impossible."

"Do we accept this work then for our group?" Cries of "No" from the floor. Walter smiled. "So now you see how it works. We must all be frank and then the artist can learn from his own mistakes instead of just trying to cover them up." They applauded, exuded love for Walter, finally offered up some of their own works – all heavily praised and accepted, even the damned frogs. Agung was delighted. At last he was getting art.

But sorting out all such practical matters was as nothing compared with finding a name for the organisation. Various Dutch and Malay forms were proposed but all sounded like a trade union or political party and would invite Dutch disapproval. Balinese mythology was ransacked, the sun god *Surya*, the Supreme Teacher *Batara Guru*, *Saraswati*, goddess of learning, were all yoked to our wagon and proposed but failed to ignite the passion of their worshippers. Then, one evening, we were driving in the Whippet to Walter's house with a load of paintings. Aboard were Sobrat, myself, an American art historian called Clair Holt and Gusti Lempad. We were all listening to Lempad complaining as usual. I no longer recall which of his many wrongs he was rehearsing. It may have been tax, or the government or that fact that no one ever listened when he complained, but I do remember that he was in full flow. At that hour it was pitch dark and it was unfortunate that, just as we passed the cemetery, the main headlights failed, plunging us into complete obscurity. Luckily there was bright moonlight – we had been the previous day to a full-moon ritual at a nearby temple – so Walter kept going, knowing better anyway than to stop at a cemetery, in the dark, with a carload of Balinese. He shouted something about the *verfluchte grosse Scheinwerfer* being *kaputt* and this was passed around in various languages, Walter's English rendition being that "the great shine-throwers were broken". Clair Holt thought this hilarious and tried to explain why to the Balinese. Gusti Lempad, of course, understood not a word, yet from all this emerged somehow the Balinese term *Pita Maha*, the Great Shining. It dropped like a stone into our conversation. We all knew it immediately for what it was. This then became the name of our organisation, invented by a dicky seat full of uncomprehending Balinese who were totally in the dark.

* * *

"Tuan Walter," said sad-faced Resem, "is in the garden." His voice sank to a tone of hushed awe. "He is crying."

"Do you know why?"

He opened his eyes wide and shrugged as if to say, "These crazy *bule*. Who knows why they do anything."

I made my way down the steps and the little path that skirted the river. It was a bright, cool day. The butterflies were aflutter. Bougainvillea and hibiscus provided splashes of colour against a dark green backdrop. A black cat lay on a rock and blessed me with a smile and a contented closing of both eyes. It had a smooth, long tail not the kinked tail of a Balinese cat. There was something feline, it occurred to me at that moment, about Walter – the same ability to do absolutely nothing without suffering boredom, the infinite capacity for soaking up affection and then just stalking off without attendant burden of guilt. But crying. Oh God. It must be his mother. It could *only* be his mother. I began to rehearse various scenarios in my mind. Would he go home? If so, would he return? I found him, out of sight of the house, hunched – very small, shaded by a cluster of rustling bamboo. He turned a tear-stained face towards me. Only then did I see the cockatoo perched on his shoulder and tugging at his hair as if arranging it for a mad scene.

"It's Plumpe," he said. Plumpe? Who the hell was Plumpe? Was it one of the other animals? Plumpe sounded like a hedgehog. I flicked quickly through the list of those I could remember, ready to adjust my response anywhere between commiseration and joshing disbelief. He groped blindly in his top pocket and pushed a letter at me. Not an animal then.

It was from a firm of Moneterey attorneys, Habgood and Waymark, announcing the death of their client, Friedrich Murnau, né Plumpe – I had forgotten – and a substantial bequest, in his will, in favour of Walter. The only problem lay in the contestation of the will by a former business partner, the freezing of all his estate's rights in his latest film and the expectation of a complex coroner's hearing, owing to the unusual circumstances of his death. As a result, it was impossible to place a figure upon the cash value of the inheritance. Even at this remove, the lawyers could be heard licking their lips at fat fees. I looked at the date. It was three months old.

"I was going through that pile of letters about the museum that I had left unopened and found this one. There was another from Temp who had heard from Hub who met Garbo after the funeral in Berlin." He sighed and suddenly gripped his knees in a spasm of anguish. The cockatoo complained and flapped away to a tree. "He always told me I was the love of his life. When someone says that it's like a curse and when they say it as you are leaving them it's a determination to make their whole life a tragedy out of spite. And when your first love dies it's like a little taste of your own death."

As usual, I did not know what to say but all he needed was someone he could talk to frankly and without dissimulation, someone who would not be shocked by the sort of emotions of which he would speak. "Did *you* love *him*?" I asked.

"Of course. In fact I still do. That he is dead makes no difference. In fact, some people are easier to love when they are dead than when they were alive."

"Where is Conrad?" I asked somewhat desperately.

"Oh," he batted the question away. "We had a young lady visitor, some friend of Claudette Colbert. He has taken her off to an *odalan* festival at Tampaksiring."

I had noticed that, nowadays, Conrad always took the ladies, Walter the men. This household was becoming totally an economy of seduction. I sat down awkwardly and took his hand. He seized mine and gripped with cold flesh.

"He always told me his money was safe in Switzerland, so I don't know ... When I knew him he didn't have two extras to rub together. You know that during the war he was a pilot and went up on a reconnaissance mission. From up there, the whole world looked like hell except for Switzerland where all was peace and quiet, no tracks even to be seen in the snow, like in a silent film, so he landed there with a tale of mechanical and compass malfunction and they interned him in a nice chalet till the end of the war. He was supposed to come here this year. He was sick of Hollywood, had fallen out with Fox. Like Nosferatu, he wanted a place where he could step out into the light and just be himself. I told him Bali was that place. He had bought a yacht and even named it 'Bali'. If only he hadn't made that last stupid film first."

"What was that?"

He wiped snot on the back of his hand and dried his eyes with his sleeve like a little boy. It was no good, every instinct made me desperately want to mother him.

"It was called 'Tabu', some silly romance about tragic love and magic in a South Seas paradise, lots of tits and bums and palm trees." It sounded rather like one of Walter's films. At the end of "Island of Demons" they had even inserted two scenes of male and female nude bathing that included the boys from the house. They had screamed with embarrassment when Walter showed them the stills. I held out the letter and he took it back with a shaking hand and stowed it away. "He had two of my paintings. I wonder if I could get them back." Already, he was thinking like an artist.

"What were the unusual circumstances?" He looked blank. "In the letter. It says something about unusual circumstances?"

Walter cleared his throat and swallowed, straightened up and smiled, as if for a closeup. "He was killed on the way to the premier of that damn film. Aristotelian tragedy and so on, undone by own *hubris*. He was in one of those big cabrioletts the Americans like, with the roof down – it was a clear sunny day – and was thrown out when it hit a lanternpole."

I frowned. "A lamppost? How come it hit a lamppost? Was he drunk?"

"That's not clear, though with Plumpe you can bet he'd had a drink or two. When I first knew him I was very young and innocent and thought he was very wise and sophisticated, then I realised he was just drunk all the time. I was with him the last time they dried him out and you could tell it didn't take. You can't make someone give it up till they are ready – and he wasn't. Hub says Garbo told him Plumpe wasn't even at the wheel but the studio are hushing it up. It seems he had a young Filipino valet. *He* was at the wheel and Plumpe's head was, for some unimaginable reason, beneath the instrumentboard."

I thought about it. "Do you suppose ...?" We were both grinning. Walter rested his forehead hotly against mine. I smoothed his hair and rubbed his ears like a cat's. It just seemed the right thing to do.

"Let us hope so, Bonnetchen. Simultaneity of symbolisms and so on. Corny I know, but the critics love it. Like in one of his films. All comes together in the end. He would have liked that."

9

"Of course, I have no formal qualifications in music," said Walter, executing a particularly difficult arabesque, "as I told Leo Stokowski when he was here – but then neither have the Balinese. You might say," he twinkled, "that, as musicians, they are an unqualified success." All this going down well enough with guests Colin McPhee and wife Jane Belo, both formally degreed up to the ears and taking Walter's remarks as deference not the dismissal I was sure they were. They had met the Covarrubiases in Paris, seen the Balinese show at the Colonial Exhibition and just embarked on a hymn of praise to Sayers, the artist who had executed the murals – "though, of course, they, themselves, had no formal qualifications in art".

McPhee might not be impressed by Walter's playing – he was, after all, a concert virtuoso himself, as well as a recognised composer of the modernist school – but he was by the dropping of Stokowski's name. His enemies, of course, maintained that the mercurial conductor and showman was born pedestrian Leonard Stokes in London and had confected his exotic accent, leonine mane and exuberant mannerisms from scratch. The disdaining of the normal baton and the arrangement of concert-hall lights to focus on his hands and the dramatic shadows they threw had come about after his experience of the Balinese shadow play. He had also made a speciality of bedding Garbo and marrying an heiress. McPhee had followed him in that. It was Belo's family money that had subsidised this pelagic excursion.

McPhee, pale, Canadian, red-haired and weakly handsome, very pink, exhibiting the first signs of what Walter would term "porculence", about thirty in – of all things – a suit . Belo, of the same age, even paler, strawlike blond hair cropped boyishly short, very thin with a wealth of nervous mannerisms and wearing a simple cotton shift like a nightgown, as if she had been snatched from a sanatorium in the middle of the night. The pair, freshly married but uncovarrubiously distant, living as in parallel but never touching.

Conrad had been present at dinner, looked her over in silence and clearly decided that – as an intellectual – she was Walter's patch rather than his. He had left to go to the village where he claimed, as so often nowadays, to have a lesson in Balinese. Possibly, but – if so – then the improvement in linguistic skill did not match the time and effort he was putting in. I suspected a love interest. And why not? He was young and undeviant.

But what was striking now was the blatant buzz of sexual transmission between McPhee and Walter to which she and I remained resolutely deaf. It was, if nothing else, embarrassingly rude to his bride. Pert little Resem had just served coffee with great grace, patting the cups into perfect alignment with delicate fingertips as only the Balinese do and McPhee had given him a look that virtually ripped the sarong from his loins. I felt a flare of paternal outrage over such molestation.

Jane had told me that she was here to work on trance in ritual and performance, that she was a trained cinematographer hoping to make some films, but that her deeper mission was the "exploration of herself and her key sexual configurations". I detected resonances of years of psychoanalysis, just the thing that has led Americans to see themselves as particularly deep and interesting, whereas nothing could be further from the truth. It was only my blushes that stifled my yawns. I took it that she had been early introduced into the lesbic-leaning sororities of the Ivy League and was now having doubts. These expressed themselves in the usual anthropological form of the conflict between nature and nurture, that would allow her to discover a totally fictitious "real" her, to which she could henceforth be true. Marriage to McPhee – it seemed obvious to me – had been the clearest possible way of situating herself in a heavily defended sexual no-man's land. Temp, I could not help thinking, might have been a more suitable spouse, a marriage made – if not I heaven – at least at Harvard. Her talk that night was all girlish gush of her mentor, Ruth Benedict, and a book she was writing which, she assured me, would reshape the entire subject. I don't believe I ever heard of it again.

"So tell me, Walter, what do the Balinese make of Western music?" Walter stopped playing and turned on his stool, slid out from behind the piano and began walking up and down. An academic audience was as good as a musical one.

"That's an interesting question, Colin. Jazz interests them. After *gamelan* practice once, I played them some records of Ted Lewis, you know New Orleans style, and they nodded along and said that was fun – so everybody *was* happy. Then I played them some Beethoven, one of the piano sonatas. They said it was too busy, too many tunes at the same time, that man needed to sit down and think a bit more and decide what he wanted. So then I gave them a Chopin prelude and some light Mendelssohn. They didn't think much of those. Just like the Opera Stamboul they said – you know – the Malay opera, all screeching and syrupy melodies – the kind of thing the Chinese love to sit around listening to in torn vests. So then I banged out a Bach prelude and they just sat there entranced. Now, *that*, they said was real music."

McPhee laughed and slid behind the keyboard himself, began to allow something slender and Debussyish to flow from his fingertips. Debussy – himself inspired by the music of the Indies at a previous colonial exposition, but Javanese, the sort that was so vapid it sent Balinese to sleep.

"So," said Walter, rubbing his hands, suddenly businesslike, "tomorrow we can get you started on the musical tour, bamboo *gamelans*, iron *gamelans*, north versus south, old versus new. I can introduce you to the major musicians and dancers. There's so much going on at the moment. The only problem is petrol. Up here it's worth its weight in gold …" He looked off into space theatrically and chewed his lip as though in thought.

I recognised the opening manoeuvres to reel them in and get them to pay up in advance. So, he was broke again. Murnau's money – referred to in the house as "the American royalties" – had yet to plump up his account. The signs had been there in the incoherent dinner, the vegetable course being my own contribution from the palace, the rest all stuff from the garden packed out with cheap buys in the market, the whole masked as an amusing introduction to local exotica. Oleg came in with *brem*, rice spirit, a present from one of the neighbours. The whisky must have all been used up. To coos of appreciation, Walter passed round rustic Balinese cigarettes wrapped in corn husk and a wind of string.

Oleg had grown, and – it must be said – grown ugly. Under the impact of Walter's kitchen, he had put on weight, one of the few Balinese who would look better in a shirt. Yet he remained as sweet-natured as ever and enjoyed the favours of a very pretty girl down in the village where he now passed the night. And he moved in a very Balinese way that belied his weight. For a Westerner of his build to dance could only be a comic thing, yet Oleg still moved with grace and assurance, at ease with his own form. You could imagine him stamping out a creditable *baris*. I commented on it, then managed to corner Walter, appropriately, in a corner, nudging and whispering. "Moreover," I finished, "if you value your domestic tranquillity you should make sure Oleg – rather than Resem – looks after McPhee. He's trouble." He nodded. Was he really listening? "This is not," I added, "a matter of jealousy as you will doubtless pretend. It is out of concern for Resem's innocence. He is surely unaware of what such men are capable of."

"Mmm. You are right. About the way Oleg moves – how would you say that in English, in German something like *körperliche Gelassenheit*?"

"Grace?" I suggested. "No. Wait. Poise. He has exquisite poise."

McPhee looked up sharply, an old bloodhound picking up a distant scent borne on the wind. The corners of his mouth contracted into a shark's rictus.

"Boys?" he asked breathily. He had been knocking back the *brem* and his speech was slurred. "Did somebody say 'exquisite boys'?"

* * *

Walter raged around the island with the McPhees, showing, introducing, explaining, leading them off the beaten track to places and experiences they would never have found for themselves. It always refreshed him to show off *his* Bali, drawing strength from the admiration and pleasure of others. There was nothing jealous or proprietorial about Walter. One of his friends was Nyoman Kaler, inventor of the *oleg* dance, another Mario, inventor of the flashy *kebyiar duduk* that was a sort of gobbet compilation, a moving *rijstafel* of difficult dance moves and, of course,

Limbak of the new, improved *kecak*. He shared them all unselfishly, as a good boy does his sweets. Walter was always very firm in the view that Balinese theatre and dance did not merely entertain but showed the young how they should best behave.

TheMcPhees settled in a damp house in Kedaton, near Nyoman Kaler, where McPhee worked like a European – not a Balinese – demon, recording and transcribing music, banging out the basic tunes on an old tropicalised upright piano. Of course, in those days we had, as yet, no way of recording sound in the field so it must all be done by hand. The Balinese, themselves, had no system for noting down anything but the most basic melodies so that McPhee had to drag it all out of their heads and memories as passed down from nameless ancestral composers. Communal art as described by Miguel, except, of course, that it could be owned and one hamlet might well capitalistically buy a new tune and the secrets of its performance from another, lock, stock and barrel. The McPhee choice of residence, just across from the shelter in which the hamlet's orchestra practised, might have been seen as the triumph of duty over domestic quiet, had it not also allowed ready access to Nyoman's young and comely nephew, Made Tantra, whom – it soon became clear – McPhee was assiduously, but not monogamously, courting. He was a striking boy, with long, straight hair that he always decorated with great style. Sometimes, it was a flower tucked behind the ear, or a poignantly unopened budlet woven into his crisp forelock. On one occasion, at an evening festival, it was flashing fireflies tied into his hair with tiny threads.

"You should say something to Nyoman about his nephew," I urged. "They go everywhere together. It is shocking. How old is that child? Thirteen? Fourteen? A scandal."

Walter sighed. "Nyoman does not care about anything but his *gamelan* orchestras. Of those he is fiercely jealous. Anyway, Balinese do not count birthdays so they do not have an age. When a boy starts behaving as a man, he is a man. What is wrong with you Bonnetchen? *We* go everywhere together. You don't know what they actually get up to. It may be entirely innocent. You spend so much of your life disapproving of things, Bonnetchen, that I think sometimes you disapprove of yourself. Those ladies who buy your paintings in Batavia would be as outraged about us, as you are about Colin and Made. They would joyfully crucify you if they knew about your activities on the *lapangan kota*." What did *he* know about ...? "Look, either you believe such moral lines are universally the same or you admit they are not and then you cannot redraw them just for your own convenience. What is gravy for the female is also gravy for the male goose." Gravy for the female? Ah, sauce for the goose. "You cannot disapprove of Made and Colin on the grounds that they are simply wrong and excuse yourself as simply right. *I* should disapprove if I thought Colin were treating him badly or making him unhappy but you do see that that is quite different? Sex is not good or bad. It is how you use it to affect other people. Once you throw away universal rules you are left simply with the pagan virtues, kindness and good manners."

"Colin's out with Made. He'll be back soon," explained Jane with a sour Texas twang, as she showed me over the bare, comfortless house. "You know, I've sort of done this before. My first husband was a artist, George Biddle. He lived in Tahiti, adopted some local children. Why, he even wrote a book about it. You know, someone just made the most marvellous film about Tahiti, called 'Tabu', filmed right where he lived?" Good God – Murnau. Then – *first* husband? Jesus. How many had she had?

"Oh, Colin's only my second. We decided to get wed after I wrote a essay in anthropology at the Sorbonne. 'Is marriage a human universal?' I guess the answer they wanted was 'Yes but only if you let "marriage" be stretched so far it doesn't mean a thing any more'. You know, men marrying men, people marrying the dead, a girl taking up with a whole heap of brothers and so on – the way they do in different places. Colin and I were real close at the time in temperament. He was studying under Nadia Boulanger. There were problems but when you looked at all that marriage data, us two getting married didn't really seem so odd any more. So we just went ahead and did it. My analyst said it was a great step forward in my maturational phase to embrace a feminine man and so move towards dealing with my own temperamental inconsistency. I guess it is the same for you, having made the decision to live in partnership with dear Walter."

"Walter and I do *not* live together! We are friends."

"Oh my! Now I've embarrassed you." She resumed her tour like the guide to a palace. "Most of the furniture we just borrowed from the manager of the Bali Hotel. He was a most obliging gentleman." She prodded one of the beds and it responded with a groan. "You see? In Bali, even the beds are musical!" she smiled. "Colin says it's a B flat." Oh my God. Surely that was the bed that Dion and I had played and harmonised upon. My eyes misted. *We* had got whole chords out of it.

"I just don't know why the manager was so nice," she prattled on, "considering he's losing business on the deal. He even had his people bring it all round for us and put it in the rooms. It's just shameful, I know, but I can't help thinking it's some kind of ploy." McPhee's cue to enter hot, sweaty-browed, crying out for lemonade.

"Boy?" he enquired eagerly. "Some kind of boy? He flopped down on a chair, looking up bright-eyed. "What kind of boy?"

Then, suddenly they were gone. Walter insisted there was no mystery to it. The McPhees' visitors' permits had simply expired and so they had to either leave or go through the lengthy and expensive procedure of becoming residents. I, myself, had found it relatively easy to regularise my position owing to my Dutch nationality and have, moreover, always been punctilious in such matters. I asked Walter how he had managed it. Surely any permission he had to remain must be long defunct? He smiled.

"Oh, no. It is still funct. I did it the Balinese way," he said airily. "A friend of mine has a brother who knows someone whose wife's cousin works in the Resident's office. He arranged for my file to be lost. I am the Mata Hari of Gianyar, a ghost. I do not exist in this world."

Made Tantra took their departure badly, tearfully. In farewell, he had boldly arranged for his photograph to be taken by Mr Kasimura, the photographer of Denpasar, wearing a new suit, hair brilliantined and against a painted backdrop of the Royal Palace in Amsterdam. The buttons on his jacket were retouched, by hand, in gold, before expensive framing. I had known it would all end in tears. I am seldom wrong in these matters.

There now came a period of calm with no visitors. Walter, through rubbing shoulders with McPhee, had rediscovered himself as a musician and spent hours pencilling transcriptions of the music of the shadow-plays, leaping from piano to piano and dragging the boys away from their work to discuss versions of the flowery elaborations to the main tune that might be added by improvising accompanists. They would crouch at the foot of the piano, dusters and saucepans discarded, shaking their heads, arguing and banging out alternatives and variations on instruments looted from the *gamelan*.

In the evenings, after dinner, they set a lamp in the middle of the floor and we all gathered round as at a camp fire, myself, Walter, Resem, Alit, occasionally Oleg and Conrad, sitting cross-legged in pairs. Walter had somehow found three identical copies of Grimm's fairy tales in Denpasar, translated ruthlessly into Malay and these were used to teach the boys to read, ourselves looking tutorially over their shoulders as they passed from a world of Germanic elves, gnomes and witches via one of Malay *poleng*, *jin* and *tukang sihir* to Balinese *kala*, *tonya* and *leyak* all with lengthy oral footnotes. Through their similarity to the Balinese Tantri tales, the stories formed a bridge to the hottest news as the Balinese understood it. Prompted by their texts, the boys chatted, wide-eyed of latest events. Last year a monkey-faced man had been captured near the Western forest and locked up but such misfortune had been visited on the captors that they had sent for a diviner who had told them it was one of the invisible people, *gamang*, revealed through some enchantment, who must be freed and returned to his home. They had loaded him with gifts and sent him off and now the harvest was fruitful as never before. Other terms caused difficulty. A gingerbread house was a challenging concept in the Indies. The translator had reached for the Malay *kue kukus*, "steamed cake", deftly adapted by Walter to *kue kakus*, "shithouse cake", with such facial expressions and lugubrious rolling of the tongue that the boys became hysterical. Then he started in on *aduk*, meaning "to beat a mixture" but also Balinese slang for copulation, with shameless miming of the licking of the spoon, by which point he could calm them only by driving protesting Mas from the kitchen and establish the reality of such a cake by making one on the spot. Later, Resem would lean trustingly back against my chest, chewing the hot, steamed fruit confection and resting his hand familiarly on my leg as I tapped out the awkward rhythm of a Malay sentence on his thigh. All this was, for him, totally non-sexual, since as a friend, I might touch him anywhere but his hair, which alone would be to show excessive familiarity. For me, of course, it was very far from empty of meaning. In the cold North, the slightest physical contact had brought down on my own head all the thundering interdictions of the vengeful god of the Old Testament and his prophet, Moses. Yet here, as I felt the hot firmness of his body against my flabby own, it was with a sense not of frustration but of gentle fulfilment. I suddenly realised that, since my youth, I had been having sex with people for the greater and simpler pleasure of going to bed with them and just touching the wonder of their bare and vibrant skin.

* * *

Elli Beinhorn came with the first small rains, after a blistering hot season, like a breath of fresh air. She came, like most, in Fatimah's car, but arriving with a great sideways skid and a loud klaxoning. Bagus climbed not from the driver's but the passenger's seat, ashen-faced and reknotting his sarong, his bottle well and truly shaken by the ride. At the wheel, sat a pert and delightful young woman in a white leather flying helmet and a yellow silk scarf. She gunned the engine, cut it and leapt out without bothering to open the door. In a man, such a gesture would have been distastefully cocky. In her it was quite charming. She pulled off the helmet, shook out her luscious blond hair and stepped forward, smiling, hand outstretched for shaking. "Elli Beinhorn!" I saw, heard and felt Conrad gawp and, unbidden, we formed a sort of instinctive line, as though for deferential presentation to Queen Wilhelmina, down which she then passed. Only Walter received the confident kiss of a recognised equal on the cheek. She was wearing trousers, still an exotic sexual perversity for a woman in those days – not even slacks – with a provokingly prominent button fly.

"Hallo darling! Can I stay for a bit?"

At that time, Elli Beinhorn was one of the most famous women in the world, Germany's leading aviatrix, a sort of feminised Amelia Earhardt, a figure of unbelievable glamour and a focus of male sexual yearning from schoolboys to septuagenarians. The boys went into fits of shy giggles whenever she was around and Conrad followed her about the house with a dogged, doggy devotion, inhaling her fragrant slipstream.

She had numerous adventures under her belt, had flown across Africa and Asia, thrilled and terrified crowds with aerobatics in her little Klemm aircraft and disappeared, presumed dead, in several savage places. The papers had made much of her recent return from beyond the grave in Persia, having been forced to ditch in the desert in a sandstorm and charm the fiercely uxorious tribesmen into transporting her back to civilisation by camel. She had been part of the first expedition to photograph Mount Everest from above, the honour finally going to a more powerfully engined and mustachioed American air ace, their names romantically linked, who had been nearly killed when the photographer – innocent of the laws of aerodynamics – had stood up in the plane to get his shot and sent it into a near-fatal spin.

"My plane is in Batavia," she explained huskily over dinner, "having floats fitted in the locomotive workshops for the flight down the islands to Australia. It's a complicated business. You have to find the centre of gravity of the whole machine by suspending it on cables and attach the floats at exactly the right angle, otherwise you stick to the water like glue when you try for takeoff. Last time I had it done they dropped the plane so, this time, I couldn't bear to watch and decided to see Bali instead." She leaned forward sensually over the cruet. "So, darling, what do I see?"

What she saw was a special ceremony at Besakih, the mother temple of the whole island, built on the slopes of Gunung Agung, volcanic home of the gods. From there, she had a lofty aviatrix's view of the world as the Balinese knew it and wallowed in the sensuous music, flags, flowers and stacked ceremonial offerings as Walter probed and nitpicked and etymologised inside. He and Stutterheim had an ongoing academic war over the distant history of Bali. The broad sequence was clear enough, a primordial Bali with archaic religion of sun and moon, stone megaliths, buffalo sacrifice and simple accompanying social structure such as they still had amongst the caste-free Bali Aga and the hill peoples. Of course, the fewer the facts, the thicker and firmer are the arrows of influence and migration that archaeologists can draw on their maps. He and Stutterheim had together paced the island, measuring, recording, photographing and become jointly lacrimose over the discovery of primordial pyramids. Then had come Hinduism from India and Java, intensified by the flight of nobles, artists, craftsmen from the Majapahit kingdom of Java when it fell to Islam in the fifteenth century. But where did Buddhism fit into all this and how many people were involved in the migration of an idea? Its traces were clear enough in a division of the priesthood into those of Siva and those of Bodda but this could not be easily equated with differences of doctrine or function and both would be performing, side by side, at Besakih. Oddly, Walter was always prepared to fight his way through hours of shrugging mystical obfuscation to engage such Balinese issues, exactly the sorts of doctrinal distinctions he treated with contempt in his own life.

I had known better than to accompany them on such an arid quest, especially since the sky was growling and coiling with bilious clouds the colour of gangrene, announcing the imminent downpour. If it split now and unleashed the real monsoon rains on them, the trip through the mountains would be a slithering nightmare. Instead, I busied myself with my chicks and a visiting painter from Klungkung, pinnacle of Balinese nobility and freshly returned from punitive exile, who was a master muralist and had promised to show me the techniques he was employing in the illuminated cloth panels for the ceiling of his rajah's palace of justice. He had just embarked on a depiction of the torments of the ungodly in hell and, I confess, I was a little curious to discover whether I and my kind had our place there and – if so – how we were kept occupied.

They returned late, delayed not by rain but by the local *pedanda* priest to whom Walter had offered a lift. Being of high Brahmana caste, it was a lifelong concern that his head should not be below the heads of others. This had naturally been accommodated through the provision of a deep cushion on which he might sit. Unfortunately, the Dutch administration had recently embarked on a major programme of road-building, with the creation of cuttings in which the roads might be sunk, whilst the footpaths remained along the tops of the embankments. This was an immediate threat to the priest's ritual purity and dignity so that, each time these were encountered, he had to disembark, scramble up the bank and use the high path until it rejoined the road and he the car. He was also troubled by overhead irrigation pipes. He must pass over, not under these and so the journey was wearily prolonged by several hours. Walter, to his credit, remained supremely calm and offered the priest refreshment at the house before sending him off, with Conrad as driver, to his own compound. The old man sat there in complete self-satisfaction, sipping his pink fruit crush, as Elli bustled off to bathe and change and return all smiles. "This woman," he said with slow authority, "is much prettier than that other one we had with us in the car today." Offered a tour of the gardens, he demurred, noting that the kitchen would thus be above his own head height and observed with outrage that Walter's roofs were higher than those of the old royal temple on the other bank.

"Not so," said Walter. "It is an optical illusion caused by the shape of the banks and the fact that the eye assumes that the river is level, whereas it is dropping away quite rapidly. I had Dr Goris come with his surveying equipment and he assures me that the roofs over there are fully two meters higher than my own." The old man was unconvinced, set his face firmly against all but the evidence of his eyes. When he finally left, Walter roared, tore at his hair and stood on his head for a full five minutes in refutation. The boys came and watched in amazement, laughing nervously. No Balinese could do that, only a demon. To stand on your head was to deliberately disorder the universe. The Balinese have no somersaulting acrobats.

Still the rains did not come and the weather continued like a boil that would not burst. Even the Balinese sat slumped in the shade, sweat running down their chests and hid from the sun. It was too hot and heavy to eat, too hot to sleep and no sex could have been had by anyone on the island for several weeks. We were worn and bored, Walter prostrate over the great table in desperation for a cool surface to rub his face against, speaking wildly of ice and snow and the glory of feeling cold. Conrad was outside, sitting alone on a rock in the cool river, his loins plunged into the stream, which probably met several of his needs at once. Then Resem let slip that witches were known to be dancing nightly in the overgrown graveyard a couple of miles down the road. Elli lit up. She needs must go. Please, please, Wälti. When would she ever be able to have such an opportunity again? Wasn't he curious to see which kind of dance they did? At first, Resem begged us not to. We had no idea how dangerous such creatures could be. Then, when Walter and Elli's resolve was set, he refused all entreaties and blandishments to go along as guide.

"You should listen to him, Walter," I urged. "If he was talking about rice-growing you wouldn't dismiss his knowledge so easily."

"But Elli isn't interested in rice-growing."

"Then I absolutely refuse to have anything to do with it. What would the Balinese think if they caught us creeping about in a graveyard at this time of night? *We* should be seen as witches."

Twenty minutes later we were drawing up outside the graveyard, perched – like Walter's house – between the edge of a village and a deep ravine. As we pulled up, a dog started barking, detonating the calls of other dogs that ricocheted around the village, rose to a crescendo and then died slowly away, each dog unwilling to let its rivals have the last word. "For God's sake," I said, "drive past, pull off the road and let's walk back only if it's all clear." Walter continued another twenty meters, yanked on the brake and climbed out, slipping on the gravel at the roadside and falling flat on his backside in a classic pratfall. Elli immediately exploded in giggles, Walter caught the infection and the two of them howled till they were gasping for air over the bonnet, Walter developing into a sound rather like a braying donkey.

"For God's sake," I stage-whispered. "Be quiet! You'd waken the dead." That set them off again. They teetered along the road, arms around each other like two drunks. Reluctantly I followed, not wishing to be left alone in such an eerie spot.

A Balinese graveyard is a desolate place, not the well-tended plot seen elsewhere in the archipelago, covered in low scrub and the debris of cremations with lumps of stone and wood to mark the spots where the dead await the final freeing of their souls in fire and water. It is not a place much frequented by visitors except for the witches who may come to dine there, their favourite meal being the entrails of an unborn child. The mere sight of the place seemed to sober my companions like a bucket of cold water. There were odd emanations, an unmistakable stench, a chill, mist where no mist – surely – could form at this season. Walter pointed.

"Look!" I turned, thinking it was another silly joke then caught my breath. Moving around the far end was a ball of lambent blue fire as though from the flambéd cognac of French cuisine.

"Perhaps," I suggested, "we should …"

"Come on." Walter was already through the gate and stumble-tripping towards the thing, Elli unhesitatingly in pursuit.

"Elli!" I shout-whispered. "Walter! You can't!" But nobody heeded me. The flame paused, as if considering them, then seemed to dance up and down on the spot in derision. As we neared, individual coiling flames could be clearly seen and the thing's rotation was evident. It danced back and forth, like someone trying to block your way in a corridor, then shot up a tree and disappeared. Walter paused, bemused as I panted up, having twisted my ankle rather nastily on a rock. The tree was empty. Then the thing reappeared several hundred meters off and bounced up and down again, only to vanish once more as soon as we approached. Then it seemed to come up out of the very ground a few meters to out left, shot wildly from side to side, zigzagged haphazardly away at speed and disappeared. We paused and looked at each other.

"Well," said Walter, impressed. "What do you make of that?"

"Marsh gas," said Elli. "Tell people about it and they'll just say it was marsh gas. They always do. Pilots see all sorts of things but learn to keep their mouths shut. On my way to Timbuktu, I was pursued for miles across the desert by a sheet of orange flame. Inside a cloud in Katmandu, I saw … well, I cannot tell you what I saw but I never want to see it again."

"For God's sake," I said, not liking the tone of hysteria creeping into my own voice, "what are we doing here? Let's go home. If anyone sees us here there'll be real trouble." But when we arrived back at the car, it was as if a hurricane had dumped it full of rubbish – dead branches, clods of earth, banana skins and, on top, a curious object. Walter lit a match and examined.

"A genuine German Bockwurst!" he exclaimed in wonder like a connoisseur examining fine art. "Somewhat rotten and – look – with huge tooth marks. Where on earth would anyone have got hold of one of these in a place like this at this time of night? They don't even stock them in Denpasar. You'd have to go to Batavia to find one. How would a witch know I was German and not Dutch? Even the Balinese don't know the difference. To them, we are all *Belanda*."

"How do you know it is intended for you?"

"Oh Bonnetchen, it was in the driver's seat. Oh my God, Plumpe ate these all the time, these and booze. You don't see an empty schnapps bottle do you?"

"Be serious, Walter. Why would Murnau send you a sausage from beyond the grave?"

Walter tossed it away and began throwing rubbish in all directions. "It is not a sausage but a message. From Plumpe. I don't know what it means but I can be certain he's not sending his love. Now come on, let's clear this stuff out and clear out ourselves."

* * *

The European Protestant cemetery in Denpasar was neater than the native Balinese but still at a formative stage, the vegetation more weed than shrub, parched and, as yet, insufficiently fertilised by its lean contents. The Dutch administrative presence had so far generated little custom, since the junior officials assigned there were mostly young and vigorous whereas any senior officer who expired in Denpasar would expect to be assigned space strictly appropriate to his rank at administrative headquarters back in Buleleng. I anticipated that its most significant occupant would be Mads Lange, the nineteenth-century Danish adventurer, whose machinations had delayed Dutch intrusion by more than fifty years and earned him a painful death by poison. But no. It seemed that he had only made it as far as the Chinese cemetery in Kuta. Criteria for admission here were quite strict, then. The Balinese, whose memories were blissfully undistracted by abstractions, remembered Lange mainly as the owner of an interesting orang-utang and a unique Dalmatian dog. I could not help wondering if they would fix Walter in their minds in much the same way.

Most of the mourners were Balinese – Walter, after all, had spent as little time as possible with the bureaucrats. Smits had not come, though the assistant *controleur* of Badung and a couple of the more open-minded officials engaged in the museum project had turned out in high-buttoned tunics, and were standing by the grave, sweating for their nation and the honour of white men in general. Elli – good girl that she was – knew what was required of her, though a guest of only a week's standing, and was stifling sobs in her hankie, supported by men on either side, as the white wives speculated, thin-lipped and flint-eyed, on what *exactly* had been her relationship with the deceased in that disorderly house of bachelors and hussies. The Balinese were at something of a loss, since, for many, this was the first white funeral they had attended. Because their own cremations were rather jolly affairs, they were puzzled by a public festival of depression whose only function was to make everyone infinitely more sad than they had been before. This, moreover, had been a bad death, one that in their own world brought pollution and threat yet no one here seemed to be concerned with averting that danger. Instead of wild, hammering music, there had been a mournful wailing, as of demons, before the unfamiliar groaning organ. One or two had been totally unnerved and crept quietly away. Instead of whirling processions, there had been standing about and talk and it was clear that even the white men themselves did not seem to know quite what they were supposed to be doing. The eulogy – delivered bleatingly by an annoyed-looking Dutch Reform minister – had seemed to be about someone totally unknown to me, a solid citizen snatched from the jaws of married respectability and regular employment only by his untimely death. Later, instead of general feasting, there would be horribly evocative cold meats served at the Little Harmonie Club – Europeans inside, natives on the lawn, mingling strictly limited to the no man's land of the verandah. And the problem of dress remained unresolved. Agung and his retinue had opted for the white of death and their finest jewels, standing under their umbrellas like a rehearsal for a *puputan* mass suicide. Natives in government service had chosen the black favoured by Dutchmen while those of more divided loyalties sported the black and white chequerwork of traditional *poleng* cloth about their waists. Traders had favoured loose, silk pyjamas. Oleg, Resem and Alit had turned events into an occasion for a visit to a man with a sewing machine in Denpasar and agonised deliciously for hours over the choice of shorts or long trousers, buttonholes and lapels. The resulting over-tailored outfits made them look like three pimps from Buleleng. Putting everyone else to shame was the old man who watered Walter's plants. He had simply bathed and walked down from the hills, wearing the same sarong he always wore, barefoot and barechested. Unintimidated by those around him, in his simplicity, he trod the grass like a master of the earth. Meanwhile, Mr Kasimura, the Japanese photographer, himself unversed in Dutch ritual, was hopefully erecting his camera tripod for the companionable photographs around the coffin that would surely be requested. As we watched the plain wooden box lowered into the torn earth, the rains finally broke with a crack of thunder – dramatically most effective – and hosed us down thoroughly. Plumpe would have approved.

Back at the Harmonie, I needed a stiff drink. It came with another ferreting priest, Father Robert Scruple, lurking at the bar, an expert on the more extreme heresies of the early church, now appointed to a roving commission about the Eastern Sees and here to press the Dutch to revoke their interdiction on missionary activity in Bali. Earlier baptisms had led to canny converts refusing to pay their dues for village activities, since all assumed the participation of the local gods, and they had finally been chased away like lepers amidst great ill-feeling. Not only had this caused public disorder, it also undermined the efficient system of traditional local government that saved the Dutch endless bother. I had read at length about Father Scruple in the local paper. He sported ecclesiastical black so immaculate that it glowed with a sort of well-brushed halo and he would shortly produce a report declaring the natives to be panting for the evangelisation so brutally denied by law, which convinced no one, not even the Dutch who were often only too willing to be convinced by implausible reports. He was still bristling at the indignity of having a trunkful of Bibles impounded by beachside Buleleng customs officials as "contraband literature", a term normally applied to works of political sedition and pornography. He sipped neat scotch with economical little swigs.

"The deceased, that poor young man, I gather you were a friend?" It seemed the pastoral position was habitual. He could smell out a lost soul as a sheepdog would a lost sheep or perhaps simply spot the weakest and most vulnerable in a flock as would a wolf. The accent was a curious mixture, part Italian, part Australian. I nodded. "Was he of the faith?"

I could not resist a smile, recalling Walter's usage of the expression. "Er … living where he did, it was impossible for him to attend church regularly but he was of a spiritual turn of mind."

Father Scruple's eyes gleamed behind their round lenses. This was not an answer. If there was any logic-chopping or evasion to be done around here, he, as a trained man of the cloth, should be the one doing it.

"You seem to be telling me that he was a most Christian atheist. He died unshriven, then? Answer me that, if you will."

"There was no time … It was so fast … He was not one for

formalities. But he was a good man, I would almost say that, in some ways he was almost a saintly man. Look, I'm no expert in such matters, unlike yourself, but his soul, I'm sure, was relatively pure – few sins of commission, maybe a few light ones of emission."

"I think you would mean 'omission'."

"Possibly so. As I say, I am no expert."

He settled a well-shod foot on the bar rail, at his ease in such places, in such postures. Behind me I heard a voice say, "Awkward business. I'm afraid the German reputation smells rather round here at the moment. It was that woman the Countess he sent down. She played a lot of whist and cheated rather badly. She tried it on with the *controleur* so we had to run her out of town."

"How exactly did it come about?"

I sighed, not wanting to go through it all again but perhaps the grace of a spiritual confession might prove efficacious even to as Protestant a soul as my own. My glass was shaking in my hand. God knows, I was in clear need of purgation of all this poisonous emotion.

"It was mid-afternoon and we had all decided to go for a swim. He chose the place himself, near Lebih, on the east coast. The sand is wonderful there and he had always loved the spot for the little temple of coral rock that runs down into the sea."

Father Scruple nodded grimly. "The innocent are frequently misled into confusing the merely romantic and theatrical for the truly spiritual."

I wasn't having that. "Precisely – I think – what Martin Luther used to say about the Roman church. You know people believe that whole area of Insaran is full of magic and witchcraft and is anyway too close to the island of Nusa Penida where the dead go and where epidemics come from. It is where Ratu Gede Mecaling, the demon king, lands every year, *bringing* famine and pestilence to Bali."

He smiled, a professional in the presence of an amateur. "Superstition. Superstition. My son. I beg you to remember my cloth and the terrible, insane delusions you are casting upon it."

"... Anyway, we arrived and parked and got changed." In fact, we had just thrown off our clothes like innocent children and run, laughing, straight into the sea but I would not offer him such an easy target for his disapproval. "We had not gone any distance, only up to our knees in the water. Elli – Fräulein Beinhorn – called out and asked whether there were any sharks and he laughed and said yes and started clowning and splashing about and then he just dived under. We thought it was all play and laughed too and then his head reappeared and he was screaming and the sea was all red and the look on his face ..." I paused and gulped breath. "We rushed over and grabbed him and then ... realised he was horribly light ..." I tried to drink and the glass castanetted against my teeth and sloshed down my shirt. I rested it on the polished bartop "... there was this great fin and it – the shark – came straight for me and rubbed against my leg as it passed with this great thrust of its tail." I shuddered, feeling again the insinuating silkiness of its touch, the kid-gloved caress of death. "We dragged him to the shore and we were screaming too. One leg was completely gone and the hand on that side and fingers on the other. You could see bare bone stripped to the knee, all white. We told the family that he lost consciousness at once and never suffered but it wasn't true. He just lay there and screamed and screamed." The glass in my hand was splashing little waves of whisky and clicking against the bar. Father Scruple took it gently from my grasp and set it down. My voice was getting loud. I was making a scene. I didn't care.

"Elli drove the car like a demon. We brought him to the hospital at Denpasar though we knew it was no good. What else could we do? It seemed to take hours and all the time he was still screaming." I sobbed. "Thank God the doctor was on duty. They gave him something for the pain and put him in a cool bed and he quietened and after a little while he stopped breathing altogether and it was all over. All over. We just felt relief, cowardly, I know. There was no blood, even in the car, he had bled out. There was no hope."

"There is always hope my son. We must never give way to the sin of despair." A mere ecclesiastical reflex. He sipped, clearly not despairing or at least not giving way to it.

"But you see he knew. He *knew*."

"Knew what, my son?"

"It was as if he had conjured up the monster, as if it came straight from his own imagination with the sole purpose of devouring him. A few days before, Walter turned up with this *balian*, a diviner." I saw him prick up his ears at the familiar heretical territory. "You know how they are, wild hair, muttering, that odd sackcloth outfit. You know they don't often predict the future? Their speciality is predicting the past, picking out something forgotten from before that is having bad consequences now. Walter was doing research, as always, and, when it got to divination and horoscopes, this man surprised everyone by accepting Walter's challenge to tell the future. He got out his calendars and the rest of the stuff and read off our destinies." Scruple hissed, recognising the old enemy, and gripped the cross about his neck. "He did us all, even the boys. He said the sea would take us. The boys laughed at that because, as you know, the ashes of all Balinese end up in the sea anyway. Then he said Elli and I would lead very long lives to make up for the others in the household who would die young. That shut them up, I can tell you – except Walter – 'Ars brevis vita longa est, eh Bonnetchen?' That night he had a nightmare and woke up the entire house with his screams." Screams, screams, I couldn't even stand the word any more. "They found him standing by the bedroom door staring at the image of Kala Rahu carved on it." Father Scruple frowned, resenting the unfamiliar theology. "Kala Rahu is a demon who got hold of the gods' drink of immortality and took a gulp but had its head cut off before the potion could reach its stomach. It hops around on one leg with enormous teeth and, for revenge, eats the moon at eclipses – oh my God." I saw teeth, blood and darkness. I saw the scene from Walter's film where the cackling witch – this time toothless – eclipses the sun. A tremor started, shaking me from head to foot and I had to grip the bar.

Father Scruple waved his manicured finger in admonition. "These are not things to be trifled with, young man. Divine foreknowledge is not a party trick. I see your immortal soul thrust into deadly danger here. The devil often wears a comely face as amongst these deluded and shameless brown souls. You should get down on your knees and pray, ask for forgiveness, leave this heathen island and return to Christian lands – myself, I have a great fondness for Melbourne where my sister Edna lives but you may have other ideas – where you can restore your soul and free yourself of the enchantment I have seen in this place where priests are not allowed to be about their work of salvation." He sprayed angry saliva like holy water.

"I'm sorry," I said. "It's only since I got here that I have discovered that I have a any soul at all and as for shameless, the Balinese are completely shameful – er, ashamed … er … full of shame."

A hand fell on my shoulder. I turned. "I have been telling him what happened. I'm sorry. I know I'm making a scene when it must be even worse for you."

Walter smiled sadly and gently. "Poor Conrad," he said. "We won't ever forget him. He is now part of Bali for all time. As for the rest of us, it is already too late and I think we will never leave this place. In its way, it is eating us all up, little by little, maybe as freewilling victims." He brightened. "But there is the carver outside I would like you to meet, from Batubulan. He has a version of Kala Rahu for poor Kosja's headstone with a most unusual use of perspective. A Balinese design on a Christian headstone. Imagine! Something new. Very exciting. The only problem is whether the techniques developed on soft volcanic rock can be easily applied to granite." He raised a finger as an idea struck him. "Perhaps it might make a good exercise for your chicks, Bonnetchen." Turning. "Please excuse us Father."

Father Scruple blazed disapproval and extended his hand petulantly, ring raised intimidatingly for kissing. Walter smiled politely and shook it with a formal and very secular click of the heels.

10

The motion pictures had not been a great success in Bali. At first it was thought that this was because the Dutch and English captions on the screen could not be understood by the natives and they had been replaced by Malay. The small number who spoke, let alone read, the language defeated this. So someone was paid to stand in front and deliver a shouted soundtrack in Balinese, over the thundering of the piano, played by a muscular and competitive Dutch lady. In time, this performer developed his art and attained an almost complete independence from the original storyline, inventing freely, transforming tragedies into low comedies so that heroines would be cast out into the incomprehensible snow to the accompaniment of roars of Balinese laughter and "Hearts and Flowers". Thus, irony was introduced to the Balinese. But the whole ambience was hostile to the idiom of local performing arts, where plays went on all night but were known in advance from a hundred previous tellings and required only flickering attention. Spectators would wander in and out, have loud conversations, cook snacks, engage in dalliance, breastfeed their families and, of course, pay nothing at all for the privilege. Art did not interrupt the maelstrom of life.

It was for such reasons that the picturehouses in Denpasar and Buleleng catered nowadays for a largely European audience, yet an enterprising and innovative Armenian, Mr Minas, had not let matters lie there. Seeing a gap in the market, he had bought a lightweight Japanese projection system, loaded it onto bicycles, ridden by coolies, and taken it around the villages where they set up under the immemorial *waringin* trees of the marketplace. A bedsheet was spread, the acetylene lamp was lit and the film projector turned by relays of pedalling legs. There was no spot on the island too remote to be visited by Minas and his minions and they relied, for their living, entirely upon the Balinese sense of shame. Curiosity, the boredom of village life, above all the lure of ancient and familiar Charlie Chaplin films enticed people into the market. After a brief taster to fire the appetite, the hat would be passed around before the main programme and no one risked the public scandal of giving absolutely nothing. The setting, the relaxed ambience, the absence of formal payment, all conspired to make these visits acceptable to the Balinese mind and gradually Charlie Chaplin became the only famous film star on the island.

It was a shock, born of his celebrity, that he had a dumpy younger brother called Sidney who – constantly facemopping – could nor stand the heat.

"Christ Charlie, it's hotter here than a fried fanny. I fought California was bad enough but this is drivin' me mental." He was filming us with one of the new compact cine-cameras though we were doing nothing but sitting on the verandah away from the afternoon sun. Syd was someone who filmed everything. A camera in his hand was like a dummy in his mouth.

"Please, not that word." In his childhood, Charlie's mother had been locked up in the madhouse, he and Syd in the poorhouse. His melodramatic plots were plucked from life. "Stop thinking about it, Syd. Go and sit in Walter's lovely river. Go and *drink* Walter's lovely river. Think cool thoughts. That's what Pola Negri used to tell me most mornings about two o' clock when the old devil stirred."

Charlie was urbane, in silk shirt – unbuttoned at the throat – and slacks, perfectly groomed and manicured like his vowels. The face was young for his forty-odd years but the hair – lovingly marcelled – pure white. Hollywood gossip, i.e. Plumpe, said that it had turned overnight during the vicious divorce from Lita Grey, married at sixteen and divorced a few years later with a sensational settlement of over $800,000 and a million in costs. Young girls were Charlie's undoing. He bore it like a cross.

"I'm sorry about Murnau," said Charlie, sipping guava juice. "He was a great talent. There aren't that many great talents in Hollywood. I know you were friends – more than friends. I've been asked to write something – you know – a whatsit, a review – eulogy – for the trade mags. He didn't get on with the studios." Splashing and groans from downstairs. I started. Syd was swimming down there – wallowing – somewhere out of sight. There were no sharks in rivers.

"Do you have problems with the studios?" Walter, a fellow professional, coolly swapping experiences.

"Not any more. I've been lucky enough to get control. Syd may not look much but he's a business genius. This thing I've just finished, City Lights, I did the script, acted, directed, produced and now wrote the score. But the bastards never leave you alone. You know all those old films I made in the Tramp costume? They have this new trick of recutting and remixing and releasing them as new films and I don't get zilch. Those bastards would suck the marrow from your bones. That's why Fairbanks. Pickford, Griffiths and I set up United Artists."

"That's interesting," mused Walter. "You see that's exactly the same method the Balinese use to compose new works of music. No one gets royalties there either."

I interrupted hastily. "You never wanted to do talkies, Mr Chaplin?" I was, I confess, something of a doting fan. I wanted to ask for an autograph. Walter would kill me. Charlie shook his head.

"Words are for lawyers. That's what they argue over and argue in. Have you ever noticed that the most important communication is never done in words? It's all in our eyes and in our faces. A guy doesn't have to say he loves a girl. It's just that, till he puts it in words, it's not legally binding. He sang in a good tenor voice:-

> "I can't forget
> when we first met
> Beneath the starry skies
> But most of all
> I would recall
> The magic of your eyes."

A corny, lacrimose little tune.

"I just wrote that. Singing in movies is fine but talking lowers them, brings them closer to the everyday. It'd be as stupid as putting a commentary over one of those Balinese dances Walter's so crazy about."

Walter shifted uncomfortably. He had done just that in his *kecak*. From downstairs came a strained voice in Syd's joke falsetto.

> Beautiful eyes
> What have they seen to make them so beautiful?
> Wonderful eyes
> What have they dreamed to make them so wonderful?
> Sorrowful eyes
> What have they seen to make them so sorrowful?
> Beautiful wonderful eyes.

Charlie laughed as Alit entered, unbidden – flashing a smile at the world with beautiful wonderful eyes – and served crisp rice crackers, smoking hot from the wok of Mas in the kitchen. Charlie watched the fine triangle of his back as he strolled away. "It's fantastic, the way they move. Like they're all on roller skates". He was, I recalled, an afficionado of the roller skate. "People in the West don't move like that. Maybe once they did. Now everybody slouches like I do in my pictures after I've lost the girl. They've had the crap beaten out of them. You've not been back since the Crash, Walter. Things are bad – really bad – you can't imagine. There are four million unemployed. Last year 20,000 people killed themselves. Soup lines, bread queues, little starving kids in the snow with no shoes and their arses hanging out. In Oklahoma people are *selling* their kids. Next they'll be eating them." He crunched happily on his snack. "Here everybody gets one square meal a day and has a place to sleep. I used to think things had moved on since my childhood in the East End. Now I wonder. Like I said to Churchill, Lloyd George, Ramsay MacDonald, there must be a better way. Maybe the Russians are right."

Walter choked on his juice. "I was there for the Russian Revolution." He made it sound like a first night. "The bloodshed was horrible, people behaving like beasts. The solution to politics is never more politics. Look at the Balinese. They sort out their affairs with their neighbours, each man on his own land, in peace and co-operation. There are no politicians here."

Charlie nodded. "You may be right. I've talked to the world's greatest economists, the US President. They say it's the gold standard. We've got to get off the gold standard and cut the cost of credit so the working stiff can get the decent life he's entitled to. I met Gandhi in London in some tiny terraced hellhole of a house down the East End – extraordinary little thing wrapped in a bedsheet. He said he wanted to drive industrialisation out of India and I said he was crazy. You can't put back the clock. He said that was exactly what he intended to do since it was machines that made India dependent on the West and the worst machine of all was the clock. Once India regained total, real independence, it could have the machines back on its own terms."

Walter sighed happily. They had reached consensus. He had become Balinese. He needed at least the pretence of consensus before he could draw a line and move on. "And now," he said, "a treat – *legong*. Coming Bonnetchen?"

I groaned. Those little girls. Not again. "I have things to do." I would sketch Alit. I remembered those eyes - what was it? Beautiful, wonderful? More seriously, Alit's knees still challenged me to the core of my artistic being. I could not rest until I cracked them.

The next morning I came to take my coffee. Walter's was, after all, by far the best and cheapest restaurant in Ubud. A softly tinkling piano could be heard from upstairs, constantly repeating the same phrase with occasional crashes and oaths. I recognised the sound of musical composition. Alit came in smiling, knotting his bright new sarong. It was a really good one, finest Yogya *batik*, swirling with birds and plants. Walter – I knew – would have been over there identifying the various species whereas I simply took in the beauty of the general pattern. Alit twirled for me to admire. I admired.

"Coffee, *Tuan*?"

"Coffee."

As I drank, Walter came up from the garden clutching orchids for the house, purple, white, yellow, one tiger-striped.in red.

"How did it go last night?" I asked.

"Fine. We went to Peliatan. Charlie loved the dance. Syd filmed it." He dropped his voice. "Did you know when they were in England they shared the favours of the same girl – their secretary? No wonder she got behind with the mail. Extraordinary, the things one learns. At the end of the dance, Charlie asked me whether the girls were 'available' like the girls in Tahiti." He dumped the flowers with all the self-righteous effort of an oppressed coalminer emptying his barrow.

"What did you say?"

"I said that, if he could decide right away which one he wanted to marry, I would open negotiations with the parents and, as soon as she started menstruating, we could move on to the next stage. That cooled him down a bit and then I felt guilty. So I said that really wasn't my area of expertise and he should go and talk to Le Mayeur." He pushed his hair out of his eyes and looked like a little boy ready for parental rebuke. I refused to play that game.

"What's the plan for today?"

"Before he goes anywhere near that old poseur, Le Mayeur, I have something he will want to see." He took my hand, me now the wayward child, and led me over to the space by the door where his new works acclimatised before being cast into the world. "There!"

It was not my cup of tea, of course, but there was an unmistakable magical – again childlike – quality about it that moved me. I felt aquisitiveness stir within me. This was a large painting for Walter. He had returned to his more metaphysical style, two interpenetrating worlds vertically stacked. In the upper sat a young man in red loincloth – surely those were Alit's face and the sinuous knees masterfully shown – but the body artificially stretched and tautened by the effort of firing a bow and arrow down into water that became the sky of a lower world. I recognised the stylisation of the Persian miniatures he had once painted on the wall of Murnau's Berlin villa. Below, lay the deer he had transfixed with his fatal arrow and below that the same creature frisking anew. Around and about one of Walter's jungles, at the same time adumbrated but precise, glowing with greens and yellows.

"When did you paint this?" He bit his lip.

"It was after Kosja's death. There was too much death about. I had to get it all out. I call it 'deer-hunting'." I felt tears in my eyes. It was impossible not to see it as a poignant statement about death and renewal. I sensed the torsion of the hunter in my own chest, the gasp of the expiring deer in my own throat. Walter twirled it casually in his hand. For Walter, like the Balinese, an object was only sacred if the spirit was in it, otherwise it was just wood and canvas, a dead thing. He leaned it against the table leg, at a deliberately casual angle.

"Charlie!" he called and set off up the stairs, beckoning me after.

He was seated at the Steinway, cigarette in an ashtray, trailing smoke like an incense stick, the face relaxed with real colour in it, hair flopping over his brow perhaps in emulation of Walter. On the piano top lay precious, now besmirched, music paper and a pen.

"A man could work in a place like this," he cried with unexpected relish. "Do you realise I went out last night and no one knew who I was, no crowds, no mobs, no cameras? People don't recognise me from the screen – of course, with the makeup and wig and costume, that's always impossible. What gives me away all the time is the pictures of me they keep putting in the newspapers. Here, there are no newspapers and one of the natives said I couldn't be Charlie Chaplin. I haven't got a moustache." He grinned Walterishly, stood up and walked to the parapet, looking down on the river and breathing deeply, sucking Bali, leisure, freedom into his lungs, stretching his arms. "Do you know, I once entered a Charlie Chaplin Lookalike Contest in Santa Monica and only came third. A thing like that saps a man's confidence."

Walter slid onto the stool in his place and accompanied his gestures with Grieg's "Morning", played very camply. "I don't think I mentioned," he said, "that when I first came to Java, the only way I could earn a living was by playing the piano in the cinema. I must have spent whole days looking up at Charlie Chaplin on the screen and expressing you in music." Charlie cakewalked towards the piano. Walter matched him step by step with "Felix Kept On Walking". Charlie stopped. Walter stopped. Charlie set off darting in all directions, switching, changing and Walter banged out "The Flight of the Bumblebee".

"Did I mention, Walter, that in England I went to see the king?" He plodded gravely, hands behind his back. Walter struck up the British national anthem. "Then I went to Paris." Gershwin's "American in Paris," as illustrated by Miguel. "Then Spain." Flamenco chords stamped out with stiff fingers. "Whilst in San Sebastian, I went to a bullfight." He parried invisible bulls with a cape. Walter blasted out stripped-down "Carmen". Charlie stood still and Walter immediately subsided into the undulating introduction to the big aria, rocking back and forth between repetitions of the phrase. "There is a restaurant in the bullring there that they took me to," he declaimed in mock-Shakespearean actorish. "The famous dish is the bhull's bhalls ..." He gestured artfully from the groin.. Walter punctuated with chords. "Roasted on skewers and I had to eat them, of course. They were so good that, the next day I went back. But the dish was completely different. The balls were small and dry and flavourless. So I summoned the waiter and asked him what had happened. 'Is easy, senor,' he said. 'Today the bull *he win!*' Walter *boom-boomed* two big chords. Charlie flung up his arms, blew kisses to the crowd, rushed forward to rising chords, backwards to descending, received invisible flowers copiously bestowed, coyly bowed and backed slowly – overwhelmed – off the stage to something schmalzy by Chopin and ran, finally, flutteringly, down the stairs to one of Schumann's "Kinderszenen".

Walter stood up from the piano and looked me in the eye, held up his finger, counting. "One, two, three." A clatter and an oath followed by silence from downstairs. Then ...

"Walter?" Charlie reappeared, breathless, clutching the painting, holding it out at arm's length. His face glowed. "Is this one of yours? Have you just finished it? You must let me buy it. Please! It's fantastic. I need to have it on my wall so when I go crazy I can see that there's one sane place in all the world."

"Well ..." Walter made the face of a man wrestling with simultaneous constipation and haemerrhoids. "I wasn't really thinking of selling that one but ... for you, Charlie ..."

Charlie was revived, electrified. I thought of myself all those years ago in Italy, slowly thawing in the sun. That night the men from the local *gamelan* came to rehearse and, in honour of the famous guest, performed their *baris* in full costume. Amidst the swelling and dying of the music, they danced in perfect synchronisation, arms up, elbows crooked, fingers windmilling – three white-faced figures, their dilated eyes and corked mustaches a sort of tribute to the Little Tramp. At the end of it Charlie, like the rest of us, leapt up and applauded. Then he slipped into the space before them, inhaled and gathered himself.

Charlie, of course, had never seen a *baris* in his life, let alone danced one. Yet he assumed a caricature of the pose with the unerring accuracy of one of Miguel's cartoons. Feet, elbows hands, eyes popping with terror not art, the crouched posture – everything was perfect. The actual steps had nothing of the military movements of the original – I seemed to recall them from one of his films, an ingratiating dance of courtship performed on ice – maybe he had even married that girl as so many others – but the Balinese loved it. After two or three steps, the drummer leapt for his instrument and brought the musicians in with the wild thundering beat of the introduction and they dropped cigarettes and seized their hammers and began the theme, a simple crashing up and down the scales, laughing and swaying. After a couple of minutes, Charlie became so outrageously flirtatious in his movements that they threw down the hammers, slapped their thighs and applauded, hiding their blushing faces behind each others' backs. Never one to let a crowd go when had them in his hand, Charlie moved on, gave them his "Animal Trainer" song, a music-hall number about a circus trainer laid low by the vicissitudes of life and reduced to running a flea circus:

> I found one but I won't say where
> And educated him with care
> And taught him all the facts of life
> And then he found himself a wife
> I give them board and lodging free
> And every night they dine off me
> They don't eat caviar or cake
> But they enjoy a good rump steak
> Off my anatomy
> It is an odd sensation
> When after meals they take a stroll
> Around the old plantation

I thought Walter would die under the burden of translation, so many of these concepts being unfamiliar to the audience, but he wisely followed the example of the Balinese film narrators and adjusted the original to fit the world he was in. It was, he explained, a song about a man who borrowed his good friend's clothes only to discover he had fleas. Charlie's grimacing and desperate embarrassed clutching at various parts of his anatomy had the required effect and they were soon helpless with laughter. Then the boys brought rice, chicken, fish roasted in banana leaves, palm toddy and spread them before us so that soon we were all sprawled on the floor – the boys too – eating and laughing and exuding a goodwill and happiness that lay beyond language. Syd filmed with grim determination, a stogie glued to his lower lip, as though gathering evidence for a lawsuit. It was typical that Charlie was concerned about the dancers.

"What do I do, Walter? Should I slip them a few bucks? Should I give something to the drummer? Should I pay the dancers more? Should …"

"Give each man one dollar when they leave, to show a little gratitude and respect. This is not," – was he aping my own prissy voice? – "a commercial transaction."

Syd flopped down beside us exuding a fat man's sweat.

Charlie poked him affectionately in the ribs. "We are facing lean times, Walter. The world is going through a bad moment." He expertly excised a comic film-prop fish-head-and-skeleton from the roasted flesh and lay it aside. Balinese would later seize that rejected head as the best part. "The modern age is coming after us all. Democracy is a luxury. Stay here, keep a low profile till we can afford it again. But that won't be soon. Maybe you will get away with it and the bastards will pass you by. Whatever … I'm coming back here," Charlie said fiercely, spooning rice. "Next year I want three months here. Einstein was right. Keep it simple. I met him in Germany, lived in some crappy cold-water walk-up apartment. Took them some flowers, they didn't have a vase. Put daisies on the dinner table in a jam jar. I asked him if he kept a notebook to jot down, impressions, ideas. I do. You know, the way a cat stretches, the motion of a falling leaf, the idea for a ballet where each dancer would be a single cog and they'd all fit together to make a machine, phrases – 'dance is thought made free' – that kind of thing. 'Ideas?' he said. 'But I only ever had one!' He maintained the greatest joy in his life was not mathematics but Mrs Einstein's cherry tart."

Charlie went to bed with his whole being atingle, the entire orchestra shuffling off up the road in single file, silhouetted against the moon, hands on each others' shoulders and waddling in imitation of his famous pigeon-toed walk. Penguins really but, of course, Balinese have not heard about penguins, which makes the gesture neither better nor worse. Perhaps, in years to come, another new dance will come out of it. We never really know what seed we sow or when.

* * *

"This is *not*," Walter said primly, "a hotel." He had to shout to be heard above the noise of the new rooms being constructed. Plumpe's money and the cash from Charlie's painting had sparked an expansive phase.

"Right," I said. "There are guests and they pay to stay here and eat here but it's not a hotel."

Walter wagged his finger triumphantly. "It has no fixed tariff. Hotels charge so much per night, so much per cup of coffee, so much per glass of beer. There is a written bill with taxes. Here we are not like that. I prefer it if people pay what they best think. It is more a voluntary donation. Some people," he pointed out, "like the Countess and yourself, pay nothing at all. The McPhees are not being charged." They had returned out of the blue, unexpectedly resolved to settle and commissioned Walter to build them a Campuhan-style compound a few miles up the road in Sayan, no expense spared. It was an amazing site, standing on a bold ridge and looking down over the river some 150 terraced meters below, with neatly rising ranges of mountains behind and they visited it almost daily on the horses that otherwise kicked their hooves against the walls of the new stable out back. Walter was in his element, spending someone else's money lavishly on bringing his own ideas to fruition. The rooms were to be scattered at various levels over the site, with all sorts of artful features. There would be a dance studio and a minstrels' gallery, God knew what else. After Charlie's bullring story there might be one of those too. Oh they were paying all right.

"Oh my," declared Jane. "Poor Colin is sooo frustrated. When he asks about the house, they say it is the wrong time for cutting grass for the roof, and there will be no cement for the floor till the end of the year when the sailing ships head back from Borneo with the monsoon, and the bamboo has to dry for nine months before you can use it and you can't do this because the wood has to be used the same way up as it grows and you can't do that because everything has to be an odd number. He was so pleased yesterday when he found they'd got this big room up and watertight and then they said no that was only the house for the workmen to live in once they got started on ours. They can't even break the soil till one of those priests has checked the calendar and found the right time and then there have to be the right offerings." She stuck her fingers in her hair, both sides, and pulled it out into dog's ears. "Aaargh! Colin's no help. He's spending days interviewing the staff. We have twelve so far in matching sarongs. They look so cute! And we have three secretaries alone, including Made Tantra. But I have no idea what all those boys are going to be doing."

At night McPhee took over Walter's kitchen. In Paris, he had been seized by a sudden passion for cooking and taken *cordon bleu* instruction so that he and Walter now embarked on a sustained zoological culinary quest, exploring the flora and fauna with their teeth. They filleted, diced, marinated, puréed and steamed and porcupine fricassée, hornbill goulash, anteater casserole all graced our table. The number of animals about the place had crept slowly beyond that which was tolerable. This campaign reduced them to a more reasonable substratum population defined by its inedibility.

"The offerings have been made. The ground has been broken. Tomorrow we start building!" McPhee over his flying fox and mushroom pie.

Walter made his crooked face. "It needs more chilli. Some zing extra. Tomorrow? Er, I don't think so. It's only a few days till *galungan* when the ancestors come back for a visit. Everything stops for *galungan*, Colin."

"Does it last all day?"

Walter choked. "All week, two weeks really. Then in ten days you have the next holiday of *kuningan*. We shan't see much of the boys for a bit, I'm afraid, they'll all expect to go home. It's no good fretting. Even if you threatened to fire them, they would still rather go home. That's why the Dutch prefer regular Javanese domestics. So just smile, wish them a good time and maybe give them a little extra for the journey. You, after all, have red hair, like a Balinese demon. If you want to be a good demon, you have to try harder or all sorts of stories will get out about you."

In preparation for the visit of our ancestors, the kitchen was re-equipped with new utensils and baskets and we all dressed in our best. Walter alone disdained Balinese costume, not out of pride but rather humility.

"You see how terrible Westerners look in such dress, like Balinese in shirts and shorts. Our proportions are all wrong." I had thought I looked rather nice.

The townspeople had decked the streets with artfully pendant *penjors*, long bendy bamboo poles with frilly decorations on the ends, that converted every passage into a triumphal arch. Each region, sometimes each hamlet, had its own style and there was fierce competition to be more beautiful, more elaborate than one's neighbours. The focus of Walter's interest were the *lamaks*, geometric representations of a mysterious female figure – das Ewig-Weibliche, according to both Walter and Goethe – made by pinning together contrasting green and yellow leaves of the sugar palm. The result is a beautiful fluttery creation half a meter wide but eight or nine meters long, hung from the coconut palms, or altars or rice-granaries. Their evanescent beauty is doomed to wither in a single day and be thrown away. Walter had been drawing them for years, had hundreds of designs tucked away, but somehow always recognised a new variation. There was talk of publishing a book of them. "This," he remarked, rapidly sketching on gripped pad, "is the reason why I have doubts about the museum plan. Balinese art is not supposed to be eternal like Western art, but falling apart, included in the natural cycle of things. Yet, I suppose, I sketch butterflies and dragonflies for natural history museums, that may live but a few short days and that is much the same." He shrugged.

At the cross roads was a *Barong*, the masked mythical creature that is the sworn enemy of Rangda, the witch, and most closely resembles the Chinese dragon, though the Balinese lack of literalness allows it to come indifferently in several incarnations as a lion or a pig. It was frisking and capering happily, clapping its wooden jaws to the marching *gamelan* that accompanied it. The two men inside seemed to communicate by some means that allowed synchronised footwork at front and rear. The temples had all been cleaned and decorated, were heavy with incense and flowers, offerings and fruit and feasts and festivals were on offer all over the island, Walter's presence ensuring we were welcome everywhere. In Gelgel we witnessed ancient plays whose end was marked by men going into fierce trance and turning their *krises* on their own bare – but mystically protected – flesh as they tore at live chickens with their teeth in the clouds of stamped-up dust. In the cool, jungle *pura* of Batukau, ancient royal temple of the kingdom of Tabunan, we watched serene offerings made to the gentle spirit of the lake beneath the fanned tree-ferns and afterwards a stately and disdainful *baris* executed with long spears. It was here that I realised that henceforth, *baris* dancers will always seem, to me, to be imitating Charlie.

At the time of *kuningan*, we made a pilgrimage to the watery temple of Tampaksiring, where Soekarno would later build his sacrilegious bungalow of a Ruhr industrialist above the gushing spring. Here had been shot the scenes of male and female nude bathing so scandalously cut into the end of Walter's film and I have no doubt that Soekarno, always a dirty-minded man, was, in due course, spryly active at the window with his binoculars. On his own, I know, Walter would have been in there with the water worshippers but Jane's presence made him oddly abashed. Later, the local *Barong* came snorting down the hill and cast bathers into a trance by the power of its presence and Jane annoyed the dazed victims by her pedantic questioning that – both intrusive and remote – recalled that of the therapist. "And just what word would you use for that? Uhhuh. And when you say that word how does it make you feel? Really? Oh my." Scribbling, scribbling. She was always scribbling.

***

I was hot and unhappy and regretted bitterly coming along on what was only conceivably a treat for a simple-minded anthropologist. The branches were cleared to the height of the heads of the Balinese, which was about my shoulder, so that they kept slapping back and hitting me in the face. The bees were driving me crazy settling around my eyes to drink up the sweat. I should have stayed at home and worked up one of a series of sketches I was doing on bare-breasted women of the market. The village was a good fifteen minutes' walk – Walter-walk not that of a human being – from the motor road where we had left Jane's Chevvy.

There were at least a dozen places where she could see her kris-dancing and go through her questions on trance and possession but no, it had to be Pagutan. I knew, of course, exactly why it had to be Pagutan – because of Rawa. About thirty, skin light and smooth, tall for a Balinese, staggeringly handsome with his black hair unfashionably long, magnificent chest and thighs – a firm favourite of Walter's – Rawa. Of course, Rawa was the local ladies' man, a great climber over compound walls after dark, father it was alleged, of half the beautiful children in the village, his own foaming sperm hosing away that of skinny, weakling, ugly rivals. "Waste of a good man," Walter had stated, headshaking. The thought of seeing Rawa, alone, kept my feet moving through the evanescent dusk. He was, I realised with sudden sad insight, what Luigi would have grown to be. And then we came out onto the space before the temple and there he was, muscular arms folded over bare chest, a sarong of virginal white, short even for a Balinese sarong, matching immaculately tied headcloth. I cleaned my sweaty glasses. He was dressed to act as a priest this evening then but, even so, Rawa liked the ladies to see what they did not need to go on missing. His smile of welcome glowed equally white through the gloom. He shook hands. He liked shaking hands, and now that he had mastered the gesture, he did it every fifteen minutes or so.

"Tuan Walter. Tuan Rudi." His hot eyes rested on Jane. He had not had one of those yet. He swept forward and set his smiling face endearingly at an angle as does a puppy. "*Nyonya*." The voice was husky and seared like the baking inland winds of the hot season. Walter slipped his arm around Rawa's consenting shoulders and they moved off to arrange the performance of the evening, the usual conflict between good Barong and evil Rangda. What interested Jane most, of course, were the points at which performers went into trance, either as performers or, at the end, when the men, having failed to kill Rangda, turned their daggers against themselves in *nguruk*. The advantages of doing it here were that Rawa was reliable as a middleman, the dancers excellent, they performed as agreed, on the dot, and they had even built a handy sort of grandstand so visitors could get the shots they wanted, for this was a regular spot for tourists to come. We knew, as Jane would not, that the men here were going into trance three times a week. Walter returned smiling. I could smell Rawa's aromatic sweat on him, like the scent of a tom cat. Walter himself never sweated.

The performance ran its course as at Gelgel. The Barong transformed from friendly pet to savage guard dog, dived and charged and swerved and cowered. Rangda was appropriately revealed in the smoke of detonating fireworks, waving her talons and stomping. Walter gave Jane a running commentary and Rawa, I noted, came and sat at Walter's feet, casually plucking hairs from his chin between two coins, then rested his beautiful head on Walter's knee, who lightly stroked his shoulders as you might run your hand down the glossy flank of a quivering stallion. Nothing in the least homoerotic there for a Balinese, though Walter seemed very much not to mind making the gesture. Rawa was an outsider, a *sentana*, a man who had come to live in his father-in-law's house. He never seemed to have a special friend like the other men but was aloof and lonely. Doubtless, his nocturnal ramblings were resented in many a household. Possibly this was why he was so welcoming to Westerners who gave him the approval he sought in vain at home. I looked back at the performance. The Barong was rushing at Rangda and they fought, the quadruped finally vanquished and rolling in the dust by the mother of witches. At this point, his supporters went into trance on cue, yelling and waving their daggers, she, spitting curses and raising a white cloth against them so that they were ensorcelled and turned their knives against themselves. They twisted and pirouetted, some wept and rolled on the ground, pressing their daggers against their invulnerable chests. Suddenly Rawa stiffened and leapt to his feet with an animal cry, rushed into the arena, snatched up a dropped dagger and slashed at his chest. He, too, had entered a trance. But wait. This was not the miracle expected. A red line appeared under his left breast, blood gushed, spurting with each beat of his heart, between surprised fingers. Attendants leapt forward, caught him as he collapsed, carried him off. "Oh my!" cried Jane, writing desperately. Walter was on his feet, round the back as they pressed staunching betel leaves and red acacia blossom into the wound. I followed shamefaced, laiety intruding on a clerical space. This was too good an opportunity for other villagers. As he lay there, stunned, on a rock, an old man, with a beautiful peaceful face, came and kicked Rawa very deliberately in the chest, re-opening the wound, shouting about uncleanness and women. Others, still in trance, were prey to other passions, rushed up and thrust their mouths at the gushing wound, sucking down his precious lifeblood, staggering away slurping and liplicking, gore clogging their moustaches, like so many sated Noseferatus. I was strangely stirred by the violence and bloodshed and, looking into the wound, saw there only prime red steak, fresh and tender, felt the flare of a bizarre cannibal appetite. Walter hesitated, shouted to a priest, "*To! To!* – Look! Look!" then, suddenly resolved, held the ravening vampires away himself with a raised bare arm, regardless of their daggers. "Don't just stand there Bonnetchen, support him!"

Oh gladly. I took him on my knees and adopted a pose somewhat after that of the grieving Virgin in Botticelli's *Lamentation over the Dead Christ* – one that many critics at the time felt excessively odalisque. His white headcloth suggested a bandage so I untied it, wadded it into a pad and pressed it tenderly to the wound. Another man came up, apparently solicitous, then – grinning – tried to drag Rawa to his feet by the hair as he lay limp and dropped him like a broken doll back on my lap and laughed. Walter shooed the madman furiously away. A priest finally strode up, splashed cooling holy water, fumed incense. Men dropped to the ground like stones, lay still or struggled groggily to their knees. Then consciousness returned with a rush and Rawa too sat up, stared down, not badly hurt after all, but amazed at his own defilement and pain.

"I must," announced Jane pushing past, "interview this man."

Soon I could hear her say, bending over Rawa "And just what word would you use for that? Uhhuh. And when you say that word how does it make you feel? Really? Oh my." Scribbling, scribbling. She was always scribbling. My knees ached and my hands were sticky with Rawa's hot blood and sweat. I was not in a trance. I felt pain quite vividly where he had been dropped on my knees. But of course no one concerned themselves with me.

II

Walter had a natural empathy with aristocrats and they immediately regarded him as "one of us". That is not to say he was snobbish and despised us peasants, quite the reverse. It has always been the mark of true aristocrats that they are socially unassuming and spread their friendships widely. Like the English Prince of Wales, indeed, Walter saw himself as empathetically in harmony with ordinary villagers by some kind of social short circuit, enjoyed their company and was keen to help them in any way he could. And like an aristocrat, he seldom paid his debts, for any infusion of cash was seen as a windfall, something to be profligated on making the moment special before it leaked away, not to be spent on the dull and everyday. But he disliked the aggressive mediocrity of colonial life, with its invidious social distinctions and petty acquisitiveness and always favoured the special few who sought spiritual rather than worldly wealth – especially if they had plenty of money and their first impulse was to give lots of it to him. After all, the sensation of having Walter's hand in your pocket was, in many ways, not wholly disagreeable.

Barbara Hutton would, in a few short months, come of age and be quite simply the richest woman in the world and, though not an aristocrat herself, had a similar taste as Walter for them. She would soon embark on a lifelong series of failed marriages with failed European princelings – tirelessly repeating the same mistake – interrupted solely by one with Cary Grant who puzzled her by neither abusing her nor stealing her money. Consequently, he bored her. The present candidate was one Alexis Mdivani, a soi-disant Georgian prince and fortune-hunter whose relentless attentions were the motive for this world trip. Although she had good lawyers, in contrast to the Woolworths stores on which her fortune was based, in love she bought expensively and sold cheap. Her mother had committed suicide. Her father had abandoned her. Homing in on her tragic private life, the newspapers had started calling her the "poor little rich girl" after Noel Coward's song. Bing Crosby had recently driven her into hiding with his popular offering of "I found a million dollar baby in a 5 and 10c store". She was dumpy and shy and insecure and might as well have been walking around with a large target painted on her back. She talked with that odd honking accent that used to be the sound of Fifth Avenue but has now, I believe, entirely disappeared from the world apart from the call of the Canada goose. Her companions were the Kinnerleys – Jean and Morley – wealthy Anglo-Americans in their late thirties, she from a titled English house, he a successful publisher. Slim, sophisticated, assured, they knew everyone by their first names and assumed everyone else held the key. "David" was the Prince of Wales, "Mary" the English queen. Morley talked constantly of some new poet – "Eliot" – whom he considered a personal discovery, though I never found out his surname.

Perhaps it was the horse that first attracted her. The equestrian pose is inherently aristocratic. Portrait painters have known that for centuries. And it displays a man's thighs to advantage. I have always noted women to be particularly vulnerable to thighs. Then again there was Walter's Russian accent, the blond smile, the gigolo charm that he instinctively turned on full blast, with too much eye contact, laughing at things that weren't funny and so on. Her laugh, in return, was particularly irritating – a sort of equine snort. In brief, he was as catmint to her and in a few days she was clearly smitten and swept off her feet by the heated exoticism of it all. If only Walter had had a title. I began to wonder whether she had been padding up those stairs to the Kala Rahu door but surely etiquette required that he visit her, that she "receive" rather than "present". By close questioning, I had established from the boys that no Russian piano music had been played in the house – not that it was any of my business. They all went riding every morning and often ended up at the McPhees'. Inevitably, Bärbli – as she suffered herself to be called though she had spent a life fighting against "Babs" – knew Jane. It seems they had shared an analyst together which is apparently the American equivalent of an in-law relationship.

One morning I was sitting in the garden sketching one of the hornbills as it chewed on its own feet when she came and sat beside me. She had let it be known that she was a poet and had recently published – privately – a book of her poems. They all held themselves to be well-versed in poetry. Morley described the book shiftily as "not entirely devoid of merit" though the process of versification seemed to consist entirely of her wandering around with a pained expression and sucking a pencil. That morning, she was, I confess, radiant, transformed by an inner light. I had an urge – swiftly suppressed – to ask her to pose.

"Hi, Rudi," she honked, laid down her sucked pencil and replaced it with a cigarette, clearly expecting me to leap forward and light it for her. I ignored that and concentrated on my hornbill's scaly feet. "Tell, me. Why does Walter call you 'Bonnetchen'?"

"Why does he call you 'Bärbli'? Walter is like one of those early explorers who feels he has the right to rename everything since it is only when *he* sees it for the first time that it really exists."

She gave up on the cigarette and stuck out her lower lip like a child. "You don't seem to like Walter very much today. I thought you were his friend. I think he's just darling."

I pressed too hard and broke the point of my pencil. "Damn and blast!" The bird, reacting to my voice, flew off. I lay down my own pad and pencil, sighing. "Look," I said, very calmly. "Barbara. You are very young and innocent and there are certain things you may not have realised about Walter." I took a deep breath. I was not quite sure how I should put this. I groped for thoughts and words to put them in. "Walter is not as other men."

"You mean," she finally lit her own cigarette, "that Walter is homosexual?"

"Well, yes." I was genuinely surprised. She laughed. It was not such a bad laugh really.

"Like cousin Jimmy," she smiled. "Jimmy is absolutely my best friend in the whole world and he adores the New York theatre – all those costumes and chorus boys and Ethel Merman. He takes me to all the openings and I have to keep him in little presents for his little friends who can be quite cold otherwise. He is devastatingly handsome of course. His father was just the same way. Jimmy says that playing football does not mean you can't enjoy the odd game of tennis. Both are just a matter of ball control." I was shocked. She was less innocent about Walter than I had been. No wonder she got on with Jane. Perhaps they were both reproducing the wisdoms of that same seedy analyst. I had never played tennis in my life. "It's so peaceful here. You know what drove me away from New York?" I shook my head. "I went to Cartier's with Jimmy. Oh we were very naughty. I spent $150,000 on trinkets, little things that caught my eye, and when we got back to the Rolls there was a crowd of street people, dirty, ragged, thin. They knew who I was and they looked so angry when they saw the Cartier bags. I guess it was a mistake to wear furs and diamonds in daylight. Oh those mean, horrid faces! They started shouting and banging on the roof and spitting and the driver just sat there and – can you believe it? – wouldn't move just in case he knocked a couple of them down. Then, thank God, the police arrived and drove them away with their nightsticks. I fired the driver, of course. But here everyone is happy and well-fed and loved and everyone just adores the princes." She had met Agung who had charmed her over tea and softpedalled his way into her favour by placing his regal foot gently on hers under the table. "My father hired a detective after that but I soon got rid of him."

"How did you manage that?"

She laughed again. I now realised she had a whole expensive wardrobe of laughs. This was a nasty off-the-peg snicker, wet with saliva. "I seduced him of course. A very brutal man. Jesus, my fanny was black and blue for a week."

Oh my God! I began to feel a little sorry for Walter and lit a cigarette of my own, chuckling. "I heard there was another man after you at the moment."

Her pudgy little face looked sly. She tried to throw her hair back dramatically but that gesture doesn't work when the hair is mousey and short. I detected a need for drama in her life. Poor Walter!

"My prince! Alexis. My father hates him, says he's one of the 'marrying Mdavis'. They just happen to be deathly attractive to rich women. Like I say, why have money if you don't buy what you fancy? And he can't leave me alone. Jimmy has a habit of taking showers in the sports clubs downtown and says Alexis is hung like one of his own polo ponies." She preened queenily. I was puzzled – shocked too – but more puzzled than shocked.

"But didn't you come here to get away from him?"

She snorted. "Just till his honeymoon with that bitch he married for her money is over. One must observe the decencies. There's also the matter of my coming of age in a few months. That's why we came."

We were interrupted by a splashing. It was Morley, paddling in the stream. He paused, swaying off balance, nearly tumbled, grabbed a rock.

"I grow old, I grow old. I shall wear the bottoms of my trousers rolled," he chanted, smiling a greeting. "Did I hear you explaining how we came to be here? Most extraordinary coincidence, really. Jean and Barbara went to this film in New York – *Love Powder*, that was the name of it – and it turned out to be about Bali and Walter was credited. Outside, it was wet and cold and raining and Bali seemed like a good place to run off to – take a powder as we say in America – so the girls made up their minds then and there and here we are."

"Halloo, dahlinks." Walter's Russian accent was becoming absurd, a parody of itself. He appeared on the balcony as in *Romeo and Juliet*, wearing multi-spattered shorts and that silly calabash hat he wore for painting. But wait. There had been none of the usual dramas, Ubud had not been required to go into mourning while he was easing himself at the easel, the boys were not walking around on eggs and talking in whispers lest they frighten his muse. "Morley, where is dear Jean?" he called down.

"She went to the market with Resem to buy cloth. Oh yes. I was going to ask. What should she give him as a thank you?" It was impossible that had completed anything in half a day.

Walter leaned on the rail. "I think you usually find a cloth about right for a small service, don't you, Bonnetchen?" Painting always drained him utterly. There was no sign of any of the inevitable exhaustion. And yet, when we arrived upstairs, there were three new paintings, stood in a line like serving maids with their hands out for a tip, not – it must be confessed – his best, in fact rather repetitious with none of the poignancy that comes from leaving something just unsaid. I looked at one showing juxtaposed scenes of village life, men driving cattle, the dark forest beyond, night and day side by side, Rembrandtesque pools of light in between.

"What's this?" I asked suspiciously. Walter looked uppity.

"You know the way I work, Bonnetchen. He winked, slipped an arm Balinesically about my shoulders and squeezed a little too hard for comfort. "I labour away at a painting for months, simply bleeding into it, and then, sometimes, I just can't quite bring myself to kill it off and end the relationship. It is a relationship of the soul." He looked soulful and touched his heart. "You feel it, Bärbli. You are a poet. So I start another. And before I can finish the first, I have to wait for inspiration to come. I'm sure you know how it is, Bonnetchen." I knew no such thing. I knew that Walter was like the whole of Bali – nothing was ever quite finished, or, if it was, something else had fallen down in the meanwhile, so the list of things to do never got any shorter. I sneered.

"Well it looks as if inspiration turned up today – by truck – which reminds me why I came." How many paintings had he got tucked away in that studio that no one was ever allowed into?

"Oh Walter!" Barbara interrupted. She picked one up and twirled. "They're beautiful, the true voice of Bali," she honked. "Look, there are three of them and three of us. It's as if it were planned. It was meant to be. You must let me buy them all!"

Walter looked bashful, a little boy praised extravagantly by his mother in front of guests. "All three? Well ... really ... I honestly didn't expect ..." I could not stand it any more.

"Walter," I said. "I really came to say that I'm off to Java. An exhibition. Next week in Batavia. My own works and some of the Pita Maha. Lee King has a truck leaving adventitiously tomorrow and has offered to take us and the paintings on highly favourable terms. I would have asked whether you had anything new you wanted to include but you are obviously quite spent."

***

The Hotel des Indes had not greatly changed. At this hour of the afternoon, it was still overswept and -polished, overstaffed and doubtless still overcharged. The marble-tiled vestibule echoed with the clicking heels of those busily engaged in the world economy from which I had seceded. Theirs was a sphere of rustling Dutch banknotes, mine one of chinking Chinese *cash*. I started at a strange sound, then remembered – the shrilling of a telephone. I could no longer afford to stay here myself and had taken lodgings with a respectable widow near the Protestant Church, conveniently near the *Lapangan Gambir*, where, in the shadow of the railway station, occurred those nocturnal activities traditional to a town square in the Indies. The news stand snarled with the concerns of a wider world. Adolf Hitler had become chancellor in Germany. Paraguay and Bolivia had clashed. Peru and Columbia were at war. The Japanese were still in Shanghai and quailing before threatening Western powers. Nothing to do with me. Off to one side, three willowy, becummerbunded Eurasians were playing something syncopated and South American – possibly Peruvian – with excessively martial maracas. Exhibitions in those days were organised mostly by little circles of art-lovers, principally Dutch ladies of a certain age. I had spent the last week in a desert of small-talk and stolid food. My guts and ears were clogged with stodge. Yesterday, I had given the circle a talk on Rembrandt, to a packed sitting-room, that had indeed led on to a vigorous discussion, but unfortunately about the perennial problem of mildew in the tropics. I deserved a little treat and made my way to the bar where the golden glow of the sun through the shades gave light without heat and the overhead fans rustled the leaves of the palms like the wind in distant Bali. Another brief moment of shock at so many white faces together, then, behind the bar, at which I took my place, was a delightful brown face, a new barman, sharp-featured, a fine nose but with huge, dark eyes … I heard myself groan.

"Tuan?"

"*Bir*." It came cold and frothy-headed, in a glass like a vase, on a neat coaster and delivered with a smile. It was the beer you dream about on a hot, sultry night in Ubud. I smiled back and held his eye just a little too long for normal politeness and feigned bored, time-rich idleness. I was ashamed of myself, with a sad foreknowledge of self-disgust, but the anonymity of a relatively strange town spurred on my excitement.

"How long have you been here?"

He arranged his little dishes behind the raised bartop. "A month."

"How is it?"

He seesawed with his hands. "So-so." I sipped, affecting leisurely chatter.

"Where are you from?"

"Semarang."

"A pig ... fine town, Semarang. I have friends there." The politenesses were dealt with. Now to business. "You are married?"

He blushed though there was nothing irregular in my asking the question in the Indies. When people as dark-skinned as him blush it is a thing not of colour but of heat.

"*Belum* – not yet. And you?"

I was ten years older than him, an explanation was necessary, at my age, for my singularity. "No. I am a bachelor." I paused with simulated brooding significance. "I like the company of other bachelors." The line sounded ridiculous even to myself. I looked at him. Did he get my drift? Oh yes. He got it all right and was smiling down at his hands. I leaned forward to ask what time his shift finished. I must remember to ask his name. A hand fell on my shoulder.

"Bonnetchen. Leave him alone. He is young enough to be your cousin."

My hand spasmed and sent beer flying, clutched at my wobbling glass, caught it back in the nick of time.

"Walter. What? How?"

He raised an eyebrow at the barman. "Another please, Adi."

Adi smiled. "Yes Tuan Walter." He mopped at my mess with distaste and served Walter with a bow that expressed what an unutterable pleasure and honour it was.

"Agog for your news Bonnetchen. Oh, all right, two gogs but that's my final offer. How goes the exhibition?"

"What exhibition? Oh that. The usual. Down the road at Dreckers, the book shop. We've shifted quite a few. Little Sobrat has done particularly well and has a nice sum coming. Even I have nearly sold out of my market women." A man looked up at me from a neighbouring table and frowned. Scanning the room, I saw only white linen suits. "Are you here alone?"

"Not exactly. We all came together." His face lit up. "We *flew*, Bonnetchen, from that airfield down by the beach at Kuta, actually flew! Oh, you can't imagine how marvellous it is! Now I understand Elli. The exhilaration and sense of freedom! And the luxury of it all! Hot coffee served to you from a vacuum flask as Gunung Agung glides underneath your wicker chair. You can look right down into the crater, just like looking up the skirts of the gods. It is amazing, up in the clouds just like a bird. And then you fly down the entire chain of volcanoes the length of Java and swoop down over the whole, sprawling city. Marvellous!"

"Weren't you frightened?"

"Of what. They guarantee that, no matter how high they take you, you will ultimately get back to the ground. And now we go to Bangkok and Angkor Wat, all by air! Of course Bärbli is paying for everything. It is understood that Bärbli always pays." He sipped beer and winked at Adi who winked back as if to say that, yes, he too, understood that Bärbli always paid. These beers, here, for instance, Bärbli would pay. But I had not forgiven Walter for that remark about Resem and the cloth.

"But she must be very demanding" I smirked. "I understand that she requires the most complete service and what Bärbli wants, Bärbli gets."

He looked puzzled. "You mean? ... Oh no," he laughed. "You're wide of the mark there, Bonnetchen. That's all taken care of."

On cue, the doors of brass and chrome were flung open and an extraordinary figure strode through and up to the bar in a waft of hot, spiced Batavian air, seized Walter's hand and spouted fluent Russian. He was tall and muscular, thick black hair and a bounder's moustache, a panama in his hand and – God help us – spats with parti-coloured shoes. A silk handkerchief flared from his elegantly tailored breast pocket, arranged with the care that a Balinese would expend on his headcloth. Light sparkled from his teeth. This was the first time I had encountered Hollywood capped teeth and the hand he finally extended was a work of art, professionally buffed and manicured, worthy of being drawn by my chicks.

"May I introduce His Highness Prince Alexis Mdivani, Bärbli's fiancé."

"Oh Walja," he giggled. "The title is only for formal occasions." To me. "We reactivated it after the Revolution. My father says he is the only man alive to inherit a title from his sons." He slapped my arm archly with kid gloves – to Walter "handshoes" to the Javanese "handvests" – held in the left hand, as if for the issuing of challenges to duels, and laughed. It was a dreadful noise, as though someone were giggling down a musical scale. If he and Barbara ever both heard something hysterically funny in the same room, it would be hard on the ears.

"Excuse me." I was distracted. "Is that a gold bracelet you're wearing? I don't believe I have ever seen one on a man before."

He adjusted it, not in the least abashed. "From my wife ... ex-wife; when ladies like to buy you things it is your duty to cultivate needs other men do not have."

He exuded the smell of Russian leather, a nostalgic mix of the covers of the bibles in the Sunday school of my childhood and the seats of WWI railway carriages. For some reason, it made me want to cry. Walter eyebrowed Adi across and more beer was brought. Now we received nuts, too. With Alexis, our stock was rising by the minute. The white linen suits were all staring as he settled into an elegant, Côte d'Azur, pose, arranging the pleats in his trousers.

"Your ex-wife?"

"My new ex-wife, Louise van Alen – American Fur Company. It is quite in order. It has been arranged that she is to marry my brother." I was fascinated to see the expensive commercial edition of whatever it was Walter was the rough-edged, amateur version of. "I confess when I flew here, I was a little concerned about my bride and this terrible man, Walter, who had apparently supplanted me." They looked at each other and laughed. "But now, as you see, we are the best of friends. We plan to marry in Bangkok – Barbara and I, not Walja and I – and I have asked and Walja has consented, to be my best man."

"Where is Barbara?"

He sipped beer and immediately blotted his upper lip with a second-line silk handkerchief drawn from a side pocket. The white suits had their heads together and were sniggering through curled lips. I somewhere heard the word "Poodlefaker".

"Shopping. Where else? Which reminds me. I must dash. I have to order more white lilies for the suite, to lift it a little. So glooomy! They are to be the theme of our wedding. Women like those little touches." He rose and bowed, took his time to arrange all his accessories before strolling back across the floor, hefted the heavy door open with his own fair hands, turned, fixed Adi with his eye and pointed at the table with cocked wrist. "For Miss Barbara Hutton's bill, 601."

Adi nodded, bowed, smiled, clutched the bill to his chest and looked at us in something like triumph. The name "Hutton" had the unreality of a film star glimpsed in the street and the white suits went into a frenzy of outraged whispering and strained neckwork as Walter drained his beer coolly and signalled for more with the innocence of a little boy left with a large banknote in a sweet shop.

"You can bet the flowers will go on her bill too," he smiled in mitigation. "Did you know she bought Kinnerley a Bentley? I told her my own sister was called Mercedes. Yesterday we went to see a marvellous film, *Gold Diggers of 1933*. Busby Berkeley. So original, so rich. I expected it to be about hairy miners but it was not. You should go." And when beer-carrying Adi came, Walter slipped a large tip in his top pocket, patted his rump with chaste affection and ordered another glass for me too. Such spontaneous generosity with someone else's money, remembering all the little people, is the mark of the true gentleman. I looked at Mdivani's beer, lavishly abandoned after a single sip. I could never do that.

* * *

McPhee was sweaty and red-faced and – I suspected – not entirely sober. He was running rapidly to fat and had the seedy and apologetic look of a man staggering home after an ill-advised night on the tiles. We were on the terrace of the Bali Hotel, nighttime moths fluttering around us, reminding me that I might be elsewhere.

"Coffee?" I suggested. He shrugged. I ordered. It would do him good.

"Bit of trouble at the old homestead," he confided ruefully. "Jane gets odd ideas in her head at times. She is not always stable." He looked across the table to see how all this was going down. I said nothing. He lit a clove cigarette with a shaky match and put the used residue back in the box – a very annoying habit.

"I've been away at Kuta, you see, arse-end of the universe. You know Lotring, the musician?" I nodded. I knew him, a regular visitor to Walter, thin, birdlike, a composer martyred by his art whose music came to him in tortured dreams that seemed to devour him like demons. "He brought me to Bali. I heard a recording of the old Kuta *gamelan* when I was in New York, one of his works, and couldn't get it out of my head. I listened to it over and over, drove Jane crazy. 'Balinese *gamelan* is the only thing that can save Western music from the dead end it's stuck in,' I told her. And I was right. Then, when I got here, I found the group had had a big fight over a chicken or a goat or something and broken up. Lotring and I had this plan. We revived the group, bought out the old members, recruited new players, regilded and retuned the instruments, got the big gong back from the government pawnshop. To save the orchestra and Western music cost me $150. We had a big shed under a great old tree down on the beach where no one goes. I would go down there for a week or two at a time, work with the men, Lotring composing in his dreams, them rehearsing, all of us playing together. The Dutch would never allow that in public, a white man sitting at the feet of a Balinese as his pupil but who cares. You can't imagine what it was like, being absorbed into the orchestra, that great, breathing, living, ancient creature – feeling its rhythms pounding in your body and its blood flowing along with yours. It was like a dream for me too. We got up every morning to the smell of the ocean, threw open the doors and stepped into the sea. A woman from the village brought us fresh coffee, made on an open fire, porridge and fruit. Some of the boys came along to make notes. Every evening there was the greatest sunset in the world, like a huge pink flower just opening up and the swallows swooping and diving with the blush of it on their wings. And then we'd play again far into the night." The coffee arrived – not brought by a village woman moving to ancient rhythms but a waiter choking in his tight tunic – and with all the usual unnecessary complexity of china and silverware, trays and fussy chits. "At first Jane didn't mind. She had her own work and the house. She loves that garden Walter got started for her. Then she began to feel neglected and wanted to come with me and of course that ruined it for everyone. So I stopped going for a while. Lotring would creep round the back of the house every couple of weeks and keep me informed or I'd send one of the boys on the bicycle. Then Sampih turned up."

I dispensed coffee, milk, sugar like a chemist.

"Who is Sampih?"

A haunted truculence settled at the corners of his mouth. "Sampih is my friend." He seemed to expect me to challenge him. I said nothing. It is often the best way to get people to talk – not that I cared much either way. It was getting late. I had other fish to fry. I was still a young man. The fires on which I would fry those fish still burnt hot in those days. "You know the river at the bottom of the hill? A nasty, dangerous river, prone to flash floods if there's rainfall up in the mountains. I was down there one day and suddenly the level started rising. I made the mistake of trying to get back across and found myself stranded in the middle on a rock with this great roaring sound coming from upstream. I thought I was a goner when this little kid popped up, leapt across and grabbed me by the hand and led me over, showing me where the stepping stones were under the water. Seconds later, this great wall of water came round the corner and crashed down right where I'd been standing. I looked for the kid to say thank you but he's just run off. That was Sampih." He sipped coffee, choked, went into a coughing fit and soothed it with another cigarette. "I looked for him, asked around. You know the way, here, that boys run around in gangs and feed where they can like flocks of birds. Well, finally they directed me to this little shack down on a poor scrap of land where his family lived. You can't imagine the filth and poverty of the place."

People were always telling me how many things I couldn't imagine, whereas I am actually rather good at imagining things. I could imagine all sorts of things between McPhee and this boy. The story of their meeting sounded to me rather like shopgirl fiction.

"The father's a bully, a total moron. The mother's a slut. They greeted me with all that smiling courtesy. You know the way they are. When I turned up, Sampih ran off again. Anyway, I explained what had happened, gave the father some money. I don't doubt it went on booze and gambling. But then a few days later, I saw Sampih down by the river. It was like coaxing a dog that's been beaten. If you moved suddenly or raised a hand, he would snarl or cower. I had to put cigarettes down on a rock and back away. Poor little sod had never known a kind word in his life." McPhee looked as if he needed a kind word from me. I gave him none, not greatly liking the way I saw this heading. It was too late for the *lapangan kota* now. My evening was quite spoiled.

"How old is this child?"

He shrugged. "Nobody knows. The mother says four. The father says thirteen. Balinese don't have ages. You know that. They don't think that way. What difference does it make anyway? So – back to the point – little by little, he got used to me then one day he just came to the house and silently walked around looking at things, touching them. The cook gave him some food and that was it. He came again, sat outside, then on the verandah, then in the kitchen. Soon he was working for us, helping out with the cooking and so on. He was the brightest, happiest little fellow you ever saw, so curious about everything. Jane was against it from the first. You know her first husband adopted a child in Tahiti? Well that ended rather badly." I poured more coffee, spinsterishly equitable. "Then I came back one day and caught the boys playing one of the *gamelan* records – well I say 'caught' but they have always been so careful with them that it was allowed – and there was Sampih on his knees doing this wild *kebyar* dance with the boys laughing and clapping along. All right, it was rough and crude but full of fantastic energy. Of course, they all scuttled off right away and a professional torturer couldn't have got Sampih to talk about it. But the boys told me he was crazy about dancing and, of course, I got to thinking of my own beginnings as a musician ... It must be the same with Walter and those kids he teaches how to paint."

"Yes," I assented. "Except that he somehow dumped all that on me."

He looked up, put his hand on mine. "That's because there's something about you that inspires confidence, Rudi."

I was touched – literally, metaphorically. I gaped. I, myself, do not receive many words of kindness. "Really?"

He returned, unheeding, to his story. "So I offered to find him a teacher, to arrange for lessons. He said nothing for three days and then came to me and said that if it would please Tuan, then he would do it. I rather liked that. There is nothing harder to bear than someone else's gratitude. So Nyoman Kaler came and took him on but they didn't get on. He is old and pedantic and – for a dancer – totally inflexible. Sampih could never put up with that. But now I've found him another teacher, a woman, someone he likes, a retired *legong* dancer in Bedulu. I saw him give his first performance the other night. He's blossoming. There's a fantastic talent there. But the thing is ... I have to go back to the States with Jane for a while. We have some issues. I need to get back to composing. Here, I get nothing done." He gestured futilely. "I need someone to keep an eye on him, to keep the teacher up to scratch, to make sure she gets paid and that Sampih is properly looked after. There is money in an account in Denpasar. I thought that you ..."

"Me!" I positively screeched. "But I detest children. They should only handled by experts – like corrosive waste. "Why don't you ask Walter? I'm sure Sampih would adore Walter."

He sighed. "Walter is not reliable. Where is he now? Run off to Cambodia or somewhere. Oh, he would be kind and mean well enough but once the novelty of Sampih wore off he would just forget to feed him and he would run wild – just like Walter's animals – and that can't happen again. There are fewer distractions in your life." Meaning I was deathly dull and had nothing better to do and would never displace McPhee from the boy's affections. "I hoped you might do it, not for me, or even for Sampih, but because – in some way – you feel you owe Bali something." He looked at me evenly, judgementally, like my mother reading a school report. There it was, the familiar tolling of that old bell – guilt, guilt. I would never be free of it. I groaned. He saw that my armour had been pierced and worried at the wound. "When you were younger, wasn't there something you secretly wanted more than anything but didn't dare pursue?" Of course there was. There always was with men like us. But mostly it was fairly brutish desires of the flesh that had nothing to do with cryptoterpsichoreanism. Then I remembered my art, my father, my mother.

"Look," I said. "I'm not taking him on sight unseen, a pig in a poke. I want to meet him first. Then, this has to be at a distance. He lives in Bedulu. I just act as your agent and this is strictly between the two of us."

It was as if I had waved a magic wand. The worry slipped from his face. He leapt to his feet, hugged me. "He's outside in the car."

"What?"

"Well I couldn't bring him in here could I?"

Had he been so sure of me? It seemed outrageous to leave the boy out there, on his own for so long, like a parcel on a seat, but probably he would not mind. He would just switch off, as I had seen the people here do so often, and go to sleep. Sure enough, when we arrived at the car, he was curled up, dreaming of something, whimpering under his breath and twitching like a dog chasing rabbits. A perfume of frangipani hovered above him like an aromatic halo. He looked small and vulnerable and deeply angelic. Responding to the crunch of our feet on the gravel, he opened an eye and sat up, looked around as a dancer does when first stepping on stage, "looking for danger".

"Where the fuck have you been?" he growled, tucked his hands under his armpits and stuck out his lower lip. He looked at me with the hostile eyes of a small, wild creature, peering from the depths of its burrow at an enemy. Sampih was truly the most shockingly foul-mouthed Balinese I had ever met and his Low Balinese was several degrees lower than any I had ever heard before. In a culture that treasures the smooth facade, the absence of confrontation and egotism, McPhee had found the surliest, angriest, most arrogant little demon imaginable. He turned to me with that stupid, enchanted expression that one often encounters on the faces of deluded parents.

"Isn't he cute?" he asked, laughing, one hand on the door. It reminded me of the way Balinese laugh at funerals.

* * *

It came as no surprise that Walter adored aircraft. They were noisy, expensive and impractical, just like his menagerie at home. I had been alerted to his arrival by the wonders of modern radio-telegraphy which became less modern the closer it came to Ubud, its final incarnation being the skinny youth in the peaked hat who cycled from the post office. A message, naturally, took longer to travel the few hundred meters from the post office to the palace than from Batavia to Ubud. Sometimes, it could take days.

"He's coming back," he announced, yawning. "Flying back tomorrow, your big brother, Tuan Piss. If you can't sign your name, put your thumbprint here." I signed with a pencil plucked from behind his ear and tipped him a coin that he stowed inside the other ear. He was headed for the palace kitchens to rest and re-invigorate himself but, as usual, delayed – one foot on the pedals – to favour me with his views on the world. "No good will come of all this flying," he announced. "It's not natural. How does it work anyway?" He settled to fishing a cigarette from his breast pocket and lighting it with a match flamboyantly struck on the handlebars with a conductor's gesture.

"I don't know. I don't know how bicycles work. I don't know how matches work. Why should I understand aeroplanes?"

He shrugged. "I thought white men were supposed to know these things." I felt a pang of guilt. Now I was being a bad white man. No, wait. I was an artist. This was not my job. "The *pedanda* priest says it will bring disaster down on us." This was news.

"What's so terrible about flying?"

He yawned smoke and stretched. "He says the planes fly over Gunug Agung, over the heads of the gods, and carry ordinary people over the heads of *Brahmanas*, so that the whole country is polluted and the gods insulted. He says there'll be a dreadful reckoning, sickness, plagues of mice, barren women, a volcanic eruption. We will be attacked by great demons who will tear us apart. It will be a time of Rangda and Kala Rahu." He listed the consequences with relish. Young men regard any change from dull normality as exciting, therefore desirable. "What do you think?"

"I think you should get back to the post office and under cover before it all starts or ask them for a bigger hat." He barked a laugh of worldly cynicism and cycled off, knees pointed out, deliberately wobbling from side to side just for the sheer joy of it.

I was there, down by the beach, on time, which the plane was not. In those days, the world was still very big and defied timetables and flightplans and the Bali run was classed as a "pioneer route", which translated as higher prices and even more irregular service. It was a hot, windless day and the windsock hung limp with exhaustion. A couple of military machines were parked up one end of the strip outside a basic radio hut, its roof decorated with a spider's web of wires, before which a couple of men in uniform demonstrated their mastery of football, kicking one listlessly back and forth. In the distance, stood a large *waringin* tree overshadowing a shed, where, I deduced, McPhee's *gamelan* was stored, together with his dream of saving Western music from its current impasse. A man was, most unBalinesically, playing with a tawny dog, throwing sticks into the sea and pretending to chase it as it pranced around, stiff-legged and refused to give it back. Those meeting the flight had gathered to marinate in their own juices under the trees, amongst a litter of vehicles, in attitudes of despair. Balinese beach idlers and little boys formed a sort of snack-munching chorus behind, curious to see this new thing drop from the sky. A man, reluctant to waste a crowd, had set up a satay stall in hope of their patronage. In front, stood some assorted white women who complained bitterly of the meaty smoke, a junior clerk from the governor's office, Father Scruple who ignored me – I was doubtless classed as a lost soul – and a man from the post office who was coughing anxiously into a handkerchief and examining the product. In the early years, flights were subsidised by lucrative government mail contracts and the posts made much of the fact that we were all dancing to their tune.

At length, there came an irritating buzzing and, far out to sea, a small black dot appeared, turned gradually to white, then acquired blue highlights and the little, twin-engined KNILM Fokker circled the airfield suspiciously. Finally reassured, it came in low from the sea, shot past us all in a shower of dust and sand and roared to the far end of the strip, gradually calming itself before returning, bumping over the compacted earth and stopping with a definitive clatter and a fart of blue gas. Inside were two small, white faces wearing unmistakeable expressions of relief.

As the propellor juddered to a halt, a crowd of Balinese rushed forward, cheering and racing with each other, pulling open the door and slotting a tubular steel ladder into place to begin tumbling luggage from the rear. On this airstrip, Western time ruled. The passengers were all male and clambered awkwardly down, sweaty bums turned to the world. One had a newspaper tucked under his arm with a headline reading "America repeals Prohibition". A second rush, this time of wives who kissed their returning husbands openly on the mouth with satay-flavoured lips to embarrassed Balinese giggles. Then, finally Walter, all refurbished – new suit, hat, shoes, reclaiming matching tan suitcases, doubtless Bärbli's bounty – and shaking hands in sturdy male companionship.

"Bit of a rough flight," he confided as though a seasoned flier gripping a pipe between his teeth. "A storm over Java. Threw us all over the sky and one motor *kaputt*. Most invigorating."

Over his shoulder, I saw Scruple greet a thin subaltern and have his boys trundle a large trunk swiftly over to a waiting glossily episcopal car, engine left running.

"Looks like he got replacements for those seized bibles."

Walter gazed over. "Bibles? That's nothing, Bonnetchen," he smirked and tapped his sleek attaché case. "Wait till you see what I've got in *my* luggage."

A couple of hours later, we were sat at the forest giant table. The house buzzed with happy activity, Mas cooking to fatten up poor thinned-down Walter, the boys – intoxicated with little gifts and the payment of salary arrears – fair yodelling their sire's return. Even the cockatoo had become hysterical and been forbidden the house until it returned to a state fit for human society.

"Angkor Wat was sublime, so primitive, so purely Hindu. You would have to spend a month there to see it in all its glory, these vast ruins with the forest trees thrusting up through them. It seems that they were built by the Sailendra dynasty that also constructed Borobodur in Java. I must ask Stutterheim about it. The dancing was grossly inferior to our own on Bali, a mere exercise in how long you can stand on one leg, though the costumes were stunning. Saigon was a thoroughly pointless French city. Do not," he instructed, as though I were about to pack my bags, "waste your time on it."

"So how was the wedding?"

Walter drank rich Java coffee, blew smoke from a *Sumatra Cum Laude* cigar and stretched his legs with relish in a familiar chair, the things a man does to reclaim possession of his personal place.

"Didn't happen. The whole thing was a damp squid. Bärbli was still underage and the consul refused to perform the service without permission of her parents. He was a very unimaginative man. So much *Wirrwarr*. 'Call him up then,' she said. 'I'll pay.' Can you imagine, phoning from Bangkok to New York just to fight with your family down the line at so many dollars per second? They yelled at each other for an hour and then her father obviously saw she wasn't backing down and agreed that they could get married as long as they did it in Paris in a proper way. So I got all dressed up for nothing. But …" He opened the attaché case and swivelled it round so that I could view the interior, "it wasn't entirely in vain."

"Is this a joke?"

It was crammed, as in parody of a bootlegger's suitcase, with banknotes, but not crisp packets of fresh dollar bills, neatly stacked, as in the movies. Instead, it bulged with heaped mounds of old Indies notes, higgledy-piggledy, all colours – red, green, orange – and all states of besmirched decay – some torn, some folded – like swept-up leaves in autumn. A windfall.

"No joke. Bärbli wants me to build a house here for her." He hefted a handful of notes aloft and let them flutter back onto the surface. Some were worn so thin you could see right through them, a metaphor of currency depreciation. "It will be the most beautiful house of all and she simply must have a pool." He threw a second fistful up in the air, then laughingly upended the entire suitcase. "Enough to pay off all my debts. Enough to live without having to produce paintings against the clock with Stutterheim standing over me with a whip. Finally, I won't have to work all day, every day, like a slave, like a dog as I have for donkey's years, which is a coon's age, which …"

"Shut up, Walter."

He shrugged. "Anyway, the point is I am finally free. I am the bee's knees which is the cat's whiskers." He saw my face. "You can't imagine how wonderful it feels."

"No," I said in dry agreement. "I can't."

"Moreover, while I was in Batavia, I went to see the lawyers. Plumpe's money is out of crow."

"Crow? Oh you mean escrow."

"It is on its way, is what I mean. We must keep our thumbs crossed."

"*Ma'af, Tuan,*" Alit, having pattered in on velvet feet stood at the table's edge, eyes agog, horrified by the sight of so much cash, the plenitude of it stifling his throat, cutting off speech. He coughed and spoke with difficulty, his troubled eyes fixed to the spot. "The woman from Bedulu has sent word for Tuan Rudi. There has been trouble. Sampih has stolen some money and now run away again. Since Tuan is now his father, he must please find him and sort out the affair as he promised."

Free? No. Good as I was at imagining things, I couldn't imagine that.

I was not greeted with open arms in Bedulu. It was immediately clear that most people thought I was McPhee, since all white men look the same and, it seemed, he had built up a number of local resentments of which I was now to be the beneficiary. They were polite, of course. Balinese are always polite but they have a sort of extra level of politeness that is a form of rudeness since it shunts you away and keeps you at a distance. Champlung, Sampih's teacher, was in the fields so they sat me on a solitary chair in the middle of the compound, like a garden ornament, until she might be brought. The men of the house avoided me, or rather the McPhee they thought I was. Chickens and children wandered in and out in the thickening rays of the morning sun. Everything was down at heel. They needed the money McPhee was paying.

She was a small, neat woman of middle age with all the corporeal assurance that dancers have and she was torn between dislike of Sampih and anxiety that this would mean the end of an important source of cash for the house. Even Balinese who have land and livestock and might be accounted rich, are short of cash. She came and sat at my feet, meaning that I had to lean forward because she spoke so softly.

"Tuan, he is a difficult child, cold and unloving. I tried to treat him as my own but he would not allow it." I nodded. I had seen that for myself. "It was Nyoman Kaler's fault. He came to my house with his pupil, Rindy and insisted Sampih should dance with him. I never should have allowed it. Rindy is older, more experienced. He is tall and slender. The dance has truly entered him. Sampih was shy before them both, stiff awkward. Even I would admit that. Nyoman sneered at him, made fun of him. He kept stopping him, standing behind him grabbing his arms, shouting out the beat, and forcing his body into the line that Nyoman likes, which is different from the Bedulu style. You know that he is an aristocrat, an insider? He called Sampih a peasant."

"Ah."

"He said he was ugly."

I thought about it. I found it hard to visualise Sampih's face. Only the peevish expression remained. "*Is* he ugly?"

She made a tight mouth as though at a particularly stupid pupil and her eyes flashed with contemptuous scorn. "He is dark which is the same as ugly. Nyoman laughed at the idea of anyone so dark performing as a solo dancer. Sampih was angry. His face was full of blood and he was cursing. He took the money I had made in the market and ran away." She had a small business in the folding of leaves to make religious images for altars.

"Has this happened before?"

She shifted, uncomfortably. "It has happened before. Sometimes things go missing in the house and we know it is him. We said nothing because Tuan Colin would always say that it our fault and Sampih could make him do anything he wanted."

I could see that happening too. "Where does he go?"

"He goes to the town. Then, when all the money is gone, he goes home."

A typical Balinese male, then. I wondered what he did with the money. Probably spent it on food and cigarettes. He was too young surely for drink, gambling and girls? But then, Sampih – I knew – was a precocious child. "What would you have me do? If I bring him back, will you take him?"

I saw her swallow a silent groan. The burdens of teaching, we all knew them. "I have promised Tuan Colin, so I cannot let him down, but he is a terrible trouble" … I recognised this as a renegotiation of the contract. I made up the losses and increased the fees. Now I must find Sampih.

I set out in the early morning cool to walk from Ubud to Sayan. It is just a few miles across the fields and today was one of those days when Bali is a place of magic. The air was honeyed, infused with the rich scent of frangipani, and swarmed with happy, benevolent creatures as in a Hollywood cartoon. Pigeons with little flutes under their wings circled me with music and everything was dappled with the sunlight reflected by quivering water. Green, fresh growth cascaded down the slopes and haughty, long-legged birds stalked among the rice, spearing frogs and other splashing things. Comely Balinese tended their fields, bent not in hard labour but coaxing forth fruitfulness with love and raised a hand in smiling greeting as I passed. At Sayan, the McPhees' house stood sturdy and trim on the brow of the hill. Beyond the wall, inside the yard, one of their boys was sweeping the steps with a hand brush and scattering water to lay the dust that might have offended the absent owners had they been there. A good boy, clearly.

"Have you seen Sampih?" I called across. He paused, scanned the horizon and pointed down the ridge to the river where a little blot of intense green and blue could be seen, like one of the dragonflies that haunted the spot. A fancy Pekalongan cloth, copying exuberant Chinese designs and far too expensive for most of the locals. I took the same yellowing track that the household took down the hill towards the river where he and McPhee allegedly met. It would have been impossible for me to approach him unnoticed – already his head was up like a startled deer – so I made as much noise as possible and came on as slowly as I could.

"What the fuck do you want?" The charming child was smoking.

"Good morning to you too," I *sembahed* extravagantly and sat down. He did not, after all, own the rock. "I hope your parents are both well."

He looked at me with loathing. "My father is drunk and has been beating my mother. When I came back, I found her in the field with her head laid open. One day I will have to kill that bastard."

That rather took the ironic wind out of my sails. Nevertheless, I took a deep breath and forged on in my prepared speech. "Sampih," I said gravely. "You know that Tuan McPhee has asked me, during his absence, to help you in any way that I can."

He sneered up at me. "He made me promises. He said he would look after me. I told him if he betrayed me I would kill him and pursue his soul screaming through every level of hell." His voice was thick with blood. "Now he is gone."

I allowed myself brief distraction. Did Balinese hell have levels, then? I must ask Walter. It seemed young Sampih already had a whole list of people to kill. That, Nyoman Kaler, would say, is what happens when you teach peasants to dance.

"The woman in Bedulu has agreed to take you back if you wish to go. It is entirely up to you. I too have made promises that must be kept but I have no means and no inclination to make you return if you have decided otherwise. I shall simply write to Tuan McPhee and tell him that this is the case." I spoke evenly, without heat. I had no wish to detonate his explosive mood.

"That stuck-up pig Kaler insulted me. One day I will have to ..."

"Kill the bastard. Quite so." I could see the way this worked with

McPhee, the stoking of rage until it flipped over into lust. I remained irritatingly cool. It would not be long – I foresaw – before I was added to the homicidal list. "In the meanwhile, only know that the path has been cleared for your return. Compensation has been disbursed for wrongs done and monies lost. Hurt feelings have been assuaged. If it proves necessary, a priestly offering for reconciliation can be duly made. I will keep my promise and pay all on Tuan McPhee's behalf. Only consider that the best way to make Nyoman Kaler eat his words is to outperform his pupil and so shame him before everyone. That would quite destroy him." He liked that. He liked that a lot. A week later, I heard that he had returned to his studies and was working around the clock, or rather without a clock. So much for the selflessness of art.

***

They were less co-varrubiously intertwined than before. It was no longer necessary for Rosa and Miguel to huddle on the same settee holding hands. They could even sit on separate chairs across the room from each other. After several years of marriage, this was surely not to be taken as a mark of a relationship in trouble but more likely to be a mere case of familiarity building content. More building was going on outside in a sort of athletic cabaret. A team of dusty workers were heaving thatch onto the roof of Barbara's new house, leaping up and down the bamboo scaffolding like pole-vaulters. Further off, another team, glistening with water was attacking the solid rock at the edge of the river, in an act of gigantic dentistry, with long metal picks, gouging out the new swimming pool. We sat and watched and sucked at our teeth in sympathetic pain.

"It is the duty of the gentleman," I remarked, as I thought, pointedly "to provide employment for the artisan."

"To Mother Guggenheim!" said Miguel, raising his glass in a toast. "My grant-giver who had the wisdom to see that work and fun can be the same thing." We were drinking cooled white wine. A new opulence was in the air as if we were outgrowing our student days. Rosa was still a beautiful woman but her curves had rounded and her flesh was taking on a subtly different texture like breast of chicken when overcooked. Miguel's bum had grown monstrous but he was somehow more at ease with it. Earlier, Walter had been disappointed when, at the taking of photographs, he had remained insouciantly standing instead of diving for the furniture. He was even making remarks at my own lack of steatopygic development.

"To be honest," Walter confessed regally. "We did not hope to see you both again. So many people come and say they love us, pay us a few cents and promise to return but never do. We, in Bali, are like sailors' sweethearts."

It had been a special, self-indulgent lunch of welcome, one of Walter's zoological rambles, enriched with McPhee's sauces – garlicked sea-snails, bumblebees, dragonflies, flying fox and sea cucumbers, followed by rich durian and fried acacia flowers – the last sensationally flambéd in *brem* so that the workers had stopped and gathered round, wide-eyed, to watch this wonder of Dutchmen eating fire. I didn't greatly like all this, the blue fire of *brem* being much too like that shooting from the heads of known witches but, in Bali, it is impossible to sit and eat while others fast, so fish and rice had been served to the labourers in an act of semi-biblical socialism that soothed us all.

"It makes me want to get started." Miguel sucked air through his teeth with appetite and inhaled the industry all around us like frost on a cold day. "On the book. The definitive work on Bali. I have to get it all down on paper. I have it all planned, chapter headings, fieldwork locations. I already have half the pictures from the first trip. I shall get up at dawn. I have a thousand questions for you Walter. Are you sure it wouldn't be easier if we just sat down and wrote it together? We could work non-stop. In three months it would be done. We owe it to the world."

Walter blanched like morning glory dunked in hot water. "I have someone who will be much more useful to you than I, a secretary. One moment." He shouted into the kitchen and in, from noontime shadows, stepped Made Tantra, Nyoman Kaler's nephew, McPhee's enthusiastic friend, smiling and *sembahing*. Still a dandy with a flower tucked behind his ear, but goodness, what a fine young man he had blossomed into over the last few years! Walter marketed him like a used car huckster.

"Fluent Malay, even a little English, reads and writes in all languages including Balinese. Comes with the highest possible recommendation from Colin and provides entrées to the very best musical families. Honest, hardworking, charming and – as you see- very easy on the eye."

Made Tantra, no fool, had immediately homed in on Rosa as the key to advancement and was batting his long – very long – eyelashes at her with instant, panting puppy love.

"Puppy love. Several weeks before, I had come to the house – I nearly said 'came home' – to find a puppy tied by the front door. It was adorable. Huge eyes, feet and ears and, of course, I bent down and patted it and it leapt up and licked my face, ready to give its love for a mere kind word or a tidbit. At last Walter was getting a sensible pet, a welcome change from snakes and birds and lizards and those confounded hooligan monkeys. But when I asked about it he replied.

"Oh, it's not mine. It's the priest's. He's round the back preparing an offering for displaced demons so we can break the soil for the new house." Only later did I discover that the offering *was* the puppy as Walter well knew. The experience was, to me, strangely upsetting. I had formed a relationship with the little creature and felt myself to have betrayed it. For an emotional, artistic man, Walter was strangely unsentimental in such situations. I realised suddenly that, if I were ever to suffer a long, lingering disease, he would plausibly turn up at my house, pull out a great, long gun and shoot me out of sheer dispassionate kindness – unless, of course, Sampih had already done it out of rage.

"Will he," I asked casually, nodding at desperately bobbing, incredibly handsome Made Tantra, "be living here?" There was a shout from outside, Walter's name. He rose from the table, screwing up his napkin – napkins! – and went to the verandah. The foreman was looking up, stroking his moustache and making helpless gestures in the face of – God help us – a white, ceramic toilet such as you might find in central Haarlem or Harlem.

"Time for a little cultural contribution," adjudged Walter and soon we were all looking down on him and Miguel, out there astride the thing, miming, blowing raspberry lip-farts, holding their noses with the workers falling about screaming in laughter, then Miguel sticking out and waggling his prodigious rump as Walter, head averted in stage horror, elaborately wiped it with his handkerchief.

Rosa came up beside me and smiled in a tender, almost motherly, way. "He's really needed this," she said. "We've not had a moment's peace since we were here and he got the idea of the book. You can't imagine how good it is to see him back doing some serious work again at last."

It was a time of incredible busyness. I brought my wood- and stone-carving chicks to see the new house, to design elements of it and execute them, so that it grew daily in beauty. Miguel took to instructing the Pita Maha painters in the techniques of caricature and, naturally, they devoted their new skills, gigglingly, not to the guying of his arse but to that of my face and forgot everything I had painfully taught them about naturalism. It was fortunate that Rosa's Malay was still elementary as she lectured my aristocratic chicks for hours on the advantages of workers' control of factories but perhaps it mattered little since few had any Malay, themselves, and none had any idea at all what a factory was. Miguel's book researches drove Walter to rediscover his slumbering interests in archaeology and ethnography, thrusting him out into mountain and forest. In the hills, he explored an unknown lake, ink-black and brooding, had a great raft built and lived upon it in a tent for weeks, painting delicate miniatures of water-creatures plucked from its depths, until his interest flagged. Visitors came in battalions, notably a Mrs Corrigan and entourage, the sort of eccentric millionairess Walter adored. Despite her millions, she had no fixed abode but wandered the planet dishing out handfuls of fresh, young dollars from her luggage to anyone, or any cause, she approved of. She approved greatly of Walter and his struggling museum and bestowed largesse upon both, so that he was able to rage around the island, the Whippet stupefied with expensive gasoline, buying up anything that took his fancy – gold, silver, ancient carvings and scattering them between the new house and the burgeoning museum collection, for the two were really one. One of her companions was the French Duc de la Rochefoucald, whose ancestor so eloquently preached the universality of self-interest and who had invited Charlie to visit his chateau, obliging him to foxhunt. Since Charlie had never mounted a horse in his life, he had recounted the event to us with hilarious exaggeration, acting out his panic, the bolting horse, the loss of his hat, his empathy with the departing fox. The Duc, we were gratified to hear from his own account, had noticed nothing of all that. Then, English lords, haughty and disdainful, expensively shod and baggaged but with scarecrow holes in their frayed shirts and socks, publicly displayed with amusement and poking fingers by the boys on the washing lines. Then two pipe-puffing, sheep-jawed, botany professors from Sydney and an elongated expert on snails, with matted hair. Walter treasured such contacts with the world of higher learning, loved the arcane, musty smell of academe and briefly, during their excursions, affected a briar himself. His all time favourite had been a Dutch zoologist whose expertise lay in excreta, working his way slowly towards a general classification of the ways in which the anus functioned as a pelletisation device and the shape of animal droppings was conditioned by height of release, consistency and weight, as demonstrated by graphs. Then, the Neuhaus brothers, Hans and Rolf. I distrusted them from the first. There was always something – well – fishy about them.

Their introduction to Walter was, bizarrely, the world's largest private collection of painted and varnished plaster sea creatures, cast from life. This they had compiled themselves during their stay in Java, engaged in "the import-export business". Walter had always had a little boy's enthusiasm for collections and coins, cigarette cards, train numbers were to him a prefiguring of museums in general, yet there was something unhealthy in the wonder with which he regarded these, to me, appalling objects. "They're so *solid*," he would say pathetically, turning them in his hands – he the painter in two dimensions. "They're so *real*" – he the artist of imagined worlds. The brothers were both big and fair, blue-eyed and hairy-chested, with a haze of permanent beer sweat about them. They looked like twins and were always and everywhere together, though I gathered they were not actual twins. In Bali, twins are bad news, rendering the whole area in which they are born unclean. Their parents are driven away, their house burned. It was the reaction provoked by the Neuhaus brothers – they made the Balinese' hair stand on end – that would lead Jane to write a major anthropological paper on the theme. Their sexuality was – I was almost sure – turned in on themselves. That, too, was appropriate to Balinese twinship.

"They are building an aquarium – he always pronounced it *akvarioom* – in Sanur. It will be fantastic. They will make a fortune." Walter was hopelessly optimistic in financial matters. He would believe you if you told him you could get rich by selling the Balinese bicycle clips. We were seated on the verandah, looking down. The pool was finally complete, neat stone steps, flanked by two carved stone demons clutching phallic clubs, water plants softening the edges, a real live stork washing its feet in there.

"Walter," I laughed. "No one, *ever*, made a fortune from an aquarium. You would make more money by letting people bathe in the tanks as a swimming pool."

He paused and considered. "A marvellous idea – perhaps later, but I think the *akvarioom* should come first."

A terrible realisation set in.

"Walter. Don't tell me you've invested money in it."

He shrugged and pouted. "Ja ... well ... I put in a little and they put in a little ... not so much. The fish and the water we get free! The tourists will pay to come in and be sold fish food and so pay to feed our fish and then we sell them the fish on the way out! It is not simply a matter of economics. There is an aesthetic beauty there. Maybe even locals will come – special reduction for Balinese!" He slapped his knee. His eyes were gleaming. He could see it all. In his fevered brain, he was probably busy designing the fancy uniforms the staff would wear. "The Neuhaus Brothers know everything about the technicalities. The collection of plaster casts will be a sensation. We will have a whalefish of a time. People will come from everywhere to see it – in buses. Then there will be a place where they can drink a little coffee and have cake and cold orange crush. I should like very much to drink cold orange crush." I had a vision of Walter's "profits" being drunk away in an orgy of cold orange crush. "Later a zoo. Then only maybe your swimming pool idea or maybe the best fish restaurant in the whole of the Indies. We must be practical, Bonnetchen." He was, I could see, hopelessly hooked. Would there be sharks? In Sanur? I shuddered.

Over the next few months, I took a malicious pleasure in seeing myself proved right and Walter proved wrong as each visit by the Neuhaus Brothers brought new exactions. For the construction of the tanks, vast sheets of expensive toughened glass had to be brought from Java, by road and at the owner's risk. Many did not survive. The water might be free, but to move it required a special pump from Batavia and it needed electricity to make it work. To save on glass, the tanks only used it on one side, which meant that they must now be lit from the rear with electricity, shielded from corrosive seawater with costly lead. The arguments for the undertaking no longer dwelt on the huge profits to be made but the prodigious sums already invested, that would be entirely lost, were it not to continue to completion. Walter's attaché case must be looking pretty windswept by now. I searched for, and easily detected, signs of economy. Walter decided that it was cruel to keep the horses so much shut up since there were no dry fields to graze them in and flooded land rotted their hooves. They were sold. Then, wine disappeared as swiftly as it had come, since, Walter announced, he was conducting extensive, comparative research into the qualities of different kinds of *brem* of diverse origins and only that would now be served. After the flash flood of cash, we were swinging back to drought and pinched normality.

And then, quite suddenly, it was done. We drove over one afternoon in the Whippet and there, hard by the beach, stood a solid white-stuccoed installation, shaded by palm trees, a big sign announcing it as an "akvarioom" and a bedsheet slung between two treetrunks, declaring today a grand opening. Dutch flags were waving everywhere, like alibis, and somewhere a military band oompahed a soundtrack of imperial respectability. As we climbed out of the car, the wind whipped a spray of fine grains off the sand dunes and lightly scoured our faces. I knew that, for Walter, these occasions were a martyrdom and he had increased his sufferings by squeezing into his Bärbli finery so that he was constantly easing his tight collar with an angry finger. This must all be the work of the Neuhaus Brothers and there they were, identically dressed and wearing the same smirk on the same sweaty face, oleaginating over white guests with handkissing and heel-clicking. Only a few brown faces, mostly honorary whites because of their high rank, the rest smiling, bowing staff, all suspiciously handsome and obviously chosen for their looks. The guests already had a couple of glasses of wine in them and were mellowing nicely, quick to refill, with a thirst born not of the climate but a sense of exile. Father Scruple was there, murmuring fervently in the ear of a short Balinese, presumably offering to slip him a quick Bible round the back. Smits was there, gripping a frosty beer with one chilled hand and ball-juggling with the warmed other. He saw me and leaned over to whisper something to his wife – mean mouth, parsimonious breasts, Christian faith borne like an affliction – who glared hot disapproval and crossed her arms over her chest. Probably, then, something like, "There's that dirty bugger who paints tits." Miguel and Rosa tried in vain to merge into the background, for they humbled the Dutch by the elegance of their clothes. At any moment, it seemed, they would burst into a tango and the crowd would part and fall back to make space for them to stalk and strut. They twinkled the briefest of waves. It was not entirely clear to me why they had moved back to their own quarters in Belaluan. Perhaps it was simply a matter of economy but at least Walter no longer crept around the house wall-eyed, like a Muslim in a bacon-factory, waiting for the inevitable sound of Miguel's voice. "Oh Walter! Is that you? I have a list of questions about the historical division of irrigation water in Gianyar villages."

I must admit that the tanks, under woven awnings, looked magnificent, each window some two meters high and three long, giving swirly green views onto recreated tropical reefs, swarming with multi-coloured fish, elaborate devices bubbling aeration, floors strewn with swept sand where lobsters and the more energetic shellfish scuttled. Many species were crowded together, as though, living in peace or only modest predation, they wished to set an example to the races of mankind. There were, I noted with relief, no sharks. Each window was gratifyingly crowded with pointing oohers and aahers and even the appalling plaster casts were going down well, especially with the few Balinese guests. As usual, Walter had been completely in tune with local sensibilities and Cokorda Agung was there crying "*Luar biasa*! Extraordinary! Are they for sale?" and swiftly pocketing up several without further formality. Walter's face lit up.

"Of course! An art shop! Another outlet for Pita Maha. Our Sanur members can do seascapes, still-lifes of fish. How could I have missed it? Why," he cried, staring irrelevantly up at the sky, "have *I* never painted the sea?" I had no answer to that.

Outside, oompahs had given way to the cascading tinkle of a *gamelan*. I looked up to see the Kuta group, McPhee's old orchestra, already settled and raising their hammers to rattle off into something inchoate and watery with Lothring on the female drum, hands a blur, guiding and driving them on.

"A new composition," Walter explained far too loudly, "inspired by the ocean that he saw in a very wet dream." It had ended up sounding like an imitation of Debussy at his most pastelish. Nyoman Kaler was out there too, hovering at the edge of the group, hiding vainly behind a cigarette, ears pricked for what he might borrow and puckering sourly at his orange crush. Behind me, Walter was explaining his big, new idea of an art shop exalting sea and fish to the brothers who were automatically scanning each other's faces, trying to organise a common reaction that retained symmetry. The piece ended and Lothring looked around swiftly – no time for a smoke – caught everybody's eye and immediately brought them in again with a few smart drumtaps, the introduction to *baris*. A symbolic pair of curtains had been set up, and now a dancer – properly male for once – parted them and stepped out evenly into the space, back stiffened by a long *kris* running from shoulder to shoulder, bright sunlight gleaming off the thick white makeup and painted black moustache. It was Sampih, but a Sampih transformed. Every movement of his eyes, his shoulders, his feet picked out and synchronised with something in the music. He was not performing to it, he embodied it. Even the Westerners could tell that this was something special, *luar biasa*. The music accelerated into a sudden stormy section and Sampih was all audacious fireworks, sharp muscle contractions, then riding the slowing rhythm with his breath and feeling its crests gently with his hands to cries of "Beh!" from the Balinese who were there, their eyes fixed, all sympathetically inside his body, bouncing on the balls of their own feet along with him, feeling with him, as he waited for the next explosion of sound and movement. At the end, there came a throaty Balinese roar, thunderous applause from the Europeans. Sampih, allowing no wedge between self and role, *sembahed* unsmiling and glided back through the curtains. I turned to Walter.

"What? How? Who?"

This was not the work of the Bedulu woman. This was something else. I caught Nyoman Kaler throwing down his cigarette and stamping on it before stalking off, a very choleric Kaler, a "windhead" as the Malay has it.

Walter was immensely pleased with himself. "You know Mario?"

Of course I knew him. Who did not? The most famous dancer in the whole of Bali, inventor of the flashy *kebyar duduk*, a dance that had created a sensation and set him head and shoulders above everyone else on the island. A very vain and difficult man by reputation, completely unapproachable. "He owed me a favour or two and felt uncomfortable not being able to pay me back so he agreed to take Sampih on for three months, sink or swim, and we needed a main act for the opening, so ... Well, I think he swam at our *akvarioom*, don't you?"

I was lost for words, "gobsmacked", to use one of Walter's recent acquisitions. He had taken two problems – three really – and, putting them together, created a short-circuit to make a solution. I ducked confusedly behind the curtain, looking for Sampih, wanting to congratulate him, warn him against excessive arrogance, ask him what further arrangements had been made ... He had disappeared. I asked around. Balinese shrugs. Headshakes. From the front, I heard Walter's voice, shy, squirming and embarrassed, forcing itself into a stiff speech. Now I was stuck behind the curtains until he had finished.

"Ladies and gentlemen. The Balinese just do things but, for some reason, we have to both do them and say what it is that we are doing. Sooo ... Let me thank you all for coming to this opening today. I should like ..." There was a sharp bang, a puff of blue smoke, as if in mockery of a military salute, and all the lights went out in the tanks. As I peered round the curtain, suddenly, all the fish in the main display were boiling, convulsing, one even flying through the air to land, with a wet slap, in the lap of a large – and not surprisingly, screaming – woman in a cloche hat. Another short circuit, then, this time less welcome. The crowd turned like some great mindless beast and a stampede was about to happen when Walter – in what was surely his finest hour – stopped it dead.

"Ladies and gentlemen," he called. "I should just like to announce our special surprise event for this evening." Unwillingly, they turned back and listened. The hubbub died down. Perhaps all this had been a deliberate stunt. All colonial life is about keeping up a front. Perhaps they were showing themselves up. They looked guiltily around for natives that they might be showing themselves up in front of. "We have just decided that, in about an hour, we invite you to a special, and very fresh, mixed fish barbecue on the beach." They stared and then someone started to laugh and soon they were all laughing and clapping. The military band struck up again and Walter retrieved the flying fish with great ceremony and carried it away, by its tail, to be cooked. One of the waiters caught my eye, smiled and shrugged. There were, he seemed to say, plenty more fish in the sea.

* * *

Another of those dreaded brown envelopes and Walter, headholding and gibbering over coffee.

"I won't do it. They can't make me, can they?" I opened my eyes in interrogation. He picked up the letter. "Listen: 'Following the success of the recent *akvarioom* opening and in the light of your intimate connection with the museum, the Resident has determined that you are the fitting person both to organise the reception for H.E. Governor General throughout the period of his stay in Bali, the cultural events he will witness and to show him round the installation before the official opening'. And then there is an invitation to the banquet in Singhraja. 'White tie and tails'. Tails! I hate such things! You know how I hate them. They can't make me do it." All this fuss. The boys would be thinking he was about to start another painting.

"At least the aquarium opening was a success. Now it's official. I don't really see how you can refuse, Walter. As a semi-illegal alien you need friends not enemies and you disdain to take Dutch nationality. You know Smit would love to have a reason to send you packing. The Governor General might be a good friend to have."

He groaned. "It doesn't work that way. You make friends with a dog to make friends with its owner not the other way around." He slumped over the table, showed teeth, growled and howled in pain.

"Walter, this is his first visit to Bali and he will be judgemental. Please stop that noise. Every official promoted will thank you for it whilst every one found wanting will always lay that at your door. But think of it another way. You will have a huge budget. You can order around the army and the air force, arrange them in nice, neat patterns, make Smit stand in the hot sun for hours. All the Cokordas have to do anything you say. You can turn Bali into your own personal fairyland." He raised his head. There was a flicker of interest at the back of the eyes. "You can get them to paint anything any colour you say – even Gunung Agung. You can pick the music and the food and the flowers and the dancers. You are dictator for a day."

"Must I bite into the sour apple? Will there be not just *Wirrwarr* but also *Trara*?"

"All the *Trara* you want, Walter. *Trara-boom-de-ay*."

He let his tongue loll out and panted doggishly. "God damn me, I'll do it."

* * *

"As I mentioned this morning to Charlie,
There is far too much music in Bali,
And although as a place it's entrancing,
There is also a thought too much dancing.
It appears that each Balinese native
From the womb to the tomb is creative.
From sunrise till long after sundown,
Without getting nervy or rundown,
They sculpt and they paint and they practise their songs,
They run through their dances and bang on their gongs,
Each writhe and each wriggle,
Each glamorous giggle,
Each sinuous action,
Is timed to a fraction.
And although all the 'Lovelies' and 'Pretties'
Unblushingly brandish their titties,
The whole thing's a little too clever
And there's too much artistic endeavour."

Thus Noel Coward on Bali, protesting against the onerous schedule imposed by Walter on his visitors. It has been wrongly assumed, because of the opening, that he and Charlie Chaplin came together. As a witness, I can vouch for the fact that this is emphatically not the case. The coda, with its typical cowardly sting in the tail, is habitually omitted. It runs thus, "Forgive the above-mentioned Charlie, I had to rhyme *something* with Bali".

His extreme intellectual energy masked by professional langour, The Master spent his time on Bali "trying to find the rhyme" – his habitual term for lying around doing nothing more demanding than watching the slow dissipation of his own cigarette smoke. He lay by and in, the pool. He lay on the sofa. He lay in bed. Night and day, he sported extravagant silk pyjamas from the Burlington Arcade. The boys waited on him, hand and foot, in awe, recognising his immobility and dependence as marks of status. Oleg was his particular favourite. "Your young men here are very pretty, dear boy," he would concede to Walter, "but they do not *move* me. I have been to the West Indies where the local lads make good old Anglo-Saxon terms like 'heft' and 'girth' spring to one's lips. One does not dine with tweasers. But Oleg here has 'character', what, in the movies, we term 'a good face'. Were I shooting a film about a mass murderer I should engage him at once."

Walter bemused., vainly groping amongst dark Germanic roots. "What is 'heft'? What is 'girth'?"

"Ah! Quite so. What indeed?" He sucked his ebony cigarette holder that possessed neither. Noel was perhaps, then, at the height of his powers. In his mid-thirties, slim, sleek, he had conquered the musical stage, the theatre, the recording studio. He always seemed to be rehearsing, internally, incubating and wherever he went he left sheets of paper, ditties, drafts of something or other, as other men might leave dandruff. His early *Vortex*, with its overtones of drug-fiendery and homosexuality, had been a major *succès de scandale*, since when he had effortlessly reeled off hit show after hit show with no illusions about the shallowness of his craft. He could, he always made you feel, do so much more, delve so much more deeply but simply could not be bothered, as to break into a sweat was unbecoming. Walter recognised, in him, a brother.

"But why does he speak as though his mouth is full of tennis balls?"

Mixing economy with ingenuity, Walter devised a stream of allegedly local cocktails, based on *brem* and *arak* and Noel sank them without demur, though he always wished to know their name. "Ear, Nose and Throat", "Southpour Punch", "*Puputan*", "Boy Meets Girth" and "Baliballs" were the least of it. Evenings would be spent, Noel at the piano, stemmed glass delicately balanced at the keyboard edge ready for tippling a "Jolly Todger" or whatever, in a sort of protracted cocktail lounge improvisation that recalled the competitive swapping of *pantuns* at Malay weddings.

> "The Belgians and the Greeks do it,
> Nice young men who sell antiques do it.
> Let's do it. Let's fall in love!"

Then play would begin ...

> "Piles up your arse do it,
> Members of the British upper class do it.
> Let's do it! Let's fall in love."

Or

> "Greta Garbo all alone does it,
> Marlene Dietrich with a mmmmoan does it.
> Let's do it. Let's fall in love!"

Then Walter would bumshuffle onto the stool and join in:

> "Queen Wilhelmina on her throne does it,
> Barbara Hutton slowly with the phone does it.
> Let's do it. Let's fall in love."

And Noel would soar, with his high tenor voice, into the bridging section:

> "Walter Spies, in a sarong does it, though he isn't the first,
> Rudi, though it's wrong, does it. If he didn't he'd BURST!"

"Look," I said, "I don't greatly care for ..."
Interrupted by Walter, returning to the main melody:

"The very least Balinese does it,
Separately each of the McPhees – you don't know them
– does it.
Let's do it! Let's fall in love."

Back to bridging:

"Young Rosa and Miguel do it at the drop of a hat.
Oleg on his knees does it. Well, he is rather fat."

Back to Noel:

"Charlie Chaplin as a tramp does it,
Rudi in the outside heat and damp does it …"

"What are you implying? If you mean the *lapangan kota* …"

"… Let's fall in love!"

By some extraordinary coincidence, Walter had a painting freshly finished, trailing around on the forest giant table, downstairs, ostensibly to dry. It was small painting, the sort that might obligingly fit into a traveller's luggage.

Noel looked down at it. "Ripping," he commented, "simply divine. My first lover was a painter, Philip, and I remained with him till he died – 'faithful unto death' – except perhaps for the two shillings and sixpence I earned from Sir Hugh Walpole during an otherwise tedious train journey from Philip's house, at appropriately named Looe, back to the metropolis. Perhaps that is what we are all seeking – someone to be unfaithful to. But, as artists, you will understand that what one does for money does not count, since it does not engage the heart and I might well not have fallen if the buffet car had been open." He licked his lips naughtily and dropped briefly into lower class. "I have always been a bit of a bugger for a sticky bun. Philip opened my eyes to the world of art and the other thing but then, I suppose, one's taste in neither is of the best at the age of fourteen."

"Fourteen?" I gasped.

He cast me a fatigued glance and sucked on his cigarette. "I retained my virginity so late through not going to public school. But I have retained a taste for it and am an enthusiastic practitioner though gruesomely ungifted."

"Ungifted? Who says?"

"It comes, I think, from working in watercolours."

"Oh, I see. I thought you meant …"

Walter frowning through all this, saying nothing, unable to understand the excessively fronted Mayfair vowels.

"Watercolours dilute one. Your colours, dear Walter, are so vibrant". He spoke with excessive clarity and volume as though to an aged relative, hard of hearing. "To look at them, one would think red paint cost absolutely nothing. You have found your secret place. I have yet to find mine and I envy but do not begrudge. Here you can be as you are. Nobody bothers you. The external world does not impinge with its rules and its whips. In the greasepaint world of the theatre, it is one thing, we are all merely playing our parts, but before the great shockable public, quite another. If asked about romance, I just say, 'I am informed there is still a good woman in Paddington Green who wishes to marry me and it would be cruel to shatter her dreams', or I look fleetingly downcast and whisper, 'I have only loved one person in my life and, since marriage was impossible, I have never wed'. Not exactly a lie, for I fear it may be given to us on this earth to truly love only once and that I may have already known and lost that love. Grab every scrap of happiness while you can." Oddly, years later, I would be sitting in a London theatre and hear those last words spoken by a character in a revival of one of his plays, "Greb every screp of heppiness …" But whether he was using his lines on us, or his genuine words as lines, I have never known. I suppose, for an artist, there is no difference.

* * *

"I'm gonna put on my best frock, me old ducks, paint my face and drag my sagging arse back to Blighty." So Noel, in what I took to be best cockney, the day before the Governor General's coming, the day of the grand dress rehearsal. Walter, distracted, not understanding again.

"What?"

"*Der will abhauen.*"

"*Ach so.*"

The boys, unaccustomedly, forming a line and *sembahing* low and ceremoniously as we left that afternoon in the packed Whippet. He must have tipped them generously. Oleg's cheek was glowing from a final pinch of farewell. As soon as our backs were turned, they would be off to spend their money and find their own forms of wickedness suitable to marking the public holiday. Every gateway was decorated, by decree of King Walter, with a beautiful, hanging *penjor*, the usual ornament like a great ornate chandelier of bamboo. The streets were all swept, temples painted, scrubbed and decked with cut flowers while potted hydrangeas and *nipa* palms screened off anything offensive to the eye that could not be simply whitewashed into picturesqueness. Everywhere flags, fresh from the mills of Java, waved a triple greeting with enough cloth to clothe the entire population. Young men, beautifully washed, oiled and combed, in traditional warrior dress, struck advantageous poses along the roadside with ancient spears. Every crossroads was loud with marching *gamelans* and long processions of ladies, all in their best clothes and with gold in their ears, trailed towards the temples bearing artful offerings swaying on their heads. When we reached the town and drove past the new museum, soldiers were exercising on the *lapangan kota* of ill repute and Walter looked at me and smiled but said nothing. At least half the funding for the museum had gone on the lavish gateway, dripping with fangs and foliage, and it was now decorated with hundreds of little oil lamps that spread out along the walls, calculated to create a flickering evening drama of shadows. More lamps were floating in coconut shells on ponds awaiting only the touch of a match while a dance troupe in green and gold was poised, ready to spring into torchlit action at the first sign of anything looking like a Governor General. In short, the whole island was devoted to the exhibition of its beauty, history and culture with no thought for the mundane and purely practical. It rang with music, dance and song, was become a Busby Berkeley musical, a living museum, one vast, theatrical performance and the air was heavy with incense and the smell of *frangipani* that masked – as Rosa would have put it – any trace of the sweat of human labour.

As he made his way into the shady porch of the Bali Hotel, Noel gave us his hand, world-wearily, one last time. "Thank you so much, dear boys" he said waving an arm around at all the pageantry. "You really shouldn't have gone to so much trouble just for me." And as we pulled up before the Museum, King Walter smiled in complete satisfaction and yanked on the "needbrake". He had surveyed his realm and it was good.

"You know," he concluded. "This is the very first time the Balinese have got their culture absolutely right."

* * *

"Six lines," said Walter peevishly. Another brown envelope, slit, eviscerated, discarded on the table of the Bali Hotel. "Not even from the Governor General himself, some secretary. 'His Excellency the Governor General has instructed me to write to you and express ...' I am a 'valuable contribution' and my participation is 'appreciated'. I thought they would make me at least a duke."

"I don't think we do that, Walter. The whole notion of aristocracy in Holland is very underdeveloped. Keep the letter. You never know when ..."

"How can you have a royal house without a flourishing aristocracy? What if they are childless?"

"*Then*, Walterl, they send for you." This last from Vicki Baum, short, skinny, dark, very funny, in her mid-forties. A confident and self-possessed woman with theatrical affiliations and a cutting edge, typical of the women Walter really got on with. "Anyway, darling, you should never read reviews." She reached – I was about to say for her cigarettes but Vicki never smoked or drank, which was odd in those days, and would have fitted the whole ensemble of her mannerisms – for the letter. She read, holding it out at arm's length. "It is the *first* assistant secretary, after all. Damn it. I'm getting old and I forgot to bring my reading glasses on this trip."

"There is a man in the market who does glasses," offered Walter, "Japanese but a qualified optimist."

"You mean he only sells rose-tinted glasses?" We laughed. We must have been speaking English. Vicki was Austrian, though I am not sure that she did not already have an American passport at that stage but, having been raised in the Jewish quarter of Vienna, she was mistress over a form of German even more bizarre than normal Austrian, with an oriental vocabulary and what seemed like a single very dark vowel. From being a professional harpist, she had married the orchestral conductor, worked in Berlin as a magazine editor and, as readers will know, made her great success with the book, *Grand Hotel* that had gone on to grace the stage and screen on both sides of the Atlantic and provide her with an entrée into Hollywood screenwriting. "Darling, in the writing business, you can sometimes live down a flop but never a big success." She had told how she had attended the Broadway premier, escorted by dear departed Noel, both dressed up to the nines, but forced to pick their way, giggling, through swamps of horseshit from the police horses and incontinent torrential rain. Sharp-sighted despite the words of unqualified optimists, she had seen which way the wind was blowing in Berlin and got her family snugly under cover well before that storm broke. The Nazis had comforted themselves by first banning her books and later burning them. There was no nonsense about art with Vicki. She was a focused, professional writer who wrote for money. "Darling," she would say, "I am an absolutely first-rate, second-rate writer." And Bali, to her, was bankable copy, maybe a film. Who could tell? With her was her half-brother, Fritz, very comely, long limbed and a dancer but oddly not of the faith. It was agreed that she would come and stay in Barbara's new house and work with Walter and they would recall the days, before they met, but when Plumpe had known them both, in two separate but not overlapping circles, at the Berlin Ullstein studios. Fritz, alas, would not accompany her, being bound for the Berlin operatic stage where Walter's own brother was now Director and his sister a prima ballerina. So small a world really.

* * *

"Rosa has been explaining it to me," said Vicki, clacking away on her portable typewriter, turning to look at me but not slackening her pace. Her hand pounded out the words as though crushing them with hammers. At her elbow, stood a mug of coffee. She had the gestures of a boilermaker.

In the writers' building at MGM, you had to cover a certain number of pages a day, regardless of quality, so you just kept your fingers moving. "About the Balinese struggling against feudal incomers from Java. I see my book as the battle of a noble peasant, standing two-footed on his own soil, immovable against corrupt landlords. Where we don't agree is in whether you Dutch are the heroes who free him or the villains who enslave him even more." She was in Barbara's elegant new house that still smelled of paint and the size used to fix gold leaf. Through the door of the bathroom, I could see the gleaming Western toilet. I wondered whether it worked, and, if so, just where it discharged its burden.

"My Dutchness," I smiled, "must be regarded as purely nominal, since I do not regard myself as part of the official project. After all, I hold no official position."

She stopped and looked at me with pity. "Rudi, you can't ignore the outside world. Surely you realise that a time is coming when you can't sit comfortably on the fence any more. You're going to have to choose who you are with."

"Sitting on a fence," I quibbled, "is far from a comfortable position for any male."

"Look," she finally took her hands off the keys and scraped the bamboo chair round to face me. "When I left Berlin, I was like you, like Voltaire. 'We must cultivate our garden'. But it's hard not to be political when someone in a uniform is very deliberately smashing your skull with a nightstick. At that time, all the young men I knew in the theatre, arts, films were either fervent communists or fascists and didn't talk to each other. So I had an idea. I bought a lot of beer and asked them all round so they could get to know each others' point of view. At first they just glared. Then, after a few beers, they started shouting. Then, after a few more, I realised I was on my own. They'd all paired off and crept into the dark corners and were coming to their own conclusions in a more earthy way. I thought it was a great victory for good sense, but, of course, the next day they went back to hating each other. Sex is not just a loving act that brings people together. It can be violent and contemptuous. There's a quote somewhere about men spitting not just with their mouths. Wait …" She turned and pencilled a note. "That's too good to waste. Do you suppose" – she, no more the conversationalist but the writer with the next sentence half-formed in her brain and blinding her to all else – "you Dutch committed many rapes when you invaded South Bali? Of course you did. Napoleon was wrong about armies marching on their stomachs. They march on their cocks." She stood up and marched, herself on bare feet, to the door, turned to face Walter's bedroom window and called up. "Walterl!" A dim shout in response.

"During the invasion, were there any rapes?"

"What?"

"Rapes! RAPES!" There was a pause, then a sound of pounding feet and Walter appeared red-faced and confused, swinging round the doorframe, clad only in a frayed towel and gripping a rather nice hardwood sculpture of the god Tintiya, though in the new elongated style, therefore ill-fitted really to serve as a weapon of offence. Any other man would have been sweaty. Walter did not sweat.

"Vicki? Bonnetchen?" he cried incredulously. "What's happening? Thank God!" Gasping and giggling. "I thought I heard you shouting 'rape' and ran to help. I mean hinder."

Vicki laughed. "Thank you Walterl, so gallant".

"Of course, I didn't realise it was just Bonnetchen here … If there had been anything going on, *he* would have been the one screaming rape."

"The question was as to whether Rudi's people committed many rapes during the conquest?"

"Look ," I protested. "When you say 'my people' …"

He sucked in his lip and wagged his finger at me, then turned it into that hair-brushing out of eyes gesture and flopped down in a chair, legs spread, shamelessly showing all he'd got, this room become part of theatre backstage where naked bodies were just more used props without erotic charge.

"More interesting is the fact that most Balinese weddings are done *as though* they were rapes." He gestured with Tintiya in a manner that fellow Viennese, Dr Freud, would have found unsurprising then, with wide-eyed innocence, slipped it and gripped it between his legs and drummed on its head with his fingers as he spoke.

Vicki grabbed a pad and was already scribbling Islamic-looking professional shorthand all over it. "Tell me more. Spare me nothing, darling."

Walter dictated, rapidly tired, looked longingly at his pool, a prince wanting to turn back into a frog. "Enough, Vicki. Time to wallow and bathtime for the cockatoos. We had better change into bathing hose. I do not want to shock the boys."

The water was deliciously cool and the afternoon sun warm and golden on our skins . Small white flowers were floating on the surface, as if scattered in memory of one of Walter's gubernatorial receptions.

"There is a wonderful economy in Nature," declared Walter. "Flowers can attract by colour or smell and by day or by night but all night-scented flowers, like these, are white."

Was that true? He scooped one up and put it, Balinese-style, behind one ear and a white, not night-scented, cockatoo fluttered down and settled on his swimming head. It was their party trick. Walter dived underwater and the cockatoo, instead of flying off, clutched harder and followed him under, emerging coughing and gargling, like a drowning old man, when he resurfaced. Vicki's "bathing hose" were a tight black one-piece, at that time in the height of fashion and she swam with firm, efficient movements.

"I can never see swimming costumes without thinking of the tarts who worked across the street from the magazine in Berlin," she laughed between strokes. "It was forbidden to them to walk the streets, so they used to spend all day cleaning the tall windows with old lacy knickers, wearing only swimming costumes, to attract the attention of men below. That way, it wasn't strictly against the law and the *Schupos* left them alone. If anyone seemed particularly interested, the girl would accidentally drop the knickers onto the street and the kind gentleman would raise his hat, pick them up and bring them back. People always assumed they must be very clean girls because they had such wonderfully clean windows."

Clean! That reminded me. I was not entirely happy about the pool. If the new toilet discharged into the river, then it did so upstream from where we were. Consequently, we were bathing in its effluent.

"Walter," I said. "That new toilet. Does it flow into the river?"

He looked, as it seemed to me, shifty. "Of course not, Bonnetchen." He gestured vaguely. "It's piped away. Over there somewhere. Behind those trees." I was not convinced. That would have required a lot of expensive pipework. I did not recall ever seeing so much pipework on site. "But you are well aware that the rivers are always the most convenient places to shit unless there is a pig stye to hand and there is always someone upstream, even here. But you are right, Balinese decency demands that men should be upstream of women and not the other way round". He turned to Vicki: "You must remember, dear lady, if you are ever obliged to use a pig stye to check that it is empty. Sometimes the swine are so enthusiastic for your present that they gobble it down before you have quite parted company with it. Nasty injuries have been suffered."

"In Darmstadt," Vicki trod water, "they still do not have mains drainage. When I lived there, the municipality delivered this great bucket thing once a week, 'the can', and horrible little leather-clad dwarves used to take the full one away, slopping it all down the stairs. God, those were bad times. There was no coal and it was so cold." She shivered despite the tropical heat. "If you had any sense, the only time you ever left the house was to go to Aunt Dorothy's."

Walter looked puzzled. "You had an Aunt Dorothy there?"

She laughed. "An Austrian expression, *Dummkopf*. The biggest pawnshop in Wien is on the Dorotheenstrasse. So, when you needed to pawn something, you simply said you were going to see Aunt Dorothy. Of course, the can was never big enough and large families were reduced to the most appalling straits. Even friends would come round for a cup of tea at the end of the week, having held themselves all day, and pretending they just wanted a pee, dump a hundredweight of turds in your can and fill it up. There were fights over it. People even killed each other. Luckily, most of the city was starving which meant less in, less out."

"Thank you Vicki, lovely subject for a painting."

She laughed. "Walter, you've never told me where you learnt to paint."

He ducked down till the water flowed around his shoulders. "Mostly, I taught myself from books – Gaugin, Rousseau, Klee. The only real instruction I had was from Oskar Kokoschka when I was at Hellerau. Do you know him?" She did not. I did. Palsied hysterical strokes, wobbly landscapes painted through steam, a lunatic. He should never be allowed near young people.

"A great original artist. But what most attracted me to him was his character. You know he had an affair with Alma Mahler when he was little more than a schoolboy? Alma Mater he used to call her – she was very much older than him. It ended in tragedy of course and he went into the army and got wounded and had some sort of breakdown and had this full-sized mannikin made of her, precise in every detail – yes that one too – and he went around with it and spoke to it, lit its cigarettes and even took it to the opera. It was sort of his Bonnetchen." He fired me a smile to take the sting out of the joke. "The police were always after him for obscenity or something and finally he tired of being professor and resigned by leaving a note with the janitor and he just disappeared. I sometimes think I will do that too."

She grinned. "I can only use this line once, so I shall use it now. If you did, I suppose it would mean you were suffering from … Waltschmerz." We groaned, Walter laughed and splashed her in outrage. I, memorable of the possibility of effluent, forbore.

"Your book," I urged. "What will become of it? I mean, how will it end?"

She looked suddenly serious. "With the mass suicide, the *puputan*, the Balinese walking into the machine guns, dressed in all their finery. Death is always the only really convincing ending for a book. In this case, it is also the outside world breaking in, the end of the closure that allowed the Balinese to go on being themselves."

"Sometimes," said Walter, leaning back Moses-like into the bullrushes, "I wish I could build a big, high wall around Bali and keep it just as it is. No electricity and cars, no grubby blouses, especially no corrugated iron. Then I realise that God gave Man free will just so that he could make all the wrong decisions and maybe I should not try to be more than God. Leave that to the Dutch – like Bonnetchen." Before I could object, Vicki leapt in saucily.

"You mean you would build, not a wall, Walterl, but just a fence, a fence that you can sit on right alongside Rudi". *Then* I splashed her.

In *A Tale from Bali*, that was the result of all this, the story is introduced by a selfless Dutch medical man, Dr Fabius, – her acknowledgement to Walter – with a whole rigmarole about this being her retelling of his yellowed version, found in a trunk, of the life story of an ordinary illiterate Balinese. The multiple layering is an unblushing theft from Conrad's *Heart of Darkness*. As Vicki always said with her bright smile, "Ideas are free!" The names are all plucked from the household and environs, Alit, Oka (the Covarrubiases' landlord). The handsome, dancing, juvenile lead, Raka, I suspect, owes more than a small debt to our abused friend and Walter's favourite, Rawa, whom she naturally saw perform. Dull, downtrodden, unimaginative Pak, through whose deeply conventional and constipated mouth Bali speaks its truths, alone seems to have no obvious model. There is no mention of me, of course, but the book does explore love in its many forms, a discussion to which I may claim to have contributed in some small measure. When I later came to read it, I found it quite thrilling, totally professional, packed with Walter's rehydrated researches, a thoroughly good piece of knitting, yet bathed in an oddly relaxed homoerotic warmth, which was, I suppose, but an honest reflection of her actual experience in Bali. Or perhaps it was just effluent.

I2

"Walter, I'm simply dying for a Baboon's Arse," Margaret Mead gasped, wiping her brow. They were exhausted after a day of mountain trekking, being in the midst of Walter's tour-cum-assault course. I liked it when she used words like that. With her New England vowels and her first husband having been a preacher, she always sounded as if she were speaking from a pulpit and we savoured the contradiction. Walter nodded and rewound the phonograph. It was playing something syncopated and irritating that the McPhees had brought back from Europe.

"And you shall have one! I rather thought that might be the case, so I have some cooling in the river. The boys will fetch one up." A Baboon's Arse, I should explain, was a cocktail survival from Noel's visit – tinned grapefruit juice, cold jasmine tea, whisky and a shot of grenadine to give the appropriate glowing red. At least, that was the canonical formula, though, as with all cocktails, the contents of a particular batch depended on what happened to be at the back of the kitchen cupboard. In the unlikely event of polite society, it was referred to by its academic-sounding alternative title, a BA.

I had returned from a swift visit to Holland to sort out family affairs, following the death of my father. It had left me with my own cocktail of poisonous emotions – pain from all the things that touched me and guilt about the many that did not. With Margaret's arrival, it was as if the scouts and light skirmishers of anthropology had been suddenly augmented with heavy armour. I always saw Margaret as a kind of tank, smashing down all opposition and when she turned to talk to you, it was as if a grey metal turret were swivelling and bringing some great gun to bear. She often wore that peevish expression on her face that professional women have. She was in her mid-thirties, dumpy, big-chinned, with a pudding-basin hairstyle and dressed, as I always remember her, in one of those ghastly, wrapover frocks she wore on fieldwork, based on a hospital smock but with two great flat pockets in the front that she used to carry notebooks like tombstones. She always claimed they were conceived out of simple practicality – easy to wash, immune to the fluctuations of girth that fieldwork provoked – but it was clear that she yearned to have some ritual mark of her fieldwork condition, like a surgeon's gown and mask, with which she could enter the sacerdotal sphere and bring her rare specialist expertise to bear upon a comatose, but grateful subject. Or maybe she just saw herself as gravid with knowledge. Those notebooks were a form of intimidation that she used on her human as well as her anthropological contacts, whipping them out to note down any remark, no matter how trivially made, that she felt required further consideration and rebuttal. Weeks later, she might suddenly come up and say, anent an observation long forgotten, "What you said about the weather is wrong for the following seven reasons" and reel them off. The fact that she was usually right, made this no more endearing. She and Jane McPhee had clearly been trained in the same school. I had once come across the two of them in Walter's sitting room, having an everyday conversation and both taking notes.

With her, was her husband, the British anthropologist, Gregory Bateson, freshly acquired in marriage in Singapore – without, one hopes, the deployment of the fieldwork smock. They had planned to marry in Batavia but the Dutch had frigidly disapproved of her two divorces and refused, seeing themselves as sticking Dutch fingers in a dyke that held back a wave of American immorality. They had done the same to Charlie just before, robbing us of another visit from him and his latest child bride. Margaret was a dumpy five-footer, Greg a lanky six foot five. Together, they looked like a comedy double act. He was big-boned and featured, when he sat, all knees and feet, with a resonant voice and hair like an irrelevance and seemed more in awe than in love, for Margaret was a woman of firm opinions in all matters, whereas Greg was possessed of the greater gift of doubt.

"What will you have, Greg?"

"A beer, no … maybe a whisky."

"Make that well watered." This from Margaret. The McPhees, I noted, like myself, were simply offered small Arses without the option. Jane was all agog at the presence of academic eminence, willingly submitting to direction, hanging on Margaret's every word, trying not to curtsey. Greg sighed and said nothing but made a face as of a man suffering a twinge of toothache.

"So, then," Margaret summed up, "it seems, Walter – would you turn down that music? People can't hear me talk ..." He, too, made the tooth-gnashing grimace that he had learned from the grinling gibbons but meekly crouched and complied, then spoiled the effect by returning to his chair with a knuckle-dragging monkey walk "... that we have a choice as far as fieldwork location goes. We can set up shop in a town in on one of the big, fancy kingdoms with all the ritual and music and architecture and craftsmen and have a nice house and easy communications and supplies. Or, we can pick a highland area, somewhere like Bayung Gede we saw today, and be cold and hungry and get sick and work on natives who wear rags and are despised and maybe unfriendly and we'd have no way of getting in and out." Walter grinned thinly and did a monkey shrug, as if to say he had not made it that way but that's the way it was. She exchanged swift glances with Greg. "Well, I think as anthropologists there's no contest. We naturally go for the second. It sounds like paradise."

"But why?" To me it seemed crazy.

"Scientific anthropology is not meant to be easy," Margaret said with relish and made her chin even larger. "It's like the way they taught me back in Sunday school. In the field, the toughest option is probably the right one, the crude not the cute, the steep and rugged pathway not the green pastures that some go for." She looked meaningfully at Walter. "We want an unspoiled location, no schools, missions, tourists with as much pre-Hindu data as possible. The great thing is to avoid distracting events. What we want is not events but pure structure so that we can study the configuration of their culture and how it interacts with their personality." She looked around, seeing the devil of green pastures in Walter's furniture and cute paintings, looking for his concealed and distracting events. "What about a secretary?"

"I have a man for you: Made Kaler." Jesus. How many Kalers were there? Nyoman Kaler's brother? No wait. Balinese names did not work that way. "Kaler" was a common enough name anyway. He ticked off qualifications on his fingers. "He's been to secondary school in Surabaya, speaks and writes Dutch, Malay and Balinese with even a bit of English . He's really bright and reliable. The only problem will be getting him to stay in some hellhole when, like all Balinese with an education, he'd expect to move to town and buy a pair of long trousers and a chiming clock. You'll have to pay him well."

"What about a house?"

"I'll get my carpenter to build you one. It could take a week or two but you'll need that long to get your papers sorted out and do some deal on the land. They're bound to send you up to the Resident to be cleared. The people here won't want to take the responsibility."

"What about house workers?"

"I've got a couple coming to see you tomorrow. They'll be here at about ten." Margaret was impressed, despite herself. This was too easy. She was not suffering enough to make her data seem valuable. Too many events and nor enough structure. She looked unhappily on as Walter did a gibbering monkey dance – not *kecak,* pure, pre-Hindu monkey – of triumph and then shuffled over, arm-swinging – to chink Arses with her and turn the music back up.

McPhee turned to me and whispered. "Thank you for looking after Sampih." Oh Christ. I had forgotten all about him. I didn't even know where he was.

"Did you find him changed?" I asked cautiously. He glowed like a tedious pigeon-fancier suddenly allowed to talk about his hobby.

"Marvellous. He's come on so far with Mario's teaching and Rosa, before she left, was a great help. She managed to get him interested in politics as an outlet for all that rage. He now realises his enemy is not just his father but the whole structure of world capitalism." I wondered how he would set about killing that.

"Ah! Er … is that entirely a good thing?"

"Absolutely!" His eyes glowed. "Thanks to us, he has found himself. He talks about organising something like the Pita Maha for dancers, a sort of union that would break the control of the rajahs and the aristocrats and control the new sponsors, the tourists. Dance can become a weapon of social change. Even Jane is keen on the idea."

"Have you talked to Walter about this?"

He shook his head truculently. "Walter's got nothing to do with this. You know how old-fashioned he can be. This is the future."

I had just had a bit of trouble with Pita Maha and the future. One of the duties wished on me by Walter's sloth was the administration of the museum shop. It had done very nicely, bringing the tourist market and the artists together while avoiding bruising direct contact that could devalue the work they were producing. But while I had been away, behind my back, there had been some sort of campaign in the Press, alleging the incompatibility of the museum and the art business. I could not quite discover who was behind it all but I suspected the dealers in Java and Denpasar who saw valuable profits flowing back to the artists as opposed to their own ready pockets. Official pressure had been brought to bear and the shop had been closed, leaving Walter's aquarium as the only big, local outlet. The effect on the artists' income had been disastrous. Rolf Neuhaus had been treasurer of Pita Maha at the time and I went to the aquarium to find out just what happened. It was worse than I could ever have imagined.

All the flags and *Trara* had naturally been put back in their box but the shop there was flourishing and I watched a charabanc-load of tourists passing through, snapping up the most ghastly fish daubings There were acceptable Pita Maha works on sale alongside but there was something odd about them too. Round the back, I found a sort of workshop with half a dozen men working away peacefully in an open pavilion, sitting and chatting as is the Balinese way, while painting the horrors I had seen round the front. The foreman, a mature man with a charming moustache, came forward to greet me. The others rested on their arms and smiled as I passed round cigarettes and asked casually, "Who is it that you work for?"

"You speak our language? That is good. Tuan Rolf." Yes. They all nodded. And what was it they were doing there with that black and white painting? I had seen it at the Pita Maha the week before.

"Oh that is from the painters at Batuan where they only paint in black and white but Tuan Rolf says the tourists like coloured paintings better so we colour them in for the Batuan men.

And in the shop, I observed, I had noticed that the names of artists were painted on the works but it seemed to me they were the wrong names. Perhaps there had been a mistake, some confusion?

"Oh no. That is no mistake. The artists, of course, are like us, simple men who cannot write, so Tuan Rolf writes the names for them and tourists like some names, which are lucky names, and do not like others so he always chooses the most lucky names to write so they are happy." There was no dissimulation. In Bali no one has copyright or authorship. For Balinese, as for Vicki, ideas were free and objects and music were made together in groups. A signature was just another part of the design that made people happy. Now, I must drink some coffee, black and cloyed with sugar, to make *them* happy. I settled, sipped. This work, was it good work?

"Oh Yes! Much better than being fishermen which is what we did before. That was very hard and dangerous and sometimes we even enjoy the painting. There is a kind of satisfaction in it. It is best when I am allowed to use red paint but mostly, I only do the yellow bits."

Look, I told them, they must come to my classes. They could learn to paint better. They could use all colours. I would teach them in Ubud. It would cost them nothing. They giggled and blushed and shook their heads.

"That," said the mustache, "is impossible. Those classes are only for the boys from the royal houses, not outsiders, and we could not go to Ubud. It is dangerous for Sanur men there."

Was Tuan Rolf at home?

"Unfortunately both the *tuans* have gone to the market in Denpasar. If you come back in the evening, you will find them." He looked round at his fellows and whispered. "But you must be careful."

"Careful?" I echoed. "Why careful?"

He hesitated and one of the others murmured something under his breath, into his cigarette and he looked down and could not fix me in the eye. "Those two *tuans* have strange habits. That is why we do not come here at night. It is because they are twins. What can you do? It is their nature. From the womb they were too close together."

I had returned, bubbling with rage at the infamy of the Sanur operations and revealed them to Walter as he swam. It is hard to tell whether a man is shrugging as he executes the breast stroke seen from the rear. It is nothing but a series of aquatic shrugs – but I am fairly sure he did.

"It is difficult. They are my partners in the *akvaroom* but I am not sure we are partners in the art shop."

"But this is immoral, fraud ..."

He shrugged or perhaps just breast-stroked again. "There is nothing to be done. It is according to the configuration of their culture and culture is nothing but personality writ large."

"What?" I wondered, at the time, where he had got that from. Now I know ...

"What?" Walter was poking my knee.

"Don't you recognise the voice?" He had just vigorously rewound but the music still drooped with tropical langour. The wavery tenor, those absurdly fronted vowels. Of course. "It's Noel," I said. "Something about mad dogs and Englishmen."

"I still can't understand a word," complained Walter. "A mouth full of balls."

Greg grinned with a striking assortment of teeth gripped around his pipe stem. "Couldn't have put it better myself, old boy" he said.

* * *

It was not debauched Vicki who smoked but austere Margaret – like a factory chimney. She sat down there in the garden, on a deckchair, in a large floppy hat and one of those dreadful fieldwork maternity smocks, and puffed away manfully. "The important thing," she declared, "is to collect truly scientific data. Subjective impressions have their place but nothing is as good as rigorous observation and the use of tests like this allows direct comparison across cultures. It is better to have one event described by three observers than three events described by one." There was Jane, Made Kaler – a cheerful and intelligent young man with unnaturally long hands – and Margaret herself, all with notebooks drawn, triply observing. Made had been issued with a shiny, new wristwatch for professional purposes and was enjoying the sight of it shining on his wrist. Walter and the other boys sat on the ground further off and observed – presumably – subjectively. They were laughing at something

Walter was drawing in the dust with a stick, no doubt something of a satirical nature.

"Synchronise watches," Margaret commanded as if a general going into battle. "Don't forget time and date at the top of each page."

The focus of all this scientific observation was little Resem, cross-legged in the garden. He had recently grown a sweet little moustache that accentuated the cupid's bow of his mouth and, unaccustomed to it, he constantly touched it and tasted it with his tongue. He shot a shy smile up at Greg and me on the balcony. I could tell that I would soon have to sketch him again. I liked Greg. There was something terribly reliable and upright about him. He was, I suspected, a true gentleman and I could see why women liked him too. We were having one of those man-to-man talks that I have always been bad at, assuming as they do, all manner of ordinary knowledge that has never come my way.

"Margaret writes lists," whispered Greg dolefully. "You know. Things to do, questions to ask. Drives me bonkers. My mother does the same thing. I found one the other day and you'll never guess what item fourteen was. 'Sexual intercourse'. And the thing was, she'd crossed it out and written 'carry forward till tomorrow'." He had two cameras slung around his neck and his own notebook. Usually, they used both stills and cine but today, a mere rehearsal, it was just stills. "When we first met, up the Sepik river, she was still married to that crazy sod, Reo Fortune, New Zealand anthropologist, a real bargain-basement bastard. Wrote on the Dobu – nasty bunch of tossers, aggressive, jealous, always trying to kill each other with sorcery – except that's all balls. That's not the Dobu. That's Reo. You know he used to knock Margaret about? Lost a baby that way. And women are not like us, old man. They hang on to these things and bear a grudge. You can imagine what it was like with the three of us shut up in a broiling mosquito-proof room up the arse-end of New Guinea, drinking every night and arguing anthropological theory. Little by little Margaret grew away from him and towards me. I knew he'd kill me if he found out. He had a gun that he was always waving about. When it came to the point, he was quite calm. Just asked me to play him a game of chess. Odd thing is, I can't remember who won."

Margaret and Greg were centring their work on the relationship between child-rearing, personality and trance, which may not have been entirely unconnected with the fact that a crucial part of their funding was from the American Committee for Dementia Praecox. And the principal checks for schizophrenic tendencies at the time were the Holmgren and Weigl sorting tests that Resem was about to undertake. As was usually the case with Margaret, there was madness in her method.

"It's her mind that fascinates me, you see," whispered Greg, staring hungrily at her. "Margaret is about half as clever as she thinks she is, which still makes her a genius. Clear as a bell. Full of ideas and intellectual roughage. She's the most exciting woman I've ever known."

"Made." Margaret's voice was clear as a bell from below. "Have you noted down the exact words Walter used when giving our subject his instructions?"

Made nodded and flipped back the pages. "Got."

"All right." She looked up. "Are you ready Greg?" He gave her a thumbs up and grabbed his camera. "Right. Go!" My mind flashed back to von Plessen. This was not research. This was a movie.

She leant forward and handed Resem a handful of bits of wool of various colours. The idea was that he should sort them out. Everyone began scribbling though nothing at all was happening that I could see. Greg leaned forward and very deliberately took a photograph, the dull thunk! of the shutter very loud. Resem spread the threads out on the ground and began to arrange them neatly in a series of parallel lines. Like many Balinese, he had the hands of a surgeon.

"He's doing it all wrong," hissed Greg from the side of his mouth, "not sorting them out into different colours." He looked at Margaret nervously.

Having put down half the threads in this fashion, Resem turned his head sideways and now began to lay the rest carefully across them, at an angle of ninety degrees. After a couple of minutes, he looked up and smiled. "Finished."

Greg doubtfully took another photograph. Margaret looked annoyed.

"Either," she said, stubbing out her cigarette in judgement, "this young man is colourblind or he suffers from severe frontal lobe dysfunction."

"Er, actually Margaret. It's nothing like that," offered Walter, shuffling forward on his rump as dogs do when wiping their backsides. "You gave him threads and, to him, that means not just colour but cloth, so he's arranged them as you would set up a loom to weave them together and make that *ikat* cloth that you have seen all over the island."

"Bugger!" hissed Greg.

"Oh my!" said Jane.

"Data corrupted by interference of extraneous cultural patterns," intoned Margaret coldly, as she wrote in her notebook and struck out the page with a line. She made a noble and long-suffering face. "All right Jane, give him the Weigl. Go!"

The Weigl test consisted of plaques of wood in three different shapes and four different colours, so that there were many possible ways in which they could be grouped. Resem sat there in the sun and studied them, then rapidly shuffled the pack with the unexpected dexterity of a croupier handling cards and dealt them out decisively on the ground, to form a pretty starburst pattern as if in mosaic. Greg snapped again with his camera. Margaret looked very near to snapping, herself.

"I would point out," noted Walter in extrapolation, "that Resem has arranged the four basic colours according to the cardinal points, as if in a temple offering. Lots of structure there then."

"Thank you Walter." Margaret was showing all the signs of exercising a very great patience. She scribbled again and drew another thick line in her pad. "Jane, the basket of objects."

Jane rose to her feet and went over to the side of the house, pulled away a sheet and revealed a hamper of mixed goods, bought from the market – knives, spoons, crockery, tools of all descriptions. She brought them over and dumped them down before long-suffering Resem.

"Go!"

Once more, instead of sorting like with like, he shared them out, forming five or six neat piles, bigger objects at the base, smaller on top, hesitated, swopped items back and forth and then settled back on his heels.

Walter came over and whispered, nodding. "This pile," he touched, "is what you would need to gut and cook a fish. This one is most of what you need to roll a wad of chewing betel. The mat and the *kris* are together because, at marriage, the groom has to pierce such a mat with the tip of his weapon as a sign of the unflowering of the bride."

Margaret sat crumpled on her chair, cut to the quick, betrayed by science, letting her notebook droop by her side in nicotine-stained fingers. Everyone looked at her as the boys muttered and giggled at this strange and unsatisfactory new form of divination. Then she stirred and it was suddenly as if a dull cinder had burst back into flame. She rekindled herself.

"Okaaay," she drawled, sitting up, shoulders thrust back as if in school. "Change of plan." She turned to address Walter. "The other day, Walter, we were at your aquarium where there is an art shop." What was this? "I could not help noticing that several of the artists paint in a number of different styles, with far more variation than would ever occur with individual European artists. I wonder whether the reason could be that Balinese feel no need to maintain a consistent personality, that they can run several different personalities without integration. If so ..." she leaped to her feet and smiled up at Greg, "then we have shifted the notion of what constitutes an acceptable personality from the universal to the culturally specific and that would solve all our problems and fit the data we have elicited this afternoon. Painting then becomes a mere local symptom of lack of cultural homogeneity at the personal level."

"Well done old girl!" Greg enthusing down on her. "What a corker!" She glowing up at him. Both radiating a kind of intellectual excitement that manifested as sexual and physical heat. List or not, I could see what they would be doing tonight in a far from listless fashion. I had a swift prophetic vision of Greg, thrusting sweatily away under the mosquito net, Margaret moaning as he brought his mouth somehow to her ear, despite the awkward disparity of height, and orgasmically gasped, not sexual endearments, but words like "interference of extraneous cultural patterns" and "shift from the universal to the culturally specific".

"That, Margaret," said Walter in tones of ringing sincerity, " is an idea that would never have occurred to me. Is that really what I have been doing all these years when I thought I was painting?"

* * *

"Rosa and Miguel have written a book." Walter waved his copy of *The*

Island of Bali at me in proof, or rather, in evidence, since it was the final printed version that he brandished, not a proof copy, and stuffed, like an overfilled American sandwich, with cuttings from the New York press. It had come hot from the US, published by Kroeber's, elaborated with Miguel's zingy drawings and Rosa's indifferent photographs. "They have been most kind about me in it. Miguel is doing very well out of the whole thing – commissions, reviews, etc. – and has even installed a Balinese exhibition of sorts in the shop window of an American department store. Inside, you can watch his film footage and buy in leisurewear out of cloth he has based on Balinese designs. What is leisurewear?"

"I think it means clothes that don't involve a tie. What you are wearing would be leisurewear."

"Really?" He looked down at himself in astonishment, like Monsieur Jourdain being told that, all his life, what he had been speaking was prose. "The cuttings say the clothes are 'gay and abandoned'." He frowned, *stirnrunzelnd*. "Is that what I am?"

I looked inside the covers and saw the handwritten dedication with its elegant curlicues. "It says here you are generous and hospitable."

"Then that is what I must be though, according to some words I put in my dictionary the other day, I rather think I am batty and catty and ratty. Still … Vicki wrote a book. Margaret and Gregory will certainly write a book – maybe a whole shelfful of books. Jane is writing articles that will become a book, Colin has published his Balinese symphony and it has been conducted by Stokowski. Now I too shall write a book."

I looked at him doubtfully. "Walter, it takes weeks, months, years to write a book. A book is not a painting. Painters are flashy sprinters – one gasp of creativity, all over in a couple of minutes, at most a couple of days – writers are long-distance runners who just keep putting one foot in front of the other when they have long since forgotten why they ever started."

"If things had been a little different, I should already have a book." Oh God. Here it was again. The book that got away, his drawings of *lamaks*, altar decorations of palm leaf. "You know that Jane took my collection of drawings with her to America, hoping to find a publisher. It was only because she showed them to Margaret that she and Greg ended up here at all. No one would take it. Not commercial, they said. Then

Kroeber's said they would do it if I would pay in $500. $500! I did not have 500 cents. Yet they took Miguel's book." He pouted. I pointed him hastily in a different direction.

"So what is the subject matter of this work to be? Dragonflies perhaps, a work of natural history then. Or maybe your biography. That would have to be unnatural history wouldn't it?" Nasty that. Why was I being so bitchy? Too much to drink, perhaps. Or maybe I was just tired of everything. Or maybe it was because of where we were. We were at Manxi's, a new place down on the beach that Greg found more congenial than the "tight-arsed" Bali Hotel. But he was not here tonight. He would be up in the hills at Bayung Gede, pounding away at a typewriter, writing up his notes, Made's notes, Margaret's notes or maybe developing films as Margaret typed up his notes. There would be plenty of film to develop. In the course of an hour, one afternoon sitting on his porch, I had seen him fire off three rolls. Manxi's was a collection of cheap shacks of bamboo and rattan that caught the night breeze and where, in the moonlight, the ocean was reduced to a series of parallel frothy lines and a rhythmic roar beneath the tinny dance music. It was *louche*, or as near to that as Denpasar ever got, and the backbone of its dissipation was the bored, young airmen from the base next door, their sleepless hormones zithering in the tropic heat. Youthful enough to know themselves immortal – mere airboys really – and briskly omnifutuant in their tight uniforms, they danced and sported with Manxi's girls, many of whom were male beneath the silky packaging – but no questions, no packdrill, any port in a storm, one orifice as good as any other in the magic of moon- and flickering candlelight. It was certain that all this had not passed unnoticed by the authorities but was provisionally tolerated as a necessary flexibility of civilian rectitude to bring comforts to the military, although it had caused a certain dislocation of trade from the *lapangan kota* and it was mildly embarrassing to be so well known and publicly greeted by its overflow at Manxi's. The muscled Javanese barman was twinkling at me conspiratorially over Walter's shoulder as if … Had we? If so when? Manxi, it should be explained, was a gruesome buxom woman from the Isle of Man, allegedly the mistress of one of the minor princelings and simultaneously enjoyed by an expansive Dutch planter, only intermittently present, from Java. To overcome the

Balinese prejudice against red hair she had dyed hers jet black, cut it Cleopatra fashion and looked unnervingly like an exhibit in a museum of Egyptology. Walter lived in terror of her. Once she had shown him her paintings which were of a saccharine sweetness and technical incompetence that he had compared unfavourably even to my own. I could hear her laughing somewhere out on the beach. Appropriate to the darkness, she had a laugh like a screech owl. She would go on, of course, to become a radio propagandist for the Japanese and later enjoy a certain brief notoriety as "Surabaya Sue", broadcasting against the Allies during the Revolution. But I anticipate.

"Dance," said Walter so that I thought momentarily that he was inviting me to foxtrot. "It will be a book, *the* book, about Balinese dance." Two airmen were pawing at the same kohl-eyed he/she over by the bar, forming a sort of rhythmically rutting sandwich, bent at the knees but firmly locked at the groin, hands gripping beer bottles from which they occasionally swigged. "Dance on Bali is unique, not merely a highly evolved aesthetic exercise but an integral part of religious and social life." Each had his tongue in one of his/her ears which provoked loud tripartite giggling as they shimmied approximately to the shellac music. The boys' backs were wet with a Y of sweat. "Dance here is a matter of the greatest seriousness and it must be captured, explained, got down on the page for the benefit of the whole world." The he/she drew back and the two airboys kissed tenderly and then transferred their kisses laughingly to his/her cheeks.

"Walter, no one knows more about Balinese dance than you but you lack the application and ..." more kindly, "... the time."

He looked at me, bright-eyed. "Oh, someone else would have to do the actual writing. It was never intended that I should do the writing."

"Me? I'm sorry Walter ..."

He shook his head. "No, Bonnetchen. Not *you*. Beryl. Beryl de Zoete."

"Who?"

He pointed. Two of the most bizarre women on the island were coming through the door towards us. Manxi's leisurewear dress appeared to have been inspired by one of Margaret's own maternity smocks but cut from material of gross patterns and loud contrasts. I wondered how she would have fared with the schizophrenia tests. With her, was a painfully thin woman in her fifties, in height appropriate to be Greg's partner, but clad in a sort of superannuated flapper's outfit of beige tule and wearing a look of constipated discomfort on her face and a huge ring on each finger of both hands. It struck me immediately as the sort of gesture that resulted not from mere bad taste, unlike Manxi's frock, but a deliberate determination to confront. Her hair was bobbed in what was by then an old-fashioned style.

"'Allo Walter. Me and Beryl's been 'avin' a luvverly chat. I din't know you two was such old friends." Walter smiled happily. I had never actually spoke to Manxi before and realised that I was already judging, disliking, disapproving and preparing to condemn. It was not immediately obvious that hers was a voice that would go on to charm the airwaves.

"Do you remember my friend Rudi?"

Manxi giggled. "Oh yes. Everyone 'ere knows Rudi from that bit of rough field over the other side of town. Likes a bit of rough our Rudi …" I grasped her hand and, intending to shut her mouth, somehow shut my own by stupidly kissing it, catching a whiff of onion smell as she shrieked, "Ooh inne a gent?"

"Bonnetchen, this is Beryl de Zoete." Having performed one act of hand-kissing, I was now obliged to perform another but for Beryl it was somehow appropriate. In response, she etched the briefest ghost of a smile and swooned ectoplasmically into a chair. "Beryl and I are friends from my student days in Hellerau. She is one of the world's premier eurhymicists." Across the room, the two airmen had simultaneously inserted the necks of their beer bottles in their companion's mouth and watched, with awe, as they were dribblingly drained and licked. Manxi was over there in a flash, spoiling the moment, demonstrating their emptiness, demanding they buy more drink, shouting for more animated music.

Premier eurhythmicists? Where had that come from? "What," I heard myself ask, suddenly wooden-tongued, "is a eurhythmicist?"

She regarded me with pity and batted tired eyelashes. "It is a system devised by my teacher Monsieur Delcroze. He was a genius. It brings us into contact with our bodies and our bodies into a greater musical response through a series of visceral gymnastic exercises that harmonise us into immediate enraptured improvisation of dance." Right, so it was clear I would never know what eurhythmics was. I could live with that. The voice was spoken as though through an extended sigh of disappointment as though its owner could not bear to finish the sentence.

"Beryl is going to stay with me for a while. We shall have such fun! We must tour the whole island, show her every single kind of dance for our book. There are so many."

"Are you married, Beryl?" I was becoming very Balinese in my bold use of personal questions. A brave look slid over the pained one. I gestured waggishly at her hands. "Or perhaps, from all those rings, you already have eight husbands." The brave look was displaced by an even more pained one and she inhaled the frail smoke of a "Passing Clouds" and blew it, unheeding, in my face as Balinese gods are said to extract the essence from temple offerings and return the coarse matter to their worshippers.

"I once entered into what was to be a chaste and vegetarian union with a man but, unfortunately, he developed a brutish taste for beer, beefsteak and breasts, creating a rock on which shattered the fragile barque of our tryst." Goodness. Fragile barque, no less. "I have always felt that unions of the soul are more enduring than those of the flesh. My most moving act of consummation was perhaps that with an ardent young man, of a similarly poetic disposition, in my youth. We slaked our passion by removing our clothes in the moonlight, climbing two pliant poplars, side by side, and allowing our quivering leaves to gently interpenetrate."

The airmen had slumped against the bar, their elbows in the barslops and their hands jointly up under his/her frock, surprisingly innocent, rather sweet, smiles on all their faces, eyes locked and feet still shuffling in the alibi of dance. From the phonograph came high-pitched male crooning of something from Cole Porter, "You're the top. You're a dance in Bali. You're the top. You're a hot tamale". If they kept on in that fashion, the hot tamale would be, all too soon, publicly revealed. I felt tired, old, embittered. The groping hands paused, appraised, like a blind man feeling the hands on a clock. One airboy whispered in the ear of the other who looked briefly surprised, then shrugged and hugged tighter with eyes closed, arms now stretched to encompass both him/ her and his friend. The friend reached round to jointly stroke his neck in tandem tenderness. Tears started to my eyes. I envied them their shared immersion in a circle of love below the waist that involved nothing above the neck, a deep oceanic flow of accepting primordial human affection. I had a mental flash of waking in a pose of crucifixion, stiff-muscled and sated on early morning sand cooled with dew, and feeling both emptied and redeemed. Whether that was memory or intuition, I could not tell.

"This book will be my legacy. I shall not," he looked at me sharply, as though I had refused him that service, "make any babies and an individual painting can easily disappear but books are like cockroaches. The more you try to kill them, the more they proliferate". He had been reading something. Of course, probably about the Nazis and bookburning. Vicki had just written to say that her latest, on Bali, had been accorded that treatment again. It was not a political remark. Walter was incapable of politics. During the war, for him, the British emperor and the German Kaiser had been the same man, with the same face, wearing different hats. Bookburning, for Walter, would be a sign of a healthy interest in literature. When he heard of the *Anschluss*, Germany's annexation of Austria, he innocently remarked how nice it was that he and Vicki were now fellow *Landsmänner*. Walter always produced these throwaway remarks as if they were the tip of a vast submerged iceberg of wisdom, whereas that's all there was. "Dance," now pronounced Walter gravely, deploying all the eloquence of a hectoring index finger, "is quite uniquely able to cross cultural boundaries and language difference and appeal to something that moves us sympathetically across the races." For the first time in my life, I wanted to hit him. "The Balinese have a natural aesthetic sense and turn even imported novelties to that purpose. Consider the new dance genre of *janger* …" I tuned out but smiled at the recollection of an occasion when we had returned home early and surprised the boys playing with the new, brighter – but very noisy – petrol lamp borrowed by the countess. They had decided to use it in a revised shadow play, a contest to manipulate their genitals so as to cast the closest approximation of the silhouette of Queen Wilhelmina – as seen on silver coins of the realm – on the sitting room wall. Little Resem even managed to cunningly counterfeit her tiara.

"Time to go home," I urged yawningly. "Whatever you do, don't forget your book."

* * *

"The *nyonya*," I explained to the boys, "eats no flesh, no prawns, no eggs, no chicken." They looked astonished. " She drinks no beer or coffee or *arak* or gin."

"Can we still add pig's blood to the sauce?"

"No pig's blood."

"May we give her a Baboon's Arse?"

"No, keep your Baboon's Arses away from her. She only drinks much water like a camel."

"What is a camel?"

"Never mind."

"If she eats no meat, how is she to make babies?"

"She has no babies, wants no babies, does not sleep with men."

"Beh! Beh! Beh!"

"She does not like babies? Is she, then, like Rangda, Queen of the Witches?"

"She is like Rangda except that she does not drink human blood or eat the stillborn or feast on hot afterbirth." I smiled as I said it. Who, after all, could be sure? "Perhaps," I added foolishly, "she will become Rangda if you give her any of the things that are forbidden." Foolishly, for, in Bali, one does not joke about such matters and now her nickname within the house was fixed for all time and the boys were nervous at meal times, warning this unnatural woman elaborately of possible violations of her many taboos, hovering at her elbow and whipping dishes back to the kitchen before anyone had properly finished, whispering, "Rangda nearly got it – roast pig – imagine!" Propitiatory incense sticks smoked at their door and onions and garlic became favoured decorations of bedroom walls.

"Your boys are so attentive to me, Walter," she breathed. "They watch me to detect my every need. Only Hindus understand the importance of the diet and its purity."

"I think they've taken a shine to you, Beryl. We must go and watch the local orchestra later."

She looked pained. "Thank you, darling, but I must lie down. I have already seen much today. I cannot bear to see anything else until I have rested my eyes and thought about it."

But all that was as nothing compared to the excitement the first time she rose early to do her ecstatic Dance to the Dawn in the garden for, despite her air of utter extenuation, she was like those ancient prima ballerinas one has read of, who have to be carried to the wings, so that the spotlight can warm their faces, at which point they revive and leap around the stage like young gazelles.

"What is she doing?" the boys had asked. "Has she been driven mad by her learning?" It had been explained that she was dancing. "But where is her gold? Where are her beautiful decorations?" This was a mere rehearsal. "But why then is she dressed as a monkey without a tail?" It was true. In Bali, only animal parts wear tight costumes like the outrageous leotard she flaunted. She was thin enough to make it bag so that the whole became a bony *dance macabre* that did nothing to undermine the boys' terror.

She and Walter roared around Bali, photographing, interviewing, arguing and then he swam – buoyantly, boyishly – as she wrote in longhand – silver rings clicking out a fandango rhythm – or interviewed dancers in the garden and put them through their movements at *bassadanza* pace. As she worked, she would call out questions to him until he tired of it. Then, a query about dance genres would evoke: "Oh, I don't know, Beryl. It's really the music that interests me." About music: "Oh, Beryl. Ask Colin. I'm only a painter." She never repined, merely looked pained. Apparently, she lived with an orientalist from the British Museum, therefore expected little from men. One of his irksome peculiarities was to insist on the use of roller skates to avoid taxi fares.

Occasionally, at big festivals, as in a *rondeau*, they would bump into McPhee and Jane or Greg and Margaret, or the Mershons from Sanur, or Made Kaler, or me and we would all whirl briefly together as in that absurd Matisse painting in the Hermitage. Bali sometimes seemed very crowded. Margaret and Beryl hated each other on sight.

It was unfortunate that Walter had arranged for us all to converge on a *sanghyang* dance in Selat. He was not firing on all cylinders. The day before, had been a big concert he had given with McPhee, two pianos playing transcribed Balinese music in a concert at the Little Harmonie. The concert itself had been a relief after the sheer business of shifting two grand pianos from hill locations to Denpasar and retuning them but Walter, as usual, had not cared a fig for practicalities.

"Play it on the flute," I had suggested with brief malice, "better yet the piccolo."

"Concert harps," he responded in joke wistfulness. "I see a wall of great concert harps, each one specially tuned, plucked by virgins."

It had been a great success with the burghers, Bali scrubbed up, its face wiped and made to stand up straight for polite society. The Resident had applauded and spoken a few encouraging words on the positive role of Dutch civilisation in benignly developing the native gifts – though what that had to do with McPhee and Walter remained mysterious. The audience was otherwise a predictable mix of bored ladies and unwilling husbands suffering an hour's enforced sobriety, a few Balinese nobility and half-castes. The notable exception was Father Scruple and his secretary, an extraordinarily handsome Javanese who sat, straight-backed, at his feet with Scruple's papers, hat and cane clutched professionally across his knees and immaculately clad in starched and pressed shirt, knife-edged shorts and brilliantined hair. I could not forbear to steal the odd admiring look at his very fine legs and it seemed to me, tantalisingly, that there was a certain shy reciprocity of awakening interest. Scruple had seen me and decided to ignore me. He was tapping his foot to the music, his knee rubbing against the young man's back. That might just be accidental or it might be more than that. It was only halfway through the second piece, a recreational work entitled "Black Goat", that I suddenly recognised him. It was Dion. I gaped, gawped, gasped. When I next caught his eye, I executed the swift and exaggerated sideways eye movement that Balinese dancers call *sledet* and sidled, crouching, from the room like broken wind at a tea party.

It was some ten minutes before he joined me on the verandah and asked for a light. He was being careful. Other native servants were hanging about there, not being granted entry to the main room. We nodded to each other and watched a man by the gate, very deliberately booting a horse up the backside. I thought of intervening but the fact that the man wore no shoes and clearly hurt his feet in the process, mitigated the cruelty, made it part of native life. Then our eyes locked – velvet eyes – and a sudden dry mixture of lust and compassion choked me.

"Dion!" He put his finger to his lips and looked around warily.

"I'm not using that name at the moment. I'm Hendrik".

"But you used to work here for God's sake. Everybody knows you."

"They knew a Muslim with holes in his underwear. To Balinese, all Javanese look the same. Now I'm Catholic and, as you see, velly good Chlistian boy." He was very bold, confident, cool. I remembered that smile, that slight sheen on the cheek.

"Are you? What are you really up to? I came back and looked for you, you know. They mentioned the police, politics. Oh I don't know." Any attempt to construct a conversation collapsed. "Look, it's good to see you." Jealousy gnawed, sharp-toothed, at the back of my brain. "Scruple. Is he? Do you? I mean …" He looked shocked.

"Father Scruple is chaste, rather like myself at the moment. When you have something important to do, sex just clouds the brain. The Catholics know that. You should learn that too."

"Should I?" His teeth were very white, his tongue very pink. "Perhaps I never really had anything important to do." Then, "What is it that *you* are doing."

He threw down the cigarette, crushed it out like a bug. Shiny, black shoes. Sweet, white ankle socks. "You don't want to know. Just politics. We Indonesians are going to have a hard time in the next few years."

"Who? What was that word?"

"Indonesians. This is Indonesia. It's not the Dutch East Indies any more. Sooner or later, we're taking it back, one way or the other. You know the *Volksraad* is supporting the call for local autonomy but the new Governor General will oppose it? You don't know? Do you even know there *is* a new Governor General?" Wearily. "Ask your friend Sampih, he knows."

"Do you know Sampih? Is he part of it?"

He shot me a look of pity. "Look. Rudi, You're Dutch so that makes you the enemy from here on, no matter how hard you try to stay neutral. You're not a bad man. You took what you wanted but you were nicer to me than you needed to be. You're just irrelevant to what we need right now. You should go home before things get nasty and people walk all over you."

To my surprise, I felt a stirring of anger. "I had hoped that what passed between us was more important than all that, that it was more real than all this damned politics."

He sighed, reached out and plucked one of the huge bird of paradise flowers growing in the cosseted border and shredded it into confetti. "You'll never understand. This is the future". I was considerably taller than him but somehow it was as if he was looking down on me. "I have to get back before Scruple wonders where I am. This job is useful for getting me around and meeting people." He looked at me and something in his eyes softened. "I made you a promise once – to show you something. I'm afraid you'll just have to take my word for it now." He executed a twirl. "No holes any more. You see? When we're good boys and smile nicely, they dress us Indonesians up as their schoolchildren. Goodbye, Rudi." He shook my hand with the loose, pressureless shake of the Indies – Indonesia – and left, smart, even immaculate, disconcertingly purposeful, sadly delectable. I did not go back in. As he opened the door, I could hear the pianos showering down notes, working towards their inevitable conclusion, bringing all the threads busily together and then a pause and the first spatter of applause like rain. Absurd to see a man in early middle age with tears of senile emotional lability already in his eyes. Evening swallows were dive-bombing through the tired arches holding up the roof, soaring up in a steep climb, wheeling round and coming back again for another strafing run. No wait. We had not yet heard about strafing and dive-bombing or experienced the fissiparous tendencies of the new Indonesia. That lay still the future. But I had no more appetite for the future …

"… Bali's past," said Walter in his flat, deliberately boring lecturing voice and pulled down his hat against the wind. "The *sanghyang* is the uncorrupted witness of that past, perhaps the origin of all the other forms of dance." He had to shout to Beryl. A gasket, or "tightring" had blown. The Overland Whippet was getting old. Anywhere else, it would have been scrapped but in Bali, when a part broke, they did not even send for a spare, just sat down, often by the roadside, and made you a new one over a fire. "Its principal feature is that the dancers are definitely in a state of trance, often little girls who otherwise cannot dance and claim never to have even practised. But whilst they are possessed they do things of extraordinary skill and balance and so protect the whole community against the forces of evil." I tuned out, having heard and seen it all before. *Sanghyang* was something of an obsession of Walter's, it was in his film.

The roads were awash with one of those colourful Balinese crowds you find at any festival: old women, babies, men, children clutching flaming torches, the sort that makes them feel safe and happy at night. A little girl struggled past, carrying her fat younger brother who, surely, weighed more than she did. Wild shadows flickered on the compound walls as Walter braked his way delicately through the snaking crowd and drew up at a crossroads.

"Oh look," cried Beryl, "there are the Meads." She pointed but sat, waiting for me to climb out of my awkward boot seat, banging my knee nastily, so I could open the door for her and then stepped out with practised grace, swinging both legs round, knees together, to touch the ground before transferring any weight. Then she strode across lightly to Greg and Margaret. "Hallo darlings. Super to see you." Kisses on both cheeks. "What a ghastly journey. I'm an absolute wreck. Where did you park your car?"

Margaret's mouth became a straight, lipless line. "I'm afraid our fieldwork budget doesn't run to automobiles, Beryl. If we want to travel in style, we have to depend on the courtesy and consideration of our kind friends. We came by truck and walked the last few hours across the fields, carrying all our equipment. The bad part was the leeches." She exhibited bloody stigmata on wrist and shin and nodded at hollow-eyed Made Kaler, crouched, panting, over by the wall, leaning on the camera tripod like a crutch.

There came the sound of another car and the lights of a large Chevrolet swept over us. It was the McPhees, Jane driving, roof down.

"Sorry if we're late everyone. Colin was late bringing the car back. His little friend had to be taken to Sanur and it seems it just couldn't wait." There was a shit-eating grin on his face and a certain tightness around her lips. I recognised the marks of a man caught with his hand in the till or the biscuit barrel or the wrong pair of trousers – or something. Colin climbed out grumpily – no greeting for anyone – and went to sit on a low wall and sulk.

"Okaaay," said Margaret, frowning. "We should do a quick preliminary survey and decide where to arrange our observers. I don't suppose there will be enough light for useful photography, Greg, but you should obviously try to arrange something beforehand. We will need to collect the performers' names and personal details for psychological profiling and so Made can carry out follow-up interviews. He will need to be near the front so he can pick up any chance remarks they may make in Balinese, indicative of state of mind."

"Darling," Beryl interrupted, turning to me. "I wonder of you could fetch my deckchair from the car and do you suppose someone here could boil me a little water for tea?" Margaret contemplated balefully.

"More likely to tell her to go boil her head. Synchronise watches now, everyone. I have eight twenty-four, five, NOW! Remember that each individual dance sequence has to be timed separately."

Beryl glared back, eyes blazing like a cat's in the dark. "I don't need a watch darling. What was it Keats said? Something about 'a hundred handicraftsmen wore the mask of poesy'? Since dance is about the expression of the divine human soul, the only instrument I need is this." She touched her fingers delicately to her heart, then frowned. "Or was it Pope?"

"The Pope?" Walter quizzed, eyebrows raised. "What has the Pope to do with it? I must go and speak to the head of the compound. It is necessary to show respect." He fluttered away.

Margaret smiled sweetly. "Just as you wish, Beryl dear. Thank you for the offer of your heart but I think science requires something more than that somewhat mature instrument." I handed Beryl her chair and noticed Jane, fuming, tears in her eyes, drop her notebook and Greg swoop to retrieve it. He gave me a lugubrious wink as he handed it back, touching the back of her hand, bare flesh to flesh.

"I'll help Greg with the camera," I offered, Made coming with us, men scuttling instinctively from the incomprehensible and ancient wrath of women like cockroaches from the light. In Bali, the entire audience do the same anyway, splitting into two groups, women and children in one, men in the other. The spontaneous process of sorting is like watching an amoeba dividing under a microscope. We set up with our backs to a compound wall, people obligingly ducking out of our way.

"Things seem to be getting a bit sticky with that woman," Greg muttered, tightening legs and calibrating lenses. "Best to keep a low profile." He fiddled approximately in the dark. "There, that should do nicely." He withdrew and began much more complex operations and adjustments with his pipe, rolling and tamping tobacco down into its little charred crater.

"I don't think Margaret and Beryl will ever share a common vision," I ventured boldly. "Perhaps at some level they're too much alike."

He took his pipe from his mouth and stared at me as if I were mad. "What an extraordinary thing to say, old man. I've never known two women more different. No, I mean the McPhee household. A bit of trouble there unless I'm very much mistaken. Jane looks a bit of all right to me – for an older woman – but I gather Colin is a total S-H-One Teabag, contributing to neither board nor bed." He dropped his voice. "Between the two of us, I rather fancy my chances there. Get my end in with her. Take up a bit of the slack. What do you reckon? Is it worth having a crack at her?" He started puffing matches down into the bowl and showered sparks like the volcano up there on the mountain.

I was totally shocked. "But you're just married. What about Margaret?"

He lay the flat of the matchbox over the pipebowl and sucked hard through gurgling tar, then waved a cloud of smoke away and my objections with it. "Oh Margaret's got a theory about that. Fidelity is a thing of the heart." He touched his in parody of Beryl. "Not of the loins. As long as two people are honest with each other and truly close, what one's little chap gets up to is neither here nor there. It can live a life full of how's-your-father on its own in fact as well as in fantasy. She calls it her notion of the separable penis." An *arak* seller walked past with bottles slung on a long pole and caught his eye. "What about a snort?" he suggested. He haggled, sipped, coughed and turned it into a joke for the watchers.

"Look, Greg, you do realise my situation don't you? You know that I'm not exactly what you would call a ladies' man?"

He laughed, swigged more deeply and showed pipe-clenching teeth. "My word, that puts lead in your pencil." He rolled his tongue around his mouth. "Tastes like old fannies." I swiftly declined the proffered bottle. "You being a brown-hatter, you mean? Yes, of course I'd worked all that out. I went to an English public school, old man, and then Cambridge – neither of them places where you bend down in the showers to pick up the soap if you're of a nervous disposition about things like that. Sorry. Shouldn't have said that about a brown-hatter. I gather from Margaret that the proper term is an 'invert' but I've never taken to it – always makes me think of jam-making – invert sugar and so on." At that moment, we became aware of Walter, standing at his elbow in the shadows and looking apologetic, holding – perhaps inopportunely – his brown hat. He looked like a waiter come to tell us the fish was off.

"There is a slight problem." He fluttered propitiatory fingers. "It is not the *sanghyang dedari*, that of the heavenly nymphs, that is being danced to night. The news on the wind got it all wrong. It is another *sanghyang*, instead."

Greg shrugged. "Don't worry, Walter. Which one is it?"

Walter footshuffled and made his monkey-teeth grimace. "It is the *sanghyang celeng*."

Greg frowned. From behind us, Made gave a bark of laughter, swiftly stifled.

"What's that?"

"The pig. It's really quite rare, as a matter of fact. A man gets possessed and turns into a pig. They also do one for monkeys and cooking pots. You must understand what a shocking thing this is for a Balinese. Even babies are never allowed to crawl on the ground like animals. It is one of the most shaming punishments for incest."

Greg grunted. "No skin off my nose old man. Pigs, heavenly nymphs, all one to me – all cats are grey in the dark ..." Perhaps he would have made a good airman, then. Walter relaxed and grinned, slapped him on the shoulder in relief and settled his brown hat innocently back on his head. "But then, of course, I'm not the one who'd get ratty about a bit of a balls-up." Suddenly, above the roar of the audience, Margaret's voice could be heard shouting Greg's name with irritation and an edge of hysteria. The crowd went silent, shocked, swivelled their heads back and forth between the two as if at a tennis match, taking it all in.

"Better get back there," Greg said kindly, love in his voice, handing the bottle to Made and moving off. "Poor little thing needs me."

The *sanghyang celeng* was not a dance at all, but it was certainly a performance. Since people are worried about the possessed running off and doing themselves harm, it always takes place in a closed courtyard, so it turned out that we had set up the gear in the wrong place. The performer arrived in his Beryl-like leotard with clumps of palm raffia tied all over his body and settled quietly in a corner. He had a long, most unpiglike tail with a pink tip. The crowd began to sing a monotonous song about pigs and their food and the man swayed his head and upper body along with the tune and began slowly to let his head sag and grunt. As he neared trance, the crowd began a sort of rhythmic clapping and suddenly he was up on all fours, running around, rubbing his body on the walls, squealing, rushing at people and sending them screaming and scrambling onto roofs and walls. Some men threw water into the centre of the court and stirred it up, splashing with their feet till it formed a good thick ooze. "*Gelalang, geliling. Gegalang, gegiling!*" they shouted. "Wallow! Wallow!" The crowd took up the chant in that moronic, throaty voice all crowds have at football matches and the pig threw itself into the mess and rubbed its face and flanks in the filth. Then it rushed off again to drink from the gutter and threw itself in the slime on its back with the pink tip of its tail poking ambiguously up between parted legs and making copulatory motions to the huge delight of the crowd. Even little children knew full well what was going on and jumped up and down, pointing and beside themselves with glee.

"The Balinese have a notion of the separable penis," Walter remarked smoothly to Margaret, smirking at me.

"Really? That's most interesting." She scribbled notes furiously. I glared at him. How long had he stood there listening to what Greg and I were saying? Longer, anyway, than I had realised.

"It is simply part," he said in authoritative clipped tones, "of the way that their whole idea of the human body is less integrated than our own. You will have heard the story of Kala Rahu, the demon, who was dismembered and only partly reintegrated the parts of his body?" He grinned at me and thumbed his nose. Kala Rahu. Poor Conrad. This was all too easy. Giving candy to a baby. Margaret wrote notes, nodded, carried away.

"Yes! Yes! This is fantastic! It's exactly what I was saying to Greg. When he reaches for anything, his whole body is involved." She lunged forward from the waist in demonstration. "But when a Balinese does it, only the hand and the arm move. It all fits! Hence their lack of passionate participation, disengagement, withdrawal, trance even!" The pig had subsided and was sitting on its haunches, crying softly, as little boys danced around it, taunting, threatening to drag it off to market and ignominious slaughter. It wiped its eyes on its tail and, all at once, began to quiver and stiffen and men rushed up quickly, scattering the children, and doused it with jar after jar of cold water as the man re-emerged from the pig, humanly supine, limbs rigid, grief and distress very real. He was carried off to a shelter, wrapped, massaged – pinched really – by a dozen caring hands and called back with his human name. Margaret was so excited, I wondered if she weren't entranced too but – no – our culture, as she would have said, does not validate that.

When it was clear it was all over, we headed back to the cars. The Meads would be given a lift by the still-silent McPhees. Made Kaler would stay the night and collect more data in the morning. Beryl was still going on about tea. There can't have been much in tonight's spectacle to slake her thirst for expressions of the divine human soul.

"Don't forget, Made," Margaret hectored, "to collect as many accounts as possible of what people remember they saw and why they did the performance at all. Get down the actual words. Do not complete sentences for them. Even if they can offer no coherent reason, that, too, is good data, in itself." Walter went off to thank, take leave, spread a little happiness in the form of paper money for the men, coins for the children. "A time for change," he intoned, as he handed out *kepengs*. Made looked at me and shrugged.

"Why do they do it?" He rolled his eyes. "They do it because it's fun. It makes them laugh. Didn't it make *you* laugh?"

Margaret was immediately there, notebook lethally drawn. "Are you saying that in Bali expressive culture and trance are merely ways of gaining cathartic release from the demands of a repressive personality structure?"

"Huh? Er. Yes?"

Margaret's technique for eliciting information always resembled the beating of a confession out of a reluctant witness. She smirked and thrust out the prognathous chin in triumph. "QED." And made a big happy tick in her book.

* * *

It was not Margaret's flat-footed gait or machete-cropped hair that shocked. It was her occasional unexpected touches of girlishness – the shiny and dainty backstrap shoes she wore with the fieldwork maternity smocks, the unexplained appearance of earrings at her lobes. I had even seen her wear makeup and mistaken it for scabies ointment. Perhaps, the ghastly thought struck me, under all that ethnographic khaki, she wore lacy undies. But the Meads were in town and thus in their gladrags more often now. Margaret had had a nasty dose of malaria and Greg a stubborn bout of colic – "Must be more careful with the water, old boy. Bali sending a shot across our bowels" – and were putting up at the McPhees to recuperate and write up. They were working on the painters of Batuan, very close to being my patch – I had, after all, my chicks among them – and felt irritation and a sense of intrusion that made me even more impressed by Walter's complete generosity of spirit to outside researchers staging Viking raids of plunder on his work. Even so, I could not resist dropping by the McPhees' to keep an eye on what they were up to.

Walter had built the place in conformity to Balinese notions of space. So the kitchen and its fire lay to the south, this being the direction of the sun and corresponding god, the well was dug to the north and the realm of the sea god, the barn set up to the west, house shrines to the north-east and so on. It kept the servants and guests happy and drilled the importance of cardinal points into the McPhees themselves and soothed poor Made Kaler who was originally from the other side of the mountain and so totally disoriented at living ritually back to front in the south.

One of the disadvantages of Walter's position as architect-almost-on-site was that he was expected to sort out any problems that might arise, as in the present case where the well had run dry. So we found ourselves making the mid-afternoon walk, as so many times before, across the gem-like green of the ricefields towards the ridge on which their house stood with a certain high incumbence, enjoying the swish or reeds and grass against our bare legs – a memory from childhood – and steeped in the mellow clatter of wooden cowbells. "We make a beeline," said Walter, "which is as the crow flies." Arrived at the house, we were greeted with bowing regret. Tuan Colin had gone out in the car. Tuan Bayung – Gregory – had gone for a walk. It was not known when he would return. Both the *nyonyas* were taking a siesta. Perhaps we, ourselves, might care to rest downstairs, or lie down in one of the pavilions, and tea would be brought. We settled in the main living room with its great, carved beams, views out over the valley and minstrels' gallery running round all four sides. Plush cats had disposed themselves all over the furniture. The interior of the house virtually purred with them, for Jane had a weakness for cats and was nicknamed *Nyonya Meng*, "Mrs Pussy", by the Balinese. For the local builders, no detailed plans, such as Walter abhorred, had proved necessary, just a rough sketch, a wave of the hand and a walk round the site. They made the whole thing work and limited their fussing to arcane numerology – the odd and even numbers of beams and such. Traditional bamboo and thatch were forgiving media that would expand to accommodate Western architectural obsessions yet augmented the organic feel of the finished building. There was not a nail in the place, everything tied together with rattan and pegs and the whole resting lightly on the earth, more a piece of knitting than a Promethean construction. When the mountain sent out one of its many earth tremors, brick and stone split and tumbled but bamboo and wood merely yawned and stretched. We tucked our bare feet up on the soft sofas ("Sofa so good" – Walter) and I admired the quality of Nyoman Lempad's carving as Walter instinctively charmed the houseboy, poured tea and settled back, staring up at the internal spiderwork of the roof struts, impressed by his own design.

"In Bali, every house is based on the body of its owner," Walter mused, "combined in the correct proportions. So this one is saturated with the span of Colin's arms and hands and the length of his feet." The thought made me feel as if I were clutched in a pudgy, sweaty-socked embrace – quite sick. We sat in silence for a while.

Then the peace was split by a cry from upstairs, piercing and primeval, almost a sob, a reprise of the Widow Traverso's scream. It was not a cry for help but rather a noise imbued with the despair that only comes of a terrible wisdom, like the last defeated sound you will ever make in this world. We both leapt to our feet and I was halfway to the front door when I realised that Walter was not with me but halfway up the stairs. Above each door, was a transom that allowed light from the bedrooms to fall down into the gallery. I watched, appalled, as Walter skirted along the polished passageway, took a chair from against the wall and climbed on it to peer boldly in through the fanlight. He nodded, smiled, returned the chair to its place and sidled down the stairs and past me to sit on the front step and light a cigarette.

"Walter. How could you be so shameless?"

He shrugged. "Better sorry than safe. Anthropologists spend their lives looking through other people's keyholes. They must occasionally expect us to look back."

"Well ... what did you see?" He looked up at me and smiled and said nothing. Just chuckled. "Walter. Who was it? What was going on?"

He rose and dusted off the backs of his legs with irritating langour. "I think I'll go and take a look at that well." He sidled off round the corner and I heard his voice talking to one of the servants. I made to follow, paused, looked up at the transom. The cry rang out again. God help me, I had to know. I could have borne not knowing but to have Walter know and not tell was insufferable. Each step of the stairs creaked beneath my tread. At any moment, one of the boys would come and catch me red-handed and -faced. The chair stuck, then scraped on the floor, wobbled as I climbed up. Bamboo did not make good furniture. The door was hung to open outwards. If it opened now I would be pitched over the edge to a death only slightly better than the embarrassment of being caught. I put my face to the glass and looked in.

At first I could see little but my own dismembered reflection. Light was leaking into the bedroom through drawn curtains from outside. The bed was sited facing north as prescribed by Balinese notions but the head of the figure sprawled on it had its back towards me. Never mind. It was blonde and unmistakable as it twisted from side to side in denial or some agony of surrender. And crouched between its legs was another dim figure engaged in an activity that looked vaguely doggish, with hands raised to Jane's breasts like a man randomly twiddling the knobs on his wireless set to improve reception. Suddenly the whole scene shifted into focus and the dog raised its head. Not Gregory. Not one of the boys. Certainly not McPhee. Margaret! Gruesomely naked but for necklace and dangly earrings, her mouth a great red smear hinting at God knew what vampiric perversities. No wait. That was not the blood of menses nor Rangda's due of afterbirth. That was lipstick and, unless further degradations had been attempted, it had been put on her mouth and only subsequently smeared in the heat of battle. It seemed for a moment that she looked directly at the transom and saw me, but the laws of physics surely prevented that, and she returned gurgling to her task as the dreadful cry rang out again from Jane and I teetered back on the trembling chair and fled from the house.

Outside, Walter was calmly talking to Greg, over by the wall of the well, like two old men discussing the season's crop of runner beans. Surely, by rights, Greg should have been up there with Margaret, taking pictures, tripod twirled to a rakish angle, stopwatch held up to the light, ears straining to pick up any revealing slip of the native tongue. I could hear Walter showing off, reciting some fancy Malay *pantun*, full of puns on the well as a joyful source of water and the eye as a sad one, Greg all nodding, dutiful interest. On seeing me, he switched to a more Freudian mode.

"You're not going in deep enough," Walter was saying with surely calculated salaciousness, flashing glances at me. How much did Greg know? What was he prepared to put up with? "You're up here on the backbone of the ridge and, in the dry season you'll end up just scratching at a damp bottom. I reckon you need to go down another thirty meters but there's always the danger of bedrock that you'll not be able to penetrate, so you might want to think about moving down towards the river and drilling your shaft in a virgin patch." He brightened, abandoning metaphor to a better idea. "Unless you use explosives. Dynamite should get you flowing again." He could see it all in his mind, lighting the fuse, the hiss, the roar, the almighty bang. What fun. "Yes! Dynamite!" he nodded, "that's the thing."

"Walter, they'd never let you get your hands on dynamite."

"Black powder! Lee King sells firecrackers. He must have access to gunpowder. A Beryl – I mean barrel – of that should do it!"

Greg laughed and slapped Walter on the back. "Well, I was in the Officers' Training Corps and it sounds a little dodgy to me, old man, but I think we'll have to ask Jane. I don't know how long she'll be."

"Oh, I should think about another ten minutes should be about right," Walter said. We both frowned and looked questioningly at him. "Oh. I heard sounds of stirring, running water, you know." Walter's knowledge of the female sexual climax proved accurate. And ten minutes later, there they were, hand in hand no less, the adulterous minxes, taking advantage of male innocence to flaunt their Sapphic urges. Margaret had shed the harlot jewellery and wiped her mouth of Delilah's paint and looked as cleareyed and scrubbed as though she were back from singing in the church choir. With shock, I remembered that her first fieldwork had been on something like the sexuality of adolescent Samoan girls in church schools. Oh dear! It struck me then that most anthropology is really autobiography. I could not bring myself to kiss her though Walter, with a total disregard for hygiene, unhesitatingly planted a great wet kiss of greeting on her lips.

"Stay to dinner," urged Jane, looking relaxed and oddly beautiful in a simple linen dress. "We have turtle." Not just turtle but *a* turtle, presented by McPhee's Kuta musicians cum fishermen. And there it was, poor thing, turned on its back, legs pedaling the air, helplessly awaiting the butcher's knife. "Satay for everyone. I'll tell the boys." I had an unwanted vision of Margaret, red lipped, going down determinedly on the dank sea beast. I have never liked turtle meat, heavy and oily and with an attenuated taste of fish that speaks of involuntary contamination rather than true flavour, so I ate sparingly, mainly of rice and peanut sauce. Its flesh would not be wasted. The Balinese regard it as a great luxury and would spin it out amongst themselves in a web of exchange and social obligation. Beryl would be eating roots and berries back in Ubud, bringing Walter's book to term, like a dutiful wife.

It was one of those evenings like ruched satin that you can only have before age makes you constantly aware of the tinny ticking of life's clock. I recall it now in a thick wash of sepia tones. At this altitude, you looked down on the plains as from a high tower and the wind had a slight chill delicious in the tropics. Walter mixed a cunning new cocktail in an antique silver bowl and floated delicate purple and red bougainvillea blossoms on top, then decanted it into delicate little glasses.

"We shall call it 'Breast Stroke' in honour of the turtle – and various other things." I shot him a warning look. He always went too far.

"Why the tiny glasses? Looks like the product of an ant's orgasm." Greg tasted warily. Then, "I think maybe 'Walter's Dynamite'," he offered hoarsely. "*This* would certainly bore a hole through solid rock." Walter slid behind McPhee's piano and improvised some gentle bespoke variations on Balinese themes, caressing the keys breaststrokelike, the music blowing out into the darkened ricefields. I turned towards Greg.

"How did the research go in Batuan?" I asked. When conversation fails, it is always easiest to get a man talking about his work.

"Absolutely non-stop, old man." He blew air. "With Margaret as taskmaster, between work-sessions, one barely got time for a wank and a sandwich before being lashed to one's labour again."

"Don't exaggerate, Greg. It was fascinating," corrected Margaret, sweeping in and tapping ash from her cigarette. Did I imagine fishy breath? "Fulfilling. Painters make good specimens except for their notorious inability to put their art into words. Frustration breeds trancelike passivity and withdrawal from the world, a cultural validation of temperamental tendencies to dissociated states probably originally rooted in childhood toilet training." So that was it. My lessons in perspective were simply grace notes to the organisation of bowel movements. Greg clamped his mouth shut and, himself, withdrew into trance, watching with owl eyes as he displaced his own attention to the anal cleaning of his pipe bowl.

"And what do you think of their paintings? Are they any good?"

She frowned. The concept was alien to her. "Okaaay. They are neither good nor bad, Rudi. They are merely a cultural symptom like the sustained emotional passivity of our last village, Bayung Gede." Irritation flared. I had been to that village, too, knew the men she had been working with better than she did. I could see, in my mind, their thin, bony chests like those of skinned rabbits.

"And when you were in Bayung Gede, the simple fact they were malnourished, riddled with malaria, iodine-deficient and therefore prey to hypothyroid conditions – was that, too, a mere cultural symptom or part of the explanation for any passivity?"

She shook her head sadly. "No, no, no. You do not understand,

Rudi. Nature has nothing to do with it – least of all in Bali. Have you never seen a Balinese man breastfeed his baby? Look, when I was in Manus, I collected over 35,000 pieces of children's art and discovered that they are totally free of the animism that characterises Western children's paintings. They have just not been *taught* that that is what children should be doing. The whole thing was beautifully put to a colleague of mine working in the American Southwest by an old Red Indian storyteller. He told her that, at the creation, the Great Spirit had handed each people a clay cup to dip into the waters and give form to their way of life. 'But now,' he said, 'our cup has been broken'. The Balinese cup is chipped and cracked and leaking badly but it is not yet broken. What we must do is capture its outlines before it is shattered by the impact of the outside world. It is always the case that nature provides the keyboard but culture plays the tune. QED."

Over her shoulder, Walter played a – to me – very natural-sounding tune on a clearly cultural keyboard. Under the pretence of refilling my still-intact cup, I crossed the room to where Jane sat alone, staring out into darkness – dissociated some might say. I sat down beside her.

"Colin and I are getting divorced," she said coolly without preamble. Then, "Oh my!" She slumped and collapsed internally like a badly mixed soufflé. "I'm sorry, Rudi. I didn't want to make a scene. I guess I only really gave up all hope today."

"Any particular reason?" Well, what about the fact that he was off the whole time, scandalously chasing dirty little boys up and down the hills of Sayan? Maybe that's where he was at this very moment. Or that she had just been lesbically tongue-lashed by Margaret?

She smiled weakly. "It's general," she said vaguely. "He has grown, changed, developed different interests."

"And you," I asked, with more emphasis than I had intended. "Have you developed different interests?"

She turned and looked at me and smiled sadly again. "I have never been unfaithful to Colin with any other man." Ah no. I had not asked that. Anyway, she was lying through her teeth, telling the strict truth to hide it, as I had once with my mother – "No woman, mother," I had said.

"Does that mean you will be leaving Bali?"

"Not necessarily. At least not for long." A desperate look came on her face. "I have this book I am writing on trance. Margaret says it's good. I must finish that. The whole thing with Colin can be handled by efficient divorce lawyers. Margaret has been most helpful in that area." Little did we know then that poor Jane would shortly break down in acute schizophrenia and spend much of the rest of her life in and out of clinics in what they cruelly termed, in those days, 'the lithium trance'. Tears welled up in her eyes and Walter was there, on cue, the good plain uncle, without *pantuns* or dynamite, wiping them away with a broad swipe of the thumb, as though she were a little girl. Only he could have done that and made it the right thing.

"I know my playing is pretty good stuff," he smiled, "but I didn't expect to move this audience to tears. You should have come to the Little Harmonie, Jane. We could have used you with all the flinty hearts there." Margaret, seeing the tears, fluttered over and I moved away, back to Greg. This evening was becoming a curious minuet.

"Schismogenesis," he said, as if in a tutorial, and sucking his empty pipe to look wise. Did he never actually light the damned thing? "This hostility between Margaret and Beryl. There is a small disagreement between A and B that becomes progressively amplified over time, feeding on itself and driving the parties intractably asunder. I call the process schismogenesis. Where we worked before in New Guinea, you found it everywhere – basis of the feud – but there is none of it in Bali. Did you know that if two chaps just can't get along, they have a sort of ritual to declare them incompatible. Then they can avoid all the normal social contacts – don't have to say hello – not a dicky bird – and it caps the whole thing. Even the music and dance. It never gets anywhere. Every time it approaches a climax or a resolution, it just backs off and calms down again. You know Margaret calls Beryl 'Rangda'? Well, in the Balinese version, Ragda and Barong engage each other but, in the end it's just a draw. They both back off. Margaret's idea of a proper response to a slight is rather different." He laughed. "In an ideal world, she'd really like to kill her adversary in single combat, then burn down his house, slit his children's throats and rape his wife. Of course, nowadays she can only do that in the academic press but ideally a book should have, not an appendix, but a spleen. For Margaret, conflict is a *sine qua non* of life."

"What is this?" asked Walter suddenly there. "*Sine qua non*? I always though it should mean 'an impoverished Chinaman'."

Greg laughed. "And your own car, Walter, with its dodgy radiator, would be an *auto da fe*."

"Yes, yes." The drink was getting to us. We had been drinking steadily – now unsteadily – all evening. Walter dispensed more, sacerdotally, from the bowl on the piano. "And a *volte-face* would be the expression on your face when you got an electric shock."

Greg was warming up. "A *cul de sac* would be a hessian anus." He rubbed his rump, dog-like against the edge of the keyboard, gasping pantomime relief. We had the giggles, like schoolboys being naughty behind the bicycle sheds. Walter was bent double, gasping and grabbing at the …

"*Piano nobile*," I suggested daringly, "would be 'grand piano'."

"*Casus belli*," Greg thrust out his stomach in a grotesque paunch or, *feu de joie*, now clutching his groin, rolling his eyes in simulated pain and intoning roundly, "an inflammatory venereal disease."

That really set us off. And then Greg looked across the room and stiffened, straightened up, dropped his hand from his crotch, suddenly sober. Margaret and Jane were kissing with a tenderness and appetite, feeding on each other's lips, that belied any further pretence at mere compassion.

"*Noli me tangere*, Margaret," he said with an edge of American bitterness in his voice, "or, as they say in Rome, 'hands off my tangerines'."

Walter was in an expansive mood, driven to draw generalisations from the experiences of the day – in other words drunk. "You know, Bonnetchen," he stage-whispered in my ear. "I never guessed Margaret was a lesbian. It just shows how prejudiced one can be. I thought she wore those ghastly clothes because she was a Christian."

13

I may as well come clean about it. Further dissimulation would be otiose. I had not, of late, visited the *lapangan kota*. Partly, this was a financial matter. It was suddenly as if the world had seen enough of Balinese dancers and bare breasts and my paintings trailed in the art dealers' of Amsterdam. Since the museum shop had been closed and I had had Neuhaus kicked off its administrative board, Walter's shop at the *akvarioom* was closed to me, giving no direct outlet to the local tourist trade. I was not about to hawk my canvases from door to door in the hotels as Balinese did. There was also – I confess with shame – the fact that I was getting free, at home, what I might have paid for in the public domain. Putu, the palace servant who looked after me, had recently assumed new duties. Walter's description of him as "ugly" was wide of the mark. In his mid-thirties, he had always had a chunky quality, it is true, and with a dark, flat face and curly hair that Balinese themselves look down on as the mark of unrefinement. You might say that he had been created to play the role of one of Hanuman's monkey soldiers in the *kecak*, with a great, toothy grin and big ears. But it is surely the place of the artist to find beauty where others are incapable of seeing it. I could detail the soft, blue-black flue on his forearms, the delicate curl of his hair behind his ears, but these would be simply secondary justifications for a gentle passion that I would never reveal to Walter. Quite simply, his plain, hard and efficient body pleased me like the old, unfussy, Dutch country furniture I remembered from childhood. Since Putu already took care of my food, laundry and domestic cleaning, our newly physical closeness seemed – if you will permit the expression – a natural extension that he took easily in his stride. All Balinese know what a terrible thing it is to sleep alone and the fact that we had developed our sleeping to "an exchange of strokings" was unremarkable. Even strangers sleeping in the hamlet's shelter huddled together, meshing their concavities and convexities. It was a physical solace that came with no extravagant declarations and hot avowals, no agonies of identity or conscience, shrugged on almost without comment. It was a thing of the greatest possible comfort.

Beryl had left in an advanced state of literary gestation, half the book written, the rest promised, a publisher already found. Her departure was marked by an extended party with *gamelan* – Putu at the font in a new sarong, playing the cymbal-like *cengceng* – and dancers. The highpoint was an extraordinary performance, by Beryl, of a choreographically correct Moroccan bellydance that she had mastered during her researches there, Walter smacking the drums into vigorous north African tempo as Beryl gyrated her stomach as a sort of absent space, with the boys and the *gamelan* players watching agape. Afterwards, she had to be carried to her room, prostrate, and slowly revived with spoonfuls of warm goat's milk so that she might witness the anthropological tableau staged in the garden by the boys, under Walter's direction.

A sheet is suddenly dropped – ooh la la! – to reveal Resem, Oleg and Alit beneath a banner bearing the legend "Anthropology in Bali". Resem is straining astride a ceramic toilet of European manufacture, bent forward, his fine teeth set in agony, and suffering Alit's fingerwagging rebuke. Alit grips a pipe between his own teeth, some of which have been coloured down in black, and wrestles with a camera tripod, adjusted to comic collapse at every turn. Frowning Oleg holds a watch and scribbles copious notes then thrusts his hand under Resem's sarong and it re-emerges, suddenly revealed as gripping a tape-measure. He makes an astonished, then arch face and holds up a length of some thirty centimeters to the audience, rolling his eyes in envy and flapping his scorched hands. Notes are written, photographs are taken of Resem, of the toilet, up Resem's skirt, of the contents of the bowl, of Oleg's scorched hands, of the tripod. Alit has a conversation in High Balinese down the toilet bowl, cupping his ear to hear its response. Oleg and Alit shake hands in mutual congratulation, raise their arms, like triumphant prizefighters, over their heads. They are fine fellows and march off arrogantly with their haul of knowledge tucked under their arms. Resem collapses back on the toilet and a loud fart is heard from offstage.

Beryl was immensely pleased by the piece. "Reminiscent of dear Aristophanes." It had not been thought necessary to invite Margaret – which meant that we lost the pleasure of Greg – but Jane was there, looking initially haggard and somewhat lost but actually laughing at the sketch and seeming not at all to feel the need to show partisanship with Margaret and her feud. As the party staggered towards its end and the musicians shouldered their instruments back into the storage room, we sat in the garden – her on a chair, myself on the chill toilet rim abandoned by Resem – under stars that seemed, that night, mysteriously golden, as if upgraded for the evening, side by side, a final Baboon's Arse gripped in our hands. Above us, as we talked, a hornbill that habitually slept in one of the trees honked disapproval like a disturbed householder.

"Does Walter not like the idea of female researchers?"

I chuckled. "Quite the contrary, he always says he heartily approves of women in academe – after all it's scarcely a job for a grown man." There was a pause – not quite long enough – before I asked, "How are things with Mc – Colin?"

"Oh my! He's very sad. I worry about him. He needs looking after." In the distance, faint sounds of singing lingered on the wind. It could be our players, companionably stupefied with Walter's *arak* and roast pig, continuing their revels. I could visualise Oleg executing a witty version of Beryl's bellydance before an appreciative audience. But it was a full moon and there would be temple ceremonies and music all over the island and, anyway, Balinese always sang while walking at night to scare away witches. "We all need looking after." She slid her hand onto my knee. At first, I thought it was a misplaced sexual overture, then realised she was working according to Balinese rules of contact. I was a child. She was a grandmother. "Poor Rudi. You aren't very happy either are you? I sometimes think there is something wrong with our whole generation."

"Me? There's nothing wrong with me."

She looked sadly into the water like a diviner. "I mean ... the way things are between you and Walter."

I was astonished. "Me and Walter? But we are good friends."

She squeezed the knee. "Yes dear. Of course you are. In other cultures, sex is organised rather better. I'm sure you know of the

American Indian *berdaches*, men who assume a female role in society and are often the most highly prized and honoured wives, or – amongst other peoples – have important spiritual powers. And here in Asia, amongst some peoples of Java, inverts are allocated major positions in society and their relationships are recognised ..."

"Look," I said. "What is it you're trying to say?" Fireflies pulsed among the trees like cats' eyes staring at us in the dark.

"You shouldn't be sad about Walter, Rudi. Walter is a wonderful person, a unique person but, as he sails serenely through life, he doesn't always realise what waves he's making that can swamp other, shallower lives. Let me pass on to you something that Margaret said to me that you might find helpful. She said that her trouble in life was that people with whom she had passionate friendships, always ruined things by treating her like bread – to be enjoyed plainly in everyday life on a daily basis – instead of like wine – to be tasted as something heady and unusual on special occasions only. Walter, too, is like wine, not bread. Once you accept that, there is no need for you to be sad. And the fact that you and your kind have no honoured place, that your love is not recognised, is not a fact of nature, merely of our own rather odd culture."

"But ... but ..." I sputtered, dithered. How dare this woman whose own private life was in such disarray, whose own sexual proclivities ... should thus presume ... should condescend ... It is hard to be on one's high horse when astride a white toilet bowl in the middle of what I must now learn to call Indonesia.

"I do not love Walter," I protested testily. "We are merely friends." She ignored me, filtered me out. She had been professionally trained after all and I was not saying what she wanted to hear.

"I think we have something to learn from the Balinese," she lectured the river, "their lack of emotional engagement that allows them to bear things unbearable for us, their passivity ..."

"Nonsense," I snapped. "They're not like that." I thought of Putu. *He* was like that. But tonight, he would be with his wife and little daughter. Balinese thought it important to have sex at the full moon to increase the chance of conception. It suddenly occurred to me that, all over this little island, comely brown figures were rutting like rabbits. Every breath of the wind seemed to bear the dying sound of an orgasmic gasp and the musky waft of discharged semen. The conceit excited me. I thought exasperatedly of Walter, fondly of Resem, of Dion – there was a quiver of sadness over Dion – perhaps he, too, at this very moment was somewhere plodding the hill to dutiful ejaculation … But I would go home alone to face a cold empty bed. No. Wait. Not cold. A hot, empty bed. More biblical. Even worse.

* * *

The success of Miguel and Rosa's book was not without its consequences. Suddenly, there were tourists everywhere, clutching it and Walter was awash with them, for everyone who bought the book felt they had purchased intimacy with him. The Duke of Sutherland – formerly the British War Minister and a friend of Charlie's – and his Duchess passed by and promised to return, whisking Walter away in their new yacht. ("Enough of the have-nots, Bonnetchen. I am joining the have-yachts.") Ruth Draper – the Australian cabaret comedienne – spent a week whilst on her Asian tour. She had the curious gift of being able to ape the sounds and mannerisms of the speakers of any language while having no actual knowledge of it at all. Her "Russian" sent Walter into paroxysms of nostalgic delight and for days he roamed the house growling vowels and rolling "r"s. Two more guest rooms were hastily constructed, more boys hired. The world was knocking on Walter's door and Bali had become a business. Every mail delivery brought more enquiries about his paintings and a lesser man would have settled back into the comfortable mediocrity of self-repetition. But in Walter's case, success, as usual, went to his feet and his first reaction was to run away. They wanted paintings? Right. He would become exclusively a musician again and off he went on an extended concert tour of Java with Colin, repeating their performance at the Little Harmonie, to packed houses. In his absence, a new cottage, rather like the little studio in which I lived, was constructed for him at remote Iseh, in the mountains near the Besakih mother temple, and there he would flee – "to be mothersoulalone" – with one or more of the boys to paint or zoologise or intensively do nothing at all. If anyone sought him out and pestered him with questions about Bali, his answer now lay ready to hand. "No idea," he would mutter abstractedly. "My own knowledge is minumental. I should look it up in Covarrubias, if I were you."

It was at this point that he made one of the worst of those errors of judgement that characterised his life. So that he could flee the press of tourists, he hastily appointed two passing German painters to run what I can now only term his hotel at Campuhan. Walter Dreesen and Fritz Lindner he possibly judged to be compatible souls – of the faith, artistically inclined, embarrassingly enthusiastic for all things Eastern and exotic, yet – somehow – just not very nice. With fat bellies and small heads, they bullied and bossed and strutted about and, I am almost sure, engaged in gross peculation. The coffee became thin and metallic, the rice of evil quality, the addition on the bills became of an almost Italian unreliability. When they invited over the Neuhaus brothers of Walter's *akvarioom*, the place was a very Wagnerian hell. I suddenly spent a lot of time at my own house. The boys, always a trustworthy touchstone of strangers, hated them all and felt themselves callously abandoned by Walter.

Dreesen caused endless confusion by insisting that *he* was the Walter who lived at Campuhan, even accepting artistic commissions on this doubtful basis. From somewhere, he dug out a "von" to preface his name and unwisely made the boys call him "Baron" which – given his endlessly flapping jaws and straggly beard – swiftly became "*Barong*". I spoke to Walter about it and he was, as always, airily dismissive. It was a purely temporary arrangement until Miguel and Rosa blew over. If I was serious about this, why did I not myself step into their shoes and so spare the boys? If they were unhappy now, it simply showed how happy they would be when things returned to normal. But for the moment another *Barong* occupied us.

"Have you heard the big news?" asked Walter, pulling up a chair to our table. We were at Manxi's – empty at this hour, save for Greg, myself, now Walter, the endlessly jolly Javanese barman and a lugubrious youth who studied us with anthropological intensity. The *patronne* was mercifully absent. Greg pointed to a newspaper, lying steeped in beer dregs on the floor. "Japanese defeat in Battle of Lake Khasan", it declared. "Russia extinguishes Japanese imperial ambition in Asia!".

Walter looked, made a face. "No. Not that. Newspapers aren't real news." He signalled for beer. The youth, having studied us, wound the grammophone and began to sift through the records on the bartop.

"Do you mean the new constitutional arrangements," I asked, "giving Bali self-rule under the traditional kings? Should be good news, shouldn't it? Directing a bit of cash back to the palaces for cultural purposes? Are you perhaps in charge of the cerebrations – I mean celebrations?"

Walter shook his head. "Yes. No. By news, I mean the cleansing of the McPhees."

"Ah." Greg drummed his fingers on the table. He had clearly not brought his pipe and was at a loss what to do with his hands. "I heard there was to be a big bash. I like a bun fight."

"What's this?" As usual, no one had told me anything. The barman brought beer. Walter slipped his arm fondly round his waist, interrogated him minutely on the state of his family and asked after his children by name. When he had finally gone back to the bar, Walter grinned at me and answered.

"The McPhees are having a *calonarang*." He said it with enormous self-satisfaction. I nearly missed the last word, drowned under a deafening squeal of – of all things – Scottish bagpipe music. The barman looked over and did a quick thumbs-up, returned by Walter. Greg and Walter exchanged a glance and laughed.

"Holy mother of God! His job," explained Greg, biting at his nails and indicating the youth, "is to take a squint at the punters as they come in, guess who they are and what they like and pick out the music that suits them. Usually, when I'm here on my own, I get 'The Teddy Bears' Picnic', which I take as something of a compliment. Walter gets 'Night and Day' and Margaret 'Felix Keeps on Walking'. I can't imagine what you've done to deserve this."

"*Calonarang*?" I asked. Neither of them could ever stick to the matter in hand. "Whatever for? The battle of *Barong* and *Rangda*, of good and evil? You're always on about *calonarang*. You show it to tourists at Rawa's village. It's in your films. Now you think it will do something for the McPhees?"

"It's always interested me," Walter drank and made a face, "that the idea that the gods cause misfortune, sets evil safely outside the human community whereas witchcraft sees it as originating in men's envy – so all that rage goes back into the search for witches and their punishment and makes it all hotter – Greg's schismogenesis. Balinese have it both ways by making Rangda the witches' queen. Very neat." He looked at Greg, hopefully, in search of comment but Greg was covering his ears with his hands.

"Do you, perhaps, have any Scottish blood, Rudi?"

Walter pouted. "Why should it not help the McPhees? Who can tell? It is not my decision but the diviner's and so Bali's view of them. I'm sure you remember that, against everyone's advice, they never finished the boundary wall and so they are exposed to all the demons and bad spirits that live both in the graveyard and the gorge, on either side of them. With all the jolly, nocturnal picnics they hold – with or without teddy bears – feasting on entrails and afterbirth, singing and dancing to Rangda, I'm surprised anyone in that house gets any sleep. The well has run dry. Several of the boys have had nasty falls. Tinned food went bad and exploded – spaghetti bolognese all over the place, apparently, and mistaken for blood and entrails by the staff. You know for yourself that their marriage is far from good and that there has been disharmony in that household. Now blue lights have been seen at night. A bit of wallbuilding, then a *calonarang* ceremony will take care of all that." The lugubrious youth, having detected that the record was coming to an end, energetically rewound and reset the needle at the hissing beginning. Greg rocked up and down on his chair and groaned.

"I read somewhere that, before they drowned Rasputin, the Bolsheviks tortured him by playing a record of 'Yankee-doodle-dandy' outside his cell day and night. I confess I'm already ripe to be pushed beneath the bloody ice. I suppose the only way to stop the lad, without hurting his feelings, is to ask for something else." He shuffled off. Records were fanned out and discussed and he shuffled back, arms beating time as in a slow drunkard's dance, to the warbling tones of "The Teddy Bears' Picnic". "Better. Much."

"Do you mean that you support the ceremony simply to make the Balinese feel better or that you actually expect it to cure their problems? Do you mean that demons are real? What *do* you mean?"

Walter sighed. "We can argue bout this until the cows come home to roost. When you live with another people, Bonnetchen, there is only one way to do it. It's a matter of all or nothing. You can't pick and choose. You must believe *everything*."

"Drink up, chaps," urged Greg in a welcome and very sudden silence. "By the time we've got through *calonarang*, I predict that we're going to be very tired little teddy bears."

* * *

"Aw Jeez, Maaahgret. Them must be the bleedin' pudenda priests." Greg's acerbic version – I assumed – of her second, New Zealand husband, Reo Fortune. He was deliberately provoking her, playing with fire, what Walter termed "putting the bat among the pigeons". They had had a bad day, yesterday, showing Balinese Rohrshach blots. In the smeared symmetries, villagers had seen nothing at all or demons, their standard response to any violation of the forms of nature. The McPhees' houseboys, in their greater sophistication, had assumed they were being handed the Tuans' used toilet paper. Margaret's grumpy ill-humour was the price she now paid for her assumption that every day was an opportunity for discovery and development, as opposed to Greg's view of its being just another damned thing to be got through.

"Stop it, Greg. You know full well the word is *pedanda* priests. And drop that stupid accent."

I imagined this was all something to do with the goings-on between Jane and Margaret, a sort of contagion of dysfunctionality between the two married couples. I regretted coming so early. The sky was still etched with the portents of dawn. Made Kaler and I exchanged mute looks of sympathy. Walter was lost in thought, watching guests and visitors struggling up the hill, bearing musical instruments, costumes and ritual paraphernalia, offerings of food and bamboo tubes of drink, corked with clumps of grass. Clouds the colour of a black eye coiled and twisted on either side and the ground was still slick from a nighttime downpour. But there would be no more rain today. Magic against disruptive precipitation was part of the package, bought and paid for. Bare Balinese feet gripped the slippery rock as our tyres had not. The Willy's Overland Whippet was parked off to one side, abandoned halfway up the bank, uncovered, for there would be no rain. It had developed a new quirk, refusing to start until pushed, following a collision with a buffalo from which only the beast had lumbered away intact. "Thank God it was unhurt. I have," Walter lamented, "no unsurance." At first, the small boys of Ubud had found pushing the car down the hill a heady comedic experience. After two weeks of it, the charm had palled and they tended to disappear at the sight of us.

The priests trooped disdainfully past in shoulder-length hair and twirled topknots, swaying white parasols held above their heads. In Bali, priests may be either male or female – pudenda, then, not entering into it. Female priests, if anything, have more assistants since they are not permitted to carry anything on their heads, otherwise the usual way for a woman to bear burdens. The McPhees were busy, offstage, with the musicians, so other guests were unctuously welcomed by our white faces – automatically surrogate hosts – with silent gestures of respect and by Made with hyperbolically exalted language and the stretched vowels of subservience. Three men, one woman, led by the renowned Ida Bagus Gede, a man of great age, archepiscopal aplomb and magisterial distaste. Most Balinese do not care to be drunk since it brings them to that near-panic state called *paling* where they lose awareness of where their sacred mountain is and thus their place in the world. Yet rumour had it that Ida Bagus's white-haired dignity was of the careful kind that drinkers use to mask their befuddlement. It did not matter. He was a man full of *sakti*, spiritual power, one of those explanatory principles – like "culture" and "personality" – that all peoples have and are central to their world and remain quite untranslatable and incoherent. The priests trailed off to purify themselves, change and scramble for the highest seats in the house. The existence of a minstrels' gallery above their heads would not please them.

"A fine, high-nosed man, Ida Bagus," Walter nodded, approvingly. "There has always been a stiffness between him and the Meads," he whispered. "He was upset that they first came at the time of *nyepi* and got permission to drive across the island despite the rules of religion. After all, *nyepi* is just a larger version of what we are doing today."

It was true. The New Year festival was a time of cleansing and marking boundaries, of tempting the demons away from the village to the crossroads for a feast, parading them in paper images – subsequently burnt – and sealing off the human domain thus purged. Unlike present events, however, it also involved a day of everyone staying quietly at home, no fires lit, not even a lamp or cigarette, to deceive the demons into thinking Bali was deserted. For Balinese, both Dutch and demons are inherently stupid but only Balinese find silence unearthly. Margaret, fearing no demons, sucked noisily on her cigarette.

"Personally, I have found the priests here to be the greatest of disappointments. I had expected cultural insight but they are mostly very ignorant old men who know nothing of 'Why' or 'How' and simply talk of 'What' – endless ritual prescriptions. It is the Balinese way to live within excessively tight organisation and the reason that they are quite incapable of coping with the unknown and with so little sense of the individual. The whole busyness of Bali," she snapped, "is just a great barrier against fear and terror and rituals such as this are, after all, simply a kind of whistling in the dark."

A dangerous glint appeared in Walter's eye. "Keep your haircut on," he laughed. "Personally, Margaret, I have always whistled in the dark and have no problem living by Balinese rules whose reason I do not know. Charlie Chaplin told me he had once stayed with Maurice Chevalier in the south of France. Chevalier had this game of skittles set up in the garden and it was a rule of the house that anyone who won had to go to a sort of shrank – shrine – at the bottom of the garden and press a button. The doors opened and the statue of a fat, naked lady came out mechanically and the winner had to kiss her arse. Chevalier was most insistent that it should be done. Charlie was happy to do it but could never understand whether the fat arse was a reward or a punishment. Bali is a bit like that." The total blank non-comprehension of Margaret's face was a delight. Here, at last, was a comment she did not have a view or a theory about. So she wrote it down.

Greg twinkled. "Complicated business the relationship between the collective and the individual, old man. You might say it's an old chestnut that's still a hot potato. Margaret's rather an expert on the subject …"

"Okaaay! I don't think you have quite caught my meaning. You exoticise, Walter," she sniffed. "You make people romantic, more unusual and exciting than they are, colour them in, whereas they are just following cultural prescriptions."

Walter wasn't having that. "Exotic, romantic, exciting? I think what you are saying Margaret," he spoke gently and calmly, eyes wide with innocence, "is that it is wrong to fall in love." She clamped her jaws and wrote that down too. Love, she might have said, was merely a cultural notion. But today she was not arguing against love, it forming part of her dispute with Greg. Walter was having a good day. "You see? I am backfiring on all cylinders, am I not?" Then to me. "Ida Bagus always insists on throwing his clients' money about," he remarked with envy, as though he had ever been denied that pleasure, "especially where rich *bule* are involved. And we – as you know – are the very *crème bule*. I don't know how many dogs, chickens, ducks and pigs will have been killed to feed the demons. Come on Bonnetchen. Let's go and see."

In the middle of the garden, where the gay bunting of the daily wash usually fluttered, a grim erection reared up like a crucifixion, a bamboo shrine for each of the cardinal points and one more for the centre. Five is a primordial number for Balinese. Splayed corpses of white beasts lay bespatchcocked to the north, black to the south, yellow to the east, red to the west and a veritable rainbow for the centre.

"Margaret," Walter stated with slow emphasis, "is a forceful woman. She is, perhaps, the only wife ever to urge her husband to get on with it and get to the point while they are having sex." I had no idea what he was talking about.

The priests were already installed on high chairs, rather like those used by us for the feeding of babies, refreshing themselves with McPhee's brandy, served by an unwontedly sweet-faced, honey-mouthed Sampih. A perilous arrangement of ladders and platforms would allow them access to the balcony and thus the highest room, where they would change. It seemed to me unwise to serve the brandy before the changing but, in due course, Ida Bagus was up there in a trice and, when he redescended, he was a thing of beauty – sparkling white sarong, high diadem of scarlet and gold, beads and bells and silver bowls – surely one of them that used by Walter to compound his "Dynamite" drink. Soon Ida Bagus was leading the chanting, coaxing forth and shaping the magical mantras with his slender hands, waving in the bells, addressing first the gods and then the demons, generating a booming power and will to command that rang out like thunder and cast a net of protective enchantment over the compound.

A cheer from the back of the building. I looked round and Walter had gone. The McPhees' boys and our own were round there, surrounded by the young bloods, scrabbling in the dust, cockfighting, a requirement of the ceremony since blood must be shed on the earth. But this did not preclude a little convivial gambling and soon Resem was untwining his silver *ringgit* from his waistbelt and handing it shamefacedly over to the other household, his cockerel slashed and slaughtered by its opponent. One by one, all our household was being roundly plucked and Walter was there, headshaking, striking poses from Victorian melodrama and grimly refusing any advance on pay – the heartless, mustachio-twirling skinflint – saving the boys' reputation as bold bachelors at the same time as he spared their money.

The *gamelan* struck up a fine brassy sound, the musicians grouped in the shelter, arranged around the legs of McPhee's piano, Sampih in there hammering at the keys of the *gangsa*, a long-stamened red hibiscus – conventional symbol of the penis – tucked behind one ear. McPhee and Jane were conferring with the lesser priests, poring over diagrams drawn in the dust, waving arms, pointing, trying to plan the rest of the event, for Ida Bagus had withdrawn to sleep and strengthen himself, as much power had been drained from him by the morning's work. The bottle of brandy had gone with him. The Meads flitted, photographed, observed arms-crossed, bickeringly disapproved. The coloured threads on the offerings, recalling the failed tests for schizophrenia, particularly annoyed Margaret. Despite all the activity, nothing seemed to be happening.

"Where are the dancers?" I asked.

"What dancers?"

"For the *calonarang* play." I had expected to see them transported up on the back of a lorry, standing upright like cigarettes in a fresh pack of American smokes.

"Ah, no." Walter's eyes shone. "This is something special, Bonnetchen. The play is to be done, not by human dancers but by the shadow puppets and Ida Bagus himself is to be the puppeteer, the *dalang*."

"Ah." Unlike some other parts of the archipelago and odd as it sounds, the Balinese sometimes perform shadow plays in broad daylight. That was, however, not to be the case today. The colourful sight of Ida

Bagus in full religious spate was not to be bleached out by sunlight, so we faced a long arid wait until late in the evening and then the play would run till dawn. This would be no problem for the Balinese who could – as it were – switch themselves off at will.

The event had by now gathered a full supporting cast outside, a crowd scene from Breughel – satay-sellers, gamblers, drink-peddlars cricket-fight impressarios, purveyors of little banana leaf-wrapped packages of rice or betel nut. As always, the shadow play would be not just be for gods and patrons but the world at large and the space before the compound boiled with the activities of everyday life. When spectators had nothing else to do, they groomed each others' hair. One mother dandled a tiny child on her lap that took alternate casual sucks at her breast and a long, rustic cigarette.

Walter led us across to McPhee's fine ricebarn – never yet used for rice – where a shaded platform offered rest to ourselves and a couple of comatose musicians, Ketok and Kumis – known, roused, greeted, caressed, of course, – as part of Walter's magic of universal friendship. Resem appeared with food and drink, hot rice, smoked duck, pungent fruit and misty *tuak*, shared in good fellowship. Jane's cats sprawled and stretched and preened about us. At the end, the food made a final circuit. "Cannot, cannot, cannot – *kenyang*," I declared. The Balinese tittered. It was an old crowd-pleaser but one I could not resist. *Kenyang* in Malay means "I am full", in Balinese "I have an erection". Resem, full but not erect, stayed to watch Walter teach all a raucous Viennese card game he had played with Vicki, called Tarock. *Kumis* is "moustache" and, as gratuitous motivation will creep into the affairs of men, Kumis's own was particularly luxuriant and clearly the envy of wispy Resem who constantly licked his own upper lip. The afternoon passed in great content, waves of muted sound washing over the newly demon-proofed walls, the barn like a raft afloat, its pillars great reassuring masts against which to rest our backs. A storm hissed through the vegetation across the valley. It would not come here. Ida Bagus would not permit it. Resem did surprisingly well at the game so that I wondered if Walter were not deliberately manipulating it to make good his losses. I, myself, did not play. I know that gambling is an important element of ritual, creating, as it does, more elbow room for the action of the gods, yet I am invariably unlucky and it brings me no pleasure to lose my money.

Kumis settled back amongst the scattered cards and lit a cigarette. "Do you know the story about Bali and gambling?" In Sayan, he was a known storyteller.

"What story?" In Bali, a storyteller relies on his audience for prompting questions, a monologue becomes dialogue.

"Well, it is like this. There lived a man, a *Brahmana*, called Sidi Mantra."

"Where was this?"

"In the kingdom of Daha, in Eastern Java."

"When was this?"

"Long, long ago." This becomes tedious to the Western ear. I shall omit further questions. "God had been kind to him and given him great wealth, everything but a son. Then, even that was granted and the boy was called Manik Angkeran.

"Oh how they loved that boy and how they spoiled him! Everything that he wanted was given to him. He grew into a young man who was bold and clever and very, very handsome but he had one failing. He gambled. He gambled at every opportunity and on everything. He surrounded himself with wild companions and played with them day and night. He had no thought even for women or anything else.

"He threw away everything he owned till he had nothing left. Then he borrowed more money. As security he used his parents' lands and soon that money was gone too. He went to his father and confessed and his parents' hearts were moved to pity. His father was a very holy man, full of *sakti*, and he fasted and prayed and asked the gods what he should do and suddenly they answered him on the wind.

"A voice told him. 'Go east until you come to Gunung Agung. There you will find a dragon called Naga Besakih who owns great treasure. Ask him for some in your extremity.' So that is what he did. At that time, Bali and Java were linked by a spit of sand. On each side, the waters boiled and gnawed but could not get through and the holy man walked across dry-shod.

"When he arrived at Gunung Agung he sat down and prayed and made mantras and rang his bell and called out the name of Naga Besakih until there came a great rumbling and the very earth shook. Other men would have run away in fear, but Sidi Mantra was protected by his great power and rang his bell again and boldly called out to the dragon.

"'Who dares to call me?' it asked and came out of its cave. It was huge and terrifying and covered in jewels that shone and dazzled. Then Sidi Mantra spoke in most respectful language and explained why he had come and what he wanted. The dragon laughed and even that was a terrible sound.

"'That is easy,' he said. He shook his body like a wet dog and great jewels fell off and rained down on Sidi Mantra who spread out his *kain* and gathered them up. 'Take them and save your son. But do not let him gamble ever again and never come and ask me for more, for that is all you will get.' So Sidi Mantra thanked him and went home and paid his son's debts and all was well. But the son forgot his promise and gambled again and lost again and said to himself. 'The old man went to the dragon and got money. I will go too. I am cleverer than him. He will not be able to refuse me.'

"So Manik Angkeran set off and came east and walked to Gunung Agung and called out to Naga Besakih and rang his father's bell – which was not allowed – and when the dragon came, he spoke arrogantly and most disrespectfully.

"'Dragon. My money is gone. I need more. Give me some!'

"The dragon listened and said, 'Manik Angkeran. Because your father is a very holy man, full of *sakti,* and my friend, I will give you what you ask. But I say to you again that you must change your ways. You must stop gambling and you must marry.' But as the dragon turned, Manik Angkeran saw a huge diamond on the end of its tail and was seized with greed. He drew his *kris* and chopped of the end of the dragon's tail. The dragon roared in pain, spun round and burned him to ashes.

"When Sidi Mantra heard what had happened, he was very sad. He loved his son and he was ashamed for what the boy had done. So he came to Gunung Agung and crouched down low and called out to Naga Besakih and asked his forgiveness.

"'Well,' said the dragon, 'I will restore your son to you but henceforth you must live apart, for you cannot live together.' And that is what he did. The son was restored to life and the father set off to return to Java. When he arrived at the sand spit, with tears in his eyes, the old man turned and drew his staff across the land and the water rushed in, in the blink of an eye, and now there is the deep and dangerous sea that divides us from Java. Bali became an island."

"Beh!". "Beh!". "Beh!".

I thought here to find a justification of my own views. "So," I said, eying Walter and Resem and directing the moral at them, "the story teaches us that gambling is a foolish and dangerous habit, unholy even."

Kumis looked at me in astonishment. "Nooo, Tuan" he said, and shook his head. "It says that gambling is the very root of Bali and that, without it, we would still be ruled by the Javanese."

Walter hooted with amusement. "And that we should all continue to live as bachelors or be eaten by dragons," he laughed.

I Bagus Gede returned long after the setting sun. In the darkness, lightning licked and crackled over the distant mountains and an electric charge tingled in the damp air. A bedsheet to serve as screen for the shadow play had been set up over a bamboo frame by the edge of the ravine with the musicians assembled and idling behind it. The demons and sprites that lived there would be conscripted to the audience. The great box of ornate, buffalo-skin puppets had been brought up and covered with a white cloth. Bagus Gede was meticulous about his preparations, chanting and praying, handing out the puppets to be set out, good on one side, bad on the other, by his assistants, invoking powers for strength and eloquence. Finally, the smoking lamp was lit and glowed behind the screen, the wooden hammer pinioned between his toes. A series of staccato raps with it, against the box, brought the musicians to order and they launched into the overture. The *kayon*, a representation of the holy tree of life with the sacred mountain at its base, was leaning against the screen. It would punctuate the various scenes but now was a character in its own right, being made to leap and twirl and pulsate to the rhythm of the music. It was immediately clear to me that Ida Bagus was drunk.

"You know, I think he is already in a trance!" whispered Walter, astonished. He crept over, on bent knees to avoid offence, to watch more closely. The Meads prowled, watching the audience, not the play – the play, to them, irrelevant – Greg firing off shots, each one greeted by a murmur from the crowd, Margaret pointing out victims like a Salem witchfinder.

"Nothing important at this stage," he explained through his pipe. "I just want to get them used to flash photography for later." Too good for a puppeteer to miss. Each time he did it, the characters projected on the screen jumped and made a joke about the thunderstorms in this play. Then came a series of smutty jokes about foreigners whose sex was mysterious since they covered their breasts and slept with everything, even pigs. The gang of little boys in the front row loved that, giggling and tugging at their genitals. Being spoken by servants, therefore in Balinese, as opposed to the Old Javanese of the high caste puppets, even I could understand it. Drunk or not, Ida Bagus was on fire. It was what you might call a three-star performance. Accents, gestures, refined and low, dirty jokes, cosmic themes, sound effects, songs – hands, feet and voice all engaged them on the simple screen, manipulating the rods attached to arms and legs to coax the figures into uncanny life. McPhee was round the back, where the puppets were all gold and bright colours, fussing over the constitution of the orchestra – why were there drums? – the tuning, the use of different themes. This was the spot for those who were not content just to watch the effect but were interested in the skill of the performers. Perhaps it has something to do with the obsessive Balinese distinction between *sekala*, the world of the visible, and *niskala*, that which lies beyond the senses. I do not know. The Balinese do not know. You would have to ask Margaret. QED. I picked up an air that Walter and McPhee had explored at their last piano recital.

Jane, Mrs Pussy, came and perched beside me, lit two cigarettes, handed me one, just as Rangda made her first appearance to a crash of gongs that echoed back from the other side of the ravine and a shudder ran through the crowd. The puppets for other characters were held close to the screen so that they were small and sharp but Rangda fluttered some way behind it, large and inchoate, as if still crystallising into existence.

"Rangda is the non-childbearing woman," she said, "for whom everything is jealousy and negativity. Sometimes I think that's me. Of course, sometimes it's Margaret. That's why she was so keen to use the name for Beryl. You men without babies just don't have the same things to put up with. And in the dramatic version, the kindly, protective *Barong* is the nurturing father and gets all the good lines."

I shrugged. "In the mountain villages here, men without children are not allowed to live in the centre or play a full role in life. They are considered never to have grown up, like – I suppose – Walter and myself."

"But they don't get all the evil and bad crap in the universe dumped on them, like Rangda. Margaret sees the roots of Rangda in the teasing mother as the embodiment of fear. Look ..." She pointed. A mother was ignoring her desperately struggling child, slung under one arm, staring off into space, not even at the screen. "The mother alternately plays with the child and then just ignores it, a sort of cultural schizophrenia, that makes the Balinese so passive yet permanently anxious. The convulsions of the possessed are just the tantrums of the ignored child. We may not say it but we are never far from despising those who love us. And all men marry their mothers."

Such nonsense. "Please," I said, with distaste. "I did not marry mine."

She smiled. "You sure didn't Rudi. You chose the other option and shunned all women. And, for once, in tonight's version Rangda gets it good, killed stone dead by a mighty holy man. Ida Bagus's favourite, all-male version." She threw down her cigarette and stood up stiffly like an old barren, non-childbearing witch, rested her hand softly and sadly on my shoulder and went over to the Meads. Margaret was making energetic notes in the torchlight, arguing with Greg over something. I heard him say "Oh, put a sock in it, Margaret" and I got up and went to the kitchen. Low lamps were lit, clotting the shadows in the corners. There was a jug of water on the table but in this house they drank – rashly – the water unboiled and unfiltered, straight from the well. Coffee was still warm on the stove. That would have been boiled. I looked round for a cup, found none and poured myself some into a glass that stood on a shelf over the sink. In my household, after washing, I had instructed that glasses be rinsed in boiled water. Here, I would have to take a chance. The Balinese liked to know how much everything cost in a fancy foreign home, transforming it into a museum of *bule* profligacy, so, in the McPhee household, the routine for washing glasses primarily targeted, not hygiene, but the preservation of the price tags gummed on the bottom.

"*Leyak! Leyak!*" Witch! Witch! I slopped coffee down myself, cursed and made for the side wall. Walter was already there, peering into darkness.

"What is it?" He pointed. Over in the fields, was a wavering light, dancing over the surface of water. It could be a witch, or a torch, or a lamp or the biggest firefly in the world or anything you wanted it to be. The shouting was from a child. Doubt was already creeping into its tones, dissolved in communal laughter. It was that point in the play where Rangda calls out to her acolytes, the witches, to come to her in the midnight graveyard and the *dalang* always milked it for everything is was worth. The lamp was dimmed, the orchestra fell – antimelodramatically – silent as his cracked, insane, unaccompanied voice yelled to the forces of darkness to come – right here, right now – and the audience trembled, made each other jump and squealed in delicious terror. Jane's teasing mother, out there, would be shouting "Boo!" at her screaming child and the play's success would be reckoned by the number of dead bodies, undoubted witches, children of Rangda, found in the village the next day. The performance had never wavered and now the players crashed and banged into a collective fight scene, individual blows marked by Ida Bagus's rapping toe-hammer. Good against evil. Male against female. Life went on.

14

They came in the night in trucks with shouting, crashing of gears and deliberately importunate lights. They came on New Year's Eve with no congratulatory wishes, no ingratiating bottle tucked under the arm. They came with a warrant for the arrest of Walter Spies.

The scene had been heavily over-engineered – a dozen dark Moluccan troops with rifles, *controleur* Smit at their head clutching a rolled document like a public proclamation, waving handcuffs and wearing the revolver he had never before got out of its cardboard box. They leaped from the trucks, crouched low, fanned out and approached the house as if in expectation of a withering volley of defensive fire. Alas, this tactic took no account of the fact that only a narrow staircase led down to the main building, so they were forced to crush together again and virtually fell, mutually jostling, through the front door. This disappointed them, for they had looked forward to kicking it down. Colonial troops were inordinately proud of their desperately uncomfortable but very splendid high boots that set them above the unshod local population. All this, I had later from one of the Moluccans, known to me from his regular appearances – in quite a different uniform and footwear – in the prowling after-dark parades of the *lapangan kota*. Walter, to Smit's enormous disappointment, was simply not there. Even his managers, Lindner and Dreesen, were absent – at that moment innocently looking forward to the promise of the new year through pink champagne in Manxi's bar – but there would be time for them later. The troops had to content themselves with a token amount of happy destruction and with rooting the terrified boys out from under their bed with poking rifle barrels, though they were more scared of the black faces than the guns. On principle, the boys knew nothing, swiftly rolling down the shutters of native incomprehension to turn blank, questioning faces on their colonial captors. They were rounded up and taken away in tears, it having been explained to them that they were to help the authorities in their inquiries into breaches of the Netherlands Penal Code Article 248 (2) of which they had never heard and which they did not understand. Then they came for me.

Access to my studio, insomuch as it was formally still part of the palace, involved a rather more extensive etiquette. Nevertheless, at three in the morning, the result was much the same – the sound of marching feet, the crunch of gravel, the door burst in – the eruption of the starkly political upon the nakedly domestic. My inherent modesty drove me, in those days, to the wearing of a sarong whilst sleeping, though for Smit, that, too, might be a dangerous sign of "going native". Though I rose from my chaste and lonely bed with expressions of astonishment and outrage, I must confess that none of this came as a great surprise to me. I had even considered the merits of allowing them to discover me naked, red-faced therefore not red-handed, for come they must.

The obscure act of the Penal Code in question, it should be noted, proscribed physical intimacy between adults and minors who were members of the same sex. This, I felt sure, embraced McPhee's shameful activities but not those of myself or Walter. Much was made of the affront to Queen Wilhelmina's dignity that such behaviour constituted, something which seemed to me mysterious. I could see that the motions of her genitals, involving as they did the legitimacy of the state, were a matter of concern to me but not vice versa. ("Vice versa," Walter would have quipped. "Isn't that what we're charged with, Bonnetchen?") Until the very end, poor Resem was convinced all this fuss sprang from the disrespectful manipulation of his loins into the shadowed silhouette of Her Majesty on the living room wall.

Advance warning had come via McPhee's expensive annual subscriptions to Batavian newspapers, delivered by air. When their divorce had come through, Jane had left with the Meads and he had stayed on alone in all the conditions of increasing seediness that come upon a solitary man living on scant funds. I had visited him some time afterwards to find him bearded and chainsmoking, petulant and lachrymose, drinking at ten in the morning and shockingly indiscreet in his indiscretions. Now, seeing which way the wind was blowing, he had promptly decamped, abandoning the house, Sampih and Jane's pussies to their fate, but, traps packed, he had sent one of his boys over with the front page – and much would be made of this at the trial – with an attached note that read: "In view of the precarious situation, I have decided to head back to the States at once. I think you might want to do likewise". The newspaper, it is true, was full of alarmist international news, the crumbling peace accords between Germany and the Allies since the Reich had gulped down the Sudetenland with scarcely a belch, the threatened annexation of the Polish corridor, the imminence of another European war – nothing it would be argued, that could be of relevance to us here, up a hill, in far Bali. But beneath the pinned note, lay another article with the infelicitously worded headline, "Crackdown on Boy Sex in the Indies – More Arrests to Follow".

It was with this present scene in mind that I had ensured that I would be sleeping alone and, around the room, arranged a cavorting throng of dancing and bathing Balinese ladies – as randomly disconnected as in any splodgy roundel by Matisse – comely and bare-bosomed, in oils and pastels, like some nineteenth-century deathbed tableau of the great artist and his works. They would bear strident false witness for me. I was cowering behind what Walter termed "my protective breastwork".

Smit stood there, blazing torchlight down on me, dark silhouettes crashing into each other behind him in the confined space. "Boots," I said, invoking the householder's sacred right to protect his property. "Would you mind asking your men to take off their boots? The floors here are a shallow skim of raw cement over soil, polished to a high finish. Your men's boots are wrecking it." I reached out for matches, laid ready on the bedside table, and made a pantomime of coolly lighting the lamp.

From the shadows, my ladies leapt to prominence and Smit, on reflex, took off his hat as his men gawped and started sniggering behind their hands, like schoolboys in the presence of smut.

"Alright sergeant. Take the men outside. Two to guard the door. Ten minute cigarette break." He turned to me, thrust his hands in his pockets and began nervous ball-juggling. There was nowhere to sit but the bed. He wasn't going to do that, so I did, gathering the sheet to hide my undress. "There's more to this than boots," he asserted. "Anyway, as it is, the Germans are stamping all over Europe with *their* big boots. Where's Spies?"

"Walter?" I raised both hands in a delicate gesture from Balinese dance to express my innocence. "I have no idea ..." I struck my thigh, through the thin stuff, as in one of Charlie's hammy films. Careful! Soon I would break into a song and dance routine from one of Noel's musicals. "You know of course that he has a house at Iseh? – where he paints? – I expect you will find him there. What's all this about?" I rubbed in his disappointment, mimed puzzlement. "Did you expect him to be at home? Isn't everyone out at parties, having fun anyway? It is New Year, after all – for us Europeans that is. Unless, of course, you've gone native." I fair beamed benevolence at him. Walter was, of course, not at Iseh or anywhere in that direction. With a bit of luck, he was already in Java, being looked after by friends in the administration, all shunted there from Bali by the new Governor General. He would throw them all off the trail by walking, on little paths, to Singarajah and rendezvous with a car there. In Java, he would be safe.

"I've got my eye on you, Bonnet." He delved deep into a pocket and juggled unhappily.

"That's comforting to hear, *controleur.*"

He gestured at my harem. "Don't think I don't know what you get up to with the ladies of the night on the *lapangan kota* but we can't – as yet – touch you for that. One of the traditions of the Indies, I suppose." He lit a cigarette, blew smoke, threw the used match loutishly on the floor. "We might be able to do you for underaged girls." He nodded at the paintings. "Some of those look pretty young to me and all these pictures should add up to a good long stretch behind bars, get the right judge, but that's a can of worms we don't really want to get into. That's only natural, after all. This is all about boys, corruption of male minors. Nasty. How come a Dutchman spends so much time with a" – he sneered – "shirt-lifter?" He paused, confused, Balinese seldom wore shirts, among women only prostitutes. "A sarong-lifter?" That would not do either. Male and female both wore sarongs and, in my experience, Balinese were quite finnicky about "lifting above" things of the below. "A pillow-biter?" But a fixture of the Indies was the tubular pillows, known as "Dutch wives" that you wrapped yourself round at night to allow air to circulate. We all drooled on our pillows.

"What about 'flower-boy-fancier'?" I suggested urbanely but a quiver of fear had crept into my voice. Jail? Under the sheet, I was slick with sweat. I cleared my throat. "In the old mountain villages, all boys who have their adult teeth but are, as yet, unmarried, are so designated. They are held to be particularly suitable to serve as vessels and vassals of divinity."

He grinned, despite himself, and plunged his hand back to grip his privities, like the little flower-boys do whenever they feel insecure. "I think that might fit nicely. Our colonial children must be protected."

"Look. The only 'boys' in Walter's life are the houseboys who, as you are well aware, are far from being children – the appellation a matter of social station, not age. The fact is, all sorts of people pass through Campuhan, male, female, Balinese, *bule*. Walter is very popular. Barbara Hutton – I believe – wanted to marry him. You surely can't imagine he sleeps with them all. I would guess that Walter is a very cool man sexually. You will be saying next …" I stared him coldly in the eye, "that *I* sleep with him."

Smit mouthed distaste. "No need to be offensive."

"The fact is that Walter has done more for the Dutch and for the Balinese than any other single person I know. The last Governor General would never have put up with this."

Smit sighed. "The last Governor General did not realise the trouble these damn foreigners cause, constantly interfering in Dutch affairs and setting themselves up above the law. The sooner we're shot of them, the better. Teach them a lesson they won't forget. The last Governor General did not have a son-in-law with similar vices or a wife who made his life hell about it."

"Hell", "wife" – I immediately thought of his own embittered, psalm-singing soulmate. So, judging by the look on his face, did he. This could be their ticket back to the Hague or, at least, Weltevreden, the trim Dutch quarter of Batavia, gardeners, trams, ladies' tea parties on the manicured lawn and all the other provincial comforts. That would draw her fangs a little.

"Well, I'm afraid you'll have to come with me. It doesn't end there. We'll need a statement and you've still got questions to answer. For God's sake, man, put on some white man's bloody clothes!"

As I struggled into a pair of presentable trousers and a shirt, Smit turned, shocked, away from the sight of my undress and contemplated the heaped-up, naked female flesh, unabashed. Outside, the men shambled to their feet, tucking snuffed smokes into top pockets, and fell in around me. I did not, of course, recognise my acquaintance from the *lapangan kota*. It appeared, to my relief that, for the moment at least, I was merely a witness and thus not subject to handcuffing. In the various courtyards we crossed, the silent palace residents gripped flickering torches of *damar* resin like extras from *La Bohème* and peered at me in curiosity, as though I were someone they had never set eyes on before. As the first rays of dawn struggled up from the east and I was hauled, trembling, up into the rear of the truck, I am sure I heard an excessively matinal cock somewhere crow once and then a second time.

Arrived in Denpasar, it seemed to me that the eyes of the by-now-rising Dutch residents were similarly eloquent, as I was frogmarched into the administrative buildings. "There he goes," their looks said with satisfaction. "The dirty bugger. Thought he was better than us and now he's going to be shamed in public, shown up, stripped bare, humiliated, thrown out of the country. It'll be in all the newspapers and he'll never sell another painting again. Serves him right. Someone should write to tell his mother."

The architectural icons of the eastern empires affect the grandiloquence of Greek classical styles but reduced to the proportions of the Indian bungalow. On the main administrative building, whitewashed and fluted Doric columns towered up a full ten feet to support a complex entablature incorporating the Dutch royal arms executed in soft plaster and picked out in gloss paint. I was led beneath it and across a sort of grey-hued reception area, down endless corridors, along a covered outside walkway fringed by spiky plants and through various locked, metal gates. It was only when a leprous iron door was thrown open and I was pushed into the dark interior, that I realised that this was the town jail, entered – appropriately – from the rear. As the door clanged shut, Smit's chuckling voice said, "Oh, by the way, Happy New Year", like a hat, flung in contemptuously after a drunk. Then silence. I went and sat on the bed.

I sat there, more or less, for two days. There was little else to do. It was a bare cement cell, perennially damp, with an unglazed, barred window. No furniture apart from the cot that came with a thin kapok mattress, a palimpsest of every possible form of nocturnal incontinence. Above the bed, someone had scratched a crude caricature of buggery as though in welcome or admonition. Yet it fired my imagination. In my mind, during the empty hours, I painted over it an elongated mural, depicting the life of the Indies. Against a frond and wave-draped background, muscular farmers, wiry sailors, insinuating, robed Chinese, held aloft the wealth of the archipelago – calculating each paintstroke and mixing each colour in the pallette of my head. I cursed myself for my lack of prescience. I had brought no cigarettes or matches, no money to buy provender or suborn the loyalty of the visibly Balinese guard in his blue cotton uniform. Young, swarthy, with broken teeth, it occurred to me that he might, himself, be a prisoner here. Nevertheless, he brought me food three times a day, rice and undifferentiated slop – neither exactly hot nor cold – not unlike my daily dole from the Cokorda's kitchens really but resisted all attempts at conversation or ingratiation. This is unheard of in the Indies, so I deduced that he must be acting on explicit orders. My excretory functions were dealt with by a chamber pot, emptied by the same guard once a day into a fly-buzzing bucket, brought for that purpose and already containing the effluent of others. It was of identical design to the one in which he delivered my drinking water and my disordered mind dwelt obsessively on the circumstances in which they might be confused. More troubling, I had not brought my supplies of quinine and other specifics. I could feel myself weakening at the whine of each questing insect.

After two days, the door opened again and the Trappist guard beckoned me out and led me back through the gates, the maze, the grey hallway and into an office dominated by a large, old-fashioned desk. This was the age of new technology, so the desk was dominated, in turn, by a huge bakelite telephone, the size of a flatiron, with a crank on the side, to ring a bell and so attract the attention of whoever was on the other end. Before it, sat a stranger, looking down at a dossier, with Smit off to one side.

"This," said Smit, glowing with pride, "is Mr Tonny van Diemen, a special investigator from Batavia." His awed tone connoted that Tonny knew anyone who was anyone, dined with the Governor General on a weekly basis, kissed his wife's hand as well as the G.G.'s arse, and – no doubt – made appropriately risqué jokes about his son-in-law in all the best gentlemen's clubs of Batavia. Tonny raised an eyebrow at something in the dossier and closed it softly. I could see my name on the front. Walter might not have a file at HQ but I clearly did and was genuinely surprised at how thick it was. Tonny was a man in his early fifties, sleek and groomed, dressed in a black suit and – God help us – a waistcoat that made no concessions to the climate. Thus, he would have dressed in a premium legal practice in the Hague. It was immediately clear that his well-manicured sensibilities never engaged the grubby, real world, merely the pieces of crisp official paper to which it was reduced. He appraised me with quick, dark eyes and clasped his elegant hands together to preclude any further courtesies.

"Mr Bonnet," he said smoothly. "*Controleur* Smit tells me you may be able to help us in our enquiries into this terrible business. I am sure you would welcome the opportunity to clear your name of any taint of involvement that might prejudice your further stay in our fair colony."

"As a Dutch citizen …" I began, ponderously.

"As a Dutch citizen, you have a duty of loyalty to your motherland, Mr Bonnet. Now what information do you have of the whereabouts of the renegade Spies? Your own tastes, I note from your dossier, tend in a different but no more creditable direction. Your debauchery of that poor young girl was, I am sure, nothing to write home about." He twirled an elegant pen, suggesting that he, Van Diemen, might feel compelled to do that writing home. "I remain convinced that you know something."

"Look," I said. "I don't care a hoot what you are convinced about, I …" The phone rang with a derisory little strangulated tinkle. Van Diemen snapped his fingers and pointed – as I thought most rudely – and Smit grabbed it. There was no whispering into phones in those days. You shouted. The person on the other end shouted too. Then what you heard through the earpiece was a pale, crackly voice barely emerging from the hiss and rumble of the static.

"What? When? Where? All right tomorrow. I'll tell him." Smit put his mouth to Van Diemen's ear, cupped his hands and whispered, Tonny vigorously nodding. He turned to me with a triumphant smile.

"There now, Mr Bonnet. It seems we need detain you no longer. We have apprehended Spies in Singaraja, found in a car stopped at a checkpoint. No doubt he was seeking to escape to Java. He is being brought back under guard." I suspected another trap.

"I can go?"

"Oh you can go all right," said Smit. "In fact, we insist upon it. At the moment, we're rather short of cells you see and we expect to make many more arrests. Get out but don't you try to run away to Java." I rose and paused. There were a hundred things I might have said, that I wanted to say, but there was no point. Already, they were chuckling clubbily. I had ceased to exist for them. I opened the doors and walked out into the hall, feeling uncomfortably light, like a man who has accidentally left his jacket and suitcase on a train. I was hungry, had not a rupiah to my name, no way to get home. A lanky figure rose to its feet.

"Rudi!" It was the Greg. I was suddenly, pathetically, glad to see him. I hugged him solidly. I wanted to cry. My nurturing father, my *Barong*.

"How? Why? When?" reprising Smit's telephone conversation. The hallway was full of the kind of loungers who always fill the hallways of government buildings. Waiting is an art form subsidised by governments. They stared at us, scratched and yawned, looked hopeful and expectant.

"We were in Australia when we heard the news. Jane insisted on coming back so we couldn't let her travel alone, poor little thing. At least Colin got out. That's the main thing."

"Yes," I said. "That's the main thing." Greg had been transformed into a wealthy planter, white suit, panama hat.

"You look like hell. Did they give you a bad time, old man?" he asked, patting me awkwardly on the back as one might a muddy and over-enthusiastic dog. Being British, he lacked a gesture for this situation. "I heard they'd taken you in, so I climbed into my best too-good-to be's and came right over."

"Too-good-to-be's?"

"Too-good-to-be-trews – trousers to you, old boy. Koch says the Dutch way is to lock as many people up as possible until someone confesses to something, then they offer to forget the confession if they incriminate someone else. Apparently, it works quite well," he admitted grudgingly. "They rounded up everyone at Manxi's. You can imagine what a mix they picked up there – draining the sump of Denpasar. Koch says Manxi's done a runner back to her old lover in Bangli. And that little priest, Scruple, they're trying to show he was dipping into more than the widows and orphans fund. They caught him at Manxi's and he made some unwise statement about Manxi being his Mary Magdalene that the papers loved. The bishop's in a fearful wax."

"Who's Koch?"

"Jane's lawyer. Are you ..." he dropped into a transatlantic twang, "all lawyered up? Margaret got her legal eagles in the States to check the locals out. They came up with Koch." He made it sound as if she kept a whole firm on retainer, ready to swing into action at the drop of a hat, an unnerving idea for a husband. "Where's Walter?" he whispered, through the panama, out of the corner of his mouth. The loungers pricked up their ears at the tone, looked irritated that they could not follow the words and slumped back grumpily, giving way, once more, to their boredom.

"It's no secret. They've just picked him up in Singaraja. He's on his way back." We drifted out, under the yawning lions rampant supporting blazon of armed and langued gules, towards the daytime *lapangan kota*, stripped, in daylight, of mystique and the freemasonry of deviance and reduced to a mere clump of scruffy grass on which rickshaw drivers were unselfconsciously peeing. I felt an unworthy stab of fear at the sight of it. Greg stopped and went through his complex pipe-lighting routine.

"Mm! Ah! Mm! It looks bad, him running away like that. Sayan is under a sort of military occupation. They're making a helluva stink. Margaret's up there giving them a piece of her mind – and you know she has quite a large supply of that. They're dredging through all forty-three dancers in the area, trying to find some excuse for all this. Today, they interrogated a three year old. They seem to be trying to smear Jane as some sort of child-eating Lisboan. All tommyrot of course."

"Yes," I echoed, "all tommyrot. Where's Sampih?"

"He's keeping a low profile. As I'm sure you know, they could put him on the rack and they wouldn't get a word out of him. Damned Dutch! Oh, not you old man, of course. But I'm afraid Colin, being absent, is going to be a handy scapegoat." A guilty, handy scapegoat. I bit my tongue.

"And Walter," I said. "Now, they've got Walter."

"Yes," he puffed. "There is that. I'm very much afraid they're going to crucify Walter. Manxi's for a snort? Should be nice and empty, if you can stand the bagpipe music."

* * *

"The mistake," said Walter, "was my trying to find Goris at the antiquities department in Singaraja. It was only ten in the morning and he is rarely drunk by then but he was one of the first arrested and that aroused their interest. It is always a grave mistake to be of interest. You are very lucky not to be of interest, Bonnetchen."

We were in durance vile, specifically a cell in Denpasar, not the one I had occupied but as near as makes no difference. Walter, too, should have looked like hell, his face a mass of angry, red mosquito bites, hair greasy and unwashed, unshaven for three days, clothes rumpled and stained. Instead, he looked rakishly healthy and rather dashing, like a man on a seaside holiday. My gifts of laundry and cigarettes lay, unregarded, on the bed. The same warder that had silently guarded me now waited on him, full of chat, always a smile, with little extras, wrapped in banana leaf, slid shyly onto his plate, always brought first so as to be hot, and no water in an ambiguous bucket, rather warm tea, served at regular hours. Also, he had been given furniture, a chair in which I sat.

"I was foolish to run away. I did not know where my head was. Koch has explained the legal situation to me. He says he hasn't the slightest doubt he can get me off. It all hinges on this notion of what is a minor. Of course, we can't be sure what evidence they may be able to dig out but Balinese are lining up to say that any such contacts that I may have enjoyed were regular by local standards and there is, anyway, no means of proving a Balinese to be underage. Balinese have no birth certificates therefore no official age in law."

I was aghast. "You mean you intend to confess to being ... of the faith? But that's suicidal. Don't you see? Once you admit that, they will cast around till they find some way to send you to jail. In itself, it may not be strictly a crime in the Indies, but it's undoubtedly considered immoral, unnatural, vicious ..." God knows, often enough I, myself, thought it so,

"... and they will find some way to get you. You don't have to *do*, just *be*. They will turn you into McPhee. Don't forget the Governor General himself is behind all this and no one, judge, police, local administration wants to displease him. They could so easily be fired for incompetence or corruption."

He smirked irritatingly. "Judges can now be fired for incompetence and corruption, Bonnetchen? Where will it all end?"

I ground my teeth. "Don't do it, Walter. Being German is not against the law either but they will find a way to make it so. You know they are having problems with all the Nazi supporters in Java, just like at home in Holland. Please, please, beware." A phrase from Smit swirled up into my head. "Get the right judge," he had said, cheerily. That would not be so hard in the tiny colonial world we lived in. Walter waved my objections away.

"I am very ware. Pfui! H.E. the G.G." – he made it preposterous – "has no interest in me. Anyway, Margaret has agreed to appear as an expert witness on my behalf. Which one will you put your money on, three hundred years of Dutch empire or Margaret?" He thought that was funny. As so often, I wanted to slap him. He was a simple child wandering through a world of dangerous, sharp-toothed creatures possessed by violent, tangled emotions he could never understand.

"Walter," I sighed. "How old are you? One day you will have to grow up."

"How old? I don't know. I stopped counting when I got to Bali. I am not an accountant."

The warder came back, crouched low with respect, handed him, two-handed, a packet of cigarettes that Walter immediately opened, lighting one for him and passing it back with a graceful smile. My own cigarettes lay, unregarded ... Never mind. There came a crashing thunderclap of noise, like Judgement Day, from outside.

"What the Hell?" We all crowded to the window. Down there, beyond the joyless wall, sat some fifteen men in sarongs bright as birdsong, their gleaming instruments before them, great smiles on their faces, one or two with children on their laps, pounding out a tune that I recognised as *baris*, the warrior dance of Bali.

"It's the Ubud *gamelan*!" There were tears in Walter's eyes. "Oh my

God! How very kind! How generous! Look, there is Oleg! To come all that way just to show me … just to say …" His voice choked. He stuck his arm through the bars and waved. There came an answering cheer and the music swelled and quickened. The warder laughed, threw his elbows up, dropped his knees and splayed his feet, stuck his cigarette in his mouth and went through the proper series of classic moves that transfers weight gracefully from one foot to another and was joined by Walter, fingers fluttering at the ends of his outstretched forearms as, in perfect synchrony, they launched into the proper steps of huffing and puffing advance and retreat, miraculously avoiding the chairs, the chamber pot, the comfortless bed – the whole cell become a temple courtyard, the drab prison uniform a glorious cloth of gold. I flattened myself against the wall lest I be run down by the juggernaut of art. They swayed back and forth dipped and rose, executed the swift little runs, the sudden spasming body contractions, their glaring eyes scissoring back and forth and then, at a point where they were supposed to swirl like dervishes, one went the wrong way and they collided and fell, giggling to the floor.

"Now look what you've done, ruined my fine costume!" They fell back, laughed and hugged each other in a moment of pure joy, physical and emotional, that consumed them both and, in their eyes, I saw clearly a surrender to simple, open love and respect that held nothing back, as we do. It was a flow of sheer common humanity, without barriers of culture or language, an insubstantial exchange that enriched both and impoverished neither, a moment in which there was no room for misunderstanding or meanness or cavilling .

Now there were tears in my own eyes. "That look," I thought. "That look is Walter's relationship with Bali and the Balinese. That look is his only and irrefutable defence". But how do you put a look into a legal dossier?

***

The little District Court was crammed and very hot. Outside, profiting from the crowd, the usual array of little foodstalls had sprung up for the Indies is a constantly munching maw that is always hungry. Whenever the doors were opened, smoke, noise and the aroma of roasting meat impertinently broke through the imposed sterile silence and the steely smell of righteousness. Downstairs, under the ticking fans, sat the dripping European community, dressed up, come for a good show.

"A classic rite of solidarity," stated Margaret too loudly, looking round like an entomologist at insects. "A statement and affirmation of the *status quo*. Here we all sit as one. This is our place and the room maps the proper distribution of power, Balinese excluded from the main body and on their feet, not sitting. The object is to define Walter also as 'not-one-of-us' and ship him off to limbo. In the old days it would have been to Jimbaran, of course, where the outlaws and lepers were driven off to – later, the Christian converts." She was wearing a broad straw hat that annoyed the man behind, a spotty frock – not one of her fieldwork smocks – and the kind of white clumpy shoes favoured by American nurses. Yet, other maps were here to be called upon. Upstairs in the gallery, the Balinese indeed stood, but over our heads, therefore inappropriately elevated, even above the judge on his high chair. Moreover, the judge sat to the south west and thus the lowest-status part of the room. This arrangement would cause problems with the high-caste witnesses if they were called to take the stand and even with the low-caste ones called to climb into the witness box above the heads of any superiors on the ground floor. For Balinese, it was a conceptual omelette. Only males had come but whether as the result of some local classification or a regulation imposed by the Dutch, I did not know. My Moluccan military friend was one of the guards standing to attention at the front of the court, flanking the judge in a pose that showed his fine powerful legs to advantage. I managed to catch his eye and risked a wink that sent him into suppressed giggles. From the dark wainscotting, the meaty face of Queen Wilhelmina and the smoothly handsome Jonkeer Alidius Warmoldus Lambertus Tjarda van Starkenborgh Stachouwer, His Excellency Governor General of the Netherlands East Indies and first cause of all our woe, glared down on us in photographic reproduction.

The chief judge, His Honour Herman de Jonghe, was sitting resentfully hunched in his black robe, red collar and white tabs, making it immediately clear that he was a man of powerful dislikes. Flanked on either side by foetus-faced Tweedledum and Tweedledee colleagues, he did not want to be here in the provinces and closed his eyes upon them for long periods, only his yawns showing that he was not quite asleep. The bored voice cried out that all his life, he had been plagued by the distasteful crimes of defendants, the stupid accusations of prosecutors and the specious excuses of the defence and now legal process was experienced as a measured personal affront, made worse by non-conformity of participants. He was annoyed by people who did not speak Dutch, or who refused to swear on the Bible or did not wear ties. He was bored by the presence of so many men in his court and appalled by any woman who did not know that a lawcourt was not her place. He was like a cat irritated at its own tail. Koch was busy whispering a running translation of events to Walter, as I was obliged to do for the Meads, despite the irritated coughing of the man behind and beady glares from de Jonghe. At least Walter had scrubbed up well in a nicely ironed pair of trousers and shirt, looking like everyone's favourite nephew.

Van Diemen made his opening address. It seemed that Walter was a spider at the centre of a vast web of vice and corruption, preying on the poor, the young and the weak – which was not true – and that he had absolutely no regard for the awful and lawful authority of Holland or its code – which was. Then, Tonny expatiated at length in broad slanderous statements about the character of Walter's clientèle of artists, musicians and divorcees. The countess's cheating at cards, the dancing of Beryl, the operatic endeavours of Temp were all laid at his door. Campuhan was a veritable Sodom and Gomorrah.

The first witness was called, I Wayan Ketok, to general puzzlement. I did not, of course, know the possibly convoluted ins and outs of Walter's sex life, though I had watched, with hot eyes, the comings and goings of a host of Balinese artists and dancers and others who were simply friends. The flexible sleeping arrangements of a Balinese household usually brought no breakfast revelations. But none of us had ever heard of this man. I saw Walter shaking his head vigorously but familiar Balinese can sometimes turn up under unfamiliar names, so we all waited to see exactly what might materialise in the witness box. It was a small Balinese lad who looked about fourteen and might therefore be about sixteen, again quite unknown. There was a moment of administrative dithering. Christians swear their oath upon the Bible, Muslims upon the

Koran but the Hindus had no holy text conveniently to hand. Walter hooted with laughter and I heard him suggest they use the Mahabarata, the ancient Indian epic from which Balinese and Javanese draw much of their theatre. The judges consulted hastily and settled for an affirmation facing north-east and Gunung Agung, therefore handily facing the court. My heart went out to the lad. Balinese are verbally, if not physically, reticent in sexual matters. Sex is not so much a matter of courtly love as of courtyard walls, shinned over under cover of darkness. He was deeply shamed by this public appearance, crouching in the corner of the box, as Van Diemen led him pitilessly through his statement and the Balinese in the gallery responded either with cruel laugher or by covering their mouths and eyes in embarrassment. The story was a simple one. He had gone to the house at Campuhan, looking for work and been received by a man called Walter, an artist. He had been enticed and made drunk till he had no idea where Gunung Agung was and then been horribly taken advantage of – though exactly what advantage remained somewhat unclear and then – even worse – sent away without compensation.

"And do you," asked Van Diemen through a local interpreter – himself blushing – "see the perpetrator of this foul and unnatural act in the court today?" He stared at Walter and nodded to the boy. Ketok looked around, eyes wide with terror, seemed to hesitate over Koch as a possible candidate and then said in a small voice, "How can I tell? Do not all white men look alike? And do they not even change their clothes so that they cannot be known?"

Van Diemen threw up his arms in despair. Walter hooted again and whispered furiously to Koch who rolled his eyes before he rose to cross-examine with a grin on his face.

"Wayan," he asked gently, "When did all this happen?"

Wayan Ketok bit his lip. "Just before last *galungan*."

"Are you aware that there were, at that time, in that house, *two* painters called Walter, Walter Spies – here on trial – and Walter Dreesen, the manager of the establishment?" Ketok listened to the translation, gaped, looked as if he were about to burst into tears. "Can you really tell us with absolute certainty which Walter it was that mistreated you?" Ketok seemed to shrink further. "I put it to you that it was not my client here, Walter Spies, who mistreated you but another Walter entirely."

The words were fed slowly through the translation process. Ketok rose, bewildered, to his feet.

"But why?" he cried, looking at Van Diemen, fearful yet outraged at the injustice of it. "This is stupid. How can white men all have the same names and not expect us to be confused?" There was hubbub in the court, de Jonghe shouting and banging his gavel, the Balinese mis-explaining to each other what had just happened, Margaret and Greg laughing, sundry Dutch raging in exasperation.

"Court adjourned! " shouted de Jonghe testily. "Court adjourned! Silence! Clear the court!"

As always in this world, our triumph was to be short-lived. The next day, Van Diemen returned, soothed, sleek, assured, bearing no trace of his routing. The ranks of the audience had been dramatically reduced for the Dutch found wearisome all the Balinese and the Balinese all the Dutch. The Balinese, it is true, found certain parallels with their traditional theatre, much of whose dialogue is incomprehensible, but were irked by the constraints imposed on gossip, audience participation and informal dining. Van Diemen had a star witness. It was little Resem.

They had shaved his moustache to cut years from his age, shorn his long hair and dressed him up in what was virtually a schoolboy uniform. He had lost weight. The cumulative effect was that he looked about twelve years old. Again, it was Van Diemen's task to lead him through a statement authenticated, not by his thumbprint, but by his proud written name. After all, Walter and I had taught him to read and write. It seemed, actually, to be a fairly dispassionate and accurate account of his relations both with Walter and with other unnamed partners. Jealousy sparked within me, displaced by a terrible fear that he would stand, point to me and cry, "If you don't believe me, ask that man. All these things, I did with him also." The statement was in Balinese, as one would have expected, but *in coitu*, he suddenly switched to a highly technical, latinate Dutch, medical vocabulary. Koch was onto it at once, quoting back words.

"This term, 'intercrural'. Is that a word you habitually use?"

"It is the word Mr van Diemen told me to use." Tonny began to shift uncomfortably in his chair.

"I see. Did Mr van Diemen help you otherwise with your statement?"

"Yes, Tuan. He helped me know what to say." Resem was always a good honest boy – young man.

"I see. Did he offer you anything for saying this and signing it? Some reward?" Resem shook his head.

"There was no reward. The Tuan just said that if I lied I would be sent to Java and die there and no ceremonies would be done for my death and I would wander in Hell for ever."

"So you made this statement in fear of eternal death and damnation?"

Resem smiled, innocently. "Yes, Tuan," he said. "That is why I was so careful to tell the truth."

Van Diemen harumphed triumphantly and returned to the chase. To crossexamine, he rose with intimidating dignity. "How old are you, Resem?"

Resem furrowed his brow. "I do not know. I was born in the year of many mice."

"And how long ago was that?"

"That was when I was very small, Tuan."

"According to Dutch law, you are a man – not a boy – at twenty-one years old. Are you a man – not a boy?" I felt Margaret stiffen beside me at this act of semantic highway robbery.

"I am a man since I had my teeth filed."

De Jonghe sat up. "What's that – teeth – what?" He displayed his own dentition, yellow, unfiled, defiled.

"It is a ceremony, Your Honour, at which a person's teeth are filed even, with special reference to the canines. It is regarded as the point at which a child may become an adult." De Jonghe yawned. I saw Walter grin and whisper something to Koch who frowned non-comprehension till Walter threw up his arms. I knew it was his standard joke about Balinese being the only people who got "short in the teeth" as they aged.

"Proceed."

"I shall produce evidence, Your Honour, from Dr Behrens," he snapped his fingers and pointed to his papers, "that, according to his best calculations, this young man was between fifteen and eighteen when he entered the accused's service." He turned back to the witness box. "Resem. When did you have your teeth filed?" Poor Resem looked confused.

"I cannot tell exactly. Tuan Walter paid for it to be done, so that he could see the ceremony and the music. You cannot do it without music. It was when I first came to work for him." I could see where this was going and did not greatly like it.

"So there was a time when you worked for him, when your teeth were unfiled and you were not yet a man?" Resem nodded.

"Oh yes."

Van Diemen leaned forward and spoke very slowly. "And, at that time, had you already 'played' with Tuan Walter." There was a long, slow silence that crept around the courtroom like an icy draught.

"Truly, I cannot remember, Tuan. There was no reason for me to remember. It may have been when he was comforting me from the pain and he came and sat with me." I heard my own release of breath. Sweat was running down my face. Of course, I heard the words before Van Diemen got the translation. He turned and stared at me, saw – I knew – right through me and curled his lip. I shuddered and impulsively clutched Margaret's chubby hand.

* * *

"The Balinese," said Margaret with damely emphasis, "have the good sense to see maturity as a performative, not a mere fact of biology or a matter of arbitrary clocks. If a boy *acts* like a man then he *is* a man." Hat on her knees, she was giving them the faith of cultural relativism hot and strong.

Van Diemen was not having that. "You are surely not suggesting that biology is not involved?"

Margaret sighed and fiddled with her hat. Her fingers yearned for a blackboard. "Okaaay! Look at it this way. Biology itself involves cultural concepts. In the Nile delta of Egypt, for instance, where the disease bilharzia is endemic, the first symptoms of intestinal bleeding appear in males in the early to mid- teens. This is seen as 'male menstruation' and a natural physical mark of sexual maturity corresponding to female menarche. Biology is seen through cultural eyes". Van Diemen frowned.

"You tell 'em old girl!" Greg sat beside me, eyes shining, openly admiring.

"Then, you are surely not suggesting that age is not involved?"

Margaret threw him a pitying look. "The Balinese have no sense of time as we understand it, that is, as a line extending infinitely forward and back. Balinese have a number of interlocking calendars that engage like the wheels in a gearbox so that time, in their experience, is circular. Naturally, this conforms perfectly with their notion of reincarnation."

Van Diemen made the sort of face that dentists see a lot of. This was alien territory to him, where he was at a disadvantage. He switched back to what he knew best, innuendo.

"And yet they manage to tell today from tomorrow and yesterday from today. Dr Mead, I wonder if you might clear up one thing I do not understand. The documentation here refers to you as the wife of one, Gregory Bateson. Is your true name Mrs Bateson or Mead?"

Margaret smoothed her spotty dress. "It is both. I am married to Gregory but, for professional purposes, I have retained the use of my maiden name. I do not accept that marriage should involve the total loss of my own identity."

Van Diemen flicked through papers. "I see. Oh yes and of course that would make more sense when one has been married repeatedly as I believe you have." He had established that she was a wanton woman and a bad wife.

"This is my third marriage."

"I see. You have kindly told us various things about childhood around the world. I wonder. Do you have any children yourself, Mrs Bateson – I beg your pardon – Dr Mead?"

"Not as yet."

She was a bad mother, a non-childbearing woman, a Rangda, a shrivelled academic who knew nothing of reality. The women in the audience instinctively heaved their bosoms in superior disapproval. There is something about women and their bosoms as symbols of virtue – perhaps Margaret is right and it is about childbearing – whereas breasts are a quite different matter. I have never understood, speaking as a man who has made his living at the breast, the odd alchemy by which wanton breasts become moral bosoms.

"And how well would you say you know Walter Spies?"

She looked over at him. Walter was absorbed in drawing something on a large pad. "I would say that I know him very well. He is a good friend." Walter raised sad eyes puppy-dog and threw her a weak smile.

"Are you not, as a woman, troubled by his frankly avowed sexual aberrations?"

Margaret sniffed. "I don't see what my being a woman has to do with it. Anthropologists have to confront all manner of forms of cultural difference without hysterical value-judgements. Walter is not a true invert in that he is capable of intermittent sexual arousal by the opposite sex ..." Very daring that in the 1930s. Blushes and scandalised gasps from the audience. "It is simply that his light involvement with Balinese youth fits very well with their own shallowness of emotional participation and dissociated impersonality. I should imagine that he might also be quite at home in some of those New Guinean sexual systems where sexuality is not a constant throughout a man's life but may follow a course from the passively to actively homosexual, in parallel to vigorous and simultaneous heterosexual activity. Now, in Africa ..."

"Thank you, Dr Mead. I don't think we need to go as far as Africa."

She leaned forward, getting carried away by her enthusiasms. "The point is that, although, in the West, Walter might be regarded as deviant, in that his temperament agrees very ill with our dominant character configuration, in Bali he is quite at home. Even an interest, such as Walter's, in art and aesthetics is not considered incompatible with masculinity in Bali. This entire prosecution has many of the qualities of those hysterical outbursts of paranoia that we see classically, in primitive societies, in witch-hunting. It might be said, of course, that this accords perfectly with the Dutch national character with its inherently passive-aggressive configuration that responds to pressure by external projection of internal conflict. Throughout Dutch history ..."

I had been watching de Jonghe getting increasingly irritated by all this, fiddling with his gavel, yawning compulsively, but just as he raised it over its little block of wood, to strike Margaret down, an angry voice rang out from the gallery. We all looked up to see a wiry Balinese of indeterminate age, trembling with unshallow emotion and heavy associated involvement, leaning over the rail and declaiming with wild arm movements and tears in his eyes. Beneath the full, thick hair of an adolescent, he had a face lined with the vicissitudes of age, breathtakingly beautiful in its patinated complexity, the sort of face I should have loved to explore, layer by layer, in a poignant and shadowed Rembrandtian drawing. I heard a Dutch woman shriek in alarm, "Is it a nationalist?" Another cried in terror, "Are the natives running amok?" Chairs were kicked back, a sort of stampede in undersea slow motion occurred. The Moluccan soldiers exchanged troubled looks. They had understood their role in the court to be purely ornamental and had no orders on how to deal with events such as this. This was embarrassing, so, instinctively, they raised their rifles to shoot someone. Fortunately, at this point, the old man turned on his heel and stalked away, out of sight, behind the crowd. His bare feet could be heard thudding, outside edge grounding first – good Balinese dance training – down the stairs towards the door, driving the audience back once more the way they had come. He turned, tiny, in the doorway and gobbed a final mouthful of Balinese at the judges and strode off with poise and dignity. Margaret was there, at my elbow, shielded by Greg, staring after him.

"What did he say? I couldn't follow it."

"He said we must all be mad, crazy. He was using, you understand, the lower speech register. What was all this fuss about? He said that Walter was one of the best and kindest men he ever met and that, if his son chose to spend time with him, then it could only do him good. We have just met Resem's father." I thought about it. "I suppose," I said doubtfully, "given the circumstances, it would be out of the question to ask him to model for me?"

Outside, the crowd milled around like children unexpectedly let out of school early. Standing under a tree, I spotted Cokorda Agung who beckoned me across with fluttering fingers. Had he been inside? Where could he possibly have sat without risking ritual pollution? A retainer lit an American cigarette and passed it with deference. Elegant slacks and shirt, clearly in his modern incarnation.

"Hello Mr Bonnet." I reciprocated greetings. He swallowed smoke like water and made an appreciative face. "There are some things about this whole business that I do not understand. Why do you white men seek to sleep with our sons and not your own sisters as do we Balinese?" I mimed puzzlement. "You are perhaps not aware that I am a twin? I was born with my sister and so we are held to have lived as husband and wife together inside our mother. Later, we can marry if we wish. We are of the same caste, so there is no difficulty. It is not as like a man marrying a woman of a higher caste which is a terrible crime." He shuddered to show how terrible it was. "Now, amongst poor people, for brother and sister to be husband and wife is a foul thing and makes the whole village unclean but amongst royal people it is very good and brings blessings. There are precedents, I believe, in the Mahabarata. You must ask Walter. He knows all about it. In such cases, the fields grow fertile. The rice is pleased but the Dutch are not. I do not understand why they are so interested in the fumblings of boys which are like the humping of buffalo. Such things are not forbidden. Why would they be? It is as if a man might not play with himself. Now, if Walter had copulated with some of his animals, that too would be very bad. Is that what really happened, Mr Bonnet. Was it those monkeys and you Dutch are ashamed to speak of it?"

* * *

In contrast to so much excitement, Walter's appearance on the stand was a rather muted affair. He sat there, hands loosely in his lap as the two lawyers prodded him over the fences of their interrogation. He simply maintained that – yes – he had had relations, irregular but not contrary to Dutch law, with Balinese males. He had no reason to think they were underage and – no – he would not divulge their names since that would be a betrayal of trust. Moreover, except for minor details, he did not deny that Resem had told nothing but the truth and understood fully why he had felt forced to do so. He remained calm and dignified in the face of Van Diemen's innuendos and sneers and the stony disapproval of the audience that beat against the witness box like the waves at Uluwatu. He did himself no good when asked whether he was not ashamed. "When I was young," he said simply, "no one ever told me this was wrong. When I did it, it seemed to make people very happy."

Van Diemen's final address was predictably nasty. What was at stake here, we were informed, was not the fate of one bohemian but the honour of Dutch rule and the peace and dignity of Queen Wilhelmina. The Dutch were in Bali as protective big brothers to preserve their colonial children from precisely such acts of exploitation and violence. Much had been made of the acceptability of such perverse and abhorrent relationships to the Balinese but that could not be the issue here. This was not a case to be tried according to local law. This was a matter of the Penal Code to which all were equally subject, from the highest to the lowest, Dutch or foreigner. It was clear that, in at least one proved case, established by science and government documentation, a partner of the accused had been under twenty-one, and thus a child, and the full power of the law must be brought to his defence. Failure to do so, would be to set at risk the whole civilization for which the administration and decent Dutch folk had toiled ceaselessly for hundreds of years. He asked for a sentence of not less than four years with hard labour. I gasped. Those about me clapped thunderously and smiled encouragement through hard eyes. I saw that what was to be punished here was not immorality so much as pleasure in the world and Walter's trusting improvidence. De Jonghe yawned. He, at least, appeared incapable of fuelling sustained moral outrage. He lacked the energy.

Walter looked pale. The words "hard labour" seemed to have shaken him badly. Koch rose and addressed Their Honours. "Walter Spies," he informed them, "stands before you" – actually he sat – "not as a predator but a victim, beguiled by the lethal charm of the Indies. Much has been made by the prosecution of the irrelevance of the supine Balinese attitude to sexual aberration. I say it lies at the very core of this case. You, yourselves, know the threat to your children of the effeminacy and complaisance of the people of these enchanted isles. Walter Spies came to the Indies as a fine young man, steadfast in his own moral rectitude, a rectitude that is blasted, for his very manhood has been fatally undermined by his own romantic sensibility." In other words, Resem had seduced him with dark arts, spun him round with a web of symbolism in which he had become fatally entangled. But Walter was not just assailed by oriental effeminacy, the enervating heat of these torrid latitudes had further sapped his moral fibre. "Alone and isolated in his remote hill station, amongst the bare and arid mountains, far from the comforts of a superior culture and stunned, day after day, by the rays of the pitiless sun, he made the fatal mistake of allowing himself a too great intimacy with the local people. All distinction was lost, the civilising mission of the West was thrown into reverse and he watched, with horror and disgust, his own degeneration into a Balinese. Walter Spies is a man deserving, not of your condemnation, but your deepest pity!"

* * *

"It's not the nine months in jail that I mind so much as Surabaya," Walter pouted. "As you will have seen, it is a brutal city, lacking in charm, a Javanese Hamburg." It was six months since I had set eyes on him. He was being brave of course. He had been brave on the jetty in Buleleng – "Take a terrible revenge for me. Bonnetchen. Paint a portrait of Smits's wife" – protecting me from my own lachrymose and sentimental response to the judges' verdict, the sight of him being shipped off in chains, the prison uniform too small and tight, as cut to native size. An acute visual metaphor. A painter thinks in metaphors and scenes. Absurdly, as I watched him being rowed out to the dirty ferry, I had recalled the sight of my own mother weeping as she sent me off alone on the tram, on my first day at infants' school, talismanically clutching the little bag she had sewn for me. Dr Behrens had been there, full of apology for his testimony at the trial, pressing quinine and Collis Browne's medicinal compound into his hands, Walter endlessly forgiving. "The best thing about jail is that it does cut down on the number of casual visitors, just wandering in. I have finally been able to ruthlessly organise my social diary." He was gaunt, had been ill, lost weight. My gift of cigarettes lay unregarded on the bed – no wait, that had been Denpasar. My hamper of food now lay broken open and ravaged, tins and jars scattered like jewels over the torn sheet. He must be ravenous.

"You are hungry, Walter? Oh my God! Aren't they feeding you?" He paused, a ham gripped in each hand.

"What? Food? The food's no problem, Bonnetchen, boring but enough. I am as happy as a worm in bacon and Mrs Schweinstrumpf of the art circle sends me in a hot dinner every Sunday." So he was not set beyond the reach of those that loved him. "But these I can trade with the white guards for canvas and paint!" He scrabbled through the debris, seized a jar of apricots and held it up to the light like a man appraising a diamond and his face was lit up in its golden hues, as if by stained glass in some pre-Raphaelite depiction of religious conversion. He seemed, then, to my relief, to have settled in, found his feet.

"Did you know that some 250 men have been arrested in this affair?" Not – I almost added in shame – myself.

"But of course, Bonnetchen! What do you think? Most of them are here. I saw Goris yesterday. The governor is a decent man and lets us all exercise together. I never realised there were so many of the faith, but – as I kept pointing out vainly at my trial – I am not an accountant. Why does no one ever listen to me? Can you imagine? Over two hundred homosexual men locked up together, packed four to a cell with nothing to do but lie in their beds and sweat – all in an effort to make them change their ways? It is like shutting up hundreds of alcoholickers together in a brewery, without water, so they will repent. The governor, poor man, is beside himself, fearing the happenings will get out in the newspapers and he will be transferred to a penal colony. I understand now why they call those places penal colonies." He made it sound rather jolly as if, in thirty years' time they would be holding camp little reunion dinners – from which I should, quite naturally, be excluded. Even in the world of aberrance, I was a deviant. I glared into his grin and looked around jealously.

"Do you share this cell with anyone?" It was a very nice cell, clean, dry, airy, absolutely five-star. Only one narrow bed.

"Good lord no. The chief warder is a friend of a friend and allows himself to be persuaded that I need space for my paintings. I have, of course, promised him one." The far end was an impromptu studio, an overstated film set of wild artistic disorder, several completed canvases, another in progress, paint left lying about, brushes sluttishly unwashed. My own studio was monastic and uncluttered, an aid to visual clarity. Normally, I deplored such hysterical mess in artists but, at last, he had found the solution to his disgusting sloth and I resisted an urge to tidy up. I walked over and gazed down on the work, eagerly. I had never been allowed in his studio before. I was appalled.

"Yes," he said. He came up behind me and I could feel his breath on my neck, smell his tobacco smoke. "Completely new! I have cleared out all the old rubbish and been reborn! You know how they put on bottles, 'Shake before use'? Well I have been well and truly shaken – out of my old complacency, my way of looking at things. I am finally ready for use. This is the first painting of my new life!"

It was huge and glowed with colours torn from the carapaces of iridescent beetles, metallic reds, blues, greens, a blue-black sky, harsh yellow light and orange ground. It showed cavorting creatures, half dog, half cow, all with the same staring human face, atop a wavering neck, ripped, as if by powerful searchlights – *Pita Maha* – from the darkest shades of nightmare. There was a suggestion of undersea currents, of the carrion monsters that feed on the bleached bodies of the drowned, a contrapuntal ordering that sneered at order itself, a diseased mentality. It was like a child playing with its own excrement.

"It came to me while I was ill. I had perhaps taken too much of Collis-Browne's opium and I saw with a wonderful clarity that painting and music can – must – be ultimately the same, that their rhythms and harmonies, ornamentations and dissonances are all in the same idiom. Reality and mood, I have flung away. The painting speaks only to itself. Its time is internal as in music. Its images exist only as variations of other images it contains. It is its own reality, trapped within the prison of the frame so that I retain distance from it. For the first time, I feel that it painted itself through me, that all I had to do was listen and look, just as the Balinese live their lives as an expression of a greater holiness. It is art, complete, almost an abstract formula, not art as a sweet to be sucked to compensate for the bitterness of life, but life itself. I call it *Scherzo fuer Blechinstrumente*, 'Scherzo für Tin Instruments'. It's promised to Stokowski." He seemed to expect me to say something.

"Brass," I corrected. "In English they call it brass when it's a musical instrument, tin when it's a cheap toy." *Red' kein Blech*', I thought. "Don't talk rubbish" – what Greg would call "tommyrot". "Extraordinary," I enthused, laying it aside. "It needs to be thought about, I can see that. Er ... What else have you got?"

15

"Perhaps I should have mentioned it before but it didn't really seem necessary. Anyway, at the time you had plenty of other things to worry about. I did what I could. It was all no good." He walked to the balcony and looked down on the river, drawing, perhaps, some comfort from its Heraclitean continuities. "It wasn't," I urged, "the Balinese. You know that. Behind it all was Smit. Dutch, not Balinese, ingratitude." He had been expelled from the Pita Maha by a vote of the committee. I had been the only dissenting voice. The others had been leaned on, very heavily. I had written a memorandum of protest. He turned back into the room.

"It doesn't matter. It was a foolish thing. Administration, committees, not *my* thing at all. Still ... our own children have a special power to wound us." He looked up at the wall. It was Sobrat's first painting in the new style. How many years ago now? One of his chicks. Now mine.

"That," I said, pointing out the point pointlessly, "is why he did it." God, I was turning into my mother. "He is basking in your unhappiness. Anyway, that is not why you are in a bad mood. It is the review." In the midst of all the gushing, ecstatic reception of the dance book he had produced with Beryl, in an obscure Dutch journal, was a single review that was critical. "It is not even about you, doubtless an old enemy of hers paying her back. You know how bitchy academics are."

Oleg shuffled in and served coffee. Oleg because little Resem had gone. It had been inevitable. Otherwise, a way would have been found to make him suffer, to bring him to grief. He was getting married. Someone had bought him a ricefield. He was happy. New staff were now quizzed about their age. It cast a shadow of mistrust over the house, a whiff of premeditation amongst the carefree scent of the dangling orchids.

"It is of no importance. After that prison, it is simply so good to spread my legs and stretch my wings." He sat and started painting again at the forest-giant table, exquisite filligreed studies of dragonflies, stretched and spread, viewed through a magnifying lens and the glare of the Enlightenment vision, correct to the last hair and mandible, exquisite in their clarity. The opposite of his avowed mission as stated in the Surabaya cell. "Painting," he now announced, "is inseparable from science. It is simplicity with nothing unrealised or clouded by passion." This had all been triggered by a visit to the Botanical Gardens in misty Bogor, the flattering attention of Director Lieftinck.

"But what about art and music, *Scherzo für Blechinstrumente*?"

He turned, tiny brush in hand and looked at me in exasperation. "Because various things come out of one head does not mean they have to be all same. That is the mistake that Margaret makes. You remember her telling us of places where it was normally expected that a man would take on several completely different sexual identities in the course of a single life? Well, why not the same but simultaneously? And not just with sex but also art. Margaret is obsessed with sex."

There was a timid knocking, more of a scratching really, at the door. Someone said, "Yes please?" and a head appeared to peer at us. Walter rose.

"Mr Kasimura? How unexpected. Please come in." Kasimura, the Japanese photographer from Denpasar. One forgets how many Japanese there were around, in the Indies, in those days. Most of the technicians, dentists, photographers were Japanese. Kaaimura was a thin, embittered man, locked in warfare with the Chinese merchant, Lee King, who held a monopoly in Western canned goods and had organised some sort of a boycott against him for what his kinsmen were suffering in Manchuria under the poking bayonets of Kasimura's fellow countrymen. Lee King had even set up a nephew in rivalrous business, with all the latest painted backdrops, including a sensational version of a transatlantic liner with real electric chandelier. Red-faced and panting, Kasimura was gripping the handlebars of a heavy iron bicycle that he appeared to want to bring in with him.

"Perhaps the bicycle would be better outside. It will be quite safe." Kasimura bowed and hissed and complied, shuffling off cracked shoes to enter in bare feet. "Please sit down. Some coffee? But I see you are hot.

Perhaps some water first? We have a whole river." Oleg was called, came, disposed all smoothly. There were various ways of dealing with the subject of Walter's recent imprisonment. Some ignored it. Others stammered out something about not believing a word of it, while blushing furiously. Kasimura combined both in a silent reddening to the roots of his hair, sitting on the edge of the sofa, bent forward, hands in lap, his lack of ease a form of politeness.

"You haven't cycled all the way from Denpasar, surely, Kasimura-san?"

He tittered and ran his hand through his hair. Unlined, in his fifies, he still had a good thick head of black hair, damp now, as the water transformed itself into sweat.

"No, Walter-san. I came with the bus. The bicycle is from my friend at the waterworks down the road."

"Is this a purely social visit, Mr Kasimura, or can I help you in some way?"

Japanese are the most businesslike of orientals, no need here to approach the topic like a lion stalking deer. Kasimura lay down his glass and picked up his coffee cup. He sighed, perhaps savouring occidental directness.

"Walter-san, I am travelling on behalf of a friend in Tokyo, a man who is in the sporting goods business. He wishes the Balinese to learn to play football, so that he may sell them equipment of Asian size at advantageous prices, and he has asked me to find an area of flat land, in the centre of several towns, where a football pitch might be established and to send him pictures. It seemed to me that Ubud is a good place to take pictures, very strategic." He wrestled with the knotty consonantal cluster. Football? I recalled it bleakly from icy Amsterdam winters, myself the blue-nosed-snivelling boy hanging by his own goal as the games master stamped and raged "Run up, Bonnet! Run up!" Then cold showers, the humiliation of naked exposure, finally seeping chilblains. Walter frowned. All this did not make a great deal of sense.

"But the locals have no interest whatever in football, Kasimura-san, except – I suppose – the few who play on the *lapangan kota* but they are mainly Javanese. Not much business there. They don't even wear boots. They don't wear much of anything." He smirked at me. Kasimura looked depressed. "And how is business?"

He sighed again and looked down at his pale, bony feet, unsuited to the playing of football. "Not so good since Mr Greg left."

"Ah." Greg had initially put a lot of work Kasimura's way: endless films, bought, developed, mounted on cards – that is until he and Margaret realised how extensive their photographic activity was to become. Then they had imported film directly in bulk and Greg had taken over the laborious winding onto rolls and the developing himself. Kasimura put his hand to his mouth.

"Oh, I am sorry, for I should not talk of Mr Greg since he became your enemy."

Walter looked puzzled. "You are wrong there, Mr Kasimura. He is not my enemy. He is a good friend. He stood by me in my time of trouble."

Kasimura shook his head. "No, Mr Walter. It is *you* who are wrong, yes please. You have, I see, no wireless. Perhaps you have not heard the news? Britain and France have declared war on Germany. London and Berlin are both in flames. Thousands, perhaps millions, have been killed by bombs. It is, I think, the end of the West and the beginning of the recognition of Japan's proper place in the world. This is very nice coffee." That last two sentences said with equal satisfaction. Every cloud, he seemed to imply cheerfully, a silver lining. Walter gaped. I gaped. He found his tongue first.

"A war? Jesus! So it's really happened. But what can a war in Europe possibly have to do with Japan? And you mean the next time Greg and I meet we shall be on different sides and required to shoot each other? But that is absurd." Walter sat down heavily, trying to come to terms with the news, lit a cigarette with fierce concentration. Secure in Dutch neutrality, I soothed.

"I don't think you should take a European war personally, Walter. If Greg has any sense, he's tucked away as safely in America as you are here." I would learn later that Greg, already in British uniform, spent much of the next few years paddling in the lugubrious headwaters of the Irrwaddy, plotting to turn the river sudden red in Rangoon and thus dismay the Japanese by the fulfilment of an ancient prophecy. Walter was genuinely, headshakingly bewildered. He must be worried about his family. I knew he had siblings prominent in the ballet and opera of Berlin, a mother somewhere in Germany. Unlike my own family, the Spieses did not tread lightly on the earth, leaving no tracks. He brushed the hair back from his eyes and shook his head free of confusion.

"You are right, Bonnetchen. There are larger issues. For example, I have an order for two paintings from London. Now I don't know. Should I send them or not?"

As it turned out, Mr Kasimura was unjustifiably Wagnerian in his view of the war's course, for it had entered a stage, less *Blitzkrieg* than *Sitzkrieg*, what the English called the "phony war", where each camp glared at the other from the security of its own side of the border but neither wanted to cross a conceptual line by deliberately breaking something. Political hostility had yet to be transmuted into the hard currency of personal hatred. In Europe, a long hot autumn and clement spring spun out inaction day by day – the calm before the storm. In neutral Bali, too, there seemed suddenly nothing to do but cultivate the arts of leisure, for tourists and European goods had virtually disappeared overnight, only deepening our sense of tranquil isolation and balmy security, the knowledge that Bali held aloof from a snarling world. In our boredom, we even went to a *janger* performance.

Ask about the origins of *janger*, as a dance, and you will receive the same sort of answers accorded inquiries into the sexually transmitted diseases of Europe. The French pox is the English disease is the Spanish distemper is the German plague, according to where you are. North Balinese declare *janger* to have been invented in the south, south Balinese in the north. In the east, it is from the west or even the offshore island of Nusa Penida. Everywhere, it is strange and exotic, enjoyed but despised and had swept the island as the musical sensation of the early Thirties. To dance *janger* is to be as irremediably common as a man who sits, in stained underwear, eating pickled herring straight from the jar. It has ancient origins, the same spirit-possession dances as Walter's own *kecak*, but simultaneously sweet- and soured with the dissonances of bitter Chinese opera, syrupy Malay theatre, sickly American songs and even the oompahing circus and it draws on a young teenaged pool of talent, divided ruthlessly into boys and girls. We had come at the instigation of Alit, there in the crowd, whose younger brother was an enthusiast of the genre. Inevitably, we were introduced to him – a skinny but moon-faced youth whose comrades went into sniggering elbow-digging that suggested they kept abreast of the latest law reports. As so often, I felt like a walking dirty joke. I was the titter that ran round the room.

The boys were divided into singers and *caks*, whose task was to chatter nonsense syllables in tight synchronisation, with rapid changes of speed and emphasis as Walter's monkeys did in *kecak*. They marched in and performed stylised movements of military drill – but more in the fashion of chorus girls – martial arts lunges at lightning speed and rapid dance steps. Then they leapt up onto each others' shoulders into extraordinary revolving pyramids that dissolved into gymnastic debris, reformed, bent into arches, dissolved again, all in time to a hammering *gamelan* with flute descant. Their costumes were an eclectic mix of elements of desirable modernity – tight football shorts, shoes and long stockings, bright red military tunics with gold epaulettes, white gloves, thick, corked moustaches and bibs covered with mirror fragments that sent light ricocheting like the revolving silver balls seen in common dancehalls. Their straining adolescent voices raged hoarsely. They smashed their fists into their palms, rocked, swayed undulated and crashed to a finale in – God help us – a mass Nazi salute.

Then it was the girls' turn, entering through the overarched arms of the boys, in swaying sarongs and sashes, headdresses of golden sunbursts trembling about their heads, flashing eye movements under the usual absolute control. Their voices rose in a high nasal whine, like a chorus of cats, as they took their places demurely in two seated rows, facing each other, reciprocally undulant, and the boys did the same to create a square. What happened within that square, over the next few hours, was a bizarre goulash of cultural influences. First, came a "Dutchman" in a long grey suit, spectacles and what was – surely – Walter's appalling beret, who made a long telephone call to the gods in Gunung Agung, arranging the programme for the evening, a brief song from the *arja*, or Balinese opera, an acting out of one of the more syrupy love stories of Hindu legend and a brief skit of two white people – Margaret and Greg? – being eaten by New Guineans in a comedy cannibalism scene. Then came more songs from the boys and girls, all with the same wild exuberance and intensity, a very correct rendition of Dutch nursery rhymes and an interaction between Capuk, the greedy braggart of Balinese theatre, and a dour and self-important Javanese student who made a loudly progressive political speech before being carried away for more fine dining by the New Guineans. The audience, that seemed to comprise every soul of the village regardless of age, loved it.

At midnight, we two had had enough and walked back alone through the velvet air, our feet crunching, in untheatrical modern shoes, on the gravel of the Dutch road, Walter so sunk in the Balineseness of the evening that he took my hand innocently, as one of the villagers would his friend's and swung it back and forth as we walked. "I know that was all pretty gruesome," he mused, as though I were the one always railing against the Balinese neglect of their own musical heritage, "but it all shows a wisdom we lack. Even at their silliest, they go to the heart of things. The appeal of dictators and militarism is a matter of pure choreography, supplemented by nice shiny uniforms and rough boyish games. That is *janger* in short. They have turned history into spectacle not bloodshed, into art not politics. If it is bad art that is only because it comes from our own bad politics."

I paid no heed to the rest of it, replying with grunts and mild affirmations – just as my father had when my mother was talking of shoes or hats or his children's hopes and dreams for the future, subjects in which he took no interest – the actual content of Walter's thoughts less important than the circumstances of them. My palm was tingling, in his, with a childish excitement at once sad and elated. Like many men, I had come to a point where I could say to myself, "This is not perfect but it is good enough, I can make do with this." Like many others, I had grown accustomed to ranging love and sex on separate shelves with only the weasel word "affection" to confuse the two. I was – I saw – a mere reverberator for Walter's constantly hammering keys. He stopped and looked out over the valley, lit only by the stars and the fireflies.

"Do you know *Den frohen Wandersmann*?" he asked, "The old Eichendorff poem? Plumpe and I used to recite it to each other when we went hiking," and launched into it. "'*Wem Gott will rechte Gunst erweisen, Den schickt er in die weite Welt, Dem will er seine Wunder weisen In Berg und Wald und Strom und Feld. Die Trägen die zu Hause liegen, Erquicket nich das Morgenrot. Sie wissen nur von Kinderwiegen,*

Von Sorgen, Last und Not um Brot ...' There is much more ..." It rolled on. I shut my ears to it, just listening to the music of his voice over the gushing river and suddenly, something Greg had said popped into my head.

"When you marry, old man ..." this had been at a very early stage of our friendship, "... marry an anthropologist. They will have been trained for years only to say just enough to keep *you* talking and will *never* interrupt and, deep down, that's what every man really wants more than anything, a captive audience". He paused reflectively. "That, of course, takes no account of Margaret."

* * *

Manxi's was slowly creeping back to muted but still scandalous life. The airboys were glad to have it back as an informal – no ties required – extension to their messroom and doubtless patriotic motives had been invoked to justify the granting of a licence. For legalistic reasons, local "ladies" seemed now to patrol exclusively outside on the beach with Manxi's as a sort of terminus to which they periodically returned to retouch, refuel and debrief. There was, I noted with relief, no musical signature tune of bagpipes to mark my entrance. A new, large radio of many valves was tuned to a Surabaya dance-music station, cheap music that sighed and faded over the mountains. Perhaps, like with religious offerings, the gods there were sucking the essence from it. There came just a flutter of fingers from the barman and a screech of greeting from Manxi. Walter executed a courtly bow in return. She was garbed in an extraordinary outfit, clearly of her own devising, half sarong, half plaid.

"For God's sake don't encourage her, Walter. Oh Jesus, she's coming over." She was badly in need of a tidy up, herself, fierce red roots showing in the black, pudding-basin haircut, makeup thickly applied like slapdash plaster over structural faults. We sat hurriedly.

"'Ow's my boys?" she asked, thrusting out a Macsaronged leg. Then, not waiting for an answer, "I 'eard as 'ow you'd bin in a bit of trouble, Walt." Her tone suggested that, in her career, many of her friends had encountered a bit of trouble. "Several of me gentlemen 'ad to leg it sharpish and – if you know what I mean – several of the ladies 'ad to become gentlemen again, for a bit anyway."

"For a bit of what, Manxi?"

She screeched. "Oh Walt, you are a caution. Inne? Inne a caution, Rudi? I 'ad to 'ave a little 'oliday myself, draw me 'orns in. Up in the 'ills, you know." That would be the boyfriend in Bangli. "Did some luvverly paintings. You must come round and see." I felt Walter shrink a little beside me. "Now dearie, what'll it be? One of me friends brought in a nice drop of Canadian scotch the other day. Two? Yes?" She clomped off in big, black shoes and passed the order to the barman in muscular articulations.

"Cheers," I offered, holding out one of the chipped glasses delivered to the table. He made a donkey face. I coaxed. "At least you are winning the war – Poland, Czechoslovakia, Denmark, Norway conquered, Britain and France all but beaten. All part of your glorious Reich. You are now a member of the master race, Walter. That must be nice, especially at breakfast. Thank God the political gymnastics will soon be over with minimum bloodshed and we can all get back to normal." Over by the bar, Manxi let out a shriek and pinched the cheeks of a well-fleshed airboy.

"Normal. Yes. I suppose so. Was there ever such an insane time to live in? War is even more stupid and moronic than football. I hope Kasimura breaks his neck on that bicycle and the Balinese never learn to play football. Charlie is wrong. Vicki is wrong. The Covarrubiases are most wrong of all. Real artists cannot be *engagiert*. It dulls the mind. Like your Holland, I am neutral. I am," he brightened, "a hotly disputed no-man's land in the battle of the sexes." Where had he got that from? We clinked glasses. The whisky was terrible. Two of the airboys had begun to dance, Manxi shouting about her licence and seeking to interpose herself and push them apart, like a referee at a boxing match. "Lieftinck," he said as though it were a natural progression, "from the botanical garden in Bogor, is very excited by my pictures of dragonflies and fish. Fish pictures are important because the specimens change colour when they are taken from the water and pickled, but my dragonflies are even more special. Those I found in the remote forests, they already know but those taken from the valley right outside the house are new species, totally unknown to science. They plan to name one of them after me in the taxonomical index. In German, we call dragonflies Jungfern, "maids", "virgins". So, in a few months is my forty-fifth birthday and the Dutch state, having put me in jail for sex, is about to name me an official virgin with a letter of thanks from Queen Wilhelmina."

Manxi appeared at his elbow, hot and tousled, blowing air, visibly refreshed by the scrum, and dispensed more drink, despite our protests. "Don't talk to me about being a virgin," she opined. "With me, it gets truer every day. Oi! I told you ..." The airboys were at grips again. Her grasp on the bottle switched instinctively to the neck as she hurried over, making it a weapon of offence, then – repenting of her aggression – using it merely to poke and provoke giggles. They, backing away from intimate prodding, knocked into the table of two tall Buginese "ladies", turned over glasses, screams, wiping off of splashes – oh dear let me – grasping and clutching, general mêlée that merged into a sort of joint quickstep as a cheery tune – one of Noel's – struck up on the wireless. I realised how irrevocably inappropriate it would be for me and Walter to dance, which also – according to some befuddled but inexorable logic – meant that I would also never paint him. Then, Manxi was there, hand appropriately reaching for the great knob to cut off the excuse for joy, when a voice like that of a headmaster walking in on a schoolboy brawl rang out and everyone froze.

"This is His Excellency Jonkeer Alidius Warmoldus Lambertus Tjarda van Starkenborgh Stachouwer, Governor General of the Netherlands East Indies, speaking to you all from Batavia. It is with the deepest sadness that I have to tell you the gravest news from the motherland. At 3.55 this morning, German forces launched a brutal and premeditated attack on the Royal Dutch Airforce base at Waalhaven, south of Rotterdam, but, encountering fierce and heroic resistance, were successfully driven off. Paratroopers are reported to have attempted landings in various parts of the country but have been contained and are being wiped up by victorious Dutch forces. A state of war henceforth exists between our nation and the German Reich. Naval and land forces have engaged the enemy and inflicted heavy losses. It is for us to remain calm and support the motherland in its time of need. We face a shameless and cowardly foe with steadfast courage and determination and our victory is certain. Further announcements will follow. God save the Queen!"

The airboys gawped and attempted a belated weak cheer. Manxi's jaw dropped. "Cripes!" Walter did not react. He had possibly not followed the aristocratic haw-hawing Dutch.

"Out!" I hissed, head down. "Do nothing. Say nothing. Stand up and just walk out. Now!"

* * *

"If I may say so," said Walter, saying so, "you look well in uniform." He was sitting on the ground, leaning against a tree, looking up at me. "Those with no dress sense always look their best when decisions are made for them. It is one of the few arguments that convince for marriage." This from a man wearing a collapsed straw hat, torn khaki shorts and a shirt, once red, now an indeterminate shade of pink, far too tight in the chest and revealing bare midriff, feet clad in worn sandals, the face fringed by a ratty blond beard – the sort that is born of neglect, not cultivation. He had lost weight, acquired deep lines at the sides of his mouth and the eyes had sunk to Rasputin-like profundity. He seemed bleached and shrivelled. Three plates of army stodge a day were filling me out while the military were obsessed with my regular depilation and the sharpness of my creases. We were in Ngawi, a couple of hours' drive from Solo, in Java's dry season, than which few things are drier. The regular cone of volcanic Mount Lawu towered over us like a pale imitation of Mount Fuji. I sat down reluctantly in the dust beside him.

"It is not the real army," I hastened to reassure. "Just a sort of militia, mostly aircraft-spotting and a bit of ack-ack but there was no chance of getting through the gate without a uniform. It seems everyone needs one these days. Since Holland fell, people have changed. There's more patriotism about – the call of a lost cause, perhaps. A white face is no longer enough. I am supposed to be on a gas familiarisation course in Solo. It seemed like a golden opportunity." It had not been as easy as I pretended. Visits were not encouraged. This was not a bad billet. But then internment was not supposed to be a prison. There was the inevitable tired barbed wire and bored guards, they not real army either but militia like myself. I had a swift fantasy that I would get myself posted here, become Walter's guard, protect him. Accommodation was in flimsy wooden huts but there was an adequacy of shade from trees. This had once been a teak plantation and the huge trees were everywhere. The main problem seemed to be sheer lack of space, with some five hundred men crowded into four small compounds. A skinny, buck-toothed man came, stood over us and stared silently with mad eyes, his glottis working furiously.

"Things are better than they were." Walter's own eyes were tired, red. "They took all the real Nazis and shut them up together. They used to drive us crazy, spent all their time being blond beasts, shouting slogans, drilling, marching up and down – just like bad *janger*. Finally, they paid me the compliment of putting me in the 'traitors' section with all the Jews, anti-Nazis, pro-Dutch and communists." He smiled. "The Neuhaus brothers are here. You remember them? They are very kind and sort of look after me." I offered a cigarette. Jealousy flared with the flame. I dumped several more packets, with matches, from under my shirt, down on the ground between us where the guards could not see. It was forbidden but they did not seem to mind. Still, one had to show respect. The madman laughed, pointed and danced on the spot. Walter gave him a cigarette and sent him gently away. "Did you know that this place is otherwise famous for the discovery of the remains of southeast Asia's great evolutionary leap, down there by the river – when there is a river – *homo erectus*?" He slumped in counter-illustration of erectness. "A Frenchman, Eugene Dubois. I understand there is a decent little museum somewhere if they would only let me take a look."

"The house, the animals, the servants are all being looked after till you get back. You have so many friends, you know. We are getting up a petition to have you released." He patted my knee absently and sighed and shrugged. I was the one who needed comfort. He seemed remote, like a painting behind glass. To formally visit like this, was moving us apart. This was not how I had expected him to take to internment. I had thought he would have seduced all the guards with his charm and proffered portraits, be sleeping with the handsomest of them, having his food sent in. But, of course, these were not lissom locals but implacably Dutch and of the clerkish class.

Then, it slipped out. "Oh, Walter, why didn't you take Dutch nationality years ago when it would have been so easy?"

"It seemed so stupid, Bonnetchen. Why should I applicate to be

Dutch to stay in the Indies? It would be like becoming Greek to stay in Japan. Which reminds me. Kasimura is here, though in a different compound of course. Why are Japanese here?" Some men were playing football, irritatingly close, like louts on a beach. Kasimura would, perhaps, be pleased. Through the gate, a long, dry road stretched away to fade out in a blue haze. Very Van Gogh.

"I don't suppose they give you any news?" I dropped my voice and polished my glasses to confuse spies. "I'm afraid the Japanese are on their way, six months at best before the war starts. They've joined up with the Nazis and overrun the French and the British Asian colonies and now they're leaning on the government here to let them take over – the Greater East Asia Co-Prosperity Sphere. Your friend, H.E. the G.G., has resisted their blandishments and told them that if they want the Indies, they will have to fight for them. We're pouring millions of tons of concrete into defences at Surabaya. I shouldn't be telling you this, I suppose. But neither of us ever seemed very much representatives of our nations. If they win, you will be free and you can come and visit me in a camp just like this, maybe the same camp. The Japanese will like Mount Lawu, just like Fuji. If we survive, that is but – look on the bright side – I expect they'd be too busy raping women and killing Chinese to care much about us."

Walter gulped smoke and stared down the road, seeming not to have heard. He said: "The oddest thing is that little priest, Father Scruple, you remember? The one who turned up at Conrad's funeral? He's chaplain here. I think he has designs on my immortal soul but actually I think I am turning him into a pagan. I am working on that Balinese dictionary you once helped me with and we discuss the more religious concepts. Little by little, he is being undermined. He plays an excellent game of chess."

Scruple? I wondered about Dion. Everyone was getting lost or, rather, they were still there, like the pieces of glass in a kaleidoscope, but with occasional twists so that they formed ever new and more unlikely patterns.

"I brought you stuff from the art circle in Surabaya, paint, paper, canvas, brushes and pencils. Life must be terribly boring here. No dragonflies." He smiled. I had pictured this so differently, myself showering bounty down on him. He happy, warmly grateful, relaxed.

But the spontaneity had been stolen, the goods seized in the guardhouse, quarantined to be unwrapped, searched, probed at the guards' leisure. It was like getting your Christmas presents on Boxing Day when they no longer counted and it was anyway as if Walter had purged himself of the need for artistic supplies. Perhaps he was painting on the canvas inside his head as I had that time in Denpasar.

"I have learnt a lot from this experience," Walter confided. "How very little a man requires. Yet we constantly educate ourselves to find the one thing that is wrong, that is lacking. When I get out of here, I shall be less driven, more ready to take life as it comes."

I gaped. I could not imagine who this rejected Prometheus of Walter's imagination, might be. If Walter became less driven, he would be comatose.

"I heard a story, once about a young village man who took a rich tourist fishing on the shore. He showed the man what to do and pulled out two fish in quick succession, then wanted to go home to eat them. But the tourist wanted more for his money and, as they sat, he calculated how many fish they might catch in one day and how many months it would take to buy a boat so that they could get out to the reef where the big fish are and how many years it would be before they might have twenty men working for them in boats and dominate all the fishing in the area. 'Why would I want to do that?' asked the young man. 'So that you can be rich,' replied the tourist, astonished. 'Then you could retire and go fishing.' One day I shall do the painting of that." He settled back and wiggled his buttocks down into the dust. "One day." As if I were nagging him.

My hand brushed the side of my jacket and detected the curvosity contained within. "Oh yes. I brought you this." I held out a pingpong ball. "They said at the art circle you kept asking for one." He shaded his eyes to peer into the sun, then leapt forward, mouth open, eyes wide and seized it with trembling fingers.

"A pingpong ball!"

I felt a stir of interest around us. A couple of men came up immediately and stared at it hungrily. "A ball! Walter has a ball!" A muted murmur rippled out across the compound. Voices were heard asking for confirmation.

"You must understand that for three months we have had a table and almost two bats but no ball. We have tried playing with cactus pith balls and wooden balls that we made ourselves and Kasimura-san managed to produce an origami ball that was almost round from a huge sheet of paper but it was no good. No bounce." He grasped my legs in genuine thanks. Now there were tears in his eyes. One of the men reached out to touch the orb like a holy relic, pure, clean, virginal. "Pingpong is one of the few pleasures left to me," Walter said tragically and then laughed at himself. He threw back his head, exhausted. "Bonnetchen, it is amazing for how little men will sell their own souls."

* * *

I was wrong about the Japanese. It was not months but weeks before they were on the move but then I was not alone in my mis-estimate. After the attack on the Americans at Pearl Harbour, Imperial forces spread rapidly over east Asia like a wine stain, flooding into Thailand, seeping into Malaya, the Philippines, reaching out delicate tendrils towards the great British bastion of Singapore. H.E. the G.G. was on the radio again, bowing to the inevitable with a declaration of war. Hard times ahead but victory is certain. We shall win because our cause is just. Then the first tentative airraids on unprotected cities, the first landings in Borneo. The cowardly enemy shall be defeated and their perfidy punished. Then Surabaya was bombed and strafed and we came to know what modern warfare might mean with women and children, bloody and dazed, wandering in the ruins. Then, Singapore, last bulwark in the East, fell with a crash that echoed around the world. Apparently, the British had built their impregnable redoubt with the guns pointing the wrong way. We shall fight on and never surrender. The lessons for Surabaya were obvious and perhaps the Japanese would pass through Ngawi and free Walter on their way there. American and Australian forces moved in and then out as a series of landings and set-piece naval battles were lost and the Indonesians began their own attacks, harassing Dutch forces. The Battle of the Java Sea, off the coast at Surabaya, put matters beyond any further doubt. From his camp, secure in the dark hills, perhaps Walter could see the flashes of the offshore guns and the following thuds as the armoured dinosaurs clashed and gored and the Allied fleets were torn apart in a vain attempt to reach the Japanese troop convoys heading for Java. Most went to the bottom, with only a few vessels escaping to Australia. The Japanese invasion fleet sailed on. Now we were alone.

I, of course, was very far from alone, being already under military occupation. The Japanese had landed in Bali the previous month and were settling in nicely for a long stay. H.E. the G.G. could still be heard on the radio, on pain of death if discovered, telling us that the tide would be turned at any moment. At least he was not caught in the mad rush for a plane to Australia, unlike the rest of the leadership, and would be shipped off to comfortless exile in far Japanese Manchuria.

They came, of course, like all invading forces – like the annual pestilence – to Sanur and began by devastating Walter's *akvarioom*, perhaps mistaking the empty fishtanks for strategic installations. The Dutch commander in his barracks in Denpasar, learning too late of their arrival, had sent a note to the airfield, ordering his men "not to delay in demolishing it." The local sergeant, confused by the implied double negative, did nothing as a detachment of paratroops, under the dashing Colonel Horiuchi, descended on the airbase and, finding it undefended, occupied it and adjourned to Manxi's next door. It was supposed to be very different, of course. A loyal band of 600 local troops, backbone stiffened by white officers such as myself, had been drilled to hold itself in suicidal readiness to repel seaborne invasion. But at two in the morning, on that particular night, it was pouring with rain and the invasion was not even noticed until dawn, by which time, the men's only thought was to slough off their uniforms and melt quietly into the ricefields. The Japanese vanguard had already driven, under cover of darkness, into town and the residents awoke to find the rain clearing away nicely and, not one, but two rising suns over their town.

It was Bali's good fortune to come under naval, rather than army, administration. Here, would be none of the deliberate atrocities favoured by General Imamura on Java as educative measures. There, allied POWs were packed into animal cages and shipped to Surabaya, there to be publicly thrown to the sharks, still caged, by chortling troops. I knew Walter, for the first time in his life, would be actually protected by his passport but I trembled to know him in such a terrible place. Like many others, I was herded into a vast chicken run on the *lapangan kota* and sat for two days without food and with scant water, as the fallen mighty walked about me and wore themselves out by tutting and huffing and swearing the vengeance that would be theirs, not for the invasion but the indignity. Smit was there, quivering with rage and terror, having been given a good slapping by exuberant troops. I could not decently bask in his suffering as the poor man was beside himself about the unknown fate of his wife. How often the love of others makes us, not strong, but weak and vulnerable. Then, to our general surprise, soldiers came and drove us out and made us work.

It seemed we were to offer public proof of the collapse of white rule and we were set to mend the roads and clear out the drainage ditches in the hot sun and, given no tools, we had to use our bare hands. The slightest hesitation or reluctance was rewarded by a thrashing to unconsciousness with a stout bamboo about the head and shoulders. Sometimes, the guards just hit you anyway because it had been some while since they had hit someone. At such moments, most covered their genitals. I protected my glasses. If they were broken, where would I ever get another pair? The locals goggled at this unlikely sight of our brutalisation but seemed to take no pleasure in it. One brave man I knew vaguely, was moved to compassion and even threw a quarter of a ringgit into the ditch where I was working when the guard's attention was distracted. The gesture moved me to tears. Occasionally, people would be led away. Some came back, badly knocked about. On the third night, one of these, an engineer, died after coughing blood all day. On the fourth, one of the young airmen was called forward, forced whimpering to his knees and executed before us with a sword, the head lopped off by a strutting officer who worked his shoulder afterwards and looked piqued as though he had strained himself with a tricky golf shot. Whether this was a random lottery, or for some specific reason, we never knew but we were ever-fearful of the guards' approach and watched them make their daily selection with predictable terror and guilty relief. It had sunk in that we were living in a different world and we struggled to understand its rules but the arbitrariness of violence bore the message that there were no rules any more. And after about week of this, the soldiers came for me. It was almost a relief, like knowing the disease you will finally die of.

The two who took me were very small, haunted – Margaret would have intuited – by some inferiority complex displaced into aggression. They pushed and pulled me quite unnecessarily, drove me with rifle butts, out of the compound and up the steps of the administrative building and into the Escher-provoking hallway. No longer langued and armed gules above the door, just a heap of smashed plaster and a Japanese flag, tacked up over the vacancy, as if implying a purely provisional occupation. There, they paused and the larger of the two kicked me viciously in the back of the knees so that I went down hard. He put his face very close to mine and hissed in Dutch, "White shit!" I felt saliva spray on my skin and wondered whether they had been issued with Dutch phrasebooks to be used in the proper ill-treatment of prisoners. Humiliatingly too, I was aware that he was very young, with beautiful skin and teeth and long, black hair – too long on the neck for a soldier, must be vain about it – devastatingly, muskily handsome. Desire stirred unwillingly. There came the sound of a door opening, shouts, violent slaps, a hand assisting me up from behind so that first thing I saw was my escort hunched and covering genitals with hands – not that that, alas, had been where the slapping had taken place – but in a gesture of submission. I turned, bent and hobbling like an old man, to see an officer with a long cigarette-holder and a broad smile – Kasimura.

"Kasimura-san!"

"Mr Bonnet. Thank you for coming." He shouted and hissed my escort – now humbled schoolboys – away and walked, with swift light steps, into the office, gesturing gracefully towards a chair, sitting down, himself, behind the desk once throned over by Van Diemen. A delicate teapot and handleless cups stood on a lacquered tray. He poured, proffered, disclosed the contents of a carved cedarwood cigarette box with authority. The hair was still so over-groomed as to resemble an implausible toupee.

"You are, I take it, no longer in the photography business, Kasimura-san." The cigarettes were "Peace" brand, inaugurated to mark the end of the last war. Since the government had recently forbidden the use of Western names for Japanese brands, these must be old stock. In those days, in Europe, only lavatory paper always had a Japanese brand name. The Japanese were, after all, famous for their paper.

"You are correct, Mr Bonnet. I now have the honour to be head of the *Kempeitei* in this sector." He glowed and swelled. We were already learning the basic Japanese necessary for survival. The *Kempeitei* were the military secret police. Even the Japanese lived in terror of them.

"My congratulations, Kasimura-san."

He smiled coolly. "It is just one of the changes you southern barbarians will have to get used to. Other races too. Last night, I had the pleasure of visiting my old friend Lee King at his shop – at his *former* shop. It was a great joy to re-educate him. His business is now under new management. Later today, I shall be interrogating Mr Smit." My hand shook. Perhaps it was the impact of the first nicotine on my system after so long without.

"Tell me, Mr Bonnet, about your friend Sampih. I understand that he is involved with the nationalist youth, the *Pemuda*. I should like to talk to him. Where do you suppose I might find him?"

"Sampih? I have no idea. I haven't seen him for years, not since McPhee left. As you know, he is a dancer. He will be dancing somewhere."

He pursed thin lips. "I have no intention of harming him. Do not alarm yourself. The nationalist leaders have been very co-operative. There are to be volunteer workers for the Japanese war effort. We may even recruit soldiers here to fight imperialism elsewhere. I have always felt that you were sympathetic to the cause of Indonesian independence, Mr Bonnet. I should think you would wish to help the just struggle of your friends." He looked at me icily. I changed the subject.

"The football pitches," I said. "That was clever. A diversion. Paratroops, yes?" He inclined his head graciously. "And Walter. Spies-san. Where is he? Has he been freed?" He frowned.

"I have no information on that. You will appreciate that I have more urgent concerns. I last saw him several months ago. The Dutch were moving all the white prisoners to Sumatra to avoid our advance. Us, they left behind. You should not concern yourself over him. The Dutch surrender in Sumatra was very rapid. As one of our allies, he will certainly have been freed. He will just have to sweat it out." Walter never sweated. He raised his cup and nodded towards the tea. We sipped. It became a sort of toast. "There is always the possibility that he was transported overseas."

"Overseas? But why …?"

He cleared his throat. "Towards the end, the Dutch forces behaved very … eccentrically. They had ten times as many men as us when they surrendered. They devoted their efforts to strange ends. One of the last things they did was to ship 200 communist prisoners to Australia. What will they do with them there? They could have left them. We would certainly have taken care of them. It served no military purpose. Me, of course, they should have shot immediately as of high value to the enemy. Instead, I was left behind." He seized a stack of papers from one side of the desk and bent purposefully over them. It looked like the same file Van Diemen had studied. "But to your own fate. I have spoken of you to our commander, who is a man of considerable learning, a university man, from Kyoto. We Japanese are admirers of art and civilisation. It does no good to see a man such as yourself on the *lapangan kota*." I flinched with reflex guilt. "It has been decided that you shall be released along with several other artists for the greater glory of the Japanese nation. Your house, as well as that of Walter-san, has been requisitioned by His Majesty's Imperial Forces. You will live with the painter Hofker in Abang. Should you not agree, you will be shot. You will not leave Abang, nor will you be permitted to write or enter into correspondence with anyone else until further notice. Should you disobey, you will be shot. In return for this kind mercy you will set your skills at the disposal of *Dai Nippon*. You will continue to paint and will deliver your paintings to me. Should you fail to satisfy your monthly quota of paintings, you will be shot."

I was dazed, confused. "Paintings? But what paintings? What must I paint?"

Kasimura rose up behind his desk and inflated his pigeon chest. "Breasts!" he cried, eyes gleaming behind his glasses. There was spittle at the corner of his mouth. "You will paint bare Balinese breasts!"

And so began a curious period of my life when I painted bare breasts in the service of His Imperial Majesty, The Emperor of Japan. I can only assume the paintings were sold to members of the Japanese forces and shipped back to loved ones in Tokyo as the face of the exotic east. Whether Kasimura grew rich on the proceeds, I cannot begin to guess. Abang lay just along the road from my previous studio. Walter's house was occupied by a gaunt and hagridden agronomist, Dr Nasiputi, charged with introducing strains of sticky rice more pleasing to the Japanese palate and my own house had fallen to two of my chicks of the *Pemuda* persuasion who produced stirring pro-Japanese posters exhorting young people to become smiling *ramusha*, volunteer labourers for the occupation. Thousands of them would die of neglect and ill-treatment in the forests and swamps of Burma but that we did not yet know. I wished them well but condemned their abominable use of colour

The Hofkers came as a pair, Willem and wife, Maria. They had first visited Indonesia at the instigation of the KPM shipping line, to present a state portrait of Queen Wilhelmina to the head office in Batavia, but were seduced by the charm of Bali and stayed. The public burning of said portrait was to be one of the most urgent acts of the new Japanese administration, a compliment of sorts. The Nazis burnt Vicki, the Japanese Hofker, nobody bothered to consign Bonnet to the flames. While Maria painted insects à la Walter, Willem Hofker was a formal portrait painter in the grand Renaissance tradition, and, soon after arriving in Bali, went into the Balinese beauties business, specialising in *legong* dancers. As Walter would have said archly, we became bosom friends.

In a tiny wooden bungalow, we two men and Maria played, like Marie Antoinette, at growing vegetables, raising chickens, shifting for ourselves, just as the locals did. Maria was a big, cheerful woman emotionally attuned to the making of nourishing soups, which was as well, for, as Japanese forced levies on food and raw materials increased, the markets emptied of goods. Our first attempts at cultivation were not successful. In the steambath of the hot season, Western vegetables flourished in early, rank growth, but were swiftly undermined by boring worms. As usual, Nature everywhere supplied unsought metaphors for life. Only our carrots swelled obscenely and came to fruition. Tired of carrot soup, we tried to exchange them with our neighbours but Balinese disdain *wortel* as a worthless Dutch peculiarity. Their charity proved a more solid resource, however, and, even in the worst times, we never lacked for rice. Diversifying, we branched out into beans and dutiful cabbage, fighting off the hawks that attacked our chicks and the snakes that their eggs attracted, handpicking pests from our plants' gnarled leaves. The last also served as models for Maria's busy pencil. While Dr Nasiputi was otherwise engaged, Willem and I staged a commando raid on Walter's artistic supplies cupboard and brought back tempera and oils that we eked out in increasingly weak pastel shades. There was, of course, no question of payment for our work. Other artists similarly got by. In bougainvillea-draped Sanur, Le Mayeur continued to live undisturbed with Ny Pollok, painting on burlap with flaming shades of Javanese sarong dye, while Theo Meier, patriarchally equipped with local wives, took to the hills, grew his own tobacco and brewed his own plum cordial, "swisky for Swiss mountain sailors". In town, so it was said, Manxi was often to be seen, chauffeured around, in the stately staffcar of a high-ranking officer. We all used what talents we had to survive.

Then, out of the blue, the lanky post boy brought a postcard from Walter. I was astonished to learn that the postal service still operated, albeit with great delay and intermittent delivery, rather as the basic bodily functions continue after death and surprise the living with sudden twitches and effusions of flatulence. The silly boy knew nothing of its origins. A knowledge of geography beyond Ubud was not required for the exercise of his duties and all his thought was absorbed in the hope that the arrival of the Japanese might mean that he would be issued with a new uniform involving a sword. The card itself was mysterious. It was a featureless khaki oblong marked "Censored" and written in Dutch to "Dear Rudi". Walter had never written in Dutch, though perhaps this was a restriction imposed by the authorities. He had never addressed me as "Rudi", though perhaps that, too, was to avoid overtones of excessive intimacy. Date was illegible but, in small print, I could just make out the name of "Kuta" and thought, at first, it was from the little seaside town where McPhee played the *gamelan*. Then I saw the other half, not "Kuta" but "Kutacane", a desperately small town in the highlands of Aceh, a byword for boredom and isolation amongst a joylessly Muslim people. "There is no dancing here and the only music comes from me – we have a piano – and a ragged teahouse violinist. For the local people, music is sinful, sex is sinful, paintings are sinful. I live a very sinful life with much musical painting. Many here are driven to explore their faith from boredom. Of all the peoples of the Indies, those here most closely resemble your own and the young men are very active around the camp. I have become invincible at pingpong. Send more balls. There is a terrible lack of them here." I did not know what to make of it. The "exploration of the faith" was obvious enough and the "young men" would be ambiguously the beguiling local beauties and the *Pemuda* nationalists, some of them armed, who were throwing their lot in with the Japanese. Were they a threat to Walter or a source of comfort? Was it the prisoners who lacked the balls or the guards? I could not tell. At any moment, he would walk through the door, flop down, grinning, in that chair and start talking about some new dragonfly he had found.

Then the kaleidoscope twisted again, the world briefly retreated and blurred, then sharpened into a new order. The naval commander was replaced, Kasimura disappeared. It was announced that anyone with half native blood would be released from internment and it was amusing to see how many "whites" swiftly rushed to the administrative building with written proof of their family's concealed half-caste status. Willem Hofker and I, growing cabbage in the hills, were adjudged a threat to security and found ourselves abruptly arrested and shipped off, with three hundred others, to Pare Pare in Sulawesi. As we marched through the town, on the way to the harbour, a great glossy car purred throatily past, Japanese driver honking, with what looked like Manxi sitting on the back seat with a huge black hat pulled down low – but I could not be sure since she held her hand to her face and looked steadfastly the other way.

16

It was the silence I enjoyed as I worked in the grand chamber of the town hall in Makassar. It was the sort of rich, deep-dust-carpeted silence you get after a bomb, part real, part derived from the fact that your eardrums have been stunned by what went before. Mural techniques were relatively new to me but this was no Michelangelo fresco – just painting on a wall as I might have painted on a canvas. I had had the odd public commission before but never anything on such a grandiose scale, evoking such grandiose themes and executed on a wall lit by chandeliers, a triptych, rather in the style of one of the old voyages of discovery, de Bry or some such. The idea was more or less the same "unity within diversity" that the Indonesian Republic would take – suitably classicised with Sanskrit – as its own original motto. One province, three peoples.

Over to the left, were sturdy Makasarese, their fisherman role conveyed by ankle-deeep foam and the shells and starfish disposed about their feet – bearing nets, baskets of sprats and great barbed, pouting fish. In the distance, we see their bright outriggers. Foreground figures tastefully unclothed, pubic bulge apparent. Those in the rear, bare-buttocked and apple-cheeked, sporting in the surf. There is nothing harder to invent than a face, so all painters' canvases are a gallery of those they have known. The foremost borrowed little Resem's sweet countenance and grafted it onto Alit's firm legs. As my brush licked their muscled chests and tendons into shape, my only critic was Yurang, a pedal rickshaw driver, unsaddled through advancing years and delegated to bring me the daily tea, coffee and snacks that my contract stipulated.

"There are no women," he observed, standing back and offering up coconut cream and pandanus cakes. "There should always be women."

"No women," I said firmly. After the forced breasts of occupation, I wanted no more Amazons' chests rampaging across my canvases. "You Muslims would complain it was immoral."

He nodded and, as always, turned to his habitual theme of the joys of the open road, now denied him. A dreamy look came over his face and he scratched his crotch nostalgically. "Still. Down by the sea. It reminds me. When I was on the bike, you know the best sex I ever had? It's the rickshaw, puts a terrible strain on the groin that needs easing after a day in the saddle. I used to peddle down to the docks after dark. If the girls had had a thin night, they were glad of a lift home and would pay you in kind, on the nail, right there on the crossbar in the shadow of the fish market."

In the centre, I set the Torajan hill-farmers, romantically loinclothed with an immaculateness of *blanchisserie* available only in Art. They are seen bending rhythmically, as in dance, stretched in the planting-out of rice seedlings, bodies glistening with rain, sweat – whatever – but glistening and, in the rear, rising up, a tropic Arcadia of palms, exotic hills and peaceful buffalo. In the far distance, loom the ancient carved and painted houses for which they are famous, their bird-wing roofs riding lightly on stilts. When the fighting ended, the bodies of the Torajans who had died were said to have climbed up from their graves and marched, all grinning rictus and tattered cerements, back into the hills for the elaborate funerals to which they were entitled, with their massacres of buffalo in the glow of burning villages. There was no shortage of people who would tell you they had seen it with their own eyes.

"Headhunters!" declared Yurang, laying down a dish of *kue lapisan*, striped durian cake. "Unclean. Uncircumcised. You wouldn't catch me up in those mountains." He shuddered. "They'd have the head of a good Muslim off his shoulders before he could say 'Allah!' Mind you. The best sex I ever had was with a Torajan girl. She would do things you wouldn't believe. But since you're not married, it would be ungodly to tell you and get you all hot and drive you to what must be a sin except in marriage."

Over to the right and balancing the composition, the Buginese, Yurang's own people, in primitive breechclouts of soft, clinging cotton. As their main hero, I gave them Oleg but serene and doe-eyed, with the tapered chest and pared waist of his dreams and the nose had been adjusted to Buginese notions of beauty, for Buginese pride themselves on their high, straight noses, claiming they resemble the prows of their great wooden sailing vessels – conveniently depicted in the background – of whose size and prominence they also boast and called – Margaret please note – *pinisi*. Slung over one caramel shoulder, they wear the chequered, silk sarongs that their women weave. A good quality one is so fine that it may be drawn with ease through a wedding ring. Indeed, I believe there is some ancient ceremonial where this is done. I cannot be sure – I cannot be expected to remember everything – but riding easily beside their Muslim faith, they retain an ancient tradition of transvestite or possibly hermaphrodite priests. Having once been the long-distance traders of the archipelago, they were disbarred by greedy Dutch monopoly and so became smugglers and pirates. Oleg bears on his shoulder a jar of perishable goods in token of ancient seaways and in the foreground market place, the transformed Ubud postboy disposes, with gawky adolescence, a banana-leaf box of cloth. I found the work surprisingly easy to execute after all that festered time in the camp, where I had produced nothing. I had been in limbo, frozen and could only count the days, months, years. The whole work was, of course, based on that mural I had painted in my mind in the bare cell in Denpasar. It had slowly cooked for years.

"A fine-looking people." Yurang nodded approvingly. "If you wanted, I could model for you. It's a face the ladies liked in their day. The best sex I ever had was with a Chinese widow who got excited watching me pedaling from behind. I had a regular appointment to take her shopping three afternoons a week but, on the way back, when I had worked up a good sweat, we'd call in at that little park at the end of the sea wall. I had a friend who had a hut there and he'd look the other way while we had our fun." He set down a dish of raw turtles' eggs, a great treat but not one I liked. They always reminded me of pingpong balls.

I had sent Walter more balls but never received any acknowledgement. I had always expected him to turn up, looking for me in the camp and, on some days, the certainty that he was about to appear was almost tangible, an imminent windfall that was just another paralysing part of being in limbo. He would come and rescue me, not on a white charger, but in a great ticking staff car or in an aeroplane, bearing credentials of the highest order to which the Japanese would immediately defer. Then, one day, the capricious time machine that was the postal service spewed out another card, delivered by the Red Cross. It had come from Ubud and I thank the lanky postboy for forwarding it. Again in Dutch and therefore from the world before.

Dear Rudi,

How I envy you your freedom! To be able to go where you like and eat what you like! My only relief here is to pour myself into a new painting. It is *The Vision of Ezekiel* and it is the most impressing thing I have ever done. I will try to get it to you so you can see for yourself. The face of Ezekiel may strike you as familiar but without your glasses! That would have been too much. It shows the godhead but as a great crushing machine, with wings and animal and human heads like my *Scherzo*, and there is a Balinese sense of the world as a turning, revolving apparatus with wheels that mesh together like Balinese time so that the more a thing moves, the more it is the same. Father Scruple lent me a Bible to look it up. As a schoolboy, I only read Ezekiel for the Whore of Babylon part where she was seduced by the wall paintings showing beautiful young men dressed all in blue, the first human depraved by art! It even drove me to go to Berlin to see the Assyrian walls myself and, as a boy, I was amazed by the complexity of the soldiers' knees though I did not like their beards and found the men not at all beautiful.

I feel the time coming when I, too, shall be free. All I think about is Bali. The people here are not as graceful as those in Bali, the trees are less tall, the water less fresh, the sky not as high. Once I get back, I swear I shall never leave again and I *shall* get back even if I have to crawl all the way from this camp.

My own camp had really not been all that bad. Naturally, Hofker had blandly assumed that his wife would be receiving gentler treatment in the women's camp in Java but, at that time, we knew nothing of the vicious atrocities and deliberate starvation imposed by Imamura and the Japanese 16th army. Our own guards were easy-going, middleaged men, headed by cylindrical Sergeant Yoshida, cynical conscripts not stiff-legged professionals, who – like us – mainly just wanted to survive and knew that this involved our co-operation. There were five of them to guard 650 of us. The private property of the inmates was respected and many had brought large sums with them that could be used to buy food or medicines – Pare Pare was literally a hotbed of malaria. In return, the guards appropriated all the allowances intended for our maintenance and installed themselves in a sort of cosy Japanese *kampung* where Yoshida could be seen having his white hairs daily plucked by a giggling local woman. Fields of good black earth were allocated to us to grow food. We traded in goats and cattle. We were allowed to fish from the beach. Life was hard but not impossibly harsh, monastically challenging rather than lethal. Our numbers were augmented, in the early months, by dribs and drabs of new arrivals seeping down from Java and, on one such day, a familiar figure clambered from the back of the truck. He was no longer in clerical garb of immaculate conception but worn *khaki mufti* into which he was sweating

"Father Scruple!" He turned furtively and eyed me with caution. "Don't you remember? We met in Denpasar. Then Ngawi. I was visiting my friend, Walter."

He frowned. "No I don't believe ... Which Walter would that be then?"

"Yes. Yes. You must remember. Walter Spies. You played chess with him every day and argued about his Balinese dictionary. A painter. A musician."

He sighed. "My son. In my line of business, one meets so many people". He turned to go but, of course, did not know where to go and dithered.

"Look," I said. "I don't know what it is you're up to but I don't believe you don't remember him. Think! He played the piano. There can't have been that many piano-playing Walters at Ngawi."

"Well, now. Perhaps I vaguely recall someone like that. He was at Kutacane, too. A strange man. When the piano fell apart, he took the keyboard and played it silently for hours. A little odd in the head. I shouldn't believe much of what he says, if I were you." A sudden thought struck him. "He's not here, is he?" he asked, in some alarm.

"No," I said. "He's not here. I don't know where he is. That's the point. When was the last time you saw him?"

He screwed up his face. "That would have been in Kutacane. It was all confused towards the end. We weren't sure whether the Dutch had already surrendered or not. There was talk of moving the prisoners again. Some of the men just deserted, or maybe they went to do some real fighting. It was hard to know. When there was no point in staying, I left. The Japanese are not always great respecters of the cloth, you know. My own capture in Palembang was terrible. They burst into the church, firing, halfway through 'Rock of Ages'. I thought we were all to be killed. All the priests were seized, all the workers, even the choir. I never got to deliver my sermon. My assistant, Hendrik, was the only one to get away." Coincidence? I thought not but was glad Dion was still free. He sighed. "Look, Walter had been working on this painting, *The Vision of Ezekiel*, he asked me to look after it in the camp, to put it in a safe place. It was an ungodly great thing. The Japanese were said to be twelve miles away and when we moved there was no space for luggage and the camp was burned. I'm sorry, my son, but there it is. All I took was my Bible. It was God's will. If it is any comfort, I am not entirely sure it was not a heretical work. The face of the prophet was most inappropriate, the face of a depraved idiot. Anyway, it was *sauve qui peut*."

"*Sauve qui peut*. For Walter that would mean 'Italian wine for anyone who can bear to drink it'." He looked at me as if I were mad. "Soave – it's a kind of Italian wine – it was a game we played – never mind." I remained calm but my voice broke. "So you saved a bible that could be replaced anywhere and burnt a major work of art, the summation of a man's life? It was possibly a water closet – I mean a watershed – of western art. That's like burning his soul."

He wasn't having that. "You know nothing of theology or of burning souls, of ... of ..." He was turning crimson. "Down, down on your knees now, bow your head and pray with me for guidance."

I turned on my heel. "If I were you, father, I'd get out of the habit of kneeling down, head bowed, when there are Japanese about."

After that, we saw little of each other in the camp. Father Scruple was finally killed in the last of the regular Allied airraids, one Sunday morning – regular since the camp was always mistaken for a Japanese barracks – so he never got to deliver his sermon, on the unpredictability of divine grace, that day either. They moved us inland, upland and our last few months were the worst – the cold, the rain, all the animals dying from standing around knee-deep in water. Then, one day, we got up to find Yoshida and his men had driven off and we were completely alone, abandoned orphans in the storm. We had won the war. It seemed that – to our great surprise and doubtless his own – H.E. the G.G., Jonkeer Alidius Warmoldus Lambertus Tjarda van Starkenborgh Stachouwer, had told us nothing but the truth. It wasn't safe any more, with the *Pemuda* wandering around and making probing raids to work up their courage, so we drifted down to the city of Makassar, mostly on foot, walking through redemptive green fields beside the swirling waves of the South China Sea.

No one can imagine the confusion and mental dislocation of those times. The Japanese had notionally surrendered and were, theoretically, acting under Allied orders, until they could be disarmed and replaced. Some supported the *Pemuda*, giving them weapons, others fought them in the streets. Crucially, Soekarno had been allowed to read out a formal declaration of independence under Japanese tutelage, while the Dutch intended to blandly resume government just as before the war with no concessions to changed realities. In Surabaya, the British Indian Army was fighting a pitched battle against an emerging Indonesian force, with terrible loss of life and everywhere were young men, inflamed by the highest political rhetoric, committing the most terrible atrocities against civilians that would soon be repaid in kind by the Dutch. The heady smell of freedom was already tainted with the stench of blood and corruption. In a bar, Hofker and I found some sort of Dutch welfare officer, who lent us thirty florins a month to live on, and settled in a room in an old abandoned bungalow. It wasn't much but was more than the Indonesians had, yet the improvidence of unsecured loans troubled me. In the evenings, we sat in the dark and listened to the news on a looted wireless whose glowing tuning dial was our only illumination. Seeded among the Dutch broadcasts, were strident new voices, some in Indonesian and English, mostly ranting of injustice. One particularly struck me. It was clearly ultimately English, female, and saying the most offensive things possible about the Allies and rapidly became known as that of "Surabaya Sue", a sort of lesser sister of "Tokyo Rose". But there could be no mistaking those intonations. It was Manxi busily still surviving. It was at this point, roaming the hot and devastated city, that I discovered the Japanese teahouse.

The Grand Hotel reared up, like a beached whale, in the more gracious area of the city, overshaded by dusty palm and eucalyptus, a great white colonial structure of approximately Palladian pretensions. The houses on either side lay shattered as though it had vastly shrugged but, in the hotel, only the gardens had suffered. It had served as the social and cultural centre of the Japanese occupation and behind, in the grounds, stood a new addition, a classic Japanese teahouse of grained wood, tatami mats and formally exuberant rooftiles. It had the most curious effect on me. After years of the temporary, the requisitioned, the grimed, worn down and abraided, it sparkled with crisp freshness, cool rational control, mastery over matter, precision of purpose and I looked at it and felt a lump in my throat for all that had been lost. The door consisted of two sliding sections leading off a passage of pure dove-grey granite and gave onto a series of sere galleries divided by panels of wood and heavy, oiled paper panels. In the main room, these had been painted in a delightful eighteenth-century style with pictures of *kimono*-clad ladies and gentlemen of the floating world. They strolled, gossiped, posed, took tea and – oh my God was there no escape – bared breasts, geishaed variously and played musical instruments. The artist had begun one of the ceiling panels, a scene of a bucolic pleasure-garden with little red hump-backed bridges, lakes, peach trees in blossom. Half a lady floated, free of the ground, like a Balinese *leyak*. He had left before her legs could be finished. His paints lay in a heap on the floor, his brush discarded beside them. It was like finding the ancient imprint of a hand on a rock wall, as I once had in Italy. It is impossible not to lay your own hand over it. I knew at once what I would do. I would set my hand where his hand had been, let his *anima* flow into me as he had let that of the Edo period enter him. I would finish those legs. I would finish the ceiling. I sought out the manager, a bewildered Armenian whose neutrality status was so complicated that the Japanese had never finally decided whether he was friend or foe, and brooked no contradiction. At first he was suspicious, hesitant of local reaction. He had been thinking of organising the burning of the tea-house as a social event. Sell a few tickets. Throw in a beer or two. I argued, not on grounds of aesthetics, but utility. The port was awash with the Allied soldiery – British, Dutch, Australian, American – their pockets stuffed with unconvertible military scrip. Of course, no one but the Japanese would ever want to eat filthy Japanese food but this would make the finest Chinese restaurant. It was agreed that the ceiling would be painted. I should even be paid.

The next six weeks were spent working with an energy I had never known, though I moved, only stiffly at first, back into the pathways of my former craft. Birds twittered and blossoms flowered from my brush, slowly and then in gathering spate. The opening – a grand affair to which the mayor came and made a clumsy speech about the beating of swords into ploughshares and – ha! ha! – paintbrushes. I was surrounded by high-ranking Canadian officers, though of what service I could not divine. There is no reticence in uniforms. A detailed biography of military violence ran through the badges punctuating their sleeves and the ribbons swarming over their chests but this was a language I could not read. At one stage, one of them passed me his military handbook and stabbed a finger at page four. A bold title read, "Women" and underneath the single sentence, "Always remember the Japs were here before you."

"The *lapangan kota*," I said wearily. "The town field. Over behind the fort." My own fieldwork days, I was almost sure, were over. Then at some stage, over red-eyed coffee and cigarettes, the mayor asked me to do something with the townhall, its interior freshly replastered after the hacking away of Nippon military insignia. The great powers were like little boys, running round the world scribbling on each others' walls.

The honorarium paid for a passage aboard one of those high-nosed Buginese ships, a voyage of six days shared with rough but cheery lads, sunburned skin like sandpaper, all inveterate gigglers, who lived simply on rice and fish and prayed every day and invited me into the fishy communal bed where we all slept, chastely entangled, in restfully non-co-varrubious propinquity. And then we were in Buleleng. Hugs, waves, a packet of rice and fish and a fervent prayer for the journey – for seamen, any journey on land was full of danger. I stepped onto the same beach as so many years before – finally back in Bali. I was home. Black sand stuck to my feet and tears pricked at my eyes.

The rain came down, as Walter always said "not in sheets but in eiderdowns". I had thought to walk into the house and just find him there, sprawled on the sofa, cigarette spiralling into smoke, a book or an animal or some ancient artifact on his lap. But it was clear no one had lived here since Dr Nasiputi, who would not be getting his tenant's deposit back. The goats, who now claimed the sitting room as their own, had refused to be chased back out into the rain and glared satanically. One munched on a Japanese newspaper and farted, another was finding the final chapter of Walter's book on dance rather hard going. Everything had been systematically looted, except for the books which were of interest to no one – all the contents, some of the beams, the doors carved by Lempad. Rain was streaming down the walls, where ferns nested in with the insolence of all life, through the eroded thatch. Soon the cement would start to crumble. I could still see Walter, in my head, as he once sat there over the river, Vicki snipping away at his hair and the birds swooping down to carry it away for their nests. Where Sobrat's first painting had hung, was a square of paler plaster like untanned flesh under discarded shorts. The house was returning to the earth, like water swirling down a drain, taking with it the joy and life of which it had once been the centre. Only silence remained. I had gone to the palace – looking depressed and down at heel – both it and me – and asked for Cokorda Agung. A cook whispered that he was in the prison in Denpasar, detained for the expression of views skeptical of Dutch rule and denounced by members of his own family. The kaleidoscope had been given another twist. And Tuan Walter? He shrugged. Who could tell? I knew what I must do.

The Neuhauses' old house stood across the street from Sanur beach. From here, you could see the spot where we had carried Conrad's torn body ashore. Here, the invading Dutch forces had landed, followed by the Japanese, followed and preceded indifferently by the annual plagues from Nusa Penida. The beach itself was deserted, dominated by the sound of waves throwing themselves against the coral reef, the lashing of the wind in the palm fronds, sand powdering against the fleshy plants that only Walter knew the names of. The *akvarioom* had the desolate, moss-blackened appearance of all down-at-heel seaside attractions out of season. I walked up to the warped steps of the porch, ducked under the sagging bougainvillea and knocked on the door. Inside, tired net curtains twitched. A lot of flies had decided to crawl between the net and the glass to die there. I knocked again. Hans Neuhaus opened the door a crack and stared resentfully through the gap.

"What do you want?"

"It's me." Of course it was me. Whoever I was it would still be me. "Rudolf Bonnet."

The door opened a little wider. He was unshaven, unwashed, clothes bleached and worn, a hairy belly pulsating between the flaps of a too-tight shirt and talking through a cigarette. There was a bottle of beer gripped in one paw though it was only ten in the morning. Hans had run to fat – no, not run – collapsed into fat. After the camp, I was just bones, one of those Torajan walking skeletons.

"What do you want?" he said again and sidled out on bare feet, holding the door close behind him as you do when you have someone in there you don't want seen. A whiff of something like despair seeped out. He closed it against the resistance of a sticking frame.

"Where's your brother?" I had always dealt with Rolf in my limited and unfortunate contacts with the Neuhaus brothers. There were two old chairs in a corner of the porch. He kicked one over and sat down. I took that as an invitation and sat in the other. I hoped he might offer me a beer so I could refuse it.

"You don't know? No, of course, you weren't here. You were on the other side." He looked at his great ugly feet, a shock after Balinese feet. Hairy, gnarled. There was a bunion coming there. "He's dead."

"Oh. I'm sorry." I was not particularly sorry. I had never got on with them. Social niceties were a nuisance. "When? How?"

He swigged. "Three years ago now. It was supposed to be the Japanese. We were sitting right here one day and they had troops searching the woods back there." He jerked a thumb over one shoulder. "They were chasing some guerrillas, *Pemuda*, who the hell knows what they were. There was shooting. The story is Rolf was hit by a stray bullet, right in the middle of the chest." He jabbed himself in illustration and flinched. "I got a written apology from the army. The bullet was

Japanese. Of course it was Japanese. All the bullets flying around, in those days were Japanese. You want a beer?"

"Yes please." He shuffled off. I heard voices inside. He came back with one, foaming at the neck and another for himself. I felt sorry for him, a lost twin. Wait. They were not twins.

"They say it was the Japanese but I think it was that little bastard Sampih."

"Sampih? But how? Why?"

He stretched out his legs to settle into the subject. "You know he's big in the nationalist youth round here. You Dutch have been after him. There was a patrol round the other day asking questions. He and Rolf had this big fight at the opening of the aquarium. Rolf made some joke about him and Colin and he just blew up, stalked off cursing. He said one day he'd come back and kill Rolf."

"He said that about lots of people. He said it about his own father. He probably said it about me."

He leered and belched. "Did you know his father was dead?" He nodded. "Yup. Killed one dark night as he walked through the woods. No one knows who or why. It couldn't be robbery. He hadn't got a penny. No Balinese would have gone there, in the dark, alone. They found him with his throat cut." He gestured throat-cutting with a nasty wet noise in his mouth and laughed bitterly. "Does Sampih know where you live?" I refused to entertain the notion. I had not been through so much to have my throat cut over nothing, now there was finally peace. I felt a sudden weary rage against the world. I had reined myself in long enough.

"Walter," I burst out. "What happened to Walter? The last time I saw him in Ngawi, you were in the same camp and I think you went to Kutacane with him."

He looked at me in horror. "Oh Christ! Didn't anyone tell you?" He looked shifty. "Everything was chaotic at the end. The Dutch were falling apart, the whole fucking world was falling apart." He swigged. I clutched my bottle and glugged at it the way a child does, seeking comfort. It was bitter, unpleasant. Whatever was coming, I knew, was bad. "The Japanese were supposed to be just down the road. The guards shoved us all in trucks and took us to Palembang where they had three old rustbuckets waiting. The idea was that we would be shipped off to

Ceylon where the British would put us in *their* camps. They crammed us in, men on the open decks in the sun, they didn't care. Rolf and I nearly died from the heat and lack of water. Walter was lucky. He got a cabin, well ... part of a cabin. We set sail. It was an incredibly calm, clear day and we had just got abreast of Nias when a single Japanese plane spotted us. It circled, saw we were civilian, no escort, and came in to attack with machine guns, strafing the decks. Cowardly bastard! Dozens were killed. It climbed up and headed for Java, then, it was as if it changed its mind and came back again. I could see this dot getting bigger and bigger, coming straight at us and then it pulled up again. We were just sighing with relief when the first torpedo struck, then another and the ship was going down. It was everyone for himself. The other ships, with the real Nazis on board, did nothing, just kept going. Our crew's only concern was to save themselves and they just pulled away in the lifeboats. Before we knew it, Rolf and I were in the water with hundreds of others. You could see Nias far off and there was nothing else to do but try to get there. We were lucky I suppose. The current must have been with us. We trod water and let it carry us along. Lots of the others made the mistake of trying to swim and exhausted themselves and drowned. Then, later in the day, the sharks started coming in." He shuddered. Involuntarily, I looked at the beach. "You could hear the terrible screams of the men as they were taken, one by one." I could hear them too or rather Conrad's as he lay just there, his young blood pumping into the beach and our pathetic concern not to get sand in the wound as if he were a picnic sandwich. "Anyway, we were lucky. We made it. It took us weeks to get off the island and then the Japanese sent us back here." There was silence. My mind swirled with watery confusion. I had to know. I had to make him say it.

"Walter?" I croaked.

"He must have been locked in the cabin with the others. They shouted and banged on the doors but the crew didn't even try to save them, just jumped in the boats and rowed away. The Japanese got them, of course, put them in some hellhole of a camp. I'm sure lots died." Said with unseemly satisfaction. No comfort to me. His voice fell to a whisper. "The worst part was that endless black night, with the sharks, the sea like ink, the deepest sea in the world, miles of it cold below you. At the start, there was this moon and then a shadow came over it and there was just this slice of it left. I thought it was the end of the world. Then it got bright again and by the morning we were being cut to pieces on the coral round Nias with these huge waves throwing us about. He pointed to his leg and ran one finger down a long, deep scar like a furrow. "At first, I thought it was a shark and I was a gonner but it was just coral slashing at me. Rolf got me to shore, saved my life."

My knee was shaking, knocking against the chair. "What? What was that you said about the moon?"

He shrugged. "Nothing much. Just some sort of an eclipse. Not even a total eclipse, just like someone had taken a big bite out of the moon." He wiped his hand over his face and then sat up foursquare like Abraham Lincoln in his monument, the voice defiant. "I tell you. Since then, I may sit here and look at it but, since that night, I have never set foot in that sea again and I never will." There was the sound of a door shutting softly at the back. After two minutes, a bicycle came, as if coincidentally, round the corner of the house, what was clearly a young fisherman pedalling languidly, sarong hitched up to show fine calves. He and Hans exchanged grins.

"Good morning, *Tuan*," he called too loudly and winked.

17

James Grits was talking in crossword puzzles again but my mind was distracted by my nose, a waft of scents, a very Balinese mixture of roasting meat, incense and frangipani blossom from the tree over by the gate. In Malay – now Indonesian – they called it "dead Chinaman flower" from its being found amongst the tombs of Chinese cemeteries, which detracted not one whit from its prettiness. It was favoured, these days, to aromatise lavatory air-fresheners, which rather did.

"The panoptic inscription of otherness evokes comparable chords of difference across the whole spectrum of harmonic discourse," he declared. "Painting is self-definitionally a frozen synchronicity of diacritical stigmata."

The meat smell would be my lunch, skewers of grilled and spiced chicken flesh in a peanut sauce fired specially with diced chilli by Nyoman. The Balinese palate was normally shy of chilli. In Balinese cuisine, colour is more important than taste. My mouth watered anticipatorially, a spring coaxed from an arid rock.

"The contrast, collision and accommodation inspired by such cultural intersections incite a reciprocal sense of loss mediated by a nostalgia for anachreontic similitudes. The diagnostic representational power of Walter Spies's actual works derives counterfactually from the present absence of so many of them. It is the re-factualisation of Walter Spies's works alone that can serve to de-mythologise him."

"A lost cause." I said through drool. "The war. The Japanese, the shipwreck, the deplorable failings of the postal service." Iced mango. Nyoman had perfected the trick of freezing pure mango pulp, scented with a splash of *brem*, into a cunning ready-made sorbet. I would have that after.

"It is the poignant coming-into-being of a blank canvas, the un-creation of self-declared art that validates and de-frames a dialogic reassessment of exercised repressive hegemony." Hibiscus tea, infused from blossoms gathered from my own garden. No, a glass of *Ersatz* Australian white wine

"Young man. Nobody left an account of his last work, as I am sure you know. *Scherzo* and *Urwald* were photographed in black and white, *Ezekiel* was sparingly described but *Campuhan* was completely lost. No one knows what was in it. Forget it."

The anthropologists, having rejected Walter as a sadly naive eccentric, all those years ago, were now feasting on him cannibalistically, stripping the flesh from his bones, boiling those bones down to gluey prose. They vaguely perceived him as the answer to something but could still not see the question.

"But the undetermined existential status of the later works hypostasises the materiality and the calling-back-into-presence of their absent artefactuality, informing their own alterity. Is there no chance of their being found, re-DIS-covering themselves? Remembering is a process of deliberate forgetting and the obverse is true."

I waved the smokescreen away, established another by the lighting of an indulgent clove cigarette. I permitted myself two a day.

"All vain speculation, I am afraid, Dr ... er, Mr ... Grits. We must accept the randomising process of history – the process that we call history. In this mordant climate, an untended artwork rapidly degrades. Walter did not always use the most durable materials, they were not available to us then. That was his great hope for the continued development of traditional art – the need to replace objects subject to decay. The termite and the moth the ultimate critic. Death leads to renewal, a very Balinese concept. QED. And now, I am afraid, at my age, I need to rest. I, too, have been ravaged by the tooth of time. I am sure you understand."

I rose, abruptly but firmly frail, invoking senescence as my get-out-of-jail card. Grits gathered his goods from the tabletop unwillingly, stuffed them sulkily back in his case. It was not the loss of my insights but the removal of an audience for his own opinions that he regretted. Kasimura, in his Kempetei uniform, was the true archetype of all educators. Now what had happened to *him*? I led Grits slowly towards the gate, the perfect, self-effacing host. I led him over the treacherous loose tile, that obligingly pivoted under his weight and sprayed muddy water – left from the morning watering – up his leg as he stumbled and sprawled full length, case and papers flying. Charlie would have made it funnier. I watched his confusion, unable, from age, to help, but elaborately dusted down his front as solicitude naturally required, blessed him and his works, waved him, all hot and bothered, crestfallen and pratfallen, away down the road. He would not see the comedy of it but my own tread was light enough as I headed for the kitchen to give Nyoman his orders for my lunch to be served outside. Grits's glass stood on the table undrained. I abhor waste.

Passing from the kitchen, through the sitting room, I entered the bedroom. These days, I was the only one who ever came here. The shades were rolled down against the noonday heat and threw bars of bright illumination against the far wall, lighting up the painting that hung there. It was, of course, Walter's *Campuhan*, the last painting he ever did, held back, with judicious illegality, by the leggy postboy and finally delivered years after its completion. It was a small painting, some forty centimeters square, and simply framed and he had lavished upon it all the colours I had brought to distant Ngawi. The background was one of Walter's Rousseauish jungles, overlapping, interpenetrating plants, tendrils, flowers, every vein and pistil unstintingly delineated, but dark green to black in colour, as though seen against bright light. Amongst the flora, the fauna goes about its business. A wide-eared monkey turns its back and stares into the centre of the painting, butterflies flap, birds stretch their wings, an enormous cricket stridulates like a violinist and one of Walter's big, red dragonflies launches itself, whirring, into light. To one side, the crumbling royal temple across the river stands out in ghostly white. When Balinese spoke of Walter, they had no doubt that all his ill fortune flowed from having set the roof of his house higher than that of the temple. In vain, he would protest that he had had it checked by the government surveyor and this was mere illusion. The gods, it seems, though implacable realists, have eyes but no theodolites to measure their offence. Below the temple, on the river bank, sits the hairy giant of myth, a chicken coop of entrapped and distressed *legong*-dancing virgins to hand, busily cooking the rice with which he will consume them. Two streams, one white, one blue, converge on the centre which is flooded with great shafts of light from above, an energised core, where sunbeams and water fuse into some novel compound to create a pure, swirling vortex of translucent energy. Then the rich sky above fades into tones of deepest blue and violet and there is the demon, Kala Rahu, a hideous, coarse head with bulging eyes and one hopping leg, gnawing at the moon in great tearing bites of bottomless malice.

Grits had reproached Walter for selling a vision of Bali-as-Paradise. That was not true. He had known that, in every paradise, there is a serpent but Walter had clutched it to his breast though he knew it would ultimately devour him. The myth that he purveyed was the myth of himself, as a man who had found that contentment that we all seek, who always sat in golden sunshine, who lived a life without the oppression of wage-slavery or anxiety, a Parsifalian Peter Pan for whom every day brought joy and the pleasure of beauty, what he, himself, might have called a *Lebenskünstler*, an artist *at* living. And though we knew that such a path was closed to us, the fact of another's attaining it somehow redeemed the world, as a single holy man's holiness can save us all. That was why the rich and famous beat a path to his door and laid their wealth at his feet. I fingered the stark curved initials of his signature, the magical index of his being. There was a soft tapping from the passage.

"*Nawegang, Pak Rudi. Ajengan sampun siaga.*" Nyoman, formerly the leggy postboy, grown to be my chubby helper, letting me know that lunch was ready. After the Japanese left, it had been necessary to retrain the servants not to bow and hiss as they had been taught. Then, after the Revolution, they were no longer allowed to call you *Tuan*, since this was unsuited to the allegedly egalitarian ethos of the new republic. So many shibboleths. So many taboos.

I stepped out into the sunlight, around the loose tile and settled to my small but appetising lunch, eating with my hands. My neighbour, pottering about his orchids, cackled at me, waggled his watering can in greeting and we did the little mime at each other of "come eat", "no, please go ahead", that politeness requires. Then, I lifted my glass, in a toast without words, and sipped the sharp, cold wine. *Sauve qui peut.*

TORAJA

Misadventures of an anthropologist
in Sulawesi, Indonesia

NIGEL BARLEY

In 1985, Dr Nigel Barley, then senior
anthropologist at The British Museum, taught
himself Indonesian and set off for the relatively
unknown Indonesian island of Sulawesi. Here
he hoped to find unsullied cultures to study and unspoilt natives to
investigate. Barley soon found plenty to wonder at and plenty to admire
among the Toraja, a vastly interesting people whose culture includes
headhunting, transvestite priests and the massacre of buffalo.

In witty and finely crafted prose, Barley offers fascinating insight
into the people of Sulawesi and their lifestyles, and he recounts hilarious
tales of the many memorable characters he meets there, not least the four
Torajan woodcarvers the author invites back to London to construct an
Indonesian rice barn in The British Museum. This quartet of Indonesian
Marx Brothers soon discover the joys of pornographic films and the
London Zoo, although they never get to grips with turning off bathroom
taps.

"A fascinating tour through a little-known corner of the world,
escorted by one of the wittiest guides around"
Kirkus Review

"Humorous, double-sided culture-shock tale, as the
anthropologist author persuades craftsmen from Sulawesi
to return to London with him and build a traditional Torajan
rice barn for The British Museum"
Rough Guides *Southeast Asia*

ROGUE RAIDER

The tale of Captain Lauterbach, the Singapore
Mutiny and the audacious Battle of Penang

Nigel Barley

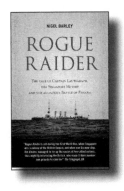

It is the First World War and Julius Lauterbach
is a German prisoner of war in the old Tanglin
barracks of Singapore. He is also a braggart, a
womaniser and a heavy drinker and through his
bored fantasies he unwittingly triggers a mutiny by Muslim troops of the
British garrison and so throws the whole course of the war in doubt. The
British lose control of the city, its European inhabitants flee to the ships
in the harbour and it is only with the help of Japanese marines that the
Empire is saved.

Rogue Raider is the adventure story of how one ship, the *Emden*, tied
up the navies of four nations off the coast of Indonesia, and audaciously
started the Battle of Penang in Malaysia, and how one man eluded Allied
Forces in a desperate yet hilarious attempt to regain his native land. It is
fictionalised history but a true history that was deliberately suppressed
by the authorities of the time as too embarrassing and dangerous to be
known. Revealed here, it brings vividly to life the Southeast Asia of the
period, its sights, its sounds and its rich mix of peoples. And through it an
unwilling participant in the war becomes an accidental hero.

"A swashbuckling adventure story, full of bawdy, uproarious fun.
Barley writes with verve and humour—settle back
and enjoy the journey"
Tash Aw, author of *The Harmony Silk Factory*

"*Rogue Raider* is an entertaining read ... the events are incredible"
The Asian Review of Books

IN THE FOOTSTEPS OF STAMFORD RAFFLES

NIGEL BARLEY

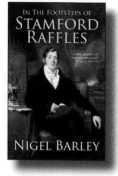

Stamford Raffles is that rarest of things — a colonial figure who is forgotten at home but still remembered with affection abroad.

Born into genteel poverty in 1781, he joined the East India Company at the age of fourteen and worked his way up to become Lieutenant Governor of Java when the British seized that island for some five years in 1811. There he fell in love with all things Javanese and vaunted it as a place of civilization as he discovered himself as a man of science as well as commerce. A humane and ever-curious figure, his administration was a period of energetic reform and boisterous research that culminated in his History of Java in 1817 and it remains the starting-point of all subsequent studies of Indonesian culture.

Personal tragedy and ill-health stalked his final years in the East. Yet, though dying at the early age of 44 and dogged by the hostility of lesser men, he would still find time to found the city-state of Singapore and guide it through its first dangerous years. Here, mythologised by the British and demonised by the Dutch, he is more than a remote founding father and remains a charter for its independence and its enduring values.

In this intriguing book, part history, part travelogue, Nigel Barley re-visits the places that were important in the life of Stamford Raffles and evaluates his heritage in an account that is both humorous and insightful.

"Barley's irreverent and amusing tone makes his work accessible to all"
New York Times Review of Books, USA

"A witty, sprightly and elegantly written book"
The Sunday Times, UK

"Alive with curiosity … a charming and affectionate book"
Times Literary Supplement, UK